SEBASTIAN'S WAY

THE PATHFINDER

For Marianne with ~~Appreciation~~ for her Friendship.

SEBASTIAN'S WAY

THE PATHFINDER

*George Steger
January 2014*

George Steger

iUniverse LLC
Bloomington

Sebastian's Way: The Pathfinder

Copyright © 2013 by George Steger.

All rights reserved. No part of this book may be used or reproduced by any means, graphic, electronic, or mechanical, including photocopying, recording, taping or by any information storage retrieval system without the written permission of the publisher except in the case of brief quotations embodied in critical articles and reviews.

This is a work of fiction. All of the characters, names, incidents, organizations, and dialogue in this novel are either the products of the author's imagination or are used fictitiously.

iUniverse books may be ordered through booksellers or by contacting:

iUniverse LLC
1663 Liberty Drive
Bloomington, IN 47403
www.iuniverse.com
1-800-Authors (1-800-288-4677)

Because of the dynamic nature of the Internet, any web addresses or links contained in this book may have changed since publication and may no longer be valid. The views expressed in this work are solely those of the author and do not necessarily reflect the views of the publisher, and the publisher hereby disclaims any responsibility for them.

Any people depicted in stock imagery provided by Thinkstock are models, and such images are being used for illustrative purposes only.
Certain stock imagery © Thinkstock.

ISBN: 978-1-4917-0896-5 (sc)
ISBN: 978-1-4917-0895-8 (hc)
ISBN: 978-1-4917-0894-1 (ebk)

Library of Congress Control Number: 2013917334

Printed in the United States of America

iUniverse rev. date: 09/27/2013

CONTENTS

The Historical Moment xiii

Prologue   Treason 1

Chapter 1   The Siege of Adalgray 7
Chapter 2   Refiner's Fire 14
Chapter 3   The Widow's Ploy 25
Chapter 4   Passing the Bar 36
Chapter 5   Fernshanz 46
Chapter 6   Venit Rex 60
Chapter 7   Saxon Hubris 70
Chapter 8   Learning to Fight 82
Chapter 9   Learning to Read—Among Other Things 93
Chapter 10 The Wolf Hunt 102
Chapter 11 The Spanish Dagger 111
Chapter 12 Worms and a New Level of Life 119
Chapter 13 Eros 133
Chapter 14 Disaster 151
Chapter 15 What a Warrior Does 158
Chapter 16 The Irminsul 166
Chapter 17 Out of the Ashes 176
Chapter 18 Andernach 188
Chapter 19 The Pilgrimage 202
Chapter 20 Wayfarers 213
Chapter 21 The Plague 223
Chapter 22 Lothar the Magician and Simon the Radhanite 234

Chapter 23	Of Silks and Success	247
Chapter 24	Gersvind	255
Chapter 25	Old Wounds	262
Chapter 26	Changing the Way	275
Chapter 27	God's Punishment	281
Chapter 28	Alas, Adelaide	294
Chapter 29	The Suntel Mountains	302
Chapter 30	Day of Reckoning	310
Chapter 31	The Third Way	320
Chapter 32	Idyll's End	331
Chapter 33	Widukind	340
Epilogue	The Torchbearer	349

For Professor Lynn Nelson, University of Kansas, whose
knowledge and love of medieval history inspired this book,

and

for Jackson, in the hope that he might always seek a different way.

PERSONS OF THE STORY

Adela	Count Gonduin's daughter
Adelaide	Count Leudegar's daughter
Anchesigal	Sergeant at Fortress Fernshanz; friend of Sebastian
Archambald	Soldier at Fernshanz; Sebastian's companion
Arno	The King's Count of the Palace at Worms
Athaulf	Count of the Fortress Adalgray and its lands; Konrad's father
Attalus	Horse Master (Constable) of Adalgray, later Lord of Fernshanz
Bardulf	Fernshanz youth, a free peasant; companion of Drogo
Baumgard	Steward of Fernshanz
Bernard	Frankish veteran soldier; personal aide of Ermengard
Bertha	Peasant woman; Father Louis's wife
Boldering	Leader of a gang of homeless peasants
Charlemagne	**Karl der Grosse**, High King, and later Emperor, of the Franks
Drogo	Fernshanz youth, a serf; companion of Bardulf
Edelrath	Count and personal vassal of Charlemagne; a general of the army and member of the *missi dominici* (king's inspectors)
Ermengard	Sebastian's mother, sister of Count Athaulf
Father Louis	Priest at Fernshanz; Sebastian's teacher
Father Pippin	Priest at Fernshanz during the rebuilding
Gersvind	Peasant girl in the village of Fernshanz; deeply attached to Sebastian

Gonduin	Lord of Andernach, Duke and general of the army; father of Adela
Grennig	Deceased Count of Adalgray; Ermengard's husband and Sebastian's assumed father
Heimdal	Blind hermit; soothsayer and advisor to Attalus and Sebastian
Herlindis	Nun of the convent of Bischofsheim, later Mother Superior; tutor and friend of Adela
Karloman	Co-King of the Franks until 771 and Charlemagne's brother
Konrad	Son of Count Athaulf; later Count of Adalgray
Laidred	Learned monk; keeper of Charlemagne's library
Leudegar	Count and Lord of Kostheim, one of Charlemagne's generals; father of Adelaide
Liesel	Bardulf's wife
Liudolf	Soldier at Fernshanz; Sebastian's companion
Liudolf, the Elder	Sergeant at Fernshanz; father of Liudolf
Lothar	Inventive serf of Fernshanz; confidant of Sebastian
Lutz	Shadow-spirited peasant boy; son of Ubrigens and brother of Gersvind
Marta	Serf and housekeeper in the lord's house at Fernshanz; medicine woman
Milo	Gersvind's son
Regwald	One of Charlemagne's personal vassals and a High Church official; member of the *missi dominici* (king's inspectors)
Sebastian	Heir of Count Grennig and Ermengard; later Lord of the Fernshanz Fortress
Simon	World traveler and trader; member of a network of Radhanite Jewish merchants ranging from Francia to the Baghdad Caliphate
Teuthardis	Hunchback leader of a band of forest brigands

Ubrigens	Frankish peasant and carpenter; father of Lutz and Gersvind, one of Sebastian's pilgrimage companions
Varnar	Captain of Charlemagne's personal guard
Welf	Count of the Saxon March (land bordering Saxon territory)
Widukind	Saxon prince and war chief

THE HISTORICAL MOMENT

At the end of the great Roman age, German tribes, held at bay by the power of the legions for four centuries, poured across the old Rhine-Danube frontier barriers and devoured the spoils of Roman Gaul. Celts and Romans gave way to Teutons until, finally, all of Western Europe lay under German hegemony.

Of all the German tribes, the Franks proved the most tenacious. By the middle of the eighth century, Karl, later called *Carolus Magnus* or Charlemagne, had ascended to power.

War is what sustained the High King Karl. He remained mighty and glorified as long as he could win victories, extend his realm, and make his wolfish nobles rich.

A tenuous balance existed between the king and his chief war leaders, especially in his early years. Those great landowners were themselves formidable fighters. They had small armies that were loyal to themselves exclusively. They prized their independence and were wary of any attempts by the king to curb their power. King Karl had not yet become "the thunderer," the invincible conqueror that men would one day call "great." In the year 768, when this story begins, he was twenty-one years old and shared the crown with his brother.

Following is a tale of Charlemagne's resolve to change the barbaric world in which he lived. As his power grew, Karl donned the Christian mantle as "Defender of the Faith," but he fought and ruled savagely, much like his pagan enemies. However, subtle forces—unlikely men—were at work to change him. It was his genius to recognize them.

Prologue

Treason

The King's Court at Thionville on the Moselle, Autumn 782 AD

Sebastian wiped the rain out of his eyes as he stood before the king, helmet in hand. He had ridden all through the dark day in a downpour and was wet to the bone. Charlemagne had not asked him to sit, nor had he looked at him since he had been admitted to the royal chambers. The king stood at a window, watching the heavy thunderbolts crashing down just beyond the palace grounds. His mood reflected the storm. Finally, he turned and fixed Sebastian with an angry glare.

"Who has told you that you may refuse to fight for your king? How dare you send me such a message? I am your king. You have a command in my heavy cavalry. If I say you will fight, you will fight."

"My king . . ." Sebastian began.

"Do you realize every officer in my army would have you executed immediately for this? Refusing to fight when you are called is high treason! How long do you think you would last if I told them about your message? Should I, your king, make excuses for you? Well? Give me a reason to keep you alive."

Sebastian dropped his eyes. For a few charged moments, he said nothing. Then, drawing a deep breath, he began again. "My liege, I have always loved you—ever since I was a small boy. I would give you the last drop of my blood. But . . . I do not refuse to fight for you . . . I refuse to murder."

"What? What are you saying, you—"

"Sire, what we did to the Saxons after the Suntel battle was a horror . . . a terrible mistake. We butchered forty-five hundred unarmed men. We cut their heads off like chickens and let them flop in front of us. And it was all unnecessary."

"Of course it was necessary, damn you. The swine swore an oath of loyalty to me, as they had done five times before. They have never kept their word. What they did was also treason. I had to set an example—finally—and they deserved to die."

"Sire, begging your pardon, hear me out. There is another way. You don't have to annihilate them. You can just divide them. Send them across the Rhine—deep into western Francia. Give them farms—good land. Treat them with respect. Take them into your army. They will make good soldiers and we could use them."

"Right!" the king said with contempt. "And who will keep them from rebelling again and sticking a knife into our backs?"

"Sire, if we divide them, there will not be enough of them in any one place to fight us and they will know it. Besides they will be happier. They will realize it is a better life, a better way."

"And how do you propose to get them to agree to such a radical plan? They will be sure to think that I plan to lure them deep into Francia to kill them all. In fact, now that you mention it, that might not be such a bad idea."

"Sire, the key is Prince Widukind."

The king started at the name. "What? I cannot believe you still propose to treat with that devil's spawn. He's the worst of the lot—by far! Have you forgotten that it was he who led the Saxons at the Suntel Mountains when they massacred my men?"

Widukind was Prince of the Westphalians, strongest and most troublesome of the Saxon tribes. In a brilliant deception, he had lured part of the Frankish eastern army into a trap and wiped out a large contingent of Charlemagne's best troops. Seven royal counts had been killed, including three of the king's personal advisors.

"That's the worst defeat I ever suffered! We lost some of the best leaders in the realm in that fiasco! And I still don't know the number of mounted fighters we lost there because of him—hundreds, though, to be sure. And you want me to parley with him. 'Please, my good prince, do come and sit down with me and let me kiss your ruddy Saxon arse!' Are you mad? I'd sooner parley with the devil himself."

"Sire, if you please, I believe I can get Widukind to come. I have met him several times. I know him better than any other Frank does. I never told you this, but I once saved one of his daughters—a bastard child, to be sure, but his nonetheless. It was during the campaign when we overwhelmed the Saxons at Syburg and took back the Eresburg fortress. Don't you remember?"

"Ha! Indeed, I do, Sebastian. We hounded them and burned their settlements all the way up to the Weser River in the very heart of Saxony. And that's precisely what I'm talking about. We decided to wage all-out war against those bloody tree worshippers in that very campaign. No more of their infernal raids! No more of their pretending to parley after we defeated them!"

The Saxons were raiding deeper and more frequently toward the Rhine, and they were building new fortresses on the cusp of Frankish territory. Whenever they were defeated, they simply pledged a new allegiance and accepted Christian baptism, only to forswear it the next time a strong leader urged an uprising. The king had reached his limit and was even at the point in his anger and frustration of contemplating genocide as a solution.

"I was ready to wipe them all out—to the last man. Still am, by God! And then we began to win, don't you know. That was the campaign that turned the tide," the king said, obviously relishing the memory.

"Uh . . . yes, sire. And that was when I rescued Widukind's daughter. He later sent me a message of thanks and a fine gold arm-ring through a Jewish merchant. You remember the man; his name was Simon and he plied his trade on the Rhine in a boat manned by Danish Vikings."

"Ah, yes. I know that clever rogue and his dodgy ways. He's the one who gave you those fantastic paper shields that fly. And he once sold me some powder he said was ground from the horn of a great beast called a rhinoceros; it was supposed to keep me stiff for a week. Didn't do a bloody thing for me, the scoundrel. But he was a charming fellow, nonetheless."

The king seemed to have lost some of his fiery intent to condemn Sebastian. He spoke more kindly. "Damn it all, boy! You know I love you like a son. You are a marvelous fighter and an extraordinary leader, with the brightest of futures before you—but you are not the king. You cannot defy me." He paused a moment. "If I forget your foolish rebellion this one time, will you vow never to try me like this again?"

In answer, Sebastian took a deep breath and said nothing. His eyes fell back to the floor.

"Damn you, Sebastian!" the king shouted.

"Sire, about Widukind. I know him. Let me go to him. I am sure he will talk to me, and there's a chance I could persuade him to come and parley with you."

"Pah! I've parleyed with that scurvy vermin before, and little good it did me, by God. I had to put up with his confounded arrogance for an entire hour! Sebastian, he has led every revolt since our first campaign against the Saxons more than ten years ago. It's Widukind who keeps the Saxons riled up year after year."

"Sire, that's exactly why we must win him over. He's the key. If we can convince Widukind to lay down his spear and move the Westphalians west across the great river into Francia, the fighting will stop."

"Oh, so I'm supposed to reward this murderous pirate with land as well as amnesty, is it?"

"My lord, begging your pardon, it's cheaper than fighting him."

"Sebastian, he'll kill you if I let you go to him. And he'll send me back your head just to taunt me."

"Well, sire," Sebastian said with a rueful smile, "you've said that you feel obliged to kill me yourself. I might as well take my chances with Widukind."

The king paused, chewing the end of his mustache as he often did when he had to make a hard choice. Finally, he took a deep breath, ground his teeth, and turned to pronounce his decision. "It's an impossible idea, Sebastian. You couldn't do it for one thing. For another, if it weren't for him, this war would be over. I cannot make peace with Widukind after all the Franks he's killed and all the trouble he's caused me. My generals would never understand."

He gave Sebastian a long look. "Give me your sword," he said. Sebastian's mouth fell open, but the king's eyes were hard and uncompromising. Sebastian unbuckled his belt and handed over the cherished weapon, scabbard and all.

"I had great plans for you, Sebastian," the king said as he looked down at the beautifully designed, gold-inlaid pommel of the sword. It was an outstanding example of the Frankish genius for making weapons. The king himself had given this long sword to Sebastian after his first fight against the Saxons. He was very proud of it.

"I was going to give you more lands than you ever dreamed of. Devil take it, I would have given you responsibility for half of Saxony after we beat them. You know I cannot do that now. I cannot even have you in my court. You would be liable to preach to me about sparing the bloody Saxons in front of my counselors." He paused. "Go home, Sebastian. Go home to your little fort at Fernshanz. Dig your fingers into the dirt as you so love to do with your damned peasants. I owe you for your exceptional service in the past, but you are done here. You are finished as a commander in my cavalry. Take your men and go home. I won't bother you; I won't even ask you to serve again. But from this moment, never come to me, and never speak of this to any of my officers. If you do, you will force me to have you executed for high treason. Do you understand?"

"Aye, my lord king," Sebastian mumbled, his eyes still on the floor.

"Then go. Get out of my sight!"

Sebastian bowed low, backed away from the king, and strode out of the chamber into the pelting rain.

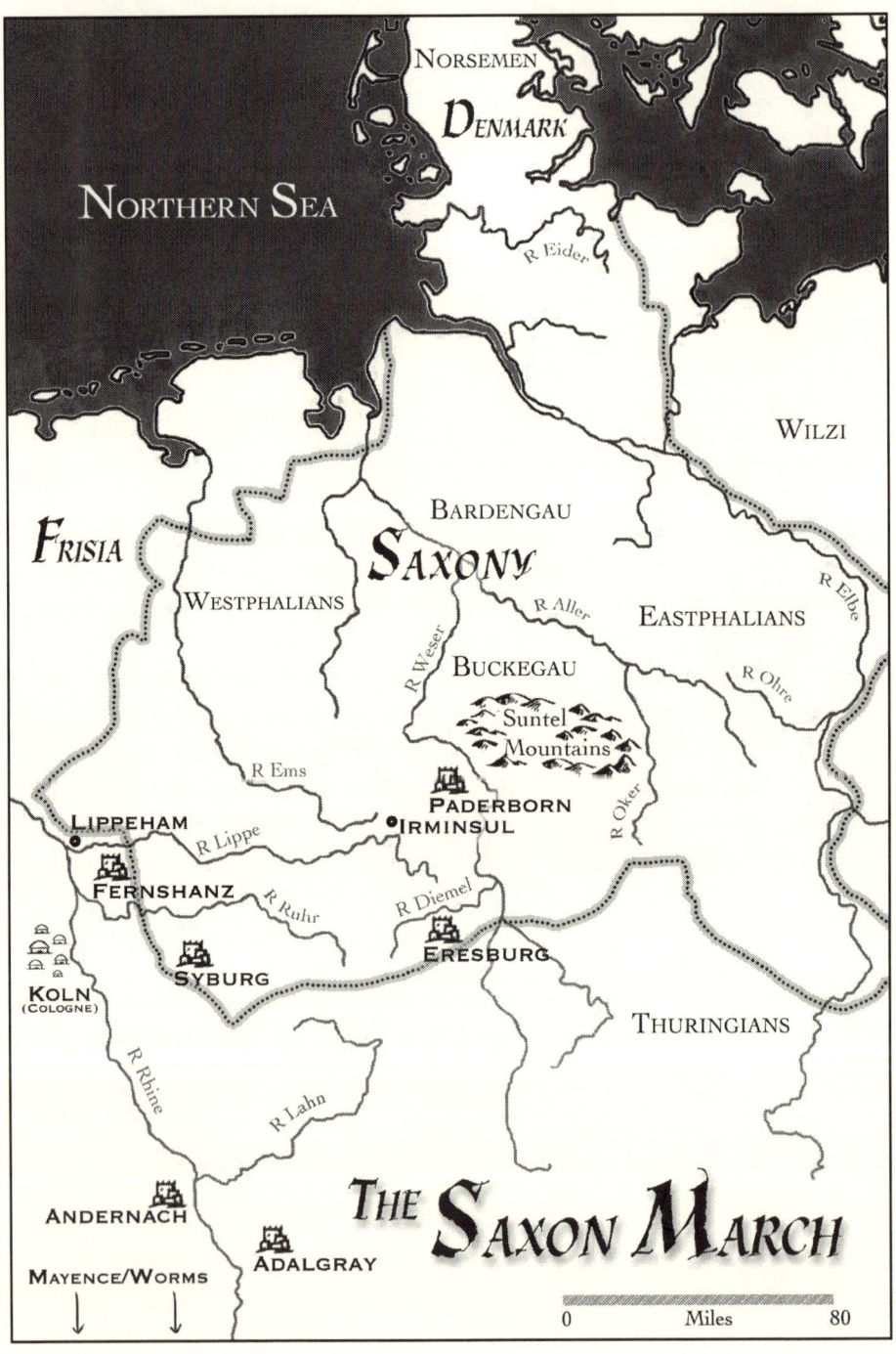

Chapter 1
The Siege of Adalgray

Autumn 768

The blind man leaned over the parapet and sniffed the air, cocking his head toward the north. "I hear chopping," he said flatly. Heimdal, the forest hermit, had been blind from his youth and relied totally on his other four senses, which resulted in making him a curiously logical man. He rejected the superstitions of the age and the narrow-mindedness and fatalism of most of the people, which ironically had the effect of creating his reputation as a legendary wise man.

An hour before dark, Heimdal had come down the rough track from the woods, tapping his way slowly through the town up to the tower gate of the old Roman fortress. The sentries obligingly helped him onto the wall walk and listened with him. They heard nothing but dared not dispute his claim, for it was well known that Heimdal could hear the grass growing.

In the forest a league away, a peasant rounding up a few skinny cattle foraging in the woods also heard the sound of axes. He quickly beat his animals back into the brush and crept to the edge of the woods. What he saw made him shudder: hundreds of grim-faced soldiers, cutting down trees and fashioning them into crude scaling ladders and heavy battering rams, with teams of oxen waiting, carts loaded with siege supplies and weapons.

The peasant watched long enough to identify the war banners on the lances. They were those of Count Welf, a ruthless and powerful noble, whose land lay between Fortress Adalgray and the Saxon territory to the north. The frightened drover made haste for Adalgray, gliding as lithely as a deer through the underbrush. He despised Welf, who abused and cheated his peasants, leaving them hungry through the winter, and he wished no harm to his own benefactor, Count Athaulf, a fair and usually generous master. The peasant arrived just at twilight as the guards began to shut the fortress gates. Heimdal nodded as he listened to the report and then persuaded the watch sergeant to send immediately for Attalus, constable and acting fortress commander.

Shortly after dawn the next morning, the sentries on the walls heard the rhythmic chanting of marching soldiers long before they saw their streaming banners.

The garrison had worked frantically all through the night to bring weapons and supplies to the walls. The town was in a panic; its people streamed through the fortress gate, where sergeants of the guard divided them immediately into groups, assigning everyone tasks to prepare for the defense. Children and mothers with babies were herded into a makeshift nursery. Serfs, slaves, and the town boys were organized into a battalion of runners, firefighters, and porters. Able-bodied women were given stations around the walls to care for the wounded and provide food, water, and other supplies. Every free man was detailed to the walls.

As the soldiers raced to ready their positions, three of Adalgray's preeminent residents confronted each other tensely in the empty great hall of the fortress: Konrad, a husky, red-haired Frank in full armor, whose bear-like young body was already sweating with excitement; Attalus, an older warrior, whose somber, heavily lined Gallic face and silver-streaked, raven hair reflected not only his Aquitanian roots but also his years of experience and responsibility; and Ermengard, a handsome Frankish lady, somewhat short and a trifle stout now with the years but still fiery, dignified, and bursting with lifelong righteous authority.

An uninvited fourth presence—Sebastian, a tense, slender youth of twelve—breathlessly watched the heated exchange from under a rug-draped bench against the wall.

A war council was in progress, and the air was thick with disagreement. Sebastian's mother, Ermengard, was barely able to contain her impatience and anger as she sat in her customary place at the table of her brother, Lord Athaulf, the absent Count of Adalgray. Ermengard's eyes never left the face of Konrad, her belligerent young nephew, the son of her brother and the heir apparent of Fortress Adalgray, her own face reflecting a mask of silent, bird-of-prey aggressiveness.

Konrad was haranguing his aunt and his father's Master of Horse, Attalus, a famous constable and soldier who was now retired from combat service. Attalus had served the counts of Adalgray for most of his life.

"We are under attack—or will be shortly! It's an outrage!" ranted the young warrior. "Count Welf, that wolf's turd! He's supposed to be my father's peer and friend, the fawning bastard! He waited until he was sure my father was out chasing Saxons with most of our soldiers, and now the jackal expects to pluck us like a ripe pear. Well, I will give him pears! We must ride out at once with our best men and strike him! You must agree, Attalus—time is essential. We must thump him now before he can organize a siege. I will lead our cavalry in a blow dead against his center. Our strength and boldness will rout him before he is even able to bring up the bulk of his men."

"What strength, Master Konrad?" questioned the constable, his calm words a marked contrast to Konrad's high-pitched, nervous tirade.

"You yourself just said that your father has most of our troops already in the field, and the best ones at that. How many mounted warriors do you suppose you could muster to throw against Count Welf's center?"

"Why, I have . . . at least a troop," stammered Konrad, after brief thought. "It would be enough for a quick strike, enough to demoralize Welf, if we strike hard and quickly."

"Aye, my lord, you do have almost enough for a troop—perhaps forty men. But your father took the best horses as well. Have you considered what you would seat your troop upon for this bold move? You would be lucky to find twenty animals one could reasonably call warhorses. And do you know at this point how many men Count Welf may put into the field?"

"His county's no larger than ours. He has no great army. I would wager no more than a few score men."

"Perhaps, my lord, but we do not know; he may have all of his men with him. If he does, he will have at least three hundred fifty. And we have scarcely fifty men at arms—counting old men and boys."

"No matter!" shouted the young lord, the veins standing out in his neck. "We can outfight them! If we counterattack now, we will have the advantage of surprise. It is our house, by God! We cannot allow this! We'll not be bottled up by this usurper, this . . . this thieving Bavarian goat."

"Konrad!" Now it was Ermengard's turn. She had waited, simmering, but she was close to boiling over. She knew her nephew would never accede to the horse master, a man he considered of low birth and no property. She rose abruptly and moved directly in front of the agitated young man. Fixing him with a cold stare, she played the one card she knew would give him pause.

"Your father has not won King Karl's favor by being a rash fool! Have you even thought of the consequences of a failed battle?" she raged at him. "You will show beyond a doubt that you are unworthy to lead your father's people. You will lose this fortress and all your father's possessions. You will lose your life and probably all of ours as well. You know you must rely on the experience of our constable. He has been a warrior three times as long as you have been alive. He has organized and commanded a hundred defenses. You must rely on his judgment! We have no time for this ridiculous bravado."

"Madame, if I may," Attalus interjected tactfully, "your nephew may indeed have a worthy idea. A successful foray may be possible—but not now, not in broad daylight. Count Welf is no fool. He will come with spear points up and ready. We can make our counterattack later, at night perhaps, when he has relaxed his guard. For now, what we really need is every available man on the battlements and a ready reserve—commanded by our most courageous fighter. I refer, of course, to yourself, Count Konrad.

"You see, sir," the old veteran continued in a soothing voice, "we won't have enough men to cover every foot of the battlements. We must wait and see where they will attack and what siege machinery they may have, and then use the reserve to plug the gaps if they break through. It is the indispensable key to any successful defense. I should think ten or fifteen of the young warriors would comprise the reserve and still leave us enough on the walls for now. Only you can command the reserve, Count Konrad. It may be the key to our survival."

The headstrong youth was mollified by the old warrior's deference and secretly pleased by Attalus's premature reference to him as *Count*. More compellingly, he was, as always, intimidated by his aunt. She had conjured up exactly what he feared most—failure in his father's eyes.

Konrad protested briefly out of pride but finally withdrew to choose his men, complaining under his breath as he went, "How long shall I have to endure fainthearted men and harping women?"

Shaken but inflated with excitement, Sebastian waited impatiently for the great room to empty before he crawled out of his hiding place and flew to the walls to watch Attalus mount the defense.

The attack on the fortress proceeded predictably. Count Welf's spies had enabled him to pick his moment carefully, taking advantage of a recent Saxon raid that had drawn Count Athaulf into a long pursuit. Welf was also counting on a sense of distraction and instability among the people caused by the division of the Frankish kingdom between two brothers. Karl, the elder, was generally regarded as the new high king, but many people said his father, King Pippin, had favored Karl's brother, Karloman, and had given him the better part of the kingdom.

Convinced that the fortress was only lightly defended, Count Welf was not expecting much of a fight. He sent three horsemen with white flags as emissaries to demand the surrender of Adalgray.

"Hear ye now, whoever commands this place," said the foremost rider, a herald, as he waved his flag back and forth in front of himself.

Attalus, as constable and fortress commander, stepped forward in the tower above the gate. He did not look like the fabled veteran of more than a score of annual campaigns during his lifetime. He never bragged or threatened but largely went about his business quietly, generally keeping his own counsel. Nevertheless, his reputation was known throughout the realm, and his very presence as a great fighter and a proven marshal visibly impressed the emissaries. He spoke now, softly but clearly, in the still air.

"Have your say, men of Welf, but be quick. We have little patience for cowards who would threaten us, and we will not listen long."

"We come on behalf of our lord, Count Welf," the herald announced in a strong, imperative voice. "He makes claim that this fortress of Adalgray is his by rights insofar as he, Count Welf, is the northern *markgrav*, and has for many years defended the Frankish realm against the Saxon menace."

"How is it, then," Attalus replied casually, "that the high king himself acknowledges that this land is in the keeping of Count Athaulf? Have we missed something?"

The emissary answered hotly: "King Pippin gave this land to Count Athaulf's brother, Grennig, who was killed fighting the Saxons. There is no charter giving the land either to Athaulf or to Grennig's wife, the lady Ermengard. Since Grennig's death, Count Welf has done far more than Athaulf to keep the Saxons at bay throughout the long wars of King Pippin. As reward, Count Welf should be the master of Adalgray."

"It has been two years now since the death of King Pippin and five since the death of Grennig," Attalus replied. "Do you not think King Karl, in his wisdom, would have seen this error and corrected it, if indeed there were such a mistake?"

"Furthermore," the herald pressed on, ignoring Attalus's reply, "there are two kings now, and King Karl's brother, Karloman, has never been consulted about this benefice. Count Welf therefore declares his intention to take Adalgray forthwith. He asks only that the defenders listen to the voice of reason and avoid the inevitable massacre should they resist."

If Welf's men expected to intimidate and frighten the defenders into giving up without a fight, Attalus's measured reply gave them no comfort.

"Tell your master that he holds his own land precariously and only at the pleasure of Karl, who is high king, and the king will find no pleasure in this affair. Tell him that he has no more than a wolf's claim here, and that we hold him in highest contempt. If he is foolish enough to attack, he will find us ready, and he had better make sure to kill us all if he can, for there will be no forgiveness, not by us and not by the king."

Withdrawing, the horse master flung over the battlement at the very feet of the messengers' horses a black Frankish lance with a white feather attached to the shaft.

Standing halfway up the ladder to the battlements, Sebastian heard every word and was filled with pride and admiration for Attalus, whom he had known since birth and loved almost as a father. Clutching his small dagger, he longed to be on the battlements himself to take part bravely in the heroic defense of his people. He would soon witness in horror the reality of such lofty notions.

Chapter 2

Refiner's Fire

Ermengard was furious. Not only had Sebastian absented himself without her permission, he had finally been found after frantic searching on the battlements at the very point of Count Welf's impending attack. Because all the available men were conscripted to the walls, Ermengard sent female household servants to bring Sebastian back to her quarters. Humiliated that women had been sent to fetch him, the boy vigorously refused to come, providing some welcome comic relief in a tense moment for nearby soldiers on the walls, behind whose legs and shields Sebastian wedged himself against the clucking corps of matrons.

Finally, Ermengard herself was forced to retrieve her son. She caused a considerable stir as she stormed up the ladder to the battlements, ordering burly men-at-arms to help her up and get out of her way. A calamitous scene between mother and child was narrowly avoided by the timely appearance of Attalus.

"Attalus! How can you allow this?" Ermengard demanded. "He is only a child!"

"Madame," hissed the constable between his teeth, "you must get down from the battlements at once. Their attack is imminent!"

"I will not get down, not without my son," she replied defiantly.

Casting a nervous eye over the walls where he could see archers assembling and ladders moving forward, Attalus quickly bent down and grasped Sebastian by his bony shoulders. He looked for a long second directly into the boy's eyes, then whispered something into his ear. Sebastian went immediately to the nearest ladder and began to climb down. Somewhat taken aback, Ermengard started to follow.

Before she could descend, Attalus touched her elbow. "Madame, a word." With a voice full of concern, he explained, "The walls are too lightly defended. We need every available man now. That includes the boys. We must have runners to bring messages and to carry water and arrows. Sebastian may be small, but he is fast and strong."

She glanced down at the boy, fear mounting in her eyes. Attalus grasped both of her elbows, brought his face close, and whispered: "Ermengard, we need him. And I have already promised him a part in this battle. He will not go with you."

On the verge of crying out, Ermengard put a hand to her mouth, sucked in her breath, and cursed the Master of Horse in a low voice. "May God damn your soul to hell, Attalus, if that boy is hurt in any way. If he dies, it's on your soul, and I will seek you out and find a way to kill you." With that she hurried down the ladder, leaving the shocked fortress commander speechless and badly distracted.

Sebastian stood sturdily at the foot of the ladder, ready to defend his decision to remain with the men. His resolve wavered, however, as he saw his mother's anguished face and the tears welling up in her eyes. She bent toward him and put her hands on his shoulders. "Sebastian, Attalus says you must stay and help with the battle. If it must be, then God wills it. But listen to me: Take no chances, stay off the battlements, and pray constantly. Pray! Do what Attalus and the others tell you, but one thing you must promise me—you must not try to fight. You are not ready. They will kill you if you do, and I couldn't bear it. Promise me that at least. Promise!" she demanded.

Abashed by her tears and worry, Sebastian could only mutter: "I promise, Mother." She embraced him briefly and hurried away, shouting something about sending him armor.

The hours that followed were filled with terror and physical exhaustion. Sebastian and the other boys too young to fight were constantly sent racing from one corner of the fortress to another bringing water, food, and additional weapons. Those who were fleetest of foot, including Sebastian, were used to convey messages from Attalus to his captains on each wall, or to Konrad, who waited with the reserve at a strategic point in the fortress yard. A horn was used to bring Konrad quickly to one wall or another but Attalus used the messengers to alert the reserve and warn it about the likely point of attack.

Fortress Adalgray had begun two hundred years earlier as a crude structure of wooden walls and blockhouses with a small town inside it. Now it was a fortress inside a town. Although the town boasted a population of some four hundred men, women, and children, its people were families of free farmers or bound serfs who worked the earth and managed only to manufacture rudimentary tools and artifacts.

Nevertheless, in times of danger the town was subject to the sacred Frankish maxim that every freeman was a warrior, regardless of his occupation or tribal origin. Thus all men who were not serfs or slaves manned the walls, though many were untrained or poorly trained for war. Few had real weapons and none had any armor. However, some could use bows skillfully, and other stocky farmers were armed with lethal ten-foot lances or the old *francisca* battle axes used by their fathers and grandfathers. Used to a hard life and constant danger, they were a collection of highly motivated and combustible men, and together they could move to fill the gaps along the walls to passable effect.

One peasant who was not so motivated was Bardulf, a gangling, raw-boned youth just beginning to get his full beard but already tall and well muscled. Bardulf's attitude toward life was simply to stay out of the way, avoiding as much work as possible and skirting any kind of pain or danger while giving free rein to whatever pleasures he could get away with. By nature he moved lackadaisically, yawning at the ant-like business of his fellow peasants and laughing at their plodding ways and unimaginative lives. He was not inherently a coward or malevolent by nature, but he was lazy and self-gratifying to the extent possible in such a poor and hardscrabble farming community. The fact that he often did manage to escape work and treat himself indulgently bore witness to his finely honed wit and resourcefulness. Furthermore, despite his indolence, he had quick reflexes and unexpected strength.

Bardulf was almost never seen without his boon companion, Drogo, a stubby, round-headed youth from a serf family that had been wiped out by disease. Drogo had replaced his family with Bardulf, whom he idolized and followed about like a shadow. Drogo was good-hearted and as friendly as a puppy, but he was also as slow-witted and unremarkable as Bardulf was clever and prickly. Most people simply ignored the fact that Drogo was a serf and should have been fulfilling his father's obligations on the land.

On this day, however, Bardulf and Drogo found themselves upon the walls.

"But Sergeant Liudolf, sir," Bardulf protested, "I don' know nothin' about fightin'. And neither does poor ol' Drogo here. Look at him, Sarge; he's just a little boy. And so am I, for that matter. We ain't old enough to be up here facing them bloodthirsty killers. We should be down there in the yard with them other boys carryin' water and that, ye know."

Liudolf the Elder, who was Senior Sergeant on the western wall of the fortress, was an old campaigner and a no-nonsense disciplinarian. "Shut yer face, ye bloody loafer. Ye'll stand this post at the far end of this wall and let me know at once if boats be launched upon the river. And if they breech the wall here, ye'll fight like any other men. If ye don't, I'll cut off yer balls, and ye know me well enough to know I'm serious as death. Ye leave this post and ye might as well be dead. By the end of the day, if they don't kill ye, I will—if ye leave this damned wall. Ye understand that, 'Master' Bardulf? Yer worst enemy is not them, it's me!"

What happened next was something neither youth had seen before nor ever could have imagined. They were given two round fighting shields, a long black spear, and a thick oaken club and told to defend the last aperture in the western wall where it ended at the river. Bardulf kept assuring Drogo that no enemy would come down far enough to threaten their position. However, when Welf's men boiled out of the woods under a shower of arrows, sure enough, one contingent of ladder bearers made straight for the end of the wall.

Both boys ducked as the arrows whistled overhead. Bardulf lifted his shield up and ducked back again as the shield caught an arrow straight away. "Get yer arses up, ye bastards. They're comin' at ye. Plug that hole!" yelled Liudolf, as he prepared to meet the onslaught farther down the wall.

Bardulf heard the shouts of the men below and jumped up just in time to see the top of a ladder being braced against the aperture. Holding the shield before him, he chanced a look down and saw a soldier in chain mail already climbing. The man was hindered by his need to hold his shield before him to protect against any blows from above while still keeping his sword at the ready. He managed it by attaching his sword tightly by a cord to his wrist and laying it across his left arm. He could then use his right hand to climb and still have his sword near to hand, but it was slow going at best.

Bardulf saw the man's predicament at once. He first tried to dislodge the climber with large rocks piled for that very purpose near his aperture. His first attempt failed to stop the climber but luckily ricocheted off the man's shield precisely into the face of the climber next in line. The man collapsed at once down the ladder, knocking into a third man on the way down.

The first climber renewed his efforts and climbed more quickly. Bardulf next tried to spear the man as he got closer, leaning well over the wall to reach him, but the man adroitly warded off his thrusts. Bardulf resorted to the stones again. This time he heaved a big one as hard as he could against the shield. The stone drove the shield down and to the man's side. Bardulf quickly struck with the lance into the exposed face of his foe. Spurting blood covered the man's eyes and left him helpless. He frantically tried to cover himself again with the shield, but Bardulf could now knock it aside easily. He plunged the spear into the man's right arm, which he was using to hold on to the ladder. The man let go and fell back into the next climber.

Archers were brought up to pin Bardulf behind the wall. He began to have a hard time seeing the progress of the climbers while holding the shield directly in front of him. "Drogo," he barked, "move yer fat arse! Bring yer shield up here and hold it in front of me while I drop these here stones. Do it! Now, ye piece of pig dung—do it!"

The petrified Drogo was shaken into movement by Bardulf's urgent commands. He leaped up and extended both their shields as far out in front of the aperture as his short arms would allow. Working under Drogo's arms, Bardulf launched rock after rock and even heaved a short wooden beam down at the climbers. Momentarily, they were halted.

"Drogo, lookee here. If they keep comin' and we can't stop 'em, I may have to let one come over the wall. While I keep him busy, ye mus' come up behind him and hit him a clout behind the ear with yer club, as hard as ye can. Do ye hear? Ye know what to do?

"Awright, Bardulf, I unnerstan'," the boy whined. "But I'm afeared I can't do it. I'm shakin' all over."

Bardulf leapt back breathlessly behind the wall and grasped Drogo by the ear. "Listen, Drogo, they're goin' to kill us unless we can stop 'em. I will try to keep 'em from getting up to the wall, but if one gets over, ye hit 'im, ye hear? And hard."

He looked his friend in the eye and patted his shoulder. "Ye can do this, Drogo. Ye mus' do it if ye don't want to see me killed, ye hear?" Drogo nodded his head in dumb assent and sank back down behind the wall.

Bardulf held his own for what seemed like an eternity. Around him down the wall, the battle raged. Some of the enemy breached the wall and were subsequently thrown back by Liudolf and a small team of gap pluggers. Bardulf refused to look, knowing his one chance was to concentrate on his own avenue of assault.

Finally, a brawny, sweating man-at-arms methodically made his way to the top in spite of all Bardulf did to try to stop him. The man forced his way through the aperture and confronted Bardulf with raised sword. "Drogo! Now! Bash the bastard. Now!" Bardulf shouted, backing away with his spear point leveled at the man. Bardulf began to scream and nearly fell off the wall into the courtyard below before Drogo finally rose up and drove the club into the back of the man's head with all the force of his chunky body. The soldier dropped his sword and ceased to function immediately.

Bardulf wasted no time in hoisting the stunned enemy up and tipping him over the wall into the dry moat below. Hugging Drogo briefly, Bardulf pushed him down to safety below the wall. "Do it again, me brave man, and we'll live to tell the tale yet." He was back to the aperture at once, heaving rocks down at the next climber.

On the first day alone the defenders lost a third of their force. As for the attackers, Count Welf threw his own men indiscriminately against the walls, a wave against one wall followed predictably by another wave against a different wall. His best men were decimated in the melee, while most of Adalgray's casualties were inexperienced soldiers or nonwarriors fighting for the first time. Losses among the core cadre of trained men-at-arms were relatively light. However, by the end of the first day, everyone was thoroughly exhausted.

One bright dimension of the fight was the courage and effectiveness of Konrad and his young warriors of the reserve. Time and time again they had been summoned to the various walls, sometimes two or three times in an hour. Konrad himself was the first up every ladder and the first to hurl himself against any attackers who managed to get over the walls.

The young lord, though short, was muscular and solid as a tree trunk. He was fearless, slamming into the foe with screams and curses and driving them back by sheer berserk ferocity. Sebastian once caught sight of him in the throes of an attack, launching himself against five heavily armored invaders who had managed to clamber over the wall and were clearing the battlements of defenders. His initial surge sent one foe flying off the battlements into the yard below and another crashing back into his comrades with a nearly severed arm. Konrad held off the remaining three men until his mates closed around him and together made short work of the survivors. Using long forked poles, they flung the assault ladders away from the walls, sending climbers careening down into the mob below. Those of Welf's warriors who had managed to reach the ramparts only to be killed were summarily flung back into the crowd.

Sebastian was woefully unprepared for the carnage, which was his first experience of death. He had never even seen a dead person before this day, his father having been killed while he was still a child too young to remember. At the end of the first day of battle, he could not stop himself from weeping, going several times to the church to pray for the souls of the friends and villagers he saw die on the ramparts, as his mother had told him to do.

After one particularly bloody and harrowing assault, he took refuge in the darkness of the chapel and threw himself down, weeping in distress in front of the altar. He was startled by a hollow voice echoing out of the gloom.

"Well, what did you expect, Sebastian? Have you discovered that war is not such a noble business after all?" The voice came from someone sitting on the floor on the other side of the church, his back to the wall. Though the figure was wrapped in a dark cloak, Sebastian could see a bald head gleaming in the half light.

"Oh, it's you, Heimdal. Thank God—I thought you were a ghost. There's so much death outside. I don't know how much of this I can stand . . . this butchery. That's why I came in here," he confessed ashamedly.

The blind man rose and tapped his way over to sit by the boy. "Listen, Sebastian, you will survive this, if any of us do. If you do, it may be a blessing for you. You had to see it eventually if you still have a mind to be a warrior. At least today you don't actually have to fight."

"What else could I be if not a warrior? Attalus is a warrior; we are all warriors in my family."

"You can become a scholar. You can learn to read and study Latin. You already show promise at it. Who knows what you can become if you can read?"

"No," Sebastian said, sitting up and wiping his eyes. "I must be what my father was, and what my uncle and cousin are. This is what I was born for. But it's horrible. I don't know if I can do it." He wiped his face and eyes with the back of his hand.

"Sebastian, let me give you something to think about. Life teaches us every day. Some lessons are much harder than others. You can learn two things today; and if you do learn them, the knowledge will make you stronger—and different from other Frankish warriors. The first lesson is that war is no game, no sport. It is not like hunting, as so many young Frankish warriors are led to think. It's a deadly serious business. Men die, homes are destroyed, women are raped, and children are lost. War is a disaster and it should be engaged in only when there is no other course. If I had my way, it would never be celebrated."

The blind man paused to listen for sounds of the battle outside. Sebastian murmured, "I don't know what to think. It is so different from what I expected. I didn't know . . ." After a moment, he added, "And the second lesson, Heimdal?"

"The second lesson is this: If you fight, there is a chance you will lose. We may lose today. But if you don't fight, there is no chance that you will lose. Is that not so, Sebastian?"

"What? I don't understand,"

"Think about it, my boy. We will speak of this later. Right now you must return to the fight. They may need you. Go, and God be with you."

After his visit with Heimdal, Sebastian was calmer and more in control of himself. He was still awed and frightened by the fighting, but he remained excited and increasingly proud of his own role. The persistent demand for his services proved a blessing. Because he was constantly on the run bearing messages from Attalus and responding to a score of voices clamoring for aid and supplies, he had no time to think about the bloodshed or to dwell on the appalling toll.

Water was the most sought after item—water to drink in the heat of battle and to pour on the endless blazes caused by the fire arrows. It was also the most difficult item to supply, for it had to be carried by heavy buckets from the several wells and cisterns inside Adalgray. Although there was plenty of water in the reservoirs, there were never enough boys to carry the buckets. Only the biggest could carry two buckets at a time. Eventually, strong townswomen were pressed into service as water bearers. Sebastian, with his slight frame, wore himself out carrying the water. It was all he could do to drag a single bucket up the battlement ladders. His value as a swift messenger saved him, for Attalus noticed his struggles and confined his duties to those of a courier.

Sebastian ate and slept with the other boys in the empty armory by the gate or directly beneath the battlements—wherever they happened to be when Attalus sent word that it was safe enough to stand down. They ate whatever was available whenever it appeared, brought by the women during lulls in the fighting.

He saw his mother only once in five days when she brought him the armor she had promised: a helmet half again the size of his head and a vest of chain mail that reached almost to his feet. He thanked her solemnly and promised to wear the items. However, he could barely move in the heavy chain mail and had to abandon it, all the more hastily when the other boys began calling him "Turtle." The helmet he continued to wear in deference to his mother, stuffing it with rags to make it stay on his head.

On the fifth day, an incident occurred that profoundly changed the kind of man Sebastian was to become. Count Welf mounted a major attack, this time surging in from two sides at once. The defenders repulsed one attack with the help of Konrad's reserve, but the second attack managed to cause a breach. A fierce melee ensued, forcing Attalus to leave the west wall unguarded in order to lead additional defenders to Konrad's aid.

Sebastian was nearly killed by an invader who had managed to scale the walls but found himself cut off when the attempt ultimately failed. Trapped, the man leapt from the ramparts and raced through the fortress grounds, desperately seeking a way out. Sebastian had been on his way back to Attalus's command post and was resting a moment, watching from the steps of the church. The invader fought his way through the town and nearly cut Sebastian down as he raced to enter the church and claim sanctuary. At the last second, he realized Sebastian was only an unarmed boy and so he stayed his blade, murmuring, "Pray for me, boy! May God help me now; pray for my soul," before he disappeared inside the chapel.

The man's efforts, however, proved pitifully in vain. A cohort of defenders in pursuit encountered Sebastian at the church. Overcome with fear and excitement, Sebastian could only point to the church door. The soldiers raced inside and quickly overwhelmed the fugitive, who was clinging to the altar. They wrestled him outside and summarily slew him on the churchyard green, as Sebastian watched in horror. They then dragged the corpse by the heels back to the wall and flung it over as if it were a rabid dog.

The scene haunted Sebastian and he could not overcome his guilt at having disclosed the man's location. He was unable to sleep and returned again and again to the church to seek relief and pray for the soul of the unfortunate soldier. For years afterward, Sebastian felt responsible for his death. Ultimately, it changed the way he would fight.

The battle raged on for another two days. Although the fortress defenders consistently held their own, they suffered casualties that could not be replaced. After a particularly difficult and costly day in which the attackers were repulsed repeatedly, another council was held. This time Attalus decided the moment had come for a gamble; he supported the idea of a foray, a mounted one, to take place during the hours of darkness just before dawn of the next day so that the raiders would be able to see well enough to withdraw successfully. The targets would be the baggage train and supply area of the enemy. Attalus knew the enemy had suffered grievously during the siege, and he suspected they were poorly provisioned as well. A successful raid might discourage their feckless leader enough to cause him to withdraw. Commanding the foray would be Konrad, who by then had emphatically proved his fighting prowess and courage.

The raid turned out to be successful beyond all expectations. The enemy supply area, including a horse paddock, was wrecked, causing the horses to scatter. Chaos prevailed in the ranks of the foe, a good many of whom perished as Konrad's cavalry swept back and forth among them. As dawn broke, the horse master experienced a moment of dismay when Konrad, intoxicated by the fight, failed to respond to the horns calling him to withdraw. The retreat nevertheless succeeded, if barely, and all but two of Konrad's raiders managed to make it back into the fortress just as the sun began to rise on the seventh day.

At the conclusion of the raid, the defenders gathered for a Mass in the courtyard to give thanks for the victory. Afterward, they lined the battlements and sang hymns, raised new battle standards over the walls and lustily shouted taunts at the disheartened ranks of the enemy.

The gambit worked; a day later the enemy withdrew, trailed by teams of Adalgray huntsmen who followed them to ensure they had abandoned the siege. After three days, the scouts reported that the enemy had completely withdrawn from Count Athaulf's lands.

Upon Athaulf's return, Attalus and Ermengard publicly gave most of the credit for the successful defense to Konrad. They treated the triumphant youth to a banquet in his honor. However, in private, Ermengard was at pains to describe to her brother in detail the course of the battle and how it truly had been won. She praised Konrad for his courage but warned Athaulf against his youth and rashness. And she extolled once again "the incomparable virtues of the Master of Horse."

Chapter 3

The Widow's Ploy

If Count Welf had succeeded in taking Adalgray, Charlemagne might have let him keep it. Such was the tenuous balance of the king's power at the time. However, Count Welf had failed, thanks to the skillful generalship of Attalus. Upon returning from the field, Athaulf had only to send a messenger to the king expressing his outrage. He could have chosen no better envoy than Konrad, whose fiery account of the siege and vitriolic hyperbole entertained the high king's court for a day and a half, sealing Count Welf's fate.

Although it was still early in the spring to mount a campaign, Charlemagne wasted no time in assembling a force. But there was to be no wetting of their spears. Welf fled as soon as he received word of the king's intentions, and he took with him only his immediate family and a few retainers. He was unable even to make off with much of his wealth. It was rumored that he had gone back to his kinsmen among the hostile Bavarians to the south, which only deepened Charlemagne's displeasure with him.

Athaulf was the chief beneficiary of this turn of events because the king, in a burst of generosity, inspired perhaps by Konrad's vivid account of the heroism of Adalgray's small garrison, decided to gift Athaulf with all of Count Welf's land and possessions. Athaulf had, after all, served the king and his father more loyally than most for the better part of twenty years, and Konrad appeared to be a worthy successor.

Unfortunately, a year or so after the siege of Adalgray, Athaulf began to grow infirm. Years of "gathering at the *Maifeld*" for long annual campaigns, first with King Pippin and then with Charlemagne, constant exposure to harsh weather, and scores of old battle bruises and wounds had eroded and exhausted his body. Increasingly, he could not get out of his bed without help in the mornings. Servants were assigned to massage him until he could use his limbs again, and even then he was in near constant pain.

At first Athaulf tried all the local healers and apothecaries and experimented with every remedy, including bleeding, all with disastrous results. Then he imported physicians at great expense, even from the court of the high king, but none could cure the slow and torturous imprisonment of his joints and the rapidly advancing deterioration of his muscles. In less than a year he became decrepit.

All other remedies having failed, Athaulf took to drink. He fell into a drunken sleep every night and woke in the morning crying for wine. He carried his cup everywhere and commissioned a household serf to follow him around and keep it filled at all times. Everyone in Adalgray knew that their lord was rapidly going insane and would soon destroy himself.

No one was more aware of this fact than Konrad, who began to act more and more like the de facto lord of the manor. His natural proclivity for arrogance asserted itself, and a streak of cruelty emerged in his character. When he was alone with the younger men of his entourage, he even mimicked the shuffling gait, wild stare, and mumbling sentences of his father. He exercised his power by ordering everyone about and criticizing anyone who was not personally attached to him.

The one person whom he dared not publicly challenge or try to humiliate was Ermengard, who refused to be commanded, intimidated, or shouted at. She stood her ground when he came into her presence, looking him straight in the eye and venting her towering anger upon him if he erred in manners or disrespected her in any way, regardless of who happened to be in the room. Her wit was too quick and her memory too long for Konrad to contest with her. He simply avoided her when he could, and when he could not, he lapsed into sullen silence. Such was the presence, dignity, and reputation of his father's sister and the widow of one of Charlemagne's most celebrated warriors.

Unlike Ermengard, Attalus was not immune to Konrad's churlish behavior and quickly became a focal point for Konrad's capricious anger and spite. Konrad resented the reputation of the Master of Horse and hated the whispered intimations that Attalus, not himself, was the one who had saved Adalgray during Count Welf's attack. Konrad took every opportunity to bait and insult the old count's most trusted officer, hurling jibes and innuendos so blatantly that Attalus gave up eating at the lord's table in the great hall. He took his meals alone and spent much of his time tending to the breeding horses in the stables and tutoring some of the young warriors in the mounted exercise field.

Ermengard observed this trend with anxiety, afraid for Attalus and convinced that Konrad's enmity toward him would one day extend to Sebastian, whom Konrad increasingly regarded with distaste and suspicion. After all, the high king could name anyone Count of Adalgray and grant its lands when Athaulf died, and Sebastian's father had been a famous Frankish warrior who had been count and commander of the fortress before Athaulf.

Ermengard had known Konrad from his rambunctious and willful childhood and knew that he was not above any means of ensuring that Sebastian did not become a serious rival. She determined that she must remove both Attalus and Sebastian from Konrad's potential wrath before he inherited the full powers of his father.

Accordingly, she confronted her brother one morning as he struggled to rise from his bed, groaning and calling for his wine cup. Athaulf was semi-lucid in the morning, and Ermengard took full advantage by ordering the count's breakfast and shushing away his servants. She fussed around her brother, smoothing his pillows and combing his hair and beard, speaking in soothing tones and with great sympathy for his pains. She had been able to manipulate him since their childhood, and Athaulf genuinely liked his spirited sister, who could be as tender as she was bold.

On this morning, Ermengard wasted little time, knowing that her window of opportunity with her brother would be open only as long as he could stave off his pain. Thus she came equipped with parchment and a plan. As her brother fussed halfheartedly with his breakfast, she directed the conversation to the Master of Horse, informing her brother of the recent births of several new colts that Attalus had been at pains to breed into a special type of warhorse. Attalus's stallions were already the most coveted mounts in the kingdom, being renowned not only for their size and strength but for their ferocity.

Athaulf loved horses and was fascinated by his sister's report. He vowed to go down to the stables that very day to see the colts. Ermengard seized the moment to press her case.

"My lord, how many years did you campaign with Attalus?" she began innocently.

"Why, more years than I can count, my dear. I cannot even remember when we did not campaign together. Until that last year when Attalus said he was getting too old, we went off together whenever King Pippin or King Karl summoned us."

"And how many times during those years did Attalus save your life?" she ventured. "You've told me many stories of fighting by his side."

"Hmm, twice, at least," the count answered enthusiastically. After pondering a bit, he added, "Probably many times, now that I think about it. By thunder, he was always at my left shoulder. I never needed to worry." The count smiled as he remembered his comrade's prowess and fidelity.

Ermengard pressed home her case. "Well, then," she said, "don't you think you should do something to reward such a good comrade who has given you so much service over these long years and protected you so well? After all, he is getting older now and has no benefice of his own, no land to support himself. You could give him a small place as a token of your appreciation. No one deserves it more. And you have plenty of land now that the high king has added Count Welf's holdings to your own."

"I will, by God," the count affirmed. "I know just the place; he can have Fernshanz. It's a good little fort, with plenty of meadows and good grass near the river. He can breed me some exceptional horses there, I'll wager. I'll tell him at the banquet tonight. It's the feast of Saint George. What better day to celebrate a real warrior?"

Ermengard was pleased. Fernshanz was an old fortress built on a tributary of the Rhine in the rolling, semi-open country on the way to the northern sea. Its proximity to the Friesian lands along the north coast as well as the Saxon border made it a convenient place for the king to rest on his frequent visits to inspect the northern and eastern defenses of his realm. It was not a large fief, but it would do nicely to support Attalus and Sebastian, and perhaps one day at Fernshanz the high king would notice her son.

Accordingly, she pressed her advantage. "My lord, what a grand idea! Attalus will continue to serve you well from that convenient window in the north. You know how clever he is. And it will be a perfect place for him to train my son to be a Frankish warrior."

"Oh," her brother remarked laconically as he spied his wine steward lurking in the doorway, "you intend to apprentice Sebastian to Attalus then?"

"What better teacher could he have, my lord? You said yourself he was one of the finest fighters you had ever seen. Sebastian is fourteen. He's old enough to train now, and he must leave Adalgray—and me—if he ever hopes to fill his father's shoes."

"Um, quite right," grunted the count, growing increasingly more impatient with the conversation. "We'll see to it," he said, waving his hand as if to dismiss her and the problem of thinking about something besides his cup of wine waiting in the doorway.

But Ermengard held her ground. "My lord, why not get this business settled quickly and be done with it? The *missi dominici* are making their rounds of the province and will surely be here within a fortnight. You must have their favor if you wish to give Attalus a part of your benefice, and they will want to know why you plan to do so. By your leave, I have had a charter composed for the king to approve. All we need do is write in the name of the benefice you will give. The priest is waiting at the door to write in the name. And, see, here is your seal. The *missi* can deliver this parchment to the king, and by the end of summer, Attalus and Sebastian can be on their way."

"What, what?" The count sputtered and fidgeted away from his sister. But she continued to push the parchment before him, clasping his hands and smiling into his eyes. "All right, all right," he grumbled in irritation. "Bring the bloody priest. Where is the damned seal? Let us do it and have done with it so a man can finish his breakfast. We can announce it all tonight."

Ermengard motioned to the cleric lurking behind the door and quickly whispered the name he was to write. Next she produced the precious seal, which she had been at considerable pains to appropriate from her brother's bedchamber. While she melted a bit of red wax with a candle, Athaulf haltingly made a tiny mark below the writing, more like a spreading branch than a signature. Ermengard then folded the parchment neatly and carefully guided the seal in her brother's shaking hand over the melted wax. Athaulf stamped the document angrily with the seal, uttering loudly, "Done, for God's sake, and finally!"

"I thank you, my kind lord and brother. I will see to everything." Ermengard touched her forehead to her brother's hand and quickly backed out of the chamber, to Athaulf's great relief. He frantically motioned for his wine steward before she was fully out of the door.

Her mind racing with the details she would need to attend to before the evening's feasting, Ermengard refused to dwell on the slim chances that her enterprise would succeed. For one thing, there was Konrad, who might explode at any time. Then there were the *missi*. Ermengard knew that all depended on the good will of these powerful men. They were the high king's inspectors general, his eyes and ears and a major tool in controlling his sprawling realm. Without their support, she had little hope. Adalgray must welcome them as if the king himself were coming.

The *missi dominici* of the king arrived three months later, in the dog days of summer. The day was so hot, even the wilted, motionless forest seemed to perspire. It was a bad start because the visitors arrived drenched in sweat, exhausted, and hungry. A guard troop of about twenty horsemen accompanied the two *missi*. The first was Bishop Regwald, a high-ranking dean of the Church, who resided permanently with the king when he was not on a mission. He was said to be one of the brightest of the king's impressive and growing collection of wise men. He was a stormy, imperious cleric of about fifty years of age, tall and solidly built but not fat, with the demeanor of a prince and the tonsure of a monk. He had the reputation for defending the king's interests with all the ardor of the entire Roman Church. In fact, Regwald fervently believed, as did so many highly placed clerics, that the safety and success of the Church depended entirely on the welfare and success of Charlemagne.

His companion was Edelrath, a royal count of the king's own court, a wiry, balding man in his early forties, who rode a horse like a much younger man and carried himself like the seasoned veteran he was. Edelrath was one of Charlemagne's generals, often entrusted with independent commands and sometimes even given charge of the king's own heavy cavalry when a fight on open ground was in the offing. Edelrath spoke little but was said to be the best judge of men in Charlemagne's court. The high king never failed to seek his counsel in the matter of choosing leaders.

The visit might have been a disaster but for Ermengard. She arranged for the two emissaries to have the best quarters available at Adalgray, which meant giving up her own comfortable rooms. Baths were readied in the rooms as soon as the *missi* arrived, and serfs were assigned to be personal servants for them, making sure they had whatever they should require. Ermengard provided wine and cups, fresh fruit and flowers, and gave orders that the *missi* were not to be disturbed until they had bathed, napped, and refreshed themselves completely. She arranged a banquet for the late evening with honey wine and singers from among the townsfolk for entertainment. A whole boar roasted slowly in the huge fireplace of the great room, filling the air with a delicious, pungent aroma. Torches on all the walls added to the festive atmosphere.

The only problem was Athaulf. His apprehension over the visit of the king's high officials had proven too great for him. By midafternoon he had drunk himself into a state of delirious stupefaction. There was nothing Ermengard could do to bring him right before the banquet began. So she greeted the emissaries herself, along with Konrad, and lied to them that the count had come down with an unusual fever and was confined to his bed. Konrad, who was in awe of the *missi* and therefore not ready to function *in loco comes*, allowed his confident aunt to take the lead. Ermengard introduced him as the count's heir but then smoothly and sweetly gave orders for the disposition of the platoon of soldiers accompanying the *missi* and guided her guests into their quarters. The cool, relatively luxurious furnishings of their apartment immediately put the legates at ease, and Ermengard left them with smiles of welcome and promises of a memorable banquet later in the evening.

And the banquet was indeed memorable. Food and wine were plentiful and the singers outdid themselves with tunes from the villages and a few which Ermengard had learned when she and her husband lived for a time at King Pippin's court. Pippin loved the *chansons de geste* and risqué ditties of the people, and Ermengard knew that Charlemagne was even fonder of them than his father had been.

Late in the evening, when the *missi* had been feasted, entertained, and honored as thoroughly as could be, Ermengard chose an appropriate moment for the real purpose of the evening. First she prevailed on Konrad to introduce Attalus to the *missi*. This was no small feat, for Konrad hated the horse master. He exploded with anger when she first approached him. He was still rankled by the memory of the Saint George's Eve banquet when Ermengard had stood behind her incapacitated brother and spoken for him the contents of the charter clutched in her brother's left hand. She had even guided Athaulf's limp arm as he labored to lift a clod of earth and place it into Attalus's hand as a symbol of the proposed gift. Konrad had been apoplectic at the time but dared not make a scene before the whole household. He had been taken completely by surprise.

Later, in a fiery confrontation with his aunt, Konrad had raged and ranted about the loss of land that one day would have been his, but he was beaten in the end by Ermengard's calm composure and her patient reminders that the deed was already done, the parchment signed and sealed, with many witnesses to the intent of the document. If Konrad should try to insert his own will in the matter, the high king himself would hear how his justice and the tradition of the Franks had been thwarted. The whole matter was facilitated by Attalus's enormous popularity at Adalgray. The old warrior was covered in honor and had a reputation for unblemished integrity and absolute loyalty to Adalgray and the king. Almost everyone thought he richly deserved his reward.

Now at the banquet for the *missi*, Ermengard played out her hand. Speaking on behalf of her sick brother, she humbly introduced her nephew, extolling his prowess as a warrior, proclaiming his steadfast love and care for his father, and giving him the credit for the generosity now about to be bestowed on an old family friend and retainer. She laid on the formal flattery and exaggerations until even Konrad felt uncomfortable, then at last yielded the floor to him to make the official presentation of the charter proposal.

Konrad had no recourse but to slip down the slope his aunt had so skillfully greased for him.

"I call the Constable Attalus forward," he began, almost shouting. "I hereby announce the intention of my father, Athaulf, Count of

Adalgray, to make over a benefice to Attalus, the Master of Horse," Konrad droned mechanically. "This benefice shall be the fortress of Fershanz and all its lands—in trust to him as long as he shall serve the high king and the Count of Adalgray loyally and fruitfully. Attalus deserves this trust because of his long service on behalf of the House of Adalgray and because of his prestigious deeds in war in service of the high king. I present this charter proposal to the emissaries of the high king and implore them to take it for his consideration. If the high king does approve, we swear we shall pronounce Attalus, Constable of the House of Adalgray, Master of Fernshanz. So speaks Konrad, son of Athaulf, Lord of Adalgray, on behalf of my father."

Konrad's whole speech before the guests lasted less than two minutes, even with long pauses for remembering the words, which Ermengard had spent the whole day laboriously schooling him to say, and he delivered the whole message in a flat, monotonous tone devoid of any enthusiasm at all. At last he sat down with a thump and remained in an angry, frustrated state for the rest of the evening.

That might have been ceremony enough for the evening. But now Ermengard brought forth her final surprise, her son Sebastian. She bade him stand before the high commissioners and made her announcement in measured tones, with great dignity and pride.

"My lord bishop, good Count Edelrath, this is my son, Sebastian. He was born of a great Frankish warrior, Count Grennig, who, everyone knows, was a favorite of the High King Pippin. Our son is much like Grennig, courageous and steadfast. He shows every promise of being a worthy successor to his father. I now propose to entrust as apprentice this precious son of ours to our faithful servant and good friend Attalus, the Constable of Adalgray. Attalus has served this house with honor for a generation, in war and hard times. He has contributed significantly to our success and prosperity. He richly deserves now to be elevated to the title of lord—Lord of Fernshanz and captain of the Saxon March."

A hum filled the great room as Ermengard's words sank in. This was the first time anyone had ever referred to the horse master as "lord." Attalus himself stood with his mouth open in surprise. She turned to him and finished her address.

"If Karl, who is the high king, wills it, I hereby entrust this brave young man to you, Lord Attalus, my son, Sebastian, whom I know you will care for and prepare to be a great servant of the king and a worthy warrior of the Frankish people in the tradition of his father, Grinnig. Do you vow to undertake this sacred trust, so help you God?"

The horse master recovered himself and looked now from Sebastian to his mother with eyes full of pride. "I do, madame, with all my heart," he replied quietly.

Ermengard continued with one final gambit. Turning to the bishop, she delivered a risky proposal into his hands. "My lord bishop, we beg your blessing on our business here this night and implore you to present our proposal favorably before the high king, not only that Attalus should come to be Lord of Fernshanz but that he should also be invested with the apprenticeship of our son and nephew, Sebastian."

Everything now hung on the disposition of Bishop Regwald at this point. If he had other plans or if he was displeased with this unorthodox petition put forth through the boldness of a woman, Ermengard's hopes could be dashed.

The bishop conferred briefly in whispers with Lord Edelrath and then motioned for Sebastian to come forward.

"Are you a Christian boy, young Sebastian?" he began, surprisingly.

"Yes, my lord bishop, I was baptized as a babe."

"Good, and has the Holy Spirit been introduced into your soul through the Sacrament of Confirmation?" The bishop frowned down upon Sebastian from his full height.

Sebastian glanced nervously at his mother and answered hesitantly, "No, my lord, er . . . at least I don't think so."

Ermengard broke in quickly, "No, my lord bishop, he has not been confirmed. He is but fourteen years old and we have had little opportunity to bring him to a confirmation ceremony.

"I see," the bishop intoned somberly. "So you wish to give this boy over to be trained as a warrior in a distant place, quite far away from this secure home where he has grown up, where there are doubtless no women to look after him and likely no priests even to shrive him, is it?"

"No, my lord; that is, we wish him to be confirmed as soon as possible. It is just that . . . I have had no . . . it is hard to bring him to a cathedral, my lord. There are none close to Adalgray."

"All right, all right," the bishop excused her from his scolding. "Would you like to have him confirmed now, while we are here?"

Ermengard instinctively grasped her son by the shoulders and pulled him to her. "Oh yes, good bishop, so soon as possible." Sebastian was visibly stiff and uncomfortable, but he did not resist his mother's embrace.

"Well, then," said the bishop, "it shall be done. Tomorrow morning at Mass I will give him the sacrament. But first he must receive the Sacrament of Penance in order to be cleansed for the Holy Spirit. Have him come to the chapel immediately after this banquet and be ready to confess his sins. Then see that he fasts accordingly and spends this night in prayer."

"Yes, my lord. Of course, my lord bishop," Ermengard exclaimed and continued to clutch her son as the bishop returned to his fruit and wine and put his head together with Count Edelrath.

Chapter 4

Passing the Bar

Sebastian had little time to prepare for his confession. His mother rehearsed with him over and over again the Latin words of the penance rite and sternly advised him to be truthful and not hide any sins. She successfully resisted the temptation to prompt him to practice his confession on her, but she sat him down across from her, held his hands, and looked intently into his eyes.

"Sebastian, it is likely you will indeed become a warrior in the king's cavalry, as you wished for so long. But before you do, you need to understand what most of those warriors are like. With few exceptions they are an ugly, brutish lot, no better than the Saxons they fight. They kill without mercy, and they rape and burn just like Widukind's pagan rabble. You must not be like them. If you are, you will be no better than your cousin, Konrad. And you know what a brute that one is, don't you?"

"Yes, mother. But surely the king is not such a man. I have heard only good of him."

"You are only partly right, my son. King Karl tries to be different in many ways. I believe he truly is trying to change this barbaric world we live in. He encourages learning, he wants to build schools, and he defends the Church and calls himself a Christian king. But when it comes to war, he is more like King David than like Christ the King. The Old Testament David is his model. He gives no quarter, especially to pagans, and he does not rest until his enemies bow low before him."

"But surely that is what the king must do, mother, if he is to defend the Christian lands and people against the pagans."

"Bah! All this war! Every year it is a new campaign. So many good men die. And do you know who has done the most to bring peace to the German tribes? It is the missionaries—the great ones, the fearless ones, like Boniface. He was not afraid to die for God. That's why he could walk unarmed into a pagan camp and proclaim the Christ. Such men had tremendous courage and great faith. Compared to what they did—and still do—it is easy to ride against the foe alongside a thousand heavily armed comrades."

"But I must be a warrior, mother. I want to read, but I do not wish to be a priest or a monk."

"And so you shall be a warrior, as your father and uncle were, as Attalus is. Just be a different kind of warrior, a smarter one, not an unthinking brute. Be a warrior who finds other ways, who takes seriously what it means to say one is a Christian. You know what I mean. I have taught you from the time you were a baby. Tell me you know! Swear to me," she exclaimed passionately, grasping Sebastian's shoulders.

Alarmed by Ermengard's intensity, Sebastian hastened to reassure her, "It's all right, mother. I know. I will remember. I swear it."

Ermengard waited patiently with Sebastian while he sat in the chapel. When the bishop finally arrived, she laid her hand on his shoulder and gracefully glided out of the room.

His mother had prepared Sebastian well, and he got through the confession with ease. His list of sins was short and confined to such misdemeanors as tardy performance of his daily duties, daydreaming at lessons, and failure to inform his mother about some of his activities, especially those which concerned occasional forays into town to meet with some of the town's boys. They had been his fellow couriers during the siege and he found them fascinating because they were relatively free to do as they pleased, while he was confined to the military training field and chores in the great hall.

Bishop Regwald was satisfied with the boy's confession and his precise knowledge of the prayer for forgiveness. Sebastian seemed well prepared. But Regwald was curious about this son of a famous father and a very bold and enterprising mother. The bishop had no doubt that it was Ermengard who had manipulated the benefice for the horse master, and because he had seen more than enough of the often murderous Frankish customs involving succession to power, he instinctively guessed that it was because of Konrad that she was arranging for her son to leave Adalgray. He was interested to see if this boy was worth all the trouble Ermengard was going to on his behalf.

"Well, boy," he began after the confession had ended with the formal absolution and blessing, "you have said one prayer tolerably well. What other prayers can you say?"

"Beside my prayer for forgiveness, I can say the *Paternoster* our blessed Lord Jesus gave us, a 'Glory Be,' and some prayers to saints for protection. My mother showed me such prayers in a priest's book."

"What, your mother can read, then, is it?" the bishop exclaimed in surprise.

"No, lord bishop, she cannot. But she wants me to be able to. She has instructed the priests to teach me, and I know a little. Not much."

"But it's your mother who taught you your prayers, is it?"

"Yes, my lord bishop, some of them," Sebastian said quietly, "but Heimdal taught me most."

"Father Heimdal, I presume," corrected the bishop.

"No, my lord, he is only Heimdal, the blind man. But he knows all the prayers in Latin. He can say many more than any of the priests I know."

"How in the world does he know them, then, if he is not a priest? Who is he?"

"He is only a blind man, lord bishop. He has always been blind," said Sebastian, suddenly afraid that he had revealed something he should not have. "But he is very good at Latin. He has taught me all I know. And he is Attalus's friend, too."

"Well, say something to me in Latin, then. Let's see how well you have been taught by this Heimdal."

Sebastian thought a moment and then said in a sing-song voice of supplication, "*Beate pauperus spiritu. Dilato os tuum, et implebo illud. Esurivi enim, et dedistis mihi manducare.*"

The bishop snorted and then guffawed. "*Blessed are the poor in spirit. Open wide your mouth that I may fill it. When I was hungry ye gave me to eat.* These are all beggars' prayers. What? Was your man Heimdal a beggar, then?"

Sebastian lowered his head and said in a low voice, "Yes, your lordship, he was. He used to beg at the gates of a monastery. That's where he learned all his prayers. The monks took him in. But Attalus brought him here. He is not a beggar now. And I have learned a great deal from him."

"Well, the next thing you will say is that this Heimdal person has taught you how to say the Mass," the bishop remarked with some skepticism. "And I suppose he taught you how to read and write in Latin, too."

"No, lord bishop, Heimdal can certainly not read or write. Neither can I. But I am learning."

"And why, pray, do you want to learn? Do you wish to become a priest?"

"Oh, no, lord bishop, I wish to be a warrior. I want to fight in the high king's cavalry. But I want to read almost as much."

Well that would be refreshing, the bishop thought to himself, *a warrior who goes into battle singing the psalms in Latin! Hmm! I thought that only I could do that. An interesting boy, unorthodox but very commendable.* Aloud he said to Sebastian, "But you still have not told me why you want to read."

Sebastian thought a moment and took a deep breath, "Heimdal says we live in only a very small part of the world and that the rest of the world is vast and much different. He says one can only learn about it if one can travel—or if one can read. I want to know about things I don't understand and how to do what I cannot do now. My mother says it would make me a great man since mostly it is only the priests who know how to read. She says the high king can read and he likes others who can."

"That is so, Sebastian, my lad. He can himself read, though he struggles with it, and he cannot write at all. But he loves a scholar." After a reflective pause he continued, "All right, then, if I could arrange for you to have a teacher when you go to Fernshanz, will you be diligent and truly learn?"

"I will, my lord. I can learn. My mother says I have a good head for it. Even Heimdal says it."

"But what about becoming a warrior? Do you still want to? What about your training? It is very hard—and long. You will not have much time to devote to reading. Do you think you can do both?"

"I can, my lord. I can do both. Attalus says I can do anything. My mother thinks so, too. I don't mind the work."

"Well, you are a bit slight for a warrior, but you look fit and strong. And I can see that you are bright. We shall see. You will go to Fernshanz and we shall see."

Sebastian spent a restless and uncomfortable night in the chapel, mostly kneeling on the hard floor with his arms and head supported by the bench in front of him. He prayed, but his prayers were short, and after praying for his mother and Attalus a dozen times, and even for his cousin, Konrad, he quickly ran out of things to pray for. He did ask to be worthy of the great sacraments he was to receive on the morrow, but at fourteen years, rather than understanding them, he was more in awe of them. He knew mainly that they were holy and that he would be strengthened by them, and this was enough for him.

He spent much of the night contemplating the next day's events. Though he knew his confirmation was of primary importance, his thoughts strayed guiltily to the breakfast celebration after the Mass, when he was to formally receive the weapons and equipment of a Frankish warrior in the heavy cavalry. He remembered clearly Attalus's words when he had first begun to teach him, and he knew exactly what he would see on the presentation table.

"Listen carefully, Sebastian," the horse master had told the wide-eyed child, as he drew each item from a blanket set before them. "To become a warrior in the heavy cavalry, which is the core of the high king's army, one needs many weapons, and one must know and master each one completely. First and foremost, one needs the principal weapon of the mounted soldier, the Frankish lance. Some call it the winged spear. See how it has the crosspiece between the shaft and the blade?"

As he drew it out of the blanket, the lance seemed two or three times Sebastian's own body length, and his heart sank with the thought that he would not even be able to lift it properly, let alone throw it or plunge it into an enemy. Next, Attalus drew one weapon after the other, sharp and gleaming, from the blanket.

"These are not toys, my boy. They are the precious, indispensable tools of the mounted fighter. And they did not come easily. The long sword alone took perhaps two hundred hours and three ox carts of charcoal to perfect. Such a Frankish sword is renowned everywhere. We are not even allowed to trade it for fear an enemy would use it against us."

Attalus paused for emphasis. "You must have a warhorse, too, a great horse, bred to be big and ferocious as well as fast and strong. Such a horse you must know so well that he becomes a part of you. You will become like a centaur in battle, horse and rider forged into one body, one mind."

"And, Sebastian," he concluded, "never forget, these invaluable things have been procured for you by the service and courage of your father. Others will be gotten for you through the love of your mother and her friends and allies. All of them together, everything I have shown you, cost a fortune. And the horse—the horse costs as much as all the weapons combined."

Those thrilling recollections notwithstanding, Sebastian still faced a very long and dark night in the chapel, lit only by a single candle. His mother had come at the beginning, but she had been asleep in her chambers for hours now. Sebastian dared not sleep for fear he would be unworthy of the sacraments and therefore unworthy to be trained as a warrior—or a scholar. He was very excited about the prospect of both of these things and about the adventure of leaving Adalgray, and it was this excitement that saved him from the embarrassment of falling asleep.

He got up and wandered about the chapel, crossing endlessly from one side to another and investigating each corner. Each time he crossed the room, he was careful to genuflect before the altar. He must have done so a hundred times or more. And so the night passed until the first faint streaks of morning light appeared. He was able then to return to his position kneeling before the bench until his mother and her attendants came to wash his face and dress him for the Mass.

"Accipe signaculum doni Spiritus Sancti," pronounced the bishop. "Be sealed with the gift of the Holy Spirit." As the bishop leaned forward and anointed his forehead with the perfumed oil, Sebastian experienced a prickling in his scalp and a lump in his throat, and he believed it to mean that something truly supernatural was happening to him. But he was mostly disappointed because he did not actually feel the Holy Spirit entering his body. He felt content, nevertheless, that he was doing what was expected of him, that he would eventually be strengthened by the Holy Spirit, and that he could now go forth to become a great warrior and a loyal servant of the High King Karl, who, he knew instinctively, would one day be the greatest king of the Franks.

All passed without incident in the chapel Mass. Sebastian bore up well and made his mother proud with his responses during the short ceremony. The bishop, too, seemed pleased. It was at the breakfast after the Mass that the scenario became unscripted. Sebastian was thrilled beyond measure to find a special table in the great room upon which lay the weapons and armament he was to be given as a prize for reaching maturity. There was the famous Frankish long sword, a gift from Attalus, which still seemed to the boy to be almost as tall as himself. There was his father's *brunia*, or mailed leather shirt, which his mother had tried to make him wear during the siege. There also lay a banded, conical helmet and a beautiful lime-wood shield with a metal rim. There, too, was Sebastian's own bow and quiver, which he had used daily since he was six years old.

As the senior military officer present, Count Edelrath stepped forward to make the presentation. "Sebastian, son of Grinnig, on behalf of the king and your uncle, Count of Adalgray, I commend to you these weapons and armor to mark the beginning of your life as a Frankish warrior. Do you swear now to undertake your training under Attalus, the Master of Horse, for as long as it shall take to make you a warrior of prowess and fidelity in the service of your count and the High King Karl?"

"I do, my lord," Sebastian eagerly replied.

"Then we welcome you as a future Frankish soldier in the ranks of the king's cavalry." As he said these words, the count bent down and beat with his fist on the heavy oaken table before him. Immediately, all the males in the room did the same, and the few women present smiled at Sebastian's embarrassment at being the center of attention.

When the count's presentation was over, Konrad stepped forward with a long black lance in hand. "Sebastian," he shouted in an almost challenging tone, "I, too, have a gift for you. It is my father's lance, the lance of Athaulf the Saxon Slayer. Let us see if you can use it as well as he." With that, he lobbed the spear sideways at the boy standing in the middle of the room. Taken by surprise, Sebastian muffed the catch and the heavy javelin fell clattering to the floor. At once, there was an eruption of raucous laughter from Konrad and his cohort of young warriors.

"Perhaps he needs another fourteen years before he can handle Athaulf's spear," a rough companion of Konrad observed.

Another commented in a stage whisper, "They say he can read. Maybe instead of a warrior he should become a priest." More laughter. Others chimed in with similar comments on Sebastian's slim physique and unwarlike appearance. It became fairly obvious that this attack was not unplanned and that Konrad meant to leave a lasting impression on the *missi* that this slight boy was certainly no potential heir to the house of Adalgray or any other fief.

Sebastian was mortified. He looked from one face to another and found them to be either in contempt of him or deeply embarrassed for him. He fixed on the sneering face of his cousin and suddenly, swept away by a rage he had never experienced in his life, he raced to the gift table, swept up his bow, and before anyone could stop him, sent three arrows whistling, one after the other, a bare meter past the right ear of Konrad, into a heavy oak beam at the far end of the hall thirty meters away.

An astonished silence fell on the assembly, the mouths of the guests open in surprise. Ermengard was the first to speak, almost screaming "My lords!" Konrad's sneer turned to a scowl as he made a menacing move toward the boy. The room suddenly became alive with startled oaths and commentary.

In the midst of this, Count Edelrath slipped in front of the boy, held up a hand to all, and strode purposefully to the oaken beam where the arrows still seemed to quiver. He measured the pattern of the arrows' grouping, each one less than a palm's breadth from the others. He then tried to pull one of the arrows from the beam, and doing so only with difficulty, he turned and walked slowly back to the boy, smiling.

"May I borrow your bow, young warrior?" said the count warmly, holding out his hands. He aimed the bow again at the beam, gauged the distance, and tested the bowstring several times. Finally, he handed the small weapon back to Sebastian and patted his shoulder. "Well shot, Sir Archer. Couldn't have done better myself." With that he strode back to his table, sat down beside Bishop Regwald, and began to eat.

Several weeks later, the charter approving the award of Fernshanz to Attalus came back by courier with the king's seal. Attalus lost no time removing himself and Sebastian from Adalgray. Such belongings as they had, their weapons and armor, and their horses had long been made ready. The atmosphere of the last few weeks had gone from grey to grim, with Konrad tromping around the great house swearing and belittling Sebastian to anyone who would listen.

"Impudent little bastard. So he can shoot a bow. Let him become a foot soldier, then. That's what they do. Takes more than that to be in the cavalry. And that runt will never make it, damn his eyes. He's a weasel, the little puker, and no mistake!"

Ermengard could not wait for the word to come. She watched the road every day, hoping for a sight of the courier. Attalus and Sebastian stayed well out of the young count's way and spent most of their days hunting in the forest or preparing their horses and gear. Attalus had the great fortune to own a magnificent stallion that he had bred himself and been gifted with by Athaulf in better days. And Ermengard had given Attalus two promising mares which belonged to her. From one of them had come Sebastian's young stallion, a peppery-black courser with an intelligent eye and a mean hind leg.

The day of their departure, Ermengard met Attalus and Sebastian at Adalgray's main gate in the early dawn. No others from the house had braved Konrad's ire to see them off or even to give them a farewell supper the prior evening. The pair preferred it that way and wished to be miles from Adalgray before most of the house or town stirred. They took no servants with them, and no freemen felt at liberty to join them lest they incur Konrad's wrath. It was somewhat risky to travel alone, a man and a boy with four horses, for the forest was full of thieves and bandits. But Attalus knew trails and passages which would minimize any hostile encounter, and the two would ride sword and bow in hand.

Ermengard was heartbroken to see them go. She studied them as they made their final preparations for the trip, marveling with some alarm at how similar they were: Attalus—lean, sun-darkened face, dark hair streaked with silver, a fan of wrinkles around each eye, a mottled mustache languishing down both sides of his thin lips; Sebastian—a wiry body, long black hair falling straight and thick halfway down his back, deep-set eyes, black except in bright sunlight when they appeared a warm brown.

Her eyes filled with tears and she could not look Attalus in the eye. She kissed her son over and over again and made him promise for the thousandth time to pray, learn to read, and stay close to Attalus, who would teach him all he would ever need to know. Finally, she saw him up on his horse, kissed his knee and bade him start out. Taking Attalus aside, she pressed his hands between hers and finally looked straight into his eyes.

"Attalus, my dear, old love," she whispered. "Take good care of my son . . . our son!" And she kissed him soundly on the mouth and ran back through the gate.

A league or so down the road, a hooded figure stepped out of the ground fog into the path of the riders. A spectral voice lifted from the gloom: "Have you got a gentle palfrey for a poor, blind man, my lord?"

"We have indeed, my old friend," answered Attalus, dismounting to help Heimdal climb up on one of Ermengard's mares.

Chapter 5

Fernshanz

The Saxon March, Autumn 770

It was not for nothing that Konrad had agreed to let Attalus command at Fernshanz. His father's old companion might be past his prime, but as a seasoned constable, he was a master of fortress defense, and the Saxon raids were now coming more boldly and with increasing frequency, almost up to the great river.

As they made their way steadily along the forest paths, Attalus schooled Sebastian about their new home. "Fernshanz is built upon the ruins of an old Roman advance fortress, which is part of what they used to call 'the Limes.'"

"Why was it built here in this wild place, Attalus? It seems so far away from anything," Sebastian asked as he peered into the dense woods.

"The Limes were a line of defensive strong points on both sides of the Rhine built against the Goths and the Alemanni."

"And also against us Franks, don't forget," piped up Heimdal from behind. "We were just another lot of stinking barbarians to the Romans."

Attalus, who was used to the blind man's critiques, continued his tutorial. "East of the river, the Limes fortresses were little more than stockades, not very big or elaborate. They served mainly as forward bases for rapid reaction and only lasted a few years before the Romans retreated behind the Rhine again. We Germans were too much for them."

"Too many, you mean," interjected Heimdal. "We've never had any trouble breeding. It's what we do best."

After awhile Attalus added, "You will be able to find many signs of the Roman occupation around Fernshanz. Farmers discover them all the time in the fields. You might find it interesting to dig around in the old mounds where we think they disposed of their refuse—even some of their dead." They rode on in silence as Sebastian imagined the legions marching along the same track as wild bands of his ancestors lurked in the surrounding thickets.

"What about the people there now, Attalus? Who are they? Will we know anybody?"

"No, lad. Many of the people who are at Fernshanz now are serfs who will farm for us, but they're not warriors. We may find about half a hundred of 'the king's free'— free Franks who did not go with Count Welf. I'm told they can be trusted, but only a few of them are soldiers. Too few, I'm afraid. Fernshanz is a dangerous place now, with the Saxons making more and more raids into Frankish territory. I've heard they've even established a walled camp with a sizable garrison not much more than a day's ride from Fernshanz. They say the Saxon Prince Widukind commands it. He's a notorious fighter."

"Yes," chimed in Heimdal, "he has the reputation of a man who loves a good brawl, and worst of all, he has the cheek to say that the land the Eresburg sits upon belongs to the Saxons. If you ask me, he will prove a considerable pain in the Frankish backside."

"The land is good," continued Attalus. "It has excellent grazing areas, good water, and it's right on a river that leads to the Rhine. There's plenty of cleared land, but there aren't enough people. Not many free farmers will come here for fear of the Saxons. And the serfs don't fight."

"Why not?" Sebastian asked.

"The serfs can't leave the land; they are bound to it. But neither do they have to put their lives at risk like the the king's free, who are soldiers as well as farmers. Every free Frank is obliged to fight. That's the price of his freedom. He can come and go as he likes, but when any Frankish territory is in danger, no matter where he is, he must fight."

"Why should the serfs fight?" Heimdal said. "What stake do they have? They are not even allowed to marry without the lord's permission."

"Well, they're still better off than the slaves," Attalus temporized evasively.

"Of whom we still have more than a few at Fernshanz," Heimdal added ruefully. "Those poor devils have nothing, and they work whenever and wherever the lord decides."

"But, Attalus, don't you own all the land?" Sebastian asked.

"Actually, son, the king owns the land—Adalgray and Fernshanz both. It's a bit complicated. You see, Fernshanz is part of a royal benefice. The king has awarded it to the counts of Adalgray in return for their service and loyalty, but he could take it back if he wanted."

Once again Heimdal added a caveat, "He's unlikely to do that. It's hard to find a good fighter and leader who is also a good manager of the land. King Karl would only take a lord's benefice away from him if it were a matter of treason or a refusal to fight when called."

"So Fernshanz is now a part of Adalgray, then?"

"Oh, yes," Attalus affirmed. "Count Welf's loss was Konrad's gain. We shall have to send some of our harvest returns back to Konrad, and he, in turn, must send gifts and a certain portion of his wealth to the king. But the main thing Konrad must do is use his land to equip himself and his men so he has what he needs when the high king calls him to go and fight somewhere. We shall have to do the same. We must have horses, weapons, armor, and men, and Fernshanz must pay for all of that."

"You've often told me that the weapons and equipment I was given were terribly expensive, the horse especially. If most of the people at Fernshanz are simple farmers, how do they pay for what we need?"

"Excellent question, my boy," Heimdal barged in blithely. "I can see you will be good at managing Fernshanz when Attalus is gone. You certainly need to know the real cost of how things get done. It's very simple, you see. Everything and everybody has a place and a role; the warriors fight, the priests pray, and the poor, empty-headed peasants work—day in and day out, from dawn to dusk, until they return to the mud they crawled out of."

Attalus sighed. "Beware of Heimdal, Sebastian. He lives in a completely different and unrealistic world. It's not as bad as all that. We must have order, and Heimdal forgets to mention that it is the warriors' job to protect the peasants."

Heimdal laughed sarcastically. "Unfortunately, he is right, Sebastian. I'm afraid God has intentionally made the peasants stupid for the benefit of the lords. If you gave the peasants the choice, most of them would rather be safe than free. I just thought you ought to know how things are managed. Well, go on, Attalus."

Attalus cleared his throat. "A responsible lord will take care of his people. It is not only the right thing but the sensible thing to do. If they starve or get sick, the lord loses his income, and so it behooves him to see that they remain healthy and as happy as may be."

"Right, Sebastian," retorted Heimdal. "Give them a celebration now and then and let them get drunk and fornicate around the fire as their old pagan ancestors did. That keeps 'em happy. And it's good for business."

"Enough, Heimdal," Attalus said sternly. "Let me continue. The serfs do have plots of land they can farm for their own benefit, but for the privilege of using this land, they must farm other land exclusively for the lord. Occasionally, they must give other labor to the lord according to his needs."

"Occasionally is a very generous word," said Heimdal. "What that actually means, Sebastian, is that they spend the bulk of their time working for the lord, and their own needs come last. Sometimes I wonder how they feed themselves. Of course, they cheat as often as they can get away with it. Why wouldn't they?"

"At least the freemen can leave if they can't abide their lord," Attalus persisted. "The serfs are bound to the land."

"If you are listening well, Sebastian," Heimdal went on, "you will understand that there's really not much difference between a serf and one of the so-called king's free. Oh, it's true the freeman can leave the land and move on if he chooses, but he still has to work for a living somewhere, and almost always it's on someone else's land. And here's the main difference—no matter where he goes the freeman has the privilege and the duty of serving in the king's army whenever he is called. Of course to do that, he has to equip himself with the necessary weapons and a horse, if he can afford one."

Attalus continued mechanically, as if he had been through the same conversation many times. "It's true, most of the freemen use land owned by a lord, but they only have to pay rent in money or in kind to use it."

"Money? Who's got money?" Heimdal interjected. "And by the way, that *only* Attalus pronounces so casually means the so-called king's freeman has got to pay his lord one-third to one-half of his harvest every year."

"That sounds like a lot," Sebastian mused. "Can such a farmer actually produce enough on the land he uses to pay for a horse and weapons?"

"No indeed, my good young man," Heimdal said approvingly. "You learn quickly. The peasant can only produce what the lord needs if he puts his wife and children to work all day every day, except Sunday. They are the ones who do odd jobs and forage through field and forest to provide for the family while the man coaxes what he can from his land. And often it is still not enough. Wait and see—the cost of weapons and a horse is often want and sometimes famine."

"It's the law, Sebastian," Attalus continued, "that any freeman who is able must equip himself with a spear, a sword and shield, a helmet, and a horse. Every freeman must be ready to fight."

"What if the man does not have enough land or can't afford to equip himself?"

"Then he must join with two or three other men and produce enough for at least one warrior. The men themselves will then select which of the four actually must go and fight."

"Hmmpf!" scoffed Heimdal. "It's not as civilized as all that. Most of them simply draw straws for the privilege of going off to be killed for the lord and king. Of course, they will buy themselves off if they can afford it. More often than not you will find it's the poorest bugger who actually winds up going."

In spite of Heimdal's harassment, Attalus was grateful for the long hours on the trail with Sebastian. He rarely had enough time at Adalgray to teach the boy about the people or how to manage the manor, things he would surely need to know. Now he was able to explain in patient detail not only the basic economics of life at Fernshanz but also how the fort accomplished its main reason for being—to help secure the borders of the Frankish lands against the Saxons.

He took a long time describing every aspect of the physical characteristics of the fortress. The lord's manor house at Fernshanz was built on top of a motte, a low hill that was flat on the top and dominated a village of about four hundred peasant souls. The manor included a tall wooden blockhouse, the keep, which was the last refuge against an attacker. In addition to the main house and hall, the fortress had other rooms and buildings, including stables, barns, kitchens and workshops, which were all connected around an inner courtyard. The hilltop citadel was circled by a wall of dirt upon which a parapet of heavy rocks and logs had been constructed. At the bottom of the hill was a ditch, over which a drawbridge conducted the road from the village into the citadel and its manor house.

The village below was also surrounded by a palisade that was built along the top of a low earthen wall. It was mostly in disrepair but was still potentially effective. From this rough, wooden fence, the fields spread out in a great semi-circle from the village, eventually ending at the edge of the forest. The river bounded one entire side of the village, including the back side of the motte. The proximity of the river was a major advantage for Fernshanz in that it could easily bring such trade as there was into the village, and it facilitated the movement of horses and men to and from the Rhine. For half a kilometer in either direction from the village the river was lined with grassy fields and marsh, ideal for grazing cattle and horses.

Several riders who had been patrolling slowly before the village walls saw the unfamiliar horsemen as soon as they came into view. They blew an alarm, immediately formed a line, and raced toward them, spears held aloft. At thirty meters, they pulled up, seeing only one warrior, a monkish figure, and a boy. Nervously scanning the woods on both sides of the road, the riders strove to keep their mounts under control as they pranced and strained to continue the charge. The men were lightly armed with only spears and bows. Attalus knew them at once as a band of free Franks—farmers, to be sure, but fighters as well. One of them called out, "Declare yerself, sir. At once!"

The horse master called back calmly, "I am Attalus, Constable of Adalgray and now Lord of Fernshanz."

The horsemen, immediately relieved, came on with javelins lowered. The spokesman, a spirited young Frank of strong build and bold eyes, bowed low over his horse's neck and greeted them. "Welcome to yer home, sir. Thank God ye are come. The Saxons are raidin'. There are signs of 'em everywhere, and only two days ago, three villages to the south on Count Athaulf's land, from whence ye've just come, were overrun and burned. They say it's Widukind who leads 'em."

The Frank paused a moment and then said, "I be Anchesigel, one of the sergeants here." Looking now straight at the boy, he included him in his welcome. "Ye must be young Master Sebastian. Welcome to Fernshanz." He bowed again. Sebastian felt a surge of pride that he had been deferred to almost on the same level as Attalus. As for the old horse master, he was simply gratified to see that their approach to the village had been so quickly noted.

Children of all ages had gathered, and as they rode up to the gate, escorted by the little troop of scouts, they were met by a stout, round-faced man with large teeth, beet-red cheeks, and gobs of reddish hair spilling over his forehead and pouring out of his clothes from every opening. The man was so bizarre it was hard to look at him without gawking. Even more unsettling, he spoke in an outrageously loud voice, as if he felt forever obliged to shout. He illustrated every sentence with grand and flowing gestures, waving his arms about and punching the sky for added emphasis.

While they were still some distance away, he boomed his greeting, "Welcome, lords! Welcome to your new home. Thank God you have arrived! I am your steward, Baumgard. You will have no better servant in all of Frankland than I; you will see for yourselves soon enough. Nothing escapes me. You will need to ask for nothing. And I will make sure that you are not cheated but are treated exactly as befits the lords of this place. I am the one who sees to everything—the planting, the harvest, the rents, everything! You can count on Baumgard, my lords. No better steward lives this side of the high king's own court. I, Baumgard, am here to live and die, if need be, for you, the lords of Fernshanz!" For emphasis he jabbed a pudgy finger in the air and finished with a low bow.

The man seemed so preposterous that Attalus nearly burst out laughing but caught himself in a cough, hiding his mouth behind a fist.

Stunned by the spectacle, Sebastian did not know what to think and almost rode into the man before he thought to stop his horse.

"My lords," boomed the steward, "we are greatly relieved to know you have come through the dangerous forest with no harm, and we sorely need you." Rolling his eyes to the heavens, he proclaimed dolefully, "The times, they are perilous! But if you will go straight away up to the manor house, some refreshments await you there, and I will come at once to bring you the news. Festus here will lead you. There's a good boy." He indicated a dirty youth about Sebastian's age, who had already attached himself to the mane of Attalus's horse.

Their first night in Fernshanz was spent in comfort and plenty thanks to the steward, who, as he promised, anticipated their every need. However, it proved to be the last night for a good while in which they would truly rest or feel at ease. The news was indeed grim. The fabled Saxon chieftain Widukind, with a war band of Saxon light cavalry, had attacked several Frankish villages to the south, destroying and pillaging as he went.

For the next several weeks, Attalus organized daily patrols of horsemen, leading them from dawn to dusk in search of the Saxon raiders. Sebastian, to his great disappointment, was instructed to stay within the walls. Moreover, he was tasked with overseeing the rebuilding of the palisade surrounding the village and clearing debris from the ditch in front of the citadel motte. It was not a job that appealed to Sebastian, and it proved to be acutely intimidating, as it was the first time he had ever been required to give orders as a lord. However, it was a good way to meet the men and boys of Fernshanz, and he immersed himself in the task.

It was late summer, and cooler but still dry. Leaves had already begun to fall for lack of moisture, and the crops ripened in the fields and gardens. The men of the village divided their labor between the fields, the wall, and the daily patrols. The village included fewer than fifty Franks who could be called warriors—peasants to be sure, but freemen or at least semi-free. All had some kind of weapon, at least a spear or a sword of sorts, but none had armor. At any one time, a third of them would be away with Attalus on patrol.

Just past his fifteenth birthday, Sebastian was growing less rapidly than some of his contemporaries, but his slender build was deceptive, belying a wiry strength and uncommon reserves of stamina and energy.

He could run on foot for hours and he was already a fearless and acrobatic horseman, able to mount from any angle, cling to his horse at all speeds and over any terrain, and control it simply with pressure from his knees. He had long since begun the grueling martial exercises Attalus prescribed, and he practiced at every opportunity. Attalus found himself needing to call Sebastian away from his exercises even to eat or sleep.

The girls of the village were thrilled with the new young lord. They marveled at the contrast between the red-bearded Franks with their copper-colored hair and this dark, handsome lad with his deep brown eyes and long black hair, almost as silky as a girl's. They were fascinated with his air of serious intensity and purposefulness. They gathered in bunches whenever he rode or walked by and watched him in between chores as he carried out Attalus's orders among the men each day. They made games of trying to get Sebastian to laugh or even smile, rarely succeeding. Some of the boldest made suggestive gestures at him, and one portly maid even lifted her skirt and presented him with the sight of her bare bottom, sticking out her tongue at him from over her shoulder. Sebastian's jaw dropped in shock and he stumbled over the rough track of the road, causing peals of laughter from the girls.

Sebastian felt weighed down by his responsibility. Attalus simply told him again and again, "You are the lord when I am absent. You have charge of everyone and everything. When I am not here, your word is law. If anyone defies you, he must be punished. Punish him yourself if you can. Do not show weakness. Beat the peasants if you must, but it is better to use patience. Show them how to do a task and then convince them that it is necessary. Have faith in your abilities. You are the son of a count."

The peasants working the fields, more than half of whom were serfs, proved to be no problem—Baumgard, the steward, saw to that. Rebuilding the outer palisade and clearing the ditch below the citadel, however, was Sebastian's job. His work crew consisted mainly of boys and a few young, dull-witted serfs. It was hard work to hew fresh trees and plant the sharpened pales. The crews had to be driven. On the first day, a group of young men and boys promptly sat down in the shade of the wall as soon as Sebastian rode off to check on the crew at the ditch. When he returned, they did not even get up but watched him laconically. When he ordered them to resume work, a lanky, big-boned lad rose slowly in defiance, yawned, and sneered to his friends, "I expec' it's just too hot to work, eh, lads? This old wall won't stop no Saxons anyhow. Besides, I don't see no lord around here, only this little, skinny lad."

The crew laughed as the youth stood squarely in front of Sebastian, hands on his hips. Sebastian turned beet red and considered riding the young man down. Instead, he took a deep breath and sat for a moment, completely still. Then he turned his horse and galloped away to the manor house, the sound of triumphant laughter trailing after him. When he returned, the boys were still lounging beside the fence. They rose, surprised and curious to see the young lord back so soon. Sebastian dismounted, black eyes flashing, and strode immediately to his adversary, carrying in each hand a long practice sword of wood.

"What is your name?" he demanded, barely able to control his anger.

The tall lad, looking increasingly uncertain about the situation, muttered, "Why, Bardulf, if it's all the same to ye. I come here from Adalgray about the same time as ye did. I fought on the walls there durin' the siege, I did. And I come here to get away from all such as that."

"Well, Bardulf, I don't care where you came from or what you did there. I am the son of a count and the ward of Attalus, Lord of Fershanz. I am responsible for this place in the absence of Attalus. We are building this wall because the Saxons may come through that forest at any minute, and we must have time to get to the inner defenses. You will build this wall, as I tell you to do, or I will knock your head off." With that, he threw the boy one of the swords and advanced upon him at once, swinging his own sword.

The fight was short. Sebastian circled and spun around the bigger boy like a wolf considering a cornered deer. With a shout and a sudden flurry of blows, he bloodied Bardulf's head in several places, drove the breath from him with a sharp poke with the point of his sword, and nearly broke Bardulf's sword arm in a riposte to a wild swing of desperation. The big lad dropped his sword and sank to his knees, howling in pain.

Sebastian was at once sorry to have hurt him, realizing that he had a far greater advantage in years of training than his opponent. However, he caught himself and said nothing to the boy.

"You men," he commanded, "get up at once and continue with your work. This section must be done before sunset. We only have two more sections to repair, and then we will be finished. You had best be praying the Saxons don't come tonight. Now, look alive, and get to it."

Sebastian picked up the swords, mounted, and loped away again toward the crew at the ditch, his heart pounding, fighting the impulse to scream aloud and ride away furiously. He had won his first fight.

A week later, the outer palisade was finished. It was constructed of a long semicircle of pointed stakes bound together by wild grape vines and enclosing an earthen wall on which the soldiers could fight to repel invaders. Although it was no real deterrent to a large force of determined aggressors, it might serve to buy just enough time for the villagers to retreat inside the motte's citadel.

Attalus's tireless patrols kept him far from Fernshanz for days at a time. His forays extended even to the seaports of the Frisian towns to the north and east, and he sent riders with reports to the king almost daily about Saxon incursions. He was particularly concerned about Widukind's efforts to forge ties with the Frisians in the port cities. Such an alliance could greatly increase Widukind's ability to resupply and reinforce himself against the Franks. Charlemagne might well worry about such intrigues.

Attalus, however, had to content himself with spying and searching, his force being too small to challenge Widukind directly. Occasionally he was able to surprise small Saxon raiding parties, and once he intercepted a train of carts with spoils the Saxons were transporting from a successful attack against a Frankish town to the south. The Saxons had become so emboldened that they now raided almost as far south as the city of Cologne. Attalus worried constantly that Fernshanz would be next on Widukind's list. Its likely salvation thus far was that it was no rich prize but a thorny nest of tough, resourceful Franks whose conquest might be more costly than it was worth. Still, every instinct told Attalus to stay home and strengthen the defenses. Only his firm conviction that he played an essential role as the eyes and ears of the king persuaded him to allow a fifteen-year-old boy to attempt the work of a trained engineer and act as the stronghold's temporary war chief.

For his part, following Attalus's meticulous instructions, Sebastian worked every day from dawn to dusk to prepare for a Saxon attack. He shored up every defense. He supervised a schedule of constant patrols and watches, and because no man knew where Sebastian might be at any one time, they all stood their watches vigilantly. If Sebastian did catch a sentry asleep, he had him thrown into stocks in the middle of the village for an entire day. He saw to the storage of grain and other food within the barns of the inner citadel and had every available cistern and barrel filled with water. He ordered peasants to amass piles of throwing rocks and logs all along the walls of the citadel, and he set the town's three fletchers to crafting arrows on a full-time basis.

When Attalus was available, the two prepared lists of battle assignments for everyone in the town, even the children. Attalus left behind work orders to be fulfilled by the townspeople for every day of his absence. At least three times a week, Sebastian drilled the few fighting men and the entire population of the town on what to do in case of an attack. At different times of the day or night he had horns sounded, calling the peasants from their beds or from the fields and sending them pell-mell behind the walls and into the inner citadel. Although they could see the logic of his preparations and were forced to admire Sebastian's thoroughness and diligence, the people groaned with the extra effort and additional duties and complained audibly about their young master. Sebastian pretended not to notice, keeping his eye fixed on the task at hand. He slept little and smiled not at all, his life consisting of little beyond worry and work.

At the end of October, the month Charlemagne was pleased to call *Windumemonath*, month of the winds, the rains began to fall with increasing frequency. Mist often hung over the fields and forests around Fernshanz until midmorning. With the harvest in and the fortress reinforced in every way he could think of, Sebastian redirected the townsfolk to collect wood for the winter. Attalus began to stay at home for longer periods. However, he went out one last time to check the nearest routes from Saxony into Frankish territory. His vigilance thus far had been one of the main reasons the Saxons had avoided Fernshanz, knowing it would be no easy target.

Ironically, the rain and cold were a comfort to Sebastian, who had begun to believe there would be no Saxon attack this year. He had been spared the test, and he might soon be able to lay down his terrible burden of responsibility. He had become so tired and tense of late that when he lay down to sleep he immediately began to weep and then fell into a deep, short sleep, followed by fitful dreams. One persistent dream found him frantically clawing up the face of a steep cliff only to find another cliff beyond the first, or plodding through mud up to his ankles in the pouring rain. He felt old, older than the eldest villager, and he awoke fearful and unrested.

In the late afternoon of the fifth day of Attalus's latest absence, as the day's fine drizzle turned into a stone-cold rain and the daylight faded suddenly and perceptibly, Sebastian stood on the parapet by the main gate preparing to call in the mounted patrols. With him were Anchesigel, a few of the free Frank soldiers on duty, and Lothar, a peasant youth of about twenty years, whose surprisingly innovative ideas about provisioning the fortress and collecting materials for its defense proved invaluable to Sebastian.

From the first, Lothar stood out from the others because of his cheerful optimism and willingness to participate in any task at hand. Though Lothar was a serf, Sebastian adopted him at once as an advisor and foreman for his projects on the defenses. Lothar not only became Sebastian's loyal ally, he daily volunteered ingenious suggestions that made the work go more quickly or efficiently. It was he who had suggested staking dogs and penning geese all around the outer walls of the fortress to act as night watch sentinels. It was also Lothar who urged that all available forage from the fields be brought inside the walls and that the peasants be allowed to butcher swine from the forest before the normal time. He even sent boys to the nearby creeks and rivers to gather heavy, round stones that would be easier to throw down from the parapets and smaller stones for use with slings.

Just as Anchesigel was preparing to sound the horn to recall the patrols for the night, those same riders came pelting down the narrow track leading from the dark forest at a wild gallop. The sentries barely had time to swing open the gates to let the riders clatter through. Behind them, emerging from the woods, were scores of dark riders with banners still clearly visible despite the wind and rain. Sebastian was struck dumb by the numbers and almost paralyzed by their approach. He shook himself and finally commanded Anchesigel to sound the alarm. As soon as he blew it, others sentinels took it up on various parts of the wall, sounding a constant, urgent alarm. Immediately the town became a cauldron of movement as the peasants burst from their houses and streamed toward the bridge leading up to the citadel, awkwardly carrying their weapons along with their children.

Sebastian saw at once that the horde of advancing riders could not be stopped at the wall. Conferring with Anchesigel, he sent word to the men on the wall to wait for the signal to fire a volley of arrows into the advancing mass of horses and riders, and then, as the horn of retreat was sounded, to make for the citadel posthaste. His heart pounding, Sebastian was about to give the command to commence firing when Anchesigel seized his arm and squeezed it hard.

"M'lord," he gasped, "m'lord!"

"What, man, what?" said Sebastian, close to panic and wincing with the pressure of the brawny sergeant's grip.

"M'lord Sebastian, stop! It is the king!"

Chapter 6

Venit Rex

Charlemagne rode near the head of his troops, just behind the advance guard, and the king and the guard arrived at the gate nearly simultaneously. The first riders began shouting and pounding on the gate, which was still firmly secured. "Open for the High King of the Franks! What goes on here? Open at once!"

Sebastian quickly gave the word to open, and the king rode in, noticing with keen interest the frantic scramble of the peasants who continued to stream across the bridge and into the citadel.

"Who's in charge here?" shouted the king. "Attalus? What the devil's going on?"

Sebastian leaped down from the parapet and breathlessly approached the king. "I, my lord . . . uh, I, sire. I'm in charge," he gasped, bowing awkwardly in his haste.

The king bent down from his horse to see Sebastian better in the fading light. "You? Why, you're only a boy. Where's Attalus?" he demanded.

Fighting to pull himself together, Sebastian became very still for a moment, took a deep breath, and bowing low and formally this time, answered in a respectful voice, "My lord high king, I am Sebastian, son of Count Grennig and ward of Lord Attalus, Master of Fernshanz. He is away on your business against the Saxons. He has entrusted me with the command of this fortress. If you will give me a moment, sire . . ."

Sebastian turned to Anchesigel and ordered him to have the soldiers stand down from the walls and the peasants return to their homes. "And tell Baumgard to prepare a supper for the king and his officers," he added.

After this stilted, overly formal address, Sebastian bowed again and then forced himself to look straight into the king's eyes, as Attalus had always advised him to do with any man. He was aching with fear that he would fail to measure up, and he had no idea what to do next.

After a terrible moment of silence, the king suddenly laughed and blurted out in a high voice, "By God, you're a plucky young greyhound! I reckon you are in command after all. And from the looks of it, you've not done a bad job, either. I never heard so much racket coming out of a fort—dogs, chickens, geese, and those confounded horns everywhere. It's enough to turn even the Saxons away! And I expect we may have just escaped getting a prick or two from your archers there, eh, lad? Well done, my boy, as far as I can see in this gloom. Have you got anything to eat?"

"Oh, yes, my lord high king," Sebastian replied with enthusiasm. "We have venison the hunters brought in just this morning, and the peasants have been slaughtering swine all week. Our steward is roasting meat for you this very moment. Will you be pleased to come with me into the citadel?"

From that point the evening proceeded wonderfully for Sebastian. The king proved to be in good humor, and Sebastian found it marvelously easy to be in his presence and converse with him. Charlemagne had a prominent, almost musical and curiously high voice, especially when he was excited or enthusiastic, but he moved with absolute authority and was comfortable with everyone. Baumgard outdid himself with hospitality, bringing in the hot, roasted meat at just the right moment after the king had finally settled into the great hall of the manor house. He also provided the only moment in the entire evening when Charlemagne was at a loss for words.

"Great High King of the Franks," boomed Baumgard as he ushered in a throng of servants with the plates of meat and pitchers of wine, "please accept these humble offerings gleaned from the fields and forests of our fair land, and know that we offer them to you, O Great King, with loyalty and admiration. May they be the nourishment of your body and an aid to your high purpose, whatever it may be!"

Stunned for a second, Charlemagne burst out laughing and the rest of the room erupted as well; but the king jumped up gamely, slapped Baumgard on the back, and thanked him heartily for his good offices. He then sloshed some wine into a cup and raised it to his companions. "Friends and comrades, this is a good beginning. Here's to the people of this place, good Franks all, and to the next few days' work. May we show the Saxons what it means to be a Frankish warrior and teach 'em a good lesson!"

Charlemagne drained his cup, as did all present. However, he would drink little more for the remainder of the evening, being content to lounge on a bench by the large stone hearth in the middle of the great room, pulling on his long mustaches and observing the proceedings keenly as his captains dispelled the cold and rain of their long ride with wine and song. The king joined in the battle songs and lays of the ancient Franks, and he devoured a prodigious amount of roasted meat. He even laughed loudly at some of the bawdy rhymes and ditties. But he would not join in the drinking or the wild boasting and banter of his counts and officers.

Sebastian remained in a state of awe for most of the evening. The high king was spectacle enough, being a head taller and bigger in frame than almost anyone in the room. He seemed a giant in comparison to some. But all the men seemed large and strong to Sebastian, who divided his time between staring at the entourage of the king and making sure the kitchen staff continued to provide whatever was required.

All of Charlemagne's captains seemed extraordinary to Sebastian. They were full of vigor and excitement, even after the long day on the road, and they pounded on the tables with their fists or the butts of their knives to emphasize their words or their appreciation for another man's remarks. The room was charged with energy as they shouted back and forth and moved about the room joking and laughing. Many were dressed more elaborately than the king, who wrapped himself in a simple blue cloak and wore no crown. Some of the men wore bright clothing and sported strange amulets on their arms and Aquitanian jewelry around their necks. As they drank, their banter became more vulgar and aggressive.

"Balderich, you son of a stable bitch, I'll be buggered if I don't kill more Saxons than you in the days ahead," shouted a young count bedecked in a yellow silk tunic and a bejeweled leather belt.

"Izzat so, my fine Theodulf? And what would the son of a Visigoth peddler and a Moorish sheep know about killing Saxons?" replied a burly, red-bearded count with close-cropped hair. "We all know you'd far rather be lounging by the seashore in Al Andalus with your seven dark virgins, wishing your book were the Qur'an instead of the Holy Bible."

Sebastian understood little of this lively, coarse banter, and he wondered that such insults did not lead to fighting. But these men, long accustomed to campaigning together against others, merely laughed with delight at each fresh barb and competed with one another to heckle their friends in the most outrageous ways. All of them were in high spirits, and though they had ridden hard for days, they could not contain their enthusiasm for the coming fight. Combat, as Sebastian would soon learn, was not only their chief occupation but their ultimate thrill, their reason for being. All else was simply prelude.

At one point in the evening, during a lull in the singing, Charlemagne noticed Sebastian still gamely trying to tend to every need of the crowd of unexpected guests. He watched him attentively for a while and then called him over to the table by the fireplace.

"Well, then, young Sebastian, what sort of lad are you? What is it that you hope to be or do when you grow to be a man?" the king began in a kindly tone.

Sebastian replied without hesitation "Why, sire, I am to be a Frankish warrior in your cavalry, if God give me strength."

"So, a warrior is it, eh? And in the heavy cavalry, no less! Well, I suppose you can ride if you've spent much time around Attalus. There's no better teacher of horsemanship in the world. I've got some good horses myself, but none as fine as those he breeds. I tried many a time to lure him to my court, but he wouldn't leave Adalgray. In truth, I never understood what hold your father and old Athaulf had on him. Well, he missed a good chance to rise high amongst the Franks, but he's always been a shrewd fighter and a superb horse master. You do well to apprentice under him."

"Thank you, my lord king," Sebastian murmured. Then, as if unable to contain himself any longer, he blurted out, "Sire, it's true I want to be a warrior, and I work hard at it, very hard. But there is something else."

"What is it, lad? What could be more important than being in the heavy cavalry?" exclaimed the king in mock surprise.

"Sire, I want to learn to read. It's not that it's more important than becoming a warrior, but I feel that there is something else . . . I want to read the Bible first and the holy stories. But I want to know more about everything. They say you have many at your court who can read. They even say you can read, sire," Sebastian finished this confession breathlessly, embarrassed that he had been bold enough to form the words. His face burned, and he cast his eyes down.

"Whoa, lad," exclaimed the king. "You're a rare one! I spend my days scouring the kingdom for men who'd like to become scholars. Most warriors have no taste for it at all and ridicule the ones who do. And here you are in the middle of the woods at the far end of the realm and you want to read! Amazing!" He paused and studied the boy.

"I can indeed read," continued the king enthusiastically. "In fact, I'm something of a scholar myself—of a sort. And I love men who are smarter than me! They might teach me something, by thunder. God knows we need such men in this wilderness."

The king leaned forward as if to get a better look at Sebastian. "Tell you what, my good young man, I'll confer with Attalus when he finally shows up, and if he supports you—and I trust his judgment entirely— I'll see to it that you get a tutor, if I have to send for one to Rome itself. Do you think you can do it all—train to fight, help run this place, and find time to learn to read as well?"

"Oh yes, my lord, I can do it. I'll do all of it," said Sebastian, sitting bolt upright and looking directly into the king's eyes.

"All right, then, my boy—it's done. I shall send a man to you before the snows begin in earnest, so you'll have all the winter months to learn to read. Then, when you've mastered it, I shall send for you, and we shall see what kind of a future you have in this land. We can never have enough scholars, and you may well prove to be one." The king reached across and squeezed the boy's shoulder. "At least, I'll give you the chance, all right?"

"Oh yes, high king. I'll not disappoint you. I will study hard, I will . . ." his words trailed off as a commotion at the door ushered in a bedraggled and rain-drenched Attalus, still cloaked and in full armament.

"My lord high king," exclaimed Attalus, coming at once and bowing low to the reclining figure by the fire.

"Attalus, old friend! Sit, man—here, next to the fire. Shed your trappings. Sebastian, get your master a drink and something to eat—there's a good lad."

And with that, Charlemagne and Attalus fell into a long and intense discussion that only ended after almost everyone else had collapsed into their blankets along the benches or on the floor. After seeing to Attalus's needs, Sebastian rested his head against a table and absently watched the smoke from the hearth fire curl lazily through the hole in the middle of the roof before he fell asleep.

The subject of Charlemagne's long council with Attalus had been nothing less than a declaration of war against the Saxons, who until recently had been content to remain north of the Lippe, the river guarded in the west by Fernshanz. However, over the past several years, the Saxons had continued to raid and push to the south toward larger Frankish settlements, and they had built a rudimentary castle on the Diemel, about five leagues farther south from the Lippe. The rustic fortification was called the Eresburg, and somewhere near it lay one of the holiest places of the Saxon religion, the mysterious Irminsul.

The Franks knew little about the Irminsul. They would soon find out that it was less a place than a sacred object—an enormous truncated dead tree, the remains of an ancient oak that might have stood in the forest for a thousand years. The Saxons regarded it as the *Yggdrasil*, Odin's horse, which the god was said to ride in order to pass between the nine worlds of Saxon legend. It also was considered to be the "universal tree" that connected heaven and earth. The barkless column of the gaunt old giant still reached its skeletal arms several hundred meters into the clammy air of the thick forest, and steps were cut into its huge sides. On the ground before it the Saxons heightened their pagan rituals by making blood offerings of bulls, horses, and other animals. It was rumored that in times of great danger or need they made human sacrifices by hanging their victims from the ancient branches of the Irminsul.

Charlemagne was determined to destroy this pagan shrine and to raze the Eresburg fortress as well. He was in a fever to do it without delay. Attalus, on the other hand, urged caution.

"My lord king," Attalus reasoned, "it is already too late this year. The snow will come soon. You will not get the supply carts through if it is heavy."

"We'll take packhorses. We won't need the carts if we go quickly," countered the king. "We've done it before with raids into Saxony any number of times—a *scarus*, a small, heavily armed force, such as I have here now—a quick strike, before they're aware. They won't suspect we're coming. We can do it, Attalus, I tell you."

"Sire, the Eresburg is a real fortress, not just some walled village. It is solidly constructed. You will not take it without siege instruments. The few Saxons we've managed to capture say Widukind himself leads the defense and dares you to attack him there. We have not been able to scout the fort itself as yet; there are constant Saxon horse patrols around it. The last time we came close to it they set upon us at once and there was a furious fight. We barely got away without losing any men. As it was, two of my warriors were seriously wounded. Only the coming of the night saved us."

"What of the Irminsul?" asked Charlemagne, leaning forward. "Where does it lie? Is it inside the fortress?"

"No, my lord, they say not. I'm told the Irminsul is hidden within a small stockade deep in the forest, but not far from the Eresburg. Only priests and a single troop of elite Saxon cavalry are said to guard it. One dying Saxon told me he wanted to be buried 'by the world tree in the deep forest' so that he might more easily make the trip to his heaven."

"We must take this place, Attalus!" the king whispered passionately. "Do you know they sacrifice men to the devil? I'm told they sometimes even eat the flesh of those they sacrifice. They must be stopped! If we can destroy the Irminsul, they will know that ours is the true God, and there is no hope in fighting against us. And when we take the Eresburg, it will drive them back into their forests and put an end to these cursed bloody raids."

"Forgive me, my king," began Attalus, reluctantly, "but such a place as the Eresburg will not be taken easily. You will need more men than you have brought, along with infantry and siege equipment and supplies enough for at least three months, in my judgment. You will accomplish nothing if you go there with only cavalry and packhorses. I believe the Saxons are ready to challenge us seriously, and you'll have war this time, not just border raiding and retaliating. They will stand and fight—especially if you threaten their holy place."

At that point their conversation was interrupted once again by a commotion at the door of the great hall. A surly voice shrilly scolded the guards. Curses and a scuffle could be heard behind the door, which burst open to reveal Varnar, the captain of Charlemagne's Praetorian guard. Behind him, in the clutches of two other sturdy guards, Konrad of Adalgray struggled and swore.

"Sire, Count Konrad begs an audience with you. He would not wait," Varnar explained apologetically.

The king was perceptibly displeased by the interruption, as he had been absorbed in his council with Attalus, whose advice he considered vital to his plans. However, he nodded at Varnar, and Konrad plowed noisily into the room. Some of the warriors half-asleep on the benches lining the walls groaned, swore, and turned away from the boisterous and unruly young count, whom they already knew only too well.

Konrad stomped up to the king and knelt clumsily. "M'lor'," he burbled and immediately belched. "M'lor', excuse me, please. I have traveled . . . long way, ver' cold . . . I come . . . beg pardon . . . missing assembly. However, my men . . . we rode day and nigh'. Please tell me we have not missed the fight." He looked up into the king's face, anxious and bleary-eyed.

"No, you have not missed the fight, Konrad. Woe to you if you had—you know it's something I will not tolerate. Suppose we had needed you?"

It was clear that Konrad had been drinking heavily while still in the saddle—honey beer or mead from the smell of it—and was nearly drunk. He weaved on one knee before the king and had to put out his hand to steady himself. The king purposefully neglected to tell him to rise.

"M' lor', I am truly sorry. We were undavoibly . . . unvoloidaby, un . . . uh, we had trouble at home, sire—with the horses and such," he finished lamely.

"Konrad," the king said sternly, bending forward for emphasis, "you know I don't tolerate lateness to the call-up. I should have you fined. As it is, you are seven days late. Therefore you are to be deprived of meat and wine for a week, and that goes for all your men as well. You should be setting them an example, but look at you—you look like the devil, and you've been drinking. How dare you come into my presence in this state? You're disgusting. If you weren't such a good man in a fight . . ." the king's voice trailed off. "Well, to sleep with you, then. Pick a place against the wall," the king said sharply as Konrad lurched to his feet. "You only have a few hours. And do it quietly!"

"Yer pardon, m'lor'," rasped the chastened count, who backed himself into a corner of the room and collapsed in a heap. In less than a minute his snores added to the general buzz of sleeping soldiers.

Before dawn Charlemagne was awake and barking orders. He had sat alone for much of the night after conferring with Attalus. The king was thorough, thinking through his plans carefully, imagining both the best and the worst—but he was also stubborn. If he made up his mind to follow a course of action, he usually saw it through, even if he knew the plan was a risk. He had set his mind to make a reconnaissance in force against the Eresberg. He would try to draw the Saxons out of the fort for a pitched cavalry battle. Meanwhile, his scouts, ranging in every direction around the fort, might come upon the fabled Irminsul.

Sebastian was astonished at how swiftly Charlemagne's warriors were ready to march. He learned later that the king's soldiers always prepared their gear and horses the night before so they would be ready when his call came. They had made all their preparations before they ate or slept.

When the king rode out at midmorning at the head of the Frankish host, Sebastian, too, rode not far from him, at Attalus's side. At the first hint of movement, Sebastian had prepared his horse and arms, provisioned two packhorses with a two weeks' supply of grain and food for himself and Attalus, and stationed himself by the door of the manor house. When Attalus saw the packs, the ready horses, and the look of determination in the boy's eyes, he knew this time Sebastian would not be denied. He said simply, "Let us go forth bravely now—for God and the king!" They mounted and joined the long line of horsemen riding out of the gate.

The march to the Eresburg was not a long journey. The Franks could have been upon it in two days time, but in the afternoon of the first day of the march, the snow began to fall.

Chapter 7

Saxon Hubris

The Eresburg Fortress, Late Autumn 770

Charlemagne's blood was up, and from the moment the Franks set forth, he strained with the desire to destroy the Saxon fort at Eresburg. As they rode on, his sense of urgency almost made him insensible, and he pushed the column of horsemen at a reckless pace into the garnering snow. Poor Attalus was bombarded with questions and was severely discomfited by his inability to answer them to the king's satisfaction.

Finally, they stopped for the first night, and still the snow fell relentlessly. It began to look as if the morrow's march was certain to founder. Late that night, as he and the king sat alone on logs around a fire, Attalus had a chance to speak quietly with him. Only Sebastian listened just outside the firelight.

"My lord king," Attalus began, pleading his case carefully, "you will march to the Eresburg most certainly, but what will you do when you get there? There will be no cavalry action. The Saxons will not dare to ride out in force to meet us in such weather, but they will be sure to set us in ambush. They will wait with bows behind every fallen log and bramble as we get closer. They will pick us off in the forest one by one as we struggle along the narrow path. You'll likely lose many a warrior before ever you see Widukind's gates.

"And when you do," Attalus continued, becoming more and more animated, "they'll hide behind their stockade, shower you with arrows as your horses struggle in the snow, and show their backsides to you, laughing, until you admit you cannot overcome them—at least not this year. Please, sire, let us come back in the spring, when we can bring siege machines, more men, and enough food and supplies to make the siege work."

Impatient and testy, the king spat angrily into the fire. "Attalus, confound it, we've come too far. I cannot go back empty-handed. The Saxons have raided against us all summer, and when we chase them, they disappear again into their confounded black forests. Now I finally know where there's a nest of them, and by God, Attalus, it's too close to us. We cannot allow them to keep moving farther and farther south. Why, the last time they raided nearly to Cologne! I must stop them and have their blood, the heathen devils! By the Lord, we must not go home without striking a single blow!"

Attalus waited, knowing too well it was foolish to argue with the king when he was riled. The fire hissed as the snow fell into it and began to grow dim. After a time, Attalus got up to tend it and began again softly, "My lord king, this time it may be enough for you to bring the army to the walls, not to attack the Eresburg but simply to make a show of force and examine its defenses. Ride boldly round it. Show yourself openly; let them know the King of the Franks marks them himself. They won't ride out against you, I am sure of it, but if they do, so much the better. No ragged line of Saxon cavalry has ever prevailed against a full-blooded Frankish charge."

Attalus paused and sat down again beside the king, looking intently at him. "And, sire, if you will, you can ask for a council."

"A council!" erupted Charlemagne. "Why would I seek a council with Saxons? They are little more than pagan savages. They live in a wilderness and make blood sacrifices to gods who live in trees. They deserve extermination, not a council! How could you suggest it? And with whom would I speak? They don't even have a king."

"Meanwhile," Attalus continued, as if he had not heard the outburst, "we'll send scouts riding in circles at various distances around the area of the Eresburg. In this snow, some of them are bound to pick up roads or tracks leading to the fortress. If we follow those tracks in reverse, we may be lucky enough to find the Irminsul."

The king snorted and then chuckled with satisfaction. "So that's your plan, is it, you fox? I should have known. We'll go and make a big show, pull the whole army up round the fort, and while we dicker about a formal council, my scouts will be ferreting out the Irminsul. Good! It might work. And even if it doesn't, we'll have had at least a couple of days to see exactly how strong they are there and what it will take to knock them off. Splendid, Attalus! Let's do it. Even if we have to go home now without wetting the spears, we'll have seen what we need to do, and I shall return in the spring with a force that will send the lot of them to the devil they worship, well and truly."

And so it happened. The next day the king drew his entire army up to the banks of the shallow Diemel River, close upon which the Eresburg hill fort had been built overlooking the ford. The Saxons were in a state of consternation, flying about to prepare a hasty defense and cramming the walls with soldiers. Ironically, the persistent snow had covered the advance of the Franks, and Charlemagne was able to take them by utter surprise, making a grand show of bringing his troops into full order of battle in front of the fortress. He then sent forth a small delegation with a flag of truce, calling for a council. Splashing in the lead through the thin ice forming on the shallow waters of the ford was the redoubtable Count Edelrath.

The Saxons manning the walls shouted at the delegation in derision, and some even threw rocks at the three horsemen, who danced their horses farther back toward the river. Finally, a small door in one side of the huge gates opened and a horseman on a white stallion came charging out. The rider recklessly sped toward the Frankish delegation and jerked his plunging beast to a halt just in front of them. The Saxons on the walls cheered wildly.

The horse continued to rear and leap about for a time, its rider showing uncommon skill merely to stay on its back. Finally the charger quieted and the rider, a large and very blond man, was able to approach the group. Unlike most of the Saxon warriors, he was well armored, with a full *brunia* of tight chain mail and a helmet. A long Saxon spear lay crosswise across his horse's neck.

"I am Widukind," he announced, smiling broadly. "You wish to have council with me?" His boldness at appearing completely alone for the parley was tempered by the fact that at least fifty Saxon archers had been covering their leader with arrows notched since he burst forth from the gate.

Count Edelrath registered no surprise at the showy arrival or the roar of insults and challenges from the Saxons lining the parapets. He appeared to be completely unimpressed with everything thus far, gazing steadily instead into the lively, almost merry, blue eyes of the Saxon chieftain, who seemed to be enjoying himself. Still, he strained forward in the saddle, tense and ready.

Edelrath broke the tension calmly, "I am come on behalf of my lord and king, Karl the Great, sovereign of all the Frankish peoples and owner of the land upon which you have built this fortress."

"You are mistaken, my friend," exploded Widukind, laughing loudly at this opening challenge. "There are no Franks here; this is Saxon land, as you can clearly see." He gestured toward the jeering mob behind him.

"And what makes your king so 'great,' may I ask?" he continued. "I don't believe he is King of all the Franks. Does he not have a brother who co-rules with him?" he said grinning. "A brother, I have heard, who does not even like him?" Widukind ended this last comment with a gleeful laugh, watching cunningly for any angry reaction in the eyes of the unruffled Frankish count. If he expected an outburst of denial, he was disappointed.

Count Edelrath merely continued evenly, "I see that you are misinformed, Prince Widukind. If you will consent to give the high king your company tomorrow at this same time, he will be happy to instruct you in what constitutes Frankish territory and what you might now do to win his favor."

Widukind erupted with a loud "Hah!" at which his stallion bucked and leaped sideways, nearly spilling its rider. "King Karl wishes to instruct me now, does he? He wishes me to curry his favor?" Widukind laughed again, and turning his horse, he waved toward the wall of Saxon soldiers and opened a wide hand pointing back to the Frankish delegation, as if to say, "Who can believe these preposterous people?" The Saxons roared their approval of his bravado.

"That is," Edelrath said pointedly, "if a Saxon prince can be found who is not afraid to meet face-to-face with the High King of the Franks."

"High king or not," shot back Widukind, "I will meet with Karl. In truth, I can think of nothing more entertaining. Bring him here tomorrow midday, and I will sit with him in the snow and drink a *schnaps*. I have some very good brew that we 'borrowed' from some of your monks. It's made from apples. They said the stuff was for medicinal purposes; alas, that lie didn't save them either," he said, laughing uproariously and slapping his leg. "I should like nothing better than to meet this 'great' king and see why he thinks it will be so easy to school a Saxon prince. He may find that it is I who will teach him."

They agreed to meet again the next day under a canopy on the bank of the river. Each side was to bring only three additional participants.

With that, the three Franks retired, backing their horses away from the Saxon. Edelrath bowed solemnly from his saddle as he withdrew. Widukind sat watching them until they had turned their horses and plunged back across the icy river. Then he kicked the white stallion briskly, making it rear and whirl about as he saluted his troops on the walls with his spear. He then raced back again as furiously as he had come. The gate swung open just in time to allow his precipitous passage.

During that day and the night that followed, Charlemagne's captains effectively sealed off the fortress from the forest around it, crossing the river in strength at several places. No road or path was left unguarded, and foot patrols moved constantly back and forth between the few narrow lanes leading out of the Eresburg. It looked, for all intents and purposes, as if Charlemagne intended to invest the fortress. He was, however, merely concealing the movement of his horse patrols as they fanned out in wide circles searching for the sanctuary of the Irminsul.

Sebastian was elated that Attalus had consented to let him go on the search. It could have been that Attalus believed the boy would be safer away from the fortress in case the negotiations turned into a real fight, and he had fully intended to lead the patrol himself. But at the last minute, the king sent for Attalus and added him to the delegation that was to meet with Widukind. Attalus attempted to decline the honor, but the king would not hear of it and ordered him to be ready on the morrow. In the end, Attalus had to be content with providing Sebastian with a small troop of the best men from Fernshanz, with Anchesigal as the sergeant in command. Sebastian insisted that the peasant Lothar, whose native wisdom he had come to trust, be allowed to accompany him. All in all, the troop included ten men.

They started off the next morning, two hours before light. The plan was to retrace their journey back to a certain cut through the forest that led directly north toward the Lippe. Attalus had given strict instructions to Anchesigal that the troop was to stay well away from the Eresburg. They were to make their way north to the Lippe, cross it, and then explore to the east, marking any roads leading south toward the Eresburg. They were under no circumstances to recross the river at any place other than the one they had already used, and they were to avoid contact with Saxons at all costs. Finally, they were enjoined to return along the same route without fail by nightfall.

All this meant that the troop would be hard-pressed even to reach the Lippe, given the snowy conditions and limited period of daylight. Anchesigal knew that all these specifics were imposed for the purpose of keeping Sebastian strictly out of harm's way. However, he did not like the set of Sebastian's jaw or the look of determination in his eyes, and he began to worry about his ability to control the headstrong boy.

As it happened, the way north was easily traversed in spite of the snow, which was dry and light. Sebastian insisted on riding at the front of the column, and he set a brisk pace. They reached the Lippe before noon, crossed with little difficulty, and turned east. After the first hour, Anchesigal began to suggest that it was time to turn back, as they had found nothing more than deer trails. However, Sebastian insisted on pushing on for at least as long as it might take to be directly north of the Eresburg.

After another hour, as Anchesigal was about to insist on turning back, Sebastian held up a hand in caution and pointed without speaking to the hoofprints of several horses leading out of a rocky ford alongside what was clearly an oxcart track. Anchesigal barely managed to grasp the boy's reins for fear he would plunge down into the ford.

"My Lord Sebastian, we cannot! Lord Attalus has strictly forbidden us to cross here. We must go back. It's a likely path; we'll mark it for our return in the spring."

"I don't want to cross, Anchesigal," Sebastian protested. "We must follow the tracks to the north. Where is that oxcart going in this snow?" With that he jerked back the reins from Anchesigal's hands and spurred up the slope into the forest. Filled with somber presentiments, the sergeant was forced again to follow in haste.

They were barely into the woods before Sebastian came upon a small clearing, and there was the cart and its occupants—two Saxon shaman-priests, who apparently had stopped to give the oxen a blow after dragging the heavily laden cart across the ford. Ahead of the cart, strung out along the path, was a small troop of Saxon horsemen.

Sebastian reined in, astonished by the scene. Anchesigal, riding close behind, cut in front of Sebastian and commanded his men. "Comrades," he cried, "Saxons! To arms! Form the line!" The Franks fell into place along a single line at once, with spears raised above their heads, as they had practiced a hundred times before. They barely had time to fall into line when Anchesigal gave the command to charge, shouting, "For God and the King!" The Franks pitched themselves pell-mell upon the astonished Saxons.

Sebastian watched from behind, dismayed that he had not had the presence of mind to join the charge. The Franks swept through the Saxons once, spearing men and horses alike. Then, without waiting for a command, they wheeled around and charged back again, finishing off most of those who had survived the first onslaught. Few of the Saxons had been astride their horses, and they were easily killed as they tried to mount. One or two attempted to stand and fight, but they were outnumbered and were at a great disadvantage against the mounted Franks. They were run over by the horses or skewered on Frankish lances before they could engage a single rider. The shaman-priests, too, were unceremoniously dispatched as they gamely tried to fight back with swords to defend the contents of the cart. Two Franks simply unlimbered their bows and shot them through at close range. The entire skirmish was over in a few minutes. The troop left no Saxons wounded, but at least two of them had escaped on horseback through the woods.

Anchesigal was desperate to leave at once. However, by now Sebastian had recovered from the shock of the encounter and, feeling embarrassed and driven by purpose, insisted on seeing what was in the cart. He had already dismounted and was going through the bulky bundles. Anchesigal quickly posted sentries at both ends of the glade and up the narrow track at a good warning distance. He refused to allow any looting for armor or weapons among the bodies. "Stay on your mounts," he commanded. "We must leave here at once!" He then leaped from his own horse and implored Sebastian to give over the search and remount immediately.

"Come at once, my lord. Two of them got away. They will bring others, and we may not outnumber them this time. I implore you, let's ride at once!"

"A moment, Anchesigal, only one moment." Sebastian waded into the crowded cart. It was full of heavy bags of provisions and many wooden tools. He rummaged around and came up with a bag marked with runic symbols. "There's something in this bag." He grunted and fell backward, pulling a heavy cast-iron statuette into his lap. It was bulky and black, the likeness of a one-eyed man or a god, ugly and unlike any figure he had ever seen. He could make out what looked like two ravens on its shoulders and a wolf at its feet. He had difficulty even carrying the image from the cart to his horse. "We must take this, Anchesigal, I'm sure it's important." Anchesigal came at once and held the figure while Sebastian mounted. He then gave it back, mounted his own horse, and gave the command to retrieve the sentries and pull out immediately.

He had no more given the command than the sentries up the trail came pounding back, shouting "The Saxons are upon us—too many! We must fly!" But it was too late. The first Saxon riders could already be seen plunging down the snowy trail.

"Fly, my lord, fly! We'll hold them off. Lothar, stay with Sebastian. Ride, man!" With that, Anchesigal gave the command to form the line again, and the small troop laid into the Saxons as they entered the glade. Sebastian caught only a glimpse of them as Lothar slapped the rump of his horse and the two bounded down to the ford and back along the trail. They galloped as well as the snow allowed most of the way back to the turn to the south, when Sebastian insisted they pull up. For anxious moments they waited, listening for the sounds of horses following. They heard nothing, only the sound of the water trickling past at the ford. Finally, Lothar convinced the boy to walk the horses into the shallows and make their way downstream until they could enter the forest without leaving conspicuous tracks. They concealed the horses in the deep woods, crept back on foot, and watched from cover to see who came up the trail—Anchesigal and his men or the Saxons.

Days later, as Charlemagne's small army made its way back through the snow toward Fernshanz, two of Anchesigal's band managed to rejoin the army. They bore the sad news that Anchesigal and all the men except themselves had been killed, either in the glade or at the ford as they tried to withdraw. Anchesigal was last seen standing astride the trail, sword in hand, his horse having been killed beneath him, as the Saxons closed in. He had urged the survivors to ride on after Sebastian. But the two, hearing the noise of pursuit behind them, had turned off into the deep woods to save themselves and wait for the night.

Sebastian and Lothar had also remained hidden in the woods all through the frigid night. They had seen the Saxons come onto the trail to the south and follow it, but the riders had returned within the hour because of the growing darkness and had gone back the way they had come. About midday on the morrow, Sebastian and Lothar, with heavy hearts and intense foreboding, had felt it was safe enough to chance the trail again and make their way back to the army.

Meanwhile, negotiations with Widukind had proceeded as expected. The Saxon prince appeared without armor this time, astonishingly naked from the waist up in spite of the cold, with only a wolf-skin cloak across his shoulders and a broad band of solid gold around his neck. He had the body of a wrestler and was openly vain about it. The meeting was short.

"What? You don't like my *schnaps*, high king?" Widukind said, laughing and slapping his leg as the king choked on the strong drink. Charlemagne tossed the remains of the raw alcohol into the fire where it caused a small explosion of flame.

"Look here, Widukind. I came here to warn you. If you continue to raid into my country as you have done this past year, and if you continue to build forts like this one on Frankish territory, you leave me no choice but to make war against you."

"What, we are not at war now? Excuse me, Karl, I thought we were. In fact, it was my impression that we have been at war since the days of your grandfather, the so-called Hammer. He could not defeat us, nor could your father, the short king." He smiled broadly and opened his arms wide, as if in wonder. The smile faded as he added, "What makes you think that you can do better than they? You may win a few battles, but you will not like the price. You see, we Saxons are like weeds, no matter how many times you cut us down, we will rise up again to choke you.

"By the way," he added, the mocking smile returning, "I am a prince of my people; if you will not use my title, I will not use yours. I don't mind."

In the end, neither side would give concessions or even suggest that any were warranted. Widukind had already been drinking, which no doubt accounted for his seeming immunity to the cold. Charlemagne found him obnoxious from the beginning but couldn't help admiring him for his pluck. Widukind was in high spirits, and his animation and boldness left no doubt that he considered himself the equal of Charlemagne and all his counts. They parted in an acrimonious atmosphere of mock courtesy and thinly veiled challenge.

Charlemagne pulled the army out during the night to avoid having to endure the taunts and provocations of the Saxons. The king was in a foul mood as the army retreated, for he was unable to shake the feeling that he had been bested by the sneering, boastful Widukind. He spoke to no one except to issue surly commands to push on without rest. In midafternoon, however, the column was halted by the arrival of Sebastian and Lothar. They were accompanied by Attalus, who, upon learning that Sebastian had not returned by nightfall, had ridden off in the night with a small detachment to find him. They had met shortly after Sebastian and Lothar emerged from their hideaway in the forest.

The meeting was both a relief and an affliction for Sebastian, who was already crushed by the burden of having to tell Attalus what had happened to Anchesigal and why it had happened. Attalus spoke little and then only to ask questions about the encounter. Without looking into Sebastian's eyes, he took the black statue from the boy and gave the order to return at once to the army. Sebastian rode back in silence, tormented by grief and shame for having been the cause of the death of Anchesigal and his men.

When Charlemagne learned of Attalus's return with the boy, he sent for them at once. As Attalus rode up to the king, Sebastian stayed back, trying to blend in with the surrounding soldiers, fearing even to raise his eyes toward the king. However, he was not to escape notice; the king sent for him almost immediately.

Charlemagne held the black statue against the pommel of his saddle. He eyed the boy keenly as Sebastian and Lothar rode up. "What happened? Tell me exactly— everything," he exclaimed with animation, pounding on the head of the black idol. "Leave out no details. Where did you get this thing? Wait. Let's get down—we'll camp here for the night. Post heavy sentries; the Saxon dogs will be sniffing after our arses. Come along, Sebastian. We'll eat. I'm hungry."

As the story of the fight in the forest glade unfolded in Sebastian's halting, strained words, the king became more and more energized. He listened attentively as he ate, tearing into a chunk of meat hastily warmed over a campfire. He asked questions about everything, occasionally exclaiming about some high point of the adventure. On hearing of Anchesigal's stand at the ford, he cried out passionately, "By the Cross, if he had lived I would have made him a count—or at least a constable. His men say he fought like a cornered bear. Ah, would that I had a thousand like him!"

"And what do you think this is, Master Sebastian?" said the king, holding up the black statue. "What devil's image have we got here, eh?"

"I don't rightly know, my lord king," mumbled Sebastian, daring to look again at the image. He paused a moment before going on, took a breath, and then spoke clearly and directly to the king. "But I think it must be important, high king. The Saxons fought hard to defend it and they chased after us halfway back to the army. I believe," and now he stammered again, "I believe it is one of their god-images. I think it must be from the Irminsul, my lord."

"And I think you are right, my boy," the king said jubilantly and slapped Sebastian on the back. "It's possible you have found nothing less than the way to the Irminsul, lad. Why else would the Saxons have had such a troop on that snowy road when they knew my army was at the Eresburg? And why would they have fought so hard for this fat piece of cold iron?"

Noting that Sebastian did not share his enthusiasm and could not raise his eyes again to the statue, the king changed his tone with sudden understanding. "It's all right, Sebastian," he said gently, laying his heavy hand on the boy's shoulder. "Men die in war. Your man Anchesigal knew it could come to that, and he fought like a hero. We'll remember him for that always. And what he gave his life for may well end up being the key of this expedition. If, as I suspect, you've stumbled onto the track to the Irminsul, then you, Anchesigal, and all his men may have made this whole expedition worthwhile, and we may have found the way to strike at the heart of the Saxons."

Although the king was greatly relieved and highly pleased with Sebastian for enabling him to avoid going home empty-handed, the road back to Fernshanz was interminable and full of remorse for Sebastian. He felt guilty about his flagrant disobedience to Attalus and rued the pride and ambition that had caused him to put his companions in danger. He couldn't share the king's elation about the statue and cared more about his estrangement from Attalus instead. The horse master had barely spoken to him since their return and rode at the head of the column in brooding silence. Sebastian knew it was because of the loss of Anchesigal and the five other men of Fernshanz. Attalus had not lost so many in the entire time since they had come north from Adalgray.

However, it was the death of Anchesigal that haunted Sebastian the most. The sturdy, loyal sergeant had been his right arm and mentor during Attalus's long absences while they prepared the defense of the fortress. He had been far and away the best soldier at Fernshanz, which is why Attalus had felt able to leave Sebastian in command. Worst of all, Anchesigal had become one of Sebastian's only friends, and the boy knew he could have prevented his death.

Chapter 8

Learning to Fight

The king stayed two days at Fernshanz, long enough to rest, feed up the horses, and provision his troops for the return to the south. He was in good humor and everywhere proclaimed Sebastian to be the hero of the moment. His exuberance, however, was not shared by Attalus or Sebastian, for very different reasons, and certainly not by Count Konrad, who was almost apoplectic about the king's praise of his young cousin. The king seemed not to notice any of this and continued to mention "Sebastian's find" as if it were a great treasure, especially after Sebastian queried Heimdal and learned from the blind man that the one-eyed figure probably represented the chief Saxon god, Odin, who was said to have traded one of his eyes for all knowledge.

As the long column of horsemen began to thread its way out of the fortress and onto the narrow track through the forest, Attalus gathered his men to honor the king's departure. As he mounted, Charlemagne called Sebastian to him once more. "My boy, you may have done me and the realm a great favor, and you will find that your king rewards good service. Keep watching this road and you will soon see what I mean. Work hard, lad, in everything, and I will not forget you. Remember, your king admires a man of many talents; use all you have and any others you can gain for yourself. Strive for the excellence of the Frankish warrior, but then rise above him—become uncommon, nay, become exceptional. I'll be watching you."

During the days that followed, Sebastian could not have conceived of a training program more demanding than the one Attalus devised for him. He gave the boy a single day to recover from the trip and to think out its results. Then, without referring to recent events or mentioning Anchesigal's name, he sat Sebastian down and outlined a training program.

If it were possible that Sebastian did not hear or heed the king's commands, Attalus certainly did, and he began to drive Sebastian with a fury in all areas of the martial arts. But he first presented him with a war horse, his own, one of the very best in all of Francia, especially bred for his size and spirit. There was no ceremony. In the dawn half light of the first training day, Attalus simply led a tall, blood bay stallion into the exercise yard and handed the reins to Sebastian. This was Attalus's stud horse, the latest in three decades of fine Spanish stallions that had given Attalus the reputation of the finest horse master in Charlemagne's realm.

The horse stood pawing the earth and sending out clouds of steam in the cold morning air, its neck perfectly arched and its powerful shoulders shivering in anticipation. In contrast to its dark, blood-red coat, its mane was silky black, and its long legs were solid black well above the knees. Its luxurious sable tail reached almost to the ground. Sebastian had long thought it must be the most beautiful horse in the world. He could not speak when Attalus told him quietly that from that moment, the famous horse was his.

Attalus's widespread reputation as a horse master, as well as his close friendship with Heimdal, began in Al Andalus, the warm brown land beyond the Spanish mountains. He was a young warrior then, unattached to any noble house and seeking his fortune by selling his sword to the highest bidder. He escorted a merchant through the brigand-infested Spanish mountains to the lovely highland river town of Sarragossa and decided to stay and learn what he could of the land and its strikingly colorful and interesting people. There he lost most his wages in games of mock combat with the invincible Andalusian warriors of Ibn al-Arabi. Their prowess stemmed, first of all, from the horses they rode, which were bigger, faster, and more intelligent than any Attalus had ever seen, and second, from devices the Moors used to stay in their saddles. They called them "stirrups," loops of rope secured to their saddles into which they placed their feet while riding. The devices made a miraculous difference in the way one could fight on horseback.

On the way back through the mountains to his home in Toulouse, Attalus found himself without prospects or money. He sought refuge in the monastery at Alta Ripa in southern Acquitania, and there he first saw Heimdal. The beggar sat chanting in Latin by the main gate as Attalus rode up, his blind eyes raised toward the sound of the hooves. Attalus was astonished at the string of High Church Latin coming out of the blind man's mouth. The sound was incongruous but at the same time mysterious and magical.

Attalus spent several days at the monastery, conversing mostly with Heimdal. He learned that the blind man had been born in a noble Frankish house west of the Rhine and that he had been blind from his youth. His affliction, however, only served to make Heimdal reflective and stubbornly intrepid. He abandoned his family and set out on the road alone, determined to find a better life or die in the search. Blessed with a quick wit and phenomenal powers of memory, he flourished on the road, learning to beg and tell stories to his companions along the way. He was entertaining and popular and so made his way in relatively prosperous fashion across Francia. He met Attalus at the end of a three-year stay at Alta Ripa, where the monks took him in and shared their knowledge with him. He not only immersed himself in the Bible stories but learned to speak the Latin language as well as any of the monks.

Heimdal was the reason Attalus became a horse master. He convinced Attalus to organize another trading venture into Spain and while there to buy some of the excellent horses he had seen. They undertook the expedition together and it became a turning point in both their lives.

On the journey back to the Rhineland, where Attalus hoped to find a lord who needed his services, everyone they met wanted to buy his horses and the ones he bred from them. He owed his life to the good use of both horses and stirrups and eventually became a constable, a renowned horse master, and a trainer in King Pippin's heavy cavalry. Wherever Attalus went, Heimdal was his constant companion.

The horse he gave to Sebastian was only the latest among the many fine stallions Attalus had bred from that first stud he had brought back from Spain, but he was one of the best. The horse was not only the finest gift he could give to this boy whom he loved more than anything but the most important one in terms of maximizing Sebastian's prowess as a warrior.

It took Sebastian a week simply to learn how to stay on the stallion's back. His thighs, knees, and arms ached at night from hours of effort to control the horse's power and direct him without one or both of his hands on the reins. He called the stallion *Joyeuse*, after a word from western Francia for the famous sword Charlemagne carried into every campaign. On this horse Sebastian hoped one day to become a chastening weapon in the service of the high king. Sebastian's Joyeuse, however, was proving to be no joy at all but a horse with ideas of his own and a highly suspicious nature. He watched everything Sebastian did out of the corner of his eye, and unless Sebastian did everything exactly as Attalus had done, the horse shied, bucked, or kicked. Sebastian fell or was thrown from the horse a score of times every day, until his bruised body ached in every bone. He groaned at night with the effort to undress and fall into bed.

But Sebastian was lean and sinewy, and although somewhat slighter, he was stronger pound for pound than most of the boys his age. He was blessed with boundless energy and could work, fight, or run all day without wearing out. Attalus occasionally called him "the pine knot" and could not help but admire the boy's durability, drive, and quickness. Gradually the old strong feelings of affection and intimacy returned, and Sebastian worked all the harder to please Attalus and make him proud.

One part of the training program, however, Sebastian came to hate passionately. It was called simply "the Rope." A thick braid of hemp hung from an old, gnarled oak in the center of the exercise yard. It had been tied into a thick knot at the end, and that knot was the focus of a diabolically interminable exercise with the heavy wooden training sword.

The knot hung waist high, and Sebastian had to stand in front of it and strike it with the sword. He then had to step quickly into the space where the knot had hung and continue striking it as it swung back toward him. The object was to strike the ball of rope as hard as possible without allowing it or any other part of the rope to touch his body. The harder he struck the knot, the more the rope swung wildly and the knot gyrated unpredictably. He could spin and step aside but was not allowed to back out of the tiny meter-wide circle directly beneath the knot. That meant, of course, that the swordsman would take the knot's place, and the knot sought relentlessly to return to its center of gravity.

The exercise was designed to build the swordsman's stamina and reaction time. When the knot or the rope touched the swordsman, it was considered a blow from an imaginary enemy. It was necessary to avoid the knot and the undulating rope for a specific period of time or be considered to have lost the fight.

When Sebastian first began to do combat with the pitiless rope, he found he could hold it off for less than a minute before the knot bucked against his hands or the rope brushed his shoulders. A few more minutes and the sweat would begin to pour off the boy's body, even on a cold winter's day. Usually, a bout was timed with a small hourglass of perhaps five minutes. Then Attalus began to use larger timing mechanisms of ten and twenty minutes. At first Attalus counted the number of times he observed the rope making contact with some part of the boy's body, but as the winter wore along, he allowed Sebastian to be his own referee and his own timekeeper. He would simply say at some point in the long day's exercises, "Now the rope," and Sebastian would take a deep breath, find the practice sword, and trudge out to the well-worn circle under the tree.

Well before the Christmas season, Sebastian arrived at a point where he managed to endure the rope for half an hour without a significant touch. When he gleefully reported his progress to the horse master, instead of congratulating him, Attalus said quietly, "Good—now go put on your chain mail and helmet and do it another time with the same hourglass." And the agony began again with renewed and incredible challenge.

Not all the martial arts were so grueling, however. Sebastian actually loved most of the exercises. Having finally won the confidence of Joyeuse, Sebastian became especially good on the big horse's back. He was a natural rider who thoroughly understood his mount and bonded with it. With spear and shield, Sebastian could ride pell-mell at a target, strike it with his spear, and careen away to the next target without touching the horse, except with his knees and the seat of his trousers. He was already uncommonly good with a bow and only needed to increase the size of it from time to time. With the sword he was as quick as a snake and had an unerring eye for weakness on the part of an opponent.

On the other hand, he was not very skilled with the heavy throwing axe, nor did he strike very deeply with a spear or javelin, which was the principal weapon of the heavy cavalry. He simply did not have the weight to put behind his blows. Against other armored riders one needed either to find an opening—the face, the throat, the groin, or the leg—or be able to pierce the chain mail of an opponent with a prodigious blow. One also might unseat a rider with the sheer force of a blow to the chest without penetrating the mail, but most successful fighters concentrated on finding an opening where they could plunge the spear.

In the attack mode, therefore, the Frankish rider held his shield almost directly in front of his chest while holding his spear aloft and slightly behind the shoulder. In a clash of two opposing warriors riding at full gallop, the horse was often the key. If it could knock the other horse aside or cause it to swerve sideways, its rider enjoyed a huge advantage. Franks usually charged in a line, with little distance between their horses, which could intimidate opposing riders and slow them down, forcing them to watch for blows from both sides. Often such a charge would disorganize the enemy and lead to panic.

In Sebastian's case, it was the clash of single combat out in the open that worried the horse master. Sebastian grew slowly; he would likely not be full grown until he was twenty-one or twenty-two, and he would not gain his full weight until he was much older. Attalus knew this because he himself had experienced the curse of a slim body and slow growth. He had grown up in Aquitaine, his mother a willowy, raven-haired Gallo-Roman, and he did not inherit the sturdy, tall body of his Frankish father or his father's grey eyes and reddish hair. Other boys around him had matured at seventeen, some even at fifteen. Attalus was twenty-two before he got his full growth and strength. The handicap had only made him work harder and invent ways to succeed in spite of it. He vowed that Sebastian would profit by his own experience.

The first trick Attalus taught Sebastian was a new way to handle the spear in a charge. Instead of teaching him to hold it high above his head, as the other mounted warriors did, he showed him a technique he had learned in Spain years ago. The Saracen riders were just beginning to experiment with it, and most of them still did not use it.

"Couch the spear under your arm, boy," Attalus coached, as they sat side by side on their horses. "Now, spur on, and as you approach the target, brace the spear tightly between your body and arm, like this. Level it just over the horse's neck. If you hold the shield close in front of your body and keep the spear point down and aligned with your horse's neck, your opponent may find it difficult to see. Aim to strike your man full in the chest or head. You'll find that you will be able to lean not only all your own weight into the spear but the full momentum of the horse as well."

They cantered together toward the distant target dummies suspended from a tree. As they rode, the horses picked up speed until they were pounding at full gallop toward the targets. The blunt practice spears smashed into the dummies with such force that they careened upward and over the heads of the riders and came down dancing crazily at the end of the ropes.

Sebastian was astonished at the effect of the charge. "Attalus," he exclaimed in wonder, "who else knows this? Why don't we all do it? It's amazing! It gives you such power, and it is so much more accurate!"

"Do you know why it's so powerful and accurate? You did it very well because you are a natural rider, but you wouldn't have been either accurate or very powerful except for one thing. What was it?"

Sebastian thought a moment, reviewing the charge in his head. "The foot ropes!" he exclaimed, exultantly. "It was the rope stirrups, wasn't it, Attalus? I could stand steady in them and not be knocked off the horse by the shock."

"That's it, lad. To do this trick right you must lean well forward and brace yourself into the rope stirrups, being careful at the same time to keep the round shield high and almost directly in front of your body. Normally, it takes a long time to learn it, but you did it the first time. I have tried to teach others, but most warriors in the heavy cavalry like to fight independently after the first charge. Many don't like this new technique. It requires the riders to advance in a tight line, strike together, and then turn and do it again. It demands a great deal of practice and discipline, but if we could master it, a line of Frankish cavalry could knock down a stone wall! Now, let's try it again with real spears."

The endless practice day after day in the dead cold of winter would have become intolerable had it not been for Sebastian's companions. The practice yard was for all the freemen of Fernshanz, as every freeman and his sons were expected to be warriors, and they trained at least part of every day in winter. Especially in the mornings, the yard was usually full of men and boys engaged in various aspects of the soldier's trade. On the Saxon March, the need to be proficient at fighting was felt by every freeman and boy, and each thought of himself first and foremost as a *miles*, a soldier in the high king's service.

Sebastian's dedication and skill drew the young men to him. They watched with admiration and envy as he wheeled and charged and managed the great stallion with only his knees. Men stopped what they were doing to watch him, and women and girls found errands to do so they could pass by the exercise yard to marvel at the slight figure sitting so easily atop the huge galloping horse.

Two of the young men became especially close to Sebastian. One was a serious lad of about seventeen named Liudolf, whose father was a sergeant and one of the few men at Fernshanz who had a full-time military role. This was the same Liudolf who had fought so well at the siege of Adalgray and later followed Attalus to Fernshanz. Since the death of Anchesigal, it was Liudolf the Elder who had charge of security on the walls. The younger Liudolf strove to follow in his father's footsteps and become a respected warrior and leader. He therefore watched and imitated anything he saw Sebastian doing, for he knew that Sebastian was being trained by the best soldier at the fortress, the famous Attalus, a veteran of many campaigns.

"Sebastian," Liudolf asked as they finished for the day, "if you were faced with an opponent who was much larger than you, what weapon would you choose to fight him?"

"Well, I suppose," Sebastian answered hesitantly, "it would depend on several things: What armor is the man wearing? What kind of weapon is he using? How experienced or confident does he seem? In general, I suppose I would start with my spear. If I could find an opening, I'd throw it. A lucky throw might bring him down, and that would save me from having to grapple with him. Failing that, I prefer my sword, but if he was just big and not very skillful with his weapons, I might try an axe. I'd turn it around and hammer at him through his shield and chain mail with the spiked end."

Although Liudolf worked as hard as Sebastian, he could never quite equal his skills. That made him cling to Sebastian even more until he became like his shadow. He was so often by his side that Sebastian came to take him for granted. The two often worked or rode for long periods of time in silence, speaking only rarely, but the trust between them was complete.

The other companion was wholly different from the tall and serious Liudolf, with his perpetual frown and mop of thick chestnut hair. He was Archambald, a cheerful, sandy-haired lad of Sebastian's age, somewhat shorter and thicker than Sebastian and a full foot and half shorter than Liudolf. Archambald would never make a great warrior; he was by nature too gentle and full of fun. He could be serious when warranted but not for long, and he was easily distracted, having a propensity to laugh and sing upon almost any occasion. Sebastian liked him because he was uninhibited and carefree, chattering away like a bird, full of gossip and stories without end. Archambald was irrepressible, garrulous, and friendly to everyone, a guaranteed good tonic on any dark day.

Sebastian passed off Liudolf's question to Archambald. "What would you do, Archambald?

"Me? If he was bigger than me, I'd run like hell," was the noble reply. The boys walked off laughing as they headed for their supper.

With these two dissimilar friends Sebastian spent nearly every waking hour of the short winter days, riding, practicing, and sometimes hunting together in the mornings and accompanying Attalus in the afternoon on endless inspection rounds of the fortress and its larder, supplies, and activities. It seemed that Attalus was always moving about, always thinking, and never resting. He was obsessed with the defense of the fortress; as well he should have been, for the people would find soon enough that Fernshanz was at the top of Widukind's list of Frankish targets.

In mid-November of that year, during a break in winter storms, an ox-drawn cart, accompanied by a squad of horsemen, emerged from the snow-clad forest. Driving the cart was a large man dressed in a monk's cowl with a heavy bearskin draped over his shoulders. Everything about him seemed big—his head and nose and rubified cheeks, his huge shoulders and bulging belly, and his short, powerful arms, ending in ham fists twice the normal size. Even his voice was big and could be heard well before the cart appeared out of the forest as the man urged the oxen along the snowy path.

Any company arriving in winter was cause for considerable excitement in the isolated village, and before the cart could cover the distance from the forest to the fortress, a good number of the Fernshanz garrison had gathered on the wall by the gate. Sebastian and his companions were among them, having just come from the practice yard.

Finally arriving at the gate, the man threw back his hood and cloak revealing a broadly smiling face and a large bronze pectoral cross on a chain around his neck. He shouted a greeting to the guards at the gate. "God bless this place and all in it!" he said in a booming voice. "Open, if you please, for a weary servant of the Lord and his gallant friends. I am Father Louis, and I come with my family and friends from the court of the great King Karl himself. Open quickly, my good men, for we are sorely in need of some comfort."

With that, he jumped down from the cart and tossed aside several other bearskin rugs to reveal a nest of children lying on the broad body of a very large woman, who immediately uttered a merry laugh as the children squealed at the sight of their father. Their frigid journey finally over, they scrambled out of the cart and clung to the legs of Father Louis, chattering and laughing as he strove to help his ample wife unwind herself from the cart. Having done so, the brood marched through the opening gates holding on to the sides of their father's cart, whispering to each other and marveling at the possibilities of their new circumstances.

In such a manner Sebastian came to see Father Louis for the first time. It was a signal occasion. Although he did not then understand the importance of the moment, he had just met his teacher and mentor, the fulfillment of the promise of Charlemagne.

Chapter 9

Learning to Read– Among Other Things

It had been a long time since Fernshanz had seen a priest. The last one to come had been an itinerant father who made his living traveling from one isolated Frankish community to another. He had arrived the previous June, close to the summer solstice, and a riot of weddings and baptisms had taken place for at least a fortnight. Every peasant serf or freeman with a personal need for a priest paid what he could afford, and the cleric was hosted by the families for whom he rendered a service of some kind. It had been a joyous time.

The whole town turned out for the baptisms on the river, and there was singing every night around a bonfire. The celebratory atmosphere and the exceptional number of weddings resulted in a surge of indulgence in beer, mulberry wine, and mead, and thus, ironically, the priest's presence instigated considerable extra-marital activity. In fact, late-night dancing around the bonfires, borrowed from old pagan rituals, came close to culminating in orgies.

Of particular importance to many persons was the opportunity to receive the sacrament of confession, which was a necessity if cardinal sins were to be forgiven. Alas, a priest often was no sooner gone than he was needed again.

Life, however, did not wait for visits by such a sometime priest. As a general practice, peasants usually forgave each other, at least for venial sins, and young couples simply found a grove of trees or a grotto that had been held sacred from pagan times and married themselves to each other. That had to suffice until the next time a priest showed up.

This situation changed with the arrival of Father Louis. Mass and the Eucharist became a weekly, if not daily, event. Weddings and baptisms became scheduled occurrences, and Church law was set immediately in vigorous opposition to widespread peasant superstitions and pagan sacrifices. Father Louis was a missionary priest who had studied under the great Abbot Sturm of Fulda, and he burned with a zealous desire to vanquish the devils of the old earth religions. He approached this daunting task, however, with a great deal of love in his heart and a generous helping of forgiveness.

He had the gift of making everyone feel that he or she was the most important person in the world at that moment, and he saw them in the very best light, deliberately sifting out the bad that might dwell in them and savoring the good. He delighted in everyone he met, and though he was a very large man, no one feared him. He was kind and gentle to everyone, and he was joyous from dawn to dusk.

He did not preach fire and brimstone or burden the hardworking and long-suffering peasants with guilt or crippling blame. Instead, he had memorized several standard homilies in the vernacular language, and he regaled them with instructive stories of the saints. Father Louis was a man of great practical wisdom, but on some subjects he was nearly fanatical. One of them was the subject of saints. He was absolutely certain that holy men and women possessed miraculous powers, and he gave them credit for far more than the piety and special gifts of preaching or healing they may have had.

"Hear me, children," he would exclaim, leaning forward over the rough wooden pulpit. "The saints truly do have supernatural powers. Why, they can even hover in the air! I've seen 'em myself, flying all around at the top of the church in Fulda—Saints Peter and Paul and even our holy Saint Martin, patron saint of the Franks!"

In fact, Father Louis had not actually seen them; they were figments of his dreams. Still, his dreams were so real to him that he was sure he must have seen them.

"And you must know this," he would say in a hushed voice, "they can be in two places at once! Why, Abbot Sturm himself has seen the sainted Boniface, gone from us now these many years, at the court of the high king and then again in the church rafters as soon as he returned to Fulda!" In the hushed silence of the chapel, he pressed home his convictions. "Ah, the holy saints are great intercessors with God, don't you know.

"But my children, mind you well, it is far from easy. You must fast and pray hard and spend a penny to light a candle in this very church, and then—and then, my precious children," he would pause here for effect, "you must *believe* with all your heart. You must have the faith of a Job or a Daniel. Believe as to move a mountain! And, lo, my children, it must surely be done for you."

Father Louis's main mission, however, was to teach Sebastian; it was for this reason he had been sent to Fernshanz. At first it was difficult to find a time for study because Sebastian already had a strict routine in the exercise yard. They finally convinced Attalus that some part of each day must be set aside so that Sebastian could learn to read. It was the wish of Charlemagne himself. Thus Sebastian rose before everyone each morning and joined the priest in the empty great room where the ashes could be stirred up and a fire started for the new day. Sebastian's instruction proceeded by firelight or primitive torchlight around a crude, little table in the cold emptiness of the chamber.

Father Louis had brought a few precious tools to help teach Sebastian to read. He owned no books himself, being a man who lived totally at the bidding of other men. As a young priest he had taken vows of poverty and obedience, if not chastity, for he already had his wonderful wife, whom he would not have given up even to be the pope in Rome. But for his mission to Fernshanz, he had managed to make significant borrowings from the library of no less a person than the venerable Fulrad, Abbot of St. Denis, Charlemagne's own archchaplain. At the request of the king, Fulrad had arranged to send to Louis a small number of goatskin parchments, upon which were copied a few favorite psalms and some standard prayers for the Mass, including the *Pater* and the *Credo*. Notable among the collection were a couple of short, standard sermons in the Frankish tongue for the occasions of Christmas and Easter and copied excerpts of key parts of the four Gospels. All were in Latin, and all were written in the wobbly, cramped Merovingian cursive.

Most remarkable, however, was a single parchment upon which was transcribed a copy of the last words of King David in Second Samuel, one of Charlemagne's favorite scripture passages. Wondrous indeed to both Father Louis and Sebastian was the way in which it was written. Instead of the shaky, unbroken scrawling of the other manuscripts, this one was written in beautifully formed letters that made clearly discernible words, and the words were separated from each other by small spaces and punctuation. Although Father Louis insisted that Sebastian should study each of the precious documents diligently, it was mainly from this new script that Sebastian learned swiftly to read and even to write in Latin.

At the beginning of his studies, he was truly a *tabula rasa*, knowing little Latin. He could recite the *Pater* and the *Credo* and a few other simple prayers in Latin, and his mother had explained to him in detail what they meant. However, although he said the prayers daily by heart, he had no way to go further with the language. And so, with a blank tablet of wax and a stylus, Father Louis began.

Sebastian progressed quickly. He found a way to practice his studies in combination with his obligations on the training field. Father Louis provided him with a precious parchment for his own use, but he was forbidden to write a word on it until he had mastered writing the word perfectly on his wax tablet. Then he was allowed to copy the word onto his parchment, which rapidly filled up and became a kind of guide. For him it was a treasured hoard of magical words, and he memorized the list and said the words out loud as he practiced against the rope or engaged in mock combat with his friends Liudolf and Archambald.

"*In nomine Patris, et Filii, et Spiritus Sancti,*" he would exclaim as he laid into them with the wooden practice sword. "*Benedicite!*" Smash! "*Ora pro nobis!*" Whack! And he would always end the practice session with a pious, "*In saecula saeculorum. Amen.*"

His friends were flabbergasted at the words that poured from Sebastian's mouth. Archambald was sure that Sebastian was uttering magic incantations to make himself invincible in battle. Liudolf merely thought it was a waste of energy. However, the two became used to the recitations and occasionally even struck a blow themselves while uttering a venerable Latin word, after which they grinned sheepishly.

Sebastian was an eager student, in spite of the fatigue of splitting his time between reading and training for war. He became adept at stealing moments here and there to study. Many of those moments occurred in Father Louis's house in the citadel compound, where his substantial wife, Bertha, ruled and raised their children, Willa, Judith, and Gisela, and little Louis, almost three years old but still very much on his mother's breast.

Bertha was as ebullient and friendly as her husband. She was strong and full of energy and had a knack of including play in her chores so that her children were always around her shouting and laughing as they competed with one another to help their mother. She immediately took a liking to the slim, serious boy who came to pore over her husband's parchments. The children, too, liked Sebastian and even got him to smile with their affection and spontaneity. They knew scores of games and tried to entice him to join them in one or another. However, after their mother helped them understand that Sebastian could not play but must be engaged in their father's work, they came up only occasionally to sit quietly in his lap or run their fingers through his shiny black hair. Sebastian came to love this gentle, innocent intimacy and looked forward to it daily. He found it in no other place in the rough, male-dominated life of Fernshanz.

The love that permeated Father Louis's house taught Sebastian more than all the writings and study ever could. He saw how much Father Louis and Bertha loved each other and their children. It colored every day and made the whole family content. Sebastian envied their life.

Father Louis sensed Sebastian's loneliness and took him into his family. They spent many hours together. At the end of one long day, after the children were asleep, Father Louis told Sebastian the secret of his happiness.

Their discussion started with a simple question: "Father, what makes you so happy? Life is so hard and full of constant strife and danger."

The priest smiled with satisfaction. "Ah, Sebastian, that's a marvelous question. The answer to it will make you wise, if you hear it well. It's simply this: you must learn to be grateful. Then you will be happy."

"Grateful for what, Father?"

"Why, for everything, lad, even for your hard lessons. God is merely teaching you when things don't go well. But you must start by being grateful for all the lovely gifts God gives you. They're all around you, everywhere! For example, the other day you saw me in the forest; what was I doing?"

"I don't know, Father. When we rode by you were hardly moving and you didn't even see us until we were right upon you."

"That's right, lad! I didn't see you because I was concentrating."

"On what, Father? There was nothing to see in the forest."

"Oh no, my boy, everything was there—all of God's grandeur. There is beauty everywhere—in the way a small, bright blue wildflower grows on the side of the path, the slow adventure of a snail finding its way over a difficult road, and the way the sun shines through the trees. Every bit of life, every season is beautiful, if only you notice it."

"Even in winter, Father," Sebastian teased, "when there are no blue flowers?"

"Ah, Sebastian, the winter is very beautiful, too. Its beauty is mainly in the silence. You see, the winter earth prays, and we must listen."

"One of my favorite things," he continued, "is to walk ever so slowly down that forest path and see the multitude of life that exists on every side. You should try it sometime. It is marvelously restful and renewing, and it is a way of entering a completely different world."

"Do you know, Sebastian," he began, "what is the greatest of all happiness on earth?"

"No, Father, I don't."

"Well, my boy, in this life, at least, it's the love between a man and a woman. Of all the treasures God gives me every day, I treasure my Bertha before them all—and of course, the children are part of that love; they can't be separated from it. And from that foundation of love between a man and a woman, one can come to love all other things and all other people. That's what our dear savior Jesu says we must do, is it not?"

He sighed deeply and went on, "Sadly, many people are unable to love others because they don't know how; they have no foundation of love with their partner. They marry for land or to increase their power and influence, or simply to ensure that they will have an heir. It is such a great mistake. Don't make it, Sebastian! See that you marry a woman you love. Then you will fall in love with life itself, and you will be as happy as any king!"

At the time, Sebastian merely attributed these sentiments to Father Louis's kind and gentle nature and the general goodwill he had toward everybody. But the conversation stayed with him, haunting him with longing for many years of his life.

Attalus was somewhat leery of Father Louis. He considered him soft and weak, and he resented the time Sebastian spent at his house. In truth, he was a bit jealous, having had no formal education in letters himself. More seriously, he suspected that the new study regime was distracting Sebastian from the more important task of becoming a highly skilled warrior. Without a doubt, Charlemagne would return in the spring with an army, and they would make war on Widukind in earnest. Sebastian was now fifteen. He was at the age when Frankish youths began to accompany their fathers or guardians to the troop gatherings. The boy—his boy—almost surely would insist on taking part in the campaign this time, and Attalus was afraid he would not be ready.

As the winter days grew ever shorter, Attalus announced his intention to travel to Adalgray to see how Ermengard fared. They had been parted for months now, and he longed to see her. He also needed to confer with Konrad about whether the men of Adalgray and Fernshanz would fight together as a unit and decide what troops and equipment to assemble should the king require men from both fortresses.

He set off in early December during a break in the weather, leaving Sebastian once again in charge of the fortress. This time, however, Fernshanz was much better prepared for an attack by the Saxons, and Sebastian had much more confidence in his ability to lead. He was even somewhat relieved to see the horse master take leave, for he felt increasingly guilty about the time he spent with Father Louis.

Weeks passed and Attalus did not return. Sebastian attributed the delay to bitter weather and heavy snow. As one slow week blended into the next, the peasants began to cope with the howling winds and gloom by gathering evergreen boughs to bring the smell of life into their fusty, poorly ventilated dwellings. Over the doors of their huts they fixed berry-laden holly boughs according to the old pagan custom of driving away ghosts and evil spirits.

In an effort to transform these ancient superstitions, Father Louis was the chief organizer of forays into the forest to collect festive decorations for the church and peasant huts. He enthusiastically regaled the villagers with the legend that the first holly trees had sprung directly from the footsteps of Christ, and he had them cut great quantities of the bright-leaved branches, as well as several perfect balsam firs. These he set upright around the entrance to the church. There he repeated over and over again the legend of the sainted Boniface, the great Christian crusader among the German peoples, who had first brought the word of the true God to so many of their brethren.

"And, children," the priest would observe keenly, "see how the shape of the tree itself speaks of the true God? Three corners it has, and what do they represent?" The children would sing back earnestly as he pointed to each corner: "The Father, the Son and the Hooooo-ly Ghost!"

Then he would take a bough of holly and quiz them again. "And what do these shiny leaves represent, children?"

"Light shining in the darkness, Father!"

"And the sharp points on the leaves?"

"Jesus's crown of thorns, Father!"

"And what," he ended with dramatic emphasis, "of the bright red berries, children?"

"The very blood of Jesus, Father."

And so the season was celebrated even as it was observed in a quiet and thoughtful way. It was Advent after all, and Advent was a time of waiting and preparing. Father Louis encouraged the people to fast and pray that their lives would be made better by the coming of the Christ child.

Still, old traditions were maintained among emerging ones, as the people also brought mistletoe into their houses to ensure happiness and good luck for the coming year, to take advantage of its magical healing powers, and especially to conjure fertility for the barren. All that notwithstanding, the pretty evergreen boughs, whether in a pagan or a Christian sense, were taken as symbols of eternal life. The peasants brought them inside to enjoy the color and smell and bring cheer to the children against the darkness of winter.

As near to the day of the winter solstice as he could figure, Father Louis said a special Mass in honor of the birth of the Christ child. Afterward there was celebration, a giant bonfire, and as much feasting as the limited means of Fernshanz could afford. Sebastian instructed Baumgard to provide some honey mead and beer.

"My good and gracious young lord!" began the vociferous steward, arms flung out wide as he warmed to his complaint. "You are giving away for free such bounty as only a great lord himself should enjoy. And you are giving it away to the lazy and least deserving. 'Tis a shame and a heavy extravagance that tramples upon the best order of things as they should be!" With his finger in the air and a scandalized expression, he even went so far as to remind Sebastian that he was not yet lord of Fernshanz.

"Baumgard . . ." Sebastian warned, his voice rising menacingly. The corpulent steward coughed once, cleared his throat, and scuttled off, grumbling, to begin to collect the mead and beer for the celebration. He had experienced the smoldering eyes of this mettlesome boy often enough to know that once provoked Sebastian would be a fierce and dogged foe who would later remember an affront. He also knew that Sebastian was no wastrel and that he was well loved by Attalus. It was merely, he thought, his solemn duty as steward to guard the assets of his master, deplore excess, and advise restraint upon all occasions.

After the celebration of the Mass the peasants piled dry wood and fir boughs high on a bed of flat stones and that night set the great pyramid ablaze. Everyone enjoyed the heat and the spectacle, but the night was bitter cold and there was no dancing. Nonetheless, it was the most memorable day of the winter season.

Chapter 10

The Wolf Hunt

The festive rejoicing of the solstice celebration lasted no longer than the following day, when the entire community was horrified to learn that two children, a boy and a girl, had been carried off by wolves. The two had gone out of the main gate early in the morning after the celebration to gather wood. When they did not return promptly, their father and a brother went looking for them and came upon a ghastly scene. During the night a large wolf pack had prowled up to the very walls of the fortress, setting the fowls and sentinel dogs into a frenzied commotion. The watch had failed to pass on the word to its relief, and the next day the wolves had picked off the children as soon as they entered the forest.

"M'lord Sebastian," entreated an agitated Liudolf the Elder, "the father of them poor killed children is layin' out on the steps of the church howlin' like a mad man. He's been there since early mornin', crazy with grief. He's pullin' his hair out and tearin' his clothes, and shoutin' at the top of his voice that the devil has come and we must pay for our sins. We need to get that bloody fool off them steps or the people are likely to panic. Trouble is, the priest won't let me haul him away and a crowd is gatherin'. I'm thinkin' we mus' hunt down them wolves, and it's yerself who needs to go down there right away and tell 'em that."

Wolves were a menace in the lives of the people, especially in winter. The great forest sheltered hundreds of the creatures, and the packs grew ravenous as snow and frigid temperatures made game scarce. The people feared them all the more because wolves were so clever and silent. Their ability to hunt as a pack seemed almost human but with a demonic twist, for they moved mostly at night and their eyes glowed yellow in the dark. They howled incessantly in deep winter, terrifying the children, and they were swift, efficient killers. A pack of wolves could bring down an ox in less than a minute and often decimated the dogs of a hunting party, sending the rest whimpering back to their masters.

"I tell ye, Lord Sebastian," Liudolf continued mournfully, "this truly might be the devil's work—or it could be the work of the Saxons. It's true, like they say, them Saxons are Satan's soldiers. They call this their 'Wolf Month,' don't ye know. And certain crazed bands of 'em have raided before in midwinter, all wearin' their foul wolf-skin cloaks and howlin' as they strike. I've heard the high king hisself has put out a special bounty on the heads of them 'wolf-men,' and has sent a troop of his best warriors to track 'em down. Is it not so, m'lord?"

"I don't know that, Liudolf," replied Sebastian calmly. "It may be true. But I do know this—what took those children last night were four-footed beasts, not Saxons. There were many of them, and they were close up to the walls. We should have been alerted, but the sentries weren't sure what was upsetting the dogs. Attalus meant to hunt the wolves in the spring and summer when we could find their dens and kills their cubs—but you are right, we cannot wait. We have to hunt them down now or no one will feel safe going into the woods for the rest of the winter. Let us go and see Olderic."

Under normal circumstances, a hunt would be a joyous occasion for the young warriors. There was no more exciting sport than to hunt the great aurochs, bear, or wolf on horseback and with the dogs. Like most communities, Fernshanz boasted a large pack of mixed hunting dogs. A good number were kept in the makeshift kennels along the walls to assist as sentries with their barking. Many others with more highly developed skills were kept in a special kennel where they were trained almost every day by handlers and pampered by little boys whose only job was to see to their care.

Such a hunt was not so fine, however, when it necessarily involved the peasants, occurred in cold or inclement weather, and required the tracking on foot of dangerous beasts, as the wolves most certainly were. In such a hunt, the peasants—women as well as men—would be obliged to trudge for miles through snow or wet and run the risk of confronting a bear or a wolf with little or no defense besides a noisemaker.

After settling the commotion at the chapel with the aid of Father Louis and Bertha, who led the grieving father of the slain children away, Sebastian went at once with Liudolf the Elder, his son, and Archambald to meet with the kennel master, Olderic, a tall, craggy peasant with huge hands and a face of leather and lines. Already with him were Bruno and Godomar, two of Fernshanz's most experienced sergeants, who were both gesticulating and talking at once in loud voices. Out of respect, they fell silent as Sebastian walked in. After the recent events at the Eresburg, most of the men regarded the young man with heightened good opinion.

"How shall we take these wolves, Olderic?" began Sebastian without preamble. "Is it not necessary to go at once, before it snows again?"

Olderic was a slow-moving, slow-thinking man. He did not immediately answer Sebastian. In the silence, the others began to urge their opinions. Sebastian held up his hand and waited for the old man to answer, knowing that Olderic would know better than anyone what to do. Finally, he raised his head and began to speak softly.

"My good lord, beggin' yer pardon, but we cannot go today. The whole village will have to help with this hunt—everyone who can be spared—because there are so many wolves. And we mus' have a good day, not too cold, not too much wind so that the people do not suffer. First, we mus' cast about with the trackin' hounds to be sure where the wolves are. Then we'll have to bait 'em, and then bring in the villagers." He paused for a long minute. "Here is how we might do it, sir."

Olderic knelt down and scratched with his knife in the dirt floor of his hut. "Here is the river, here the fortress, and here the fields. When we find the wolves, we will lure them closer to the fields by stakin' an ox in the forest, one too old to plow or pull. Once they kill and eat the ox, we will take the people into the woods, not too close to where the wolves are. They will make two lines, one on either side of the kill, but well away from it. Some hunters with the runnin' dogs must be placed at the back, betwixt the lines of the people." He drew the parallel lines and placed pebbles at the far end of the open-ended square to indicate the hunters and dogs.

Bruno, an avid, if not greatly skilled, hunter, leaned forward and interrupted excitedly. "Olderic, we don' need none of the people in this snow. The wolves'll be gorged, and we can easily track 'em and set the dogs upon 'em. The snow'll make it hard for the wolves to run, and we'll have the advantage with the horses."

"Bruno," the old man wheezed, "ye ought to know by now that the wolves will be able to run in this snow better'n yer horses. They will find trails which ye will not see. And they will not leave the cover of the forest unless ye make 'em."

He continued as Bruno harrumphed and stepped back from the circle. "At the signal, the people will start movin' in toward the wolves. The runnin' dogs'll drive the wolves down toward the fields betwixt the lines of our people. As they go by, the people'll make as much noise as they can and then close in behind 'em." He connected the two lines, drawing a large U-shaped formation with the mouth opening out to the fields.

"The people and the runnin' dogs'll drive the wolves into the open fields and toward the river. The other hunters mus' wait with the greys and the big dogs at the edges of the woods on both sides of the fields until the wolves break out from the forest. Then we'll set the greys free, and at the end, the mastiffs."

"Well, at least we will be able to use the horses then, will we not, Olderic?" asserted Bruno petulantly.

The old man hesitated, rubbing his balding head. "Ye can, Bruno, but only to get close quick. The horses will not be as light of foot in the snow, and they will be in great danger of injury. The snow'll also make it difficult fer ye to spear the wolves from the saddle, and the closeness of the dogs may make it impossible to shoot 'em with the bow. It'll be very dangerous fer yerself as well if yer horse goes down near the wolves. Ye best dismount and approach the wolves on foot while the dogs distract 'em. I would judge that some should hold the horses while others go in for the kill."

The group was silent, contemplating the plan. Sebastian knew that Attalus valued Olderic more than almost any of the other peasants. He recognized that the old man was as much an expert with the dogs as Attalus was with horses. Olderic's dogs had an enviable reputation.

Most prized were the lymers—quiet, slow hounds with a keen sense of smell for picking up the scent of game before the hunt even began. Then there were the running dogs, those with good noses and great stamina, essential for driving the game to ground or toward the waiting hunters. Once the game came into view, the sighthounds were released—long-legged greyhounds, highly valued for their speed and attack capabilities. Finally, there were the mastiffs, huge, often clumsy dogs used for fighting at the climax while the hunters moved in.

It took a day to organize the hunt and provision the people for a long trek into the woods, and they waited another day for the wind to die down. At the end of the second day, they staked an old ox in the forest. Olderic took advantage of the extra time to scout the forest with the lymers. It was a tricky business to discover the approximate location of the pack without driving it away. Sebastian was worried the dogs would alarm the wolves, but the ox had done the trick. Its plaintive, terrified bellows were heard clearly on the fortress walls as the wolves closed in; then the bellowing stopped suddenly. The next day the wolves remained close to the kill.

Well before dawn on the following day, the plan was put into action. Olderic and Liudolf the Elder set out hours before dawn with the running dogs, leading them by a circuitous route well away from the kill site so as not to alarm the wolf pack. At first light, led by Bruno and Godomar, almost every soul in the village filed out, heavily bundled against the cold, and formed two lines that marched off into the forest. Sebastian, who was in command of the two main killing parties, kept the greyhounds and bigger dogs inside the fortress until messengers arrived and reported that the people were in place and Olderic was in position at the rear of the trap. The two groups moved out quickly with the hounds as soon as the baying of Olderic's dogs could be heard.

The peasants slogged slowly but steadily through the foggy, early-morning half light, shouting, beating sticks together, and making as much noise as possible on makeshift drums and hollow pots. The beaters were impeded as much by the bushy undergrowth of the forest as they were by the knee-deep snow. It was the hardest kind of work, especially for the women and children who were old enough and strong enough to participate. The men all carried heavy clubs or spears if they owned them.

Bardulf and Drogo held back as the line was being formed and wound up on one of the legs of the U-shaped trap. The beaters on the legs were obliged to move more slowly than those on the back line, and their job was primarily to make sure that the wolves did not escape through the sides. Having been on these grueling drive hunts before, Bardulf was far more content with the slower pace of the beaters on the sides of the trap.

"God's blood, Drogo, what in hell have ye been eatin'? I can smell ye from here. You stink like a dog's fart," shouted Bardulf, as the line commenced to move out.

"It's on'y onions and a bit of garlic, Bardulf. 'S'all I had. Wasn't no more bread, and I couldn't beg none from Baumgard or ol' Marta. They told me to skirr out of the big house or else," said Drogo ruefully.

"Well," said Bardulf with a snort, "at least the stink'll keep the wolves away from us, I'll wager."

He had no sooner spoken than two large grey wolves burst out of the thicket in front of them straight into their path, pursued by several of the running dogs. Drogo backed up abruptly and promptly fell over. A wolf ran right over his body and escaped. The second wolf leaped straight at Bardulf, who instinctively swung the big club just as the wolf sprang at his face. The blow dropped the wolf in midleap, but Bardulf continued to beat it furiously until Drogo stayed his arm and pleaded, "Bardulf, ye kilt it. The wolf's done fer. Please stop hittin' it."

Bardulf had reacted entirely by reflex. Now, with the big wolf at his feet, he began to shiver. "C'mon, Drogo. That's enough fer us. We're gettin' out of here."

"But we can't, Bardulf, there'll be a hole in the line," protested Drogo.

"Damn the hole, and damn ye, too, if ye don't come on. The brush will cover us. We done our part. Oh, wait a bit, cut the ear off that beast and bring it along. It may get us out of any trouble later."

And so it did, eventually, at the end of the day.

It proved to be a cold but sunny day with little wind. The snow was abundant but not impossible for the horses. Each hunter in the killing parties was equipped as if for a campaign except for armor. Each man carried a bow, the long battle sword, a second, short sword or dagger, and the traditional long Frankish spear. Some also carried battle axes and heavy wooden clubs.

In the group farthest away from the fortress, Sebastian and Archambald waited at the mouth of the trap, shivering and impatient for the wolves to break from the forest. Young Liudolf had command of the opposite group. The entire troop, some thirty in all, excited by the sport and thrilled by the sense of imminent danger, stared nervously at the tree line, struggling to keep their mounts still and the dogs as calm as possible.

Without warning or sound, a wolf appeared at the edge of the forest. No one seemed to have seen him emerge. He was just suddenly there, turning his head quickly from side to side, sniffing, sensing the air, assessing the danger. He was an old black wolf, white at the muzzle, with battle scars all over his head. He had probably seen fifteen summers. He did not like this situation: wide open fields ahead of him, noise and commotion behind him, and the smell of horses, dogs, and men everywhere. But just as he turned to go back into the woods, several other wolves broke from cover into the open—then more, and then a running dog, snarling and barking.

Against his instinct, the old wolf turned again and raced with the others toward the river. At least twenty wolves were now out in the open. Sebastian and Liudolf loosed the greyhounds. They bounded across the snow, their long legs giving them advantage, and in a trice were nipping at the flanks of the wolves, causing them to turn and fight. The old wolf almost made it to the river before he was cut off by three greyhounds. He whirled and slashed out, snapping with his great jaws. One hound leaped from behind to catch the wolf by the back of the neck, his teeth closing instead on thick hair. The wolf turned and broke the dog's leg with a savage snap. He ripped open the side of another, all the while edging toward the woods at the bend of the river. More dogs joined the fight.

The riders closed in, several seeking a bow shot from the saddle, but the field had erupted in a score and more of close-packed, furious battles between dogs and wolves. Horses reared and screamed. Peasants emerged from the woods still beating their drums and clashing their sticks together. The men dismounted, spears at the ready. Sebastian charged into a tangle of dogs circling around a wolf, waiting for a clear opening. He missed his chance; the wolf broke free of the dogs and ran a short distance before whirling again to face his enemies. This time, Sebastian, laboring mightily in the snow, came up, and without waiting, thrust his spear just as the wolf lunged at a dog. The spear took the beast high on the shoulder blade, causing the wolf to stumble. At once the dogs were upon him. Sebastian pulled out and thrust again, this time into the heart.

"Go! Attack! Go!" Sebastian screamed at the dogs and moved off immediately to another fight. Archambald, frightened and almost unmanned, moved with him and slightly behind, nearly overcome by the mayhem and the effort.

"Pull yourself together, Archambald!" shouted Sebastian as they moved in on another wolf. The young man rallied and this time drove his own spear home just behind Sebastian's. "Well, done, Archambald! *In Nomine Patris, et Filii, et Spiritus Sancti*," intoned Sebastian, laughing in exhilaration. Archambald, however, continued to move in a state of near stupefaction and terror. Still, he slogged on as best he could behind his friend.

They reached the edge of the river where the snow was thinner and the footing better. There was the old black wolf, craftily waiting out the dogs, his rump to the river, his head moving back and forth like a snake. He wasted no motion, lunging out only when he saw a clear opening. He had already crippled a half dozen of the dogs. He edged ever closer to the safety of the forest along the river bank.

"Come on, Archambald! Let's take this old demon," Sebastian shouted as he moved into the circle of dogs looking for an opening. "Go round to the other side, Archambald. Don't let him break for the woods."

Dutifully, his heart in his throat, Archambald edged around the dogs and leveled his spear with both hands, waiting fearfully for the wolf to move closer. The greyhounds kept leaping back and forth in between. Suddenly, a giant mastiff bounded into the fray, growling savagely and foaming at the mouth. Scattering the greys, he made straight for the old wolf as if to bowl it over, but the wolf leapt nimbly aside and ripped a great gash in the throat of the mastiff, bringing it down in a pool of blood. The wolf then seized the moment and leapt out of the fray directly toward Archambald, the only obstacle between it and the forest. The lad raised his spear, but not high enough; it caught the wolf in a hind leg as it leaped over the weapon and onto Archambald, driving him into the snow. Only his thick leather coat saved his life as the wolf lunged instinctively for his throat.

Sebastian cried out as his friend fell and leaped frantically through the prancing greyhounds directly onto the back of the wolf as it struggled to find Archambald's throat. Without thinking and empowered by fear, Sebastian grasped the wolf's thick fur in one hand, wrestled his short sword out of it scabbard and drove the point with all his strength between the wolf's shoulder blades. The wolf collapsed with a shudder onto the body of Archambald, who continued to shriek and kick out against its weight.

At the end of the day, eleven dogs had been killed outright and another ten or eleven were badly maimed. Scarcely a greyhound or big dog had avoided a wound of some kind or another. However, it was a great victory for the hunters, as twenty-seven wolves lay dead in the fields.

Of the hunters, one had a mangled arm and three were badly bitten. Two beaters, a man and a woman on opposite sides of the trap, had been mauled but would survive. Bardulf and Drogo were celebrated as village heroes when they produced the ear of their wolf, the killing of which was greatly enhanced by Bardulf's extremely inventive account, with Drogo holding up the bloody ear at the exact moment of the tale's climax.

Poor Archambald had been slashed open from temple to jaw and lost a considerable amount of blood. However, he eventually recovered and thereafter became known as "Archambald Wolf's Bane." His great scar gave him notoriety, and sometimes he used it to walk about in new situations with somber dignity. But he was never able to suppress his ready smile and natural good humor for long. The young women of the village found him irresistible.

Chapter 11

The Spanish Dagger

A few days after the big hunt Attalus returned with his small escort of Fernshanz men. He was sick, almost delirious, with great pain in his stomach and chest, and he had to be helped from his horse. Sebastian was frantic to help him but had no idea what was wrong or what to do. Attalus lay groaning in his bed, sweating profusely, breathing heavily, and suffering from nausea. Sebastian never left his side, bathing his forehead and helping him drink as much water as he could. Eventually, Baumgard appeared with a crone from the village, old Marta, who must have been the oldest woman in the community. She had been a girl when Karl the Hammer had seized power, and she could remember the stories of the great victory in which he saved the Franks from the invading Saracens.

The crone wasted no time in delivering a verdict on Attalus's sickness. "Poison," she hissed. "He has drunk many times from the fruit of the *belladonna*. It is the 'devil's cherry.' He will die, but slowly."

Sebastian gasped and shouted, "No! You must do something! Save him. Give him something!" But the old woman simply sat on the edge of Attalus's bed, rocking back and forth and humming. She would not speak again.

"Baumgard," Sebastian implored, "can't you do something? Can't you force Marta to treat him?"

"My lord Sebastian, what is to be must be," the big man pontificated somberly, raising his shaggy head toward the heavens. When Sebastian reacted violently by slamming his fist down on a table, Baumgard added hastily, "On second thought, my lord, leave us now for just a bit and let me see what I can do."

Sebastian hurried from the room and began to pace just outside the door. He heard a brief screech, more a cry of indignation than pain, and Baumgard appeared at the door. "Marta will treat the master, my lord. She will do what is possible. Give her a little time to go to her hut and bring back some medicines." With that, Marta emerged, clucking and talking to herself. As she scuttled away, Baumgard began giving orders to the house serfs to bring fresh water and herbs from the kitchen. He and Sebastian then sat down by the bed to wait for what Marta would bring.

Over the next weeks, Attalus recovered somewhat, although he was much diminished. He had vomited so much during the first hours of Marta's treatment that Sebastian thought he would cough up his very lungs. They spent most of their time trying to make him drink the evil-smelling potions Marta mixed over a fire and to keep some water in his body. Attalus appeared nearly dead when he finally fell asleep after a night of such torture.

It was days before Attalus could rise from his bed. They turned him often, bathed his body to keep it cool, and tried to coax him to take liquids and some porridge laced with meat juices. He fought everything but would take a little nourishment when it was given to him by Sebastian. He would not suffer Marta in his presence for more than a minute or two, turning his head from her and groaning.

Finally, Attalus was able to get up and even walk a step or two, but he never recovered his strength and never again sat on the back of a horse. The best he could do was walk slowly with a staff around the walls of the citadel or in the exercise yard. He seemed particularly anxious to watch Sebastian train and to see him improve every day. He spent so much time in the yard that Baumgard brought out a cart with a padded chair in which Attalus could sit comfortably and watch his son and heir. Although he slept a great deal, he never grew tired of the daily routine and never left the yard until Sebastian did.

One mild, early spring day, toward the end of the yard time, Attalus motioned for Sebastian to come to him. The boy had been galloping Joyeuse at a series of dummies dangling from ropes. He was attempting to run his spear through as many of the small rings attached to the right shoulders of the dummies as he could. It was a difficult feat considering the speed of the horse and the dummies swaying in the wind. If he could snare three of the five targets, he would raise his spear high with satisfaction and look toward Attalus for approval. Once he managed all five at one go and whooped with delight.

As he rode up and dismounted, Attalus slowly unraveled himself from his blankets, and with Sebastian's help, he stepped out of the cart. He bade Sebastian to bring a belt of weapons wrapped in a blanket. They were Attalus's own swords, together with his shield, hauberk, and helmet.

"Fetch your swords and shield, lad. There is something I must show you." Sebastian did as he was told and armed himself as he saw Attalus doing. When they were fully armed and ready, Attalus stuck his long sword into the dirt and leaned on it to steady himself.

"Sebastian," he said somberly, "I am about to show you something that you need to know, but you must do nothing whatsoever to act upon this knowledge. If you do, you will sign your own death warrant, for he will certainly find a way to kill you. I'm talking about Konrad. Marta thinks my sickness was caused by poison; I'm sure she is right, and most likely it was Konrad who was the poisoner—or at least he ordered it. I saw his eyes the last night I was at Adalgray. He watched me intently, with a crooked smile on his face, and he was uncommonly attentive and polite to me, whereas before he had only smirked or scowled whenever he saw me. The change even made your mother nervous. I have already told you how worried she is about you. She only stayed at Adalgray because her brother has gone from bad to worse. Athaulf wanders about barefooted in his night shirt, drinking all the day and into the night. He will not survive long, but your mother will not leave until he dies.

"In the meantime," Attalus continued, peering intently into Sebastian's eyes, "we have no proof that Konrad poisoned me—none whatever. If I accused him, even before the high king, it would be the word of a constable turned substitute count against that of a magnate of one of the oldest and most important families in the Frankish realm. No one would believe me, and the king would be angry that I even brought the problem to him because it would put him in a dilemma, as he could not side with me."

"Attalus," Sebastian stammered, "I will fight him!"

"You will not!" Attalus exclaimed animatedly, grasping Sebastian's shoulder. "At least not now. You are not ready, and Konrad is a seasoned fighter. He's as strong as a bull, and he fights insanely. He would cut you to pieces. You must bear it. Learn, practice, and get some experience. If you have the opportunity, watch Konrad, see how he fights, and determine his weaknesses. One day you will fight him—I am sure of it. He will force you to it, for he hates you. But, God willing, it will not be before you have had a chance to do some real fighting yourself and learn what you must know."

Attalus paused, breathing heavily after so many words. Then he leaned forward and again clutched the boy's shoulder. "I must teach you now what may be the most valuable lesson you will ever learn from me. Listen well. This is a terrible maneuver, fraught with difficulty and danger. If you do not manage it perfectly, you could easily be killed. If you master it, it will enable you to defeat much stronger and more experienced men."

The old warrior reached into the blanket and pulled out a Spanish dagger in a sheath. As he drew it out, Sebastian could see that it was an elegant stiletto made of burnished steel with an ebony handle. It was not as long or as broad as the Frankish small sword. Instead, it was light and so well balanced that Sebastian felt it would make an excellent throwing knife.

As it gleamed in Sebastian's palm, beautiful and deadly, Attalus whispered, "You are a very talented fighter, Sebastian." He went on, taking the dagger from the boy's hand, "You get better every day, and I am proud of how well you have learned. But now you must learn cunning. Let me show you." Attalus fixed the dagger into his own belt.

"If you find yourself being beaten and you have no other recourse, here is what you must do. Strap the dagger so, into your own belt—on the left side. Fix it so the handle leans toward your right hand—see?—and can be freely drawn out of the scabbard."

"Now raise your sword high above your head. Pick a moment like this when your opponent drives down at you with his sword; parry the blow with your shield, then release the shield from your hand. Push it aside. It will still be attached to you by the strap around your neck. Then, while he fends off your own sword, step inside your opponent's shield, as close up to his body as you can. Grasp his chain mail at the neck with your left hand so that he cannot separate from you. Stick to him like a flea at this moment, no matter what he does. If he falls backward, fall with him. If he moves forward, let him drive you backward, but keep your feet under you, no matter what."

As he spoke, Attalus went through the motions he described. "Finally," he whispered, with his face crammed against Sebastian's, "drop your sword. It too will be attached to a cord around your wrist so that you won't completely lose it. With your right hand free, reach for the dagger. It's small enough so that you will be able to wrench it between your bodies and bring it up—to the opening right under your enemy's chin, between the chain mail and his helmet. Then drive the point straight into his throat."

Several days after this lesson on the training field, Attalus died. He had taken to his bed almost immediately and never rose again. He simply slipped into a long sleep, waking intermittently. Sebastian kept vigil at his side, sleeping with his head on the bed, eating nothing and hardly even taking a cup of water, although Baumgard, clucking and mumbling mournfully, insistently proffered both food and drink.

During one of his rare moments of consciousness, Attalus beckoned for Sebastian to lean closer. "I must tell you something, Sebastian," he rasped. After a long silence he continued, painfully, "Your mother and I . . . I loved her . . . for so long. We . . . you are my son."

Suddenly, the stoical mask that Attalus had worn for such a long time fell away, and Sebastian could see in the pleading, anxious eyes beneath him the fear and longing that Attalus had suppressed for half a lifetime. As he felt the last of his father's strength tighten and then fade away in his hand, the moment passed, pitifully brief.

Father Louis visited several times a day, administering ointments and intoning the Latin prayers for the dying over and over again. He never managed to hear Attalus's confession, though he tried to do so doggedly. Between the priest's visits, Sebastian bathed Attalus's forehead and brushed his hair, newly taken by how similar the long, silky silver-and-black locks were to his own. Whenever the old warrior revived, Sebastian held his hand. Several times Attalus recognized him and provided a hint of a smile. But the soul Sebastian could see behind his eyes slipped further and further away each time until it was finally gone.

For Sebastian, a great light went out. He descended with Attalus into the shadows and remained there for a long time, numb and desolated. Eventually, he began to think again and it came to him, oddly, that he had always known somehow but had never consciously acknowledged that Attalus was his father. The bond had always been there, though unblessed and unconfessed. His loss was magnified and Sebastian allowed himself to be carried away again by regret and a multitude of conflicting concerns.

Sebastian continued to sit by the bed of the dead man through the night and even into the evening of the next day. He would let no others into the dark room except Baumgard, who hovered by the door and occasionally renewed the lone candle. Several of the senior sergeants came and went periodically, speaking in hushed voices, afraid to approach their young leader. If anyone spoke, Sebastian turned furiously and commanded them to get out.

Finally, Liudolf and Archambald edged into the room. For a long while they feared to speak and remained standing just beyond the glow of the candlelight. Suddenly, after a long time, Archambald was seized with a fit of coughing and then he sneezed, emitting at the same time a loud fart.

Sebastian erupted from his vigil chair, grabbed the candle, and turned to see the culprit who had dared disturb his somber wake in such an unholy way. Archambald shrank, abashed, against the wall, his hand to his mouth, his eyes bugging out in fear and humiliation. Sebastian, his tearstained face contorted with grief and anger, grabbed the unfortunate boy by the neck, the candle in his face, shouting, "You, you . . ." Then he suddenly seemed to see his friend. "Archambald? What are you doing here? Why did you . . . ? What is . . . ?"

He paused, staring into Archambald's trembling face, and suddenly he broke out laughing, burying his face in Archambald's neck. The tears continued to flow, but he laughed and sobbed alternatively, clinging to his friend. Both Liudolf and Archambald hung on to him until the racking sobs and convulsive laughter ceased. Then they eased him out of the room and sat him down at the dining table, where they plied him with water and some wine. Finally, they persuaded him to eat something. After nearly three days of abstinence from food, Sebastian proved to be ravenous.

The next morning, Ermengard arrived. She had left Adalgray for good and traveled with a considerable entourage of soldiers, servants, and baggage. Poor Count Athaulf had died suddenly, having fallen—or been pushed, Ermengard reckoned—down a flight of stairs in the keep. He had lingered in a coma for two days, waking only once to shout, "Assassins! Assassins!" And then he had simply died, mercifully, in his sleep. Konrad was now the new Lord and Count of Adalgray. Ermengard left as soon as her brother's body was in the ground.

It had been a harrowing trip, as winter was still hanging on, with occasional snow and high winds. At least the cold continued to keep the roads and paths of the route solid. Count Konrad had protested his aunt's insistence on her right to property and people, but Ermengard flew into one of her fits of towering rage and threatened to go to Charlemagne himself if need be. Konrad had never been able to cope with his aunt, and in the end, he had been only too happy to see the back of her. Still, he had been up all night with his friends, drinking and carousing, and as her little caravan passed through the gates he muttered aloud and drunkenly, "Good riddance, finally, to all that rotten lot of traitors, whores, and horse masters. I know what their story is—anyone with eyes can see."

Father Louis said the Mass of the dead over the body of Attalus the next day. Everyone in Fernshanz attended the funeral, crowding into the small chapel until it overflowed. Those who could not be inside stood in prayer in the cold on the small village green before the church. Attalus had been so respected that men and women of every station promised to contribute to Masses to be said for his soul, which Father Louis was enjoined to say on the first, seventh, and thirteenth days of the month for three months after his death. More than a hundred villagers vowed to say a verse from the psalter for their dead lord every day for a month.

These were no small promises, because petitioners were expected to contribute some offering or alms, either coins or work, for any Mass said at their request. Attalus would be buried forthwith beside the chapel, under the eaves of its roof so that any rain might be considered to refresh his grave with "holy water."

Ermengard shed no tears throughout the ordeal. Instead, she took charge of all the arrangements and immersed herself in planning every detail, the servers at Mass, the incense, the songs, the readings to be given, and the refreshments afterward. There was, of course, no inappropriate gaiety, but it was obvious that the townspeople felt a keen sense of satisfaction in celebrating the life of their leader, who had been by far the wisest and best master they had experienced in their short lives. Almost all felt obliged to approach Sebastian to express their regret and sorrow. It was clear they expected him to take up Attalus's mantle.

Sebastian stood woodenly throughout the mass, dumbly pondering the double shock of Attalus's confession followed so soon by his demise. Through his tears, Sebastian had trouble seeing the face of the man he had loved so much throughout his life. Gradually, instead of the honest, noble face of a devoted father, the scowling image of Konrad intruded, souring his grief. He began to feel the hatred grow, and he knew there would be no justice. Konrad would go unpunished and would not stop until he had found a way to eliminate the son as well as the father.

Filled with rage, Sebastian could not raise his eyes to the host being lifted before the crowd by Father Louis. Instead, he turned on his heel and shouldered his way through the crowd and out of the chapel. It was clear to him that Konrad was his mortal enemy now and that a fatal reckoning between them was inevitable. He found himself clenching his teeth, the blood rushing to his head, his fingers charged with energy. He welcomed the fight, whatever its consequences, and from that moment he vowed to prepare for it.

Chapter 12

Worms and a New Level of Life

THE KING'S COURT AT WORMS, SPRING 772

Ermengard held her son at arm's length and stared into his eyes. "You must go to the king's court. You must go now, Sebastian. There is no other way. If you are to survive, you have to win the favor of the high king."

"But I can't leave now, Mother," Sebastian protested. "Attalus is gone. What about the fortress? What about you? What if Konrad decides to finish all of us?"

"He will not come here if only I remain. I am no threat to him—but who knows how low he might stoop in regard to you? He becomes more crazed every year, and he is into his wine almost as much as his poor father was. If you go to court, the king will discover you again. He will see what kind of man you are becoming and what you can do. I am sure he will be impressed. He might even make you one of his personal vassals and confirm you as lord of Fernshanz. He loves anyone who can read, but most of them are churchmen. And if you can fight as well . . ."

"But what about Fernshanz? Who will captain the fortress?"

"Rubbish! Are there no sergeants? Attalus told me there were good soldiers here and that he could depend on them. Do you think this is the first time I've had to take charge in the absence of a fortress commander? Both my husband and my brother knew they could rely on me completely."

"Mother," the boy persisted, "that was at Adalgray, a fortress four times as big as Fernshanz and with many more soldiers. The Saxons . . ."

"Pah! Don't speak to me about Saxons. You held out against the Saxons even when Attalus was gone. They know this place is strong. Besides, it's too late. The winter will soon be over and they know that King Karl will come for them as soon as the snow is gone and there's enough fodder for the horses. They will doubtless be too busy preparing for war to bother with us. If you go now, you may be able to take part in the preparations for the king's new campaign. Attalus said you've become a skillful warrior and a promising leader already. The king will see it, and he will take you with him when he marches against the Saxons, for I'm sure that is what he plans to do. He may even confirm you in command of the Fernshanz men. You must ask him for that when the time comes."

Pulling him to her breast, she whispered to him, "Don't be afraid for me, my son, I have done this before. We must think of you now. You must go to the king."

Sebastian withdrew from her grasp and said, "Mother, I've never been anywhere except here and Adalgray. I don't even know where the king is."

"I have heard he will hold this year's assembly in the town of Worms. He has a big villa there. All you have to do is go to the great river and follow it upstream. I will send my man Bernard with you; you know him well. He was your father's comrade in arms and has served our family much longer than you have been alive. He has been almost everywhere and he will lead you through several large towns where you can learn something about Francia. You can cross the river at Mayence—there's an old Roman bridge there—and make your way to Worms before the general assembly begins and the king will have no more time for you."

"Mother, it is an extremely dangerous time right now. We need to be doubly on guard now that Attalus is gone. I have a bad feeling about leaving you."

"No more arguments! I won't have it. I am perfectly capable, and you must go now, without delay. We don't know what Konrad might try to do to you."

She paused now and her voice became gentler as she took his face in her hands. "You're almost sixteen. If you were the king's son, you would be commanding troops by now. King Karl knows you; he has seen you, and you did him a great service when you found the Saxons' black statue. Did he not say he would reward you? Did he not send you a teacher? It is very unlikely he has forgotten you. In fact, I think you will impress him even more when he sees how well you have learned from Father Louis. He may even want to keep you at court. At the very least, you will certainly go on campaign with him this year."

The very next day Father Louis said a Mass for Sebastian and blessed his journey. On the church steps afterward, the priest presented his pupil and friend with a parting gift. "Sebastian, my son," he began, "I have something special for you that may help you catch the attention of the high king." He produced a cleric's sheepskin case containing several parchments of writing. "Take a look and see if you can read them."

Sebastian unrolled a parchment and found that it was an excerpt for the famous passage in Second Samuel, the last words of King David. The words had been painstakingly and beautifully copied out by Father Louis in the wonderfully clear script of the parchments he had brought from Fulrad's library. Another parchment contained the entire *Credo*, written in small but stately well-formed letters. A third contained the *Pater*. Sebastian found he could easily read them all. But the fourth parchment astonished him. It was nothing like any of the biblical readings or prayers he was used to; it was written in an unfamiliar Latin cadence and style, less formal, almost personal, containing words he had not seen before in any writing. Louis spent the rest of the day tutoring Sebastian in those words and several others that were from the same document but were not included on the single parchment. The passage was a page from a document Father Louis was sure the king would know well and cherish. It was the first page of *The City of God*, written by none other than the greatest saint of the early Christian Church, Augustine of Hippo. Sebastian had little idea at the time how crucial the page would be in determining his fate.

The Rhine lay less than a day's journey from Fernshanz. Sebastian had seen it briefly several times while on patrol with Attalus. Now they kept to the rough road that ran parallel to the huge river as they made their way upstream toward Worms and the king's court. Bernard, the professional soldier, did indeed seem to have been everywhere. He could answer, albeit reluctantly, any question Sebastian put to him about the river and the places they passed. He was a hawk-nosed old veteran with leathery skin, a tangle of wild grey hair, and a gnarled, sinewy body that never seemed to need any rest. He never spoke unless he had to, merely pointing to bring something to Sebastian's attention. Nevertheless, he often watched the boy from the corner of his eye, as if by observing the way that Sebastian sat his saddle and handled any small detail of the journey, he could assess whether Sebastian would be ready for the challenges he would surely find ahead of him.

Bernard had served Ermengard's husband, Count Grennig, and then her brother, Count Athaulf, through the wars against the Aquitanian dukes and in the intermittent back-and-forth raiding against the Saxons. He had been Attalus's cohort through every fight and his closest friend. He alone, besides Ermengard, knew Attalus's secret regarding Sebastian.

Archambald was their only other companion, Liudolf having been conscripted by his father to help with the security of the fortress. Sebastian had been deeply disappointed when his steadfast friend and closest ally was denied the trip. "I shall miss you sorely, Liudolf," he exclaimed as they prepared to ride out from the fortress, "but when I return I hope it will be to command the Fernshanz men as we march against the Saxons. And you shall be at my right hand." He touched his fist to his breast and grasped Liudolf's forearm.

For his part, Archambald was delighted with the expedition. He had seen even less of the world than Sebastian and was eager to begin the adventure. Whooping loudly when Sebastian first proposed he should come, he had not really closed his chattering mouth since then except to sleep. As soon as they left the gates, however, Bernard turned his horse around, rode straight up to him, and grasped his bridle. Looking intently into Archambald's startled face, he put a single finger to his lips. His somber face and conjuror's eyes gave Archambald his first icy lesson about traveling on a potentially dangerous road.

The rutted road proved more uncertain and perplexing than perilous. Although it stayed roughly parallel to the river, the track meandered away from the river and back again as the terrain allowed. Marshes, gullies, streams, and small rivers had to be got over or around, which often took hours of the day. On a good day, they might cover only about ten leagues, riding dawn to dusk.

Sebastian was surprised to see that in spite of the difficulties, the road was well traveled the farther south they went. They encountered knots of peasant families looking for work in new, more accommodating villages or towns. Some of them were serfs who had no freedom to abandon their lord's manor and thus were fugitives; others were branded, runaway slaves who fled off the track whenever horsemen approached. They even encountered gangs of blond Saxons or Slavs, bound together and forced to plod south to be sold as slaves in the markets of Spain. They also saw the occasional churchman who was seeking a place to preach for his supper or a parish to shepherd, though he might be little more qualified than those he would serve.

Once in a while they passed bands of rough men carrying cudgels or heavy walking staffs who moved to the side of the road and cast their eyes furtively over the heavily armed riders as they passed, obviously calculating the risks involved in interfering with them. Bernard increased the pace to a canter whenever such men were encountered and put a healthy distance between them before he allowed the small troop to relax again. More often than not they rode with bare swords in hand or a spear at the ready.

Sebastian was fascinated with the bridge at Mayence. They reached the fabled town after almost a week of tedious riding, and Archambald was wild to find an inn where they could eat something hot and rest under a roof. However, Sebastian would not go beyond the bridge until he had satisfied his curiosity about it. Built upon sturdy stone pilings and held together mysteriously for centuries by some Roman engineering magic, it comprised a framework of heavy timbers and thick planks that rumbled and creaked as the horses were led over them. Not many people dared to stay mounted while crossing over the unfamiliar structure for fear they would be thrown if the horses were spooked by the noise.

Sebastian could not believe that such a wide river as the Rhine could be spanned by stone and wood, and he begged for time to study the bridge closer, even climbing down to the pilings to get a better look. He was at a complete loss as to how the pilings had been implanted in the bed of the swift-flowing river in the first place and how the stones remained bound together against the strong current after so much time. Father Louis said the bridge had been built by the Romans not long after the birth of the Christ. Sebastian studied the bridge for at least an hour while Archambald ogled the passing throng of men and women, sighing and complaining that he would soon die of hunger.

Beyond the bridge, their first impression of Mayence was of the multitude of townsfolk. Sebastian and Archambald had never seen a large town, let alone so many people at one time and so varied. Many were dressed differently than the Franks, and some were swarthy and sharp-faced with very long beards. Once they saw a man in white robes with completely dark skin bartering on the street in sign language. The town had no significant walls or fortifications, as at Fernshanz, and no troops of armed horsemen challenging every newcomer. Carts, cattle, horses, and farmers moved continuously over the bridge into the town. Big grain bins lined the wharves by the river, and barrels of wine and bins of salt lay waiting for transport. There was activity everywhere; open workshops revealed artisans of every kind making saddles, tools, shoes, and clothes. Lumber and stones were piled high along the river beside barges. Smoke from countless fires poured out of the roofs of homes and shops. They were lucky enough to arrive on a market day, and as they passed the marketplace, they could see every kind of food available to buy or to eat at once. Bernard had to take Archambald's bridle to make him come along past the delicious smells of roasting meat and baking bread.

Finally, Bernard led them to the opposite side of town where they stopped at a small inn with an adjacent stable. Much to Archambald's chagrin, their taciturn guide did not allow a return to the marketplace, offering only the words "costly" and "unnecessary" by way of explanation. Instead, they were treated to a wooden bowl of warm beer, hot bread, cold fish, and a corner of the main room of the inn near the fireplace, where they slept wrapped in their cloaks upon the floor. Bernard slept in the stable with the horses as a double measure of security and frugality. Ermengard had given him a few silver deniers, but they were precious and Bernard would not part with them easily. The next day they were up at dawn and again on their way toward Worms. Both young men looked back often and longingly at Mayence as the intriguing town receded from their view.

If the bridge at Mayence had been a wonder, the king's palace at Worms was an astonishment for Sebastian and Archambald. Arriving late in the day, they saw little of the town and spent a short night in the monastery near the palace. Bernard had them up before dawn and at the palace gate soon after first light—and for good reason. Sebastian was surprised to see so many people already at the gate. "Petitioners!" snorted Bernard gruffly, as they took their place in the line. "Ye mus' see the count of the palace first. Nobody gets in without his authority, no matter who ye might be."

They spent the next two hours camped by the gate, waiting to be seen and interviewed by Count Arno, the mayor of the palace and its most important officer. It was he who granted interviews with other court personalities or with the king himself. He had the unenviable duty of organizing every detail of palace life for as long as the king cared to stay at Worms.

Such a job required a man of remarkable talent who was a diplomat as well as a logistics genius. Arno did not look like such a man. He had an enormous belly and waddled when he walked, which was not often. He sat most of the time behind a low table while he interviewed the various counts, vassals, clerks, and clergymen who lined up to seek privileges or benefices from the king or his officers. However, Arno was a shrewd judge and could tell in a short minute whether to favor a supplicant or simply put him off or dismiss him. One of the reasons the king stayed so often at Worms in advance of a campaign was Arno, whose organizational skills smoothed and speeded the king's business. His owlish, almost lazy demeanor belied his quick grasp of a situation and of the petitioner, and he knew the king's will exactly.

While Bernard waited patiently in the line at the gate, Sebastian spent the time walking with Archambald around the perimeter of the palace. "Look at how tall these buildings are," he marveled. "They're twice as high as the keep at Fernshanz, and most of them are made of stone!"

"We don't have a single stone building at home," Archambald observed absently. "In fact, there isn't much stone anywhere around where we live. You have to dig along the stream beds to find enough just for the defense on the walls."

"See how square the whole palace area is, Archambald? I'm sure it used to be a fortress—the buildings made the wall. See, there are hardly any doors or gates, and the windows are all high and narrow. Still, that doesn't seem like much of a defense. There aren't even any walls around the town."

"I expect that's because the king believes he has beaten all his enemies. Right, Sebastian?"

"Well, he hasn't beaten the Saxons. I can't believe he thinks the Saxons can't get down this far. They've already raided as far as Cologne. It makes me uncomfortable. I'm not used to places with no walls."

Finally, as they returned from their third jaunt around the palace, Bernard signaled frantically for them to hurry, and they were ushered immediately to the table where Arno sat, finishing his breakfast. "Name and business," he grunted indifferently, while dipping a large chunk of bread into what appeared to be a bowl of beer.

Bernard stepped forward and declared in a dignified, though gravelly voice, "Lord Sebastian, son of Count Grennig, nephew of Count Athaulf of Adalgray, and ward of the Horse Master Attalus, late of Fernshanz, seeks audience with the king."

Arno's head jerked up at once and he squinted at the group as if to assess better what was suddenly a more interesting turn to the morning's duties. From the way Sebastian and Archambald were standing, one young man earnest, attentive, and meeting his own gaze directly, and the other grinning self-consciously and fidgeting from one foot to the other, he saw at once who Bernard was introducing. There was a glint of genuine interest in his gaze as he observed the slim lad with his dark locks and piercing black eyes.

"Sebastian, is it? Seeker of the Irminsul at Eresburg, no doubt. We have heard of you." He looked Sebastian up and down as if appraising a new and promising young bull. "Lucky for you, your reputation has preceded you. The king intends to hunt this morning; he has already been to Mass and is now at his breakfast. If you hurry, you may have two minutes to see him before he departs. Go at once; follow my clerk to the king's quarters. I can assure you he will remember you." He added more pleasantly in parting, "Welcome, Sebastian. May you continue to find favor with the high king." He motioned toward a waiting clergyman who quickly turned and walked rapidly ahead from the gate room and into the palace courtyard.

The king did indeed remember Sebastian. At the announcement of his name, he bounced out of his chair behind a table laden with bread and meat and greeted the boy with a bear hug, astonishing several of the high-ranking vassals and clergymen breakfasting with him. "Sebastian, good lad! What a pleasure to see you! I was afraid I was going to have to seek you out at Fernshanz when we go against the Saxons again. Where's the horse master? Where's old Attalus?"

"My lord king, I am very sorry to tell you that Lord Attalus is dead. He died not a fortnight ago—just before I came—of . . . of an illness."

"Whoa, Sebastian, say it is not so!" the king exclaimed, his face troubled. "The horse master, dead? It cannot be! Attalus was as tough as old leather and in fine shape when last I saw him! Well, I swear!" He paused, bent his head briefly, and crossed himself. "We will offer the Mass for him this Sabbath, and we will miss him greatly. Come sit down and tell me about it. And I want to know everything about Fernshanz." The king made a place for Sebastian at his right hand, recognizing and welcoming the old soldier Bernard as well and even slapping the artless but insouciant Archambald between the shoulders as he greeted him, pushing him onto a bench on the other side of his table. Sebastian spent a frenetic quarter hour answering the king's questions, which were put sharply to him one after the other. It was clear the king was moved by the loss of one of his favorites and that he realized what Attalus's death meant for his defenses along the Saxon March.

"I would not have come, my lord king, except that my mother, the Lady Ermengard, insisted. She said you would want me to come and that if I didn't you would be displeased. She said . . ."

"Your mother was correct," the king quickly asserted. "Attalus was a key to my northern defenses and to my plans for attacking the Eresburg. Now I shall have to reconsider a number of things, including the unfortunate death of Count Athaulf, as well. Have you seen Konrad, by the way?"

"No, my lord king, my mother insisted I should come forthwith, without going first to Adalgray. She said you would understand."

"Hmm, I see," the king murmured, looking intently into the boy's eyes. "Well, I suspect it might be just as well. I'll think about it, and then we'll talk again. Meanwhile, how do you feel about a hunt? I was just on the way. I know you have just finished a long journey, but are you up for it? I should be glad to have you and your men as well."

Sebastian was more than delighted to be included. Bernard, however, begged off, claiming the need to find lodgings and tend to the horses. As they strode out of the chamber, the king called back over his shoulder to his entourage of clerks and officials. "The young Lord Sebastian and his men are to stay in the palace. Find a place for them."

Of all the pastimes a Frankish king was privileged to engage in, hunting was Charlemagne's favorite. Among the dangerous game, he hunted bears, wolves, and even the huge forest aurochs, but he would hunt anything and delighted in providing for his own supper by spearing a red stag from the saddle while racing through a thick forest. The hunt itself was a raucous affair, even a joyous one, with king and vassals competing for the prize, accompanied always by the noise of horse and hound and the excited shouts of the men, who vied with one another to demonstrate their courage and skill. It was a dangerous pastime; rarely were there no wounded, and rarer still was an excursion without a kill. Charlemagne would hunt continuously from dawn to nightfall rather than go home empty-handed.

Sebastian and Archambald were thrilled, of course, just to be a part of the excitement. Sebastian even managed to be in on a kill several times during the day. Once he found himself shoulder to shoulder with the king as they rooted out a boar from a thicket and speared him as he charged. "Steady, lad, let him come," the king had shouted. They had knelt together and let the boar impale himself upon their spears.

The day had been so productive and the weather so fine that Charlemagne had not wanted it to end. They hunted until nearly dark and went home singing. They settled for a cold supper that evening, the hour being late. But Charlemagne was in high spirits and promised a banquet with entertainment the next evening. Before retiring to his own quarters, he paused to clasp Sebastian's shoulder. "Good on you,

Sebastian, son of Grennig! You'll do. Now if you can fight with the same courage as you hunt, you'll make a fine Frank indeed." He turned to go.

"My lord king, I can read as well," Sebastian blurted out hastily. "I wanted to tell you as soon as I could for fear I wouldn't have many chances. If you remember, you sent me a priest, Father Louis, and you enjoined me to learn from him. I wanted you to know that I did, and I am deeply grateful."

The king paused and turned, looking at Sebastian keenly, as if seeing a new person. "Did you now?" he exclaimed. "Well, that is good news indeed! We shall see tomorrow. See Count Arno in the morning, and he'll find a time to bring you to me. If you read well enough, you shall sit at my own table at supper and read to us as we eat. Did you bring a reading or two?"

"I have a few scrolls, sire, but they are only partials, not whole readings."

"No matter, bring them. We will see what progress you have made in any case. Rest well. And welcome, Sebastian; you have made a good start."

The next day, the king found the time he had promised, and Sebastian began the readings with the parchment page containing the words of King David, following it with the most challenging reading, the single parchment page from Augustine's *The City of God*. He had lurched awake at first light, feeling an urgent need to spend every possible second practicing the readings. When Arno called him, he could almost have recited them by heart. The king heard the readings at his breakfast. After the first paragraph he stopped eating and became perfectly still, obviously drawn to the steady Latin cadence and the beauty of the words. "A layman who can read, by God," Charlemagne exclaimed loudly after Sebastian had finished. "Such a one is a rare specimen in any case. But a warrior who can read is truly an exception!"

Charlemagne was immensely pleased, especially by the passages Sebastian chose to read. He immediately proffered an invitation to sit with him at table amongst his family that evening and to begin the feast with the king's own copy of Augustine. Sebastian begged for a simpler text but the king insisted, and Sebastian spent the rest of the day poring over the words in the king's thick book, many of which he scarcely knew or had even seen before. Mercifully, the king had specified that

Sebastian was to read only the first two pages of the first of ten books in this long, formidable work.

That evening, Sebastian was startled to find so many women at the king's table. At Adalgray, only his mother had eaten with the men, and of course, the table at Fernshanz usually included only Attalus and Sebastian. The bold chatter of the women and their open and unembarrassed appraisal of himself as he sat down at the foot of the table unnerved Sebastian. He had been around few women in any case, and to have them look him up and down as if he were a stud horse struck him as bizarre and improper. The king noticed not at all and welcomed Sebastian warmly.

As soon as the company sat down, the boar they had killed the day before was brought in on a spit from the cooking fire, along with steaming plates of pickled cabbage and fresh-baked bread. A table with chairs had been set on a raised dais for the king and a large number of his relatives. Other tables with benches were set up at varying distances from the royal table, with seating determined by the rank of the counts, bishops, and administrators—all personal vassals of the king. The great hall of the king's quarters buzzed with a collegial spirit and the sounds of laughter and good-natured conversation. The feast began with a very short grace said in Latin by Laidred, one of the king's chaplains. He was a tall, cadaverous monk with a tonsure and an air of melancholy, who, nonetheless, smiled thinly when Charlemagne thanked him for the blessing and bade him sit at the family table. Thereafter, the monk rose periodically at Charlemagne's bidding to read selected psalms or passages from the Bible.

The king waited until after the first course, however, to introduce Sebastian. He did so with fanfare, announcing the young man as "a wonder, a keen-eyed scout, a fearless hunter, and a budding Frankish warrior—who can read!" He then proceeded to bid Sebastian to do just that. Sebastian took a last sip of wine, rose quickly, and stood at the end of the table, the king's heavy book and a candle awkwardly in hand. The monk Laidred kindly rose and held the candle as the boy began to read.

"*De Civitate Dei*," intoned Sebastian in a clear, high voice. "*Gloriosissimam ciuitatem Dei siue in hoc temporum cursu . . .*" As he read, the supper guests fell silent and listened in awe as the strange words fell on their ears like so many bewitching incantations. Gradually, they returned to their supper, but as the king listened intently, they confined their comments to hushed whispers. Even at two pages, the reading was long, and Sebastian stumbled frequently over unfamiliar words. However, neither the king nor the others at the table seemed to know the difference. All seemed mesmerized by the solemn elocution of the handsome youth, his earnest face framed in the golden light of the candle. At the end, Sebastian closed the book carefully, paused for a moment of homage, and placed it on the table. He then bowed slightly to Laidred in thanks for his help and to the king before returning to his seat.

Charlemagne was visibly moved, even elated. He cleared his throat several times, thanked Sebastian warmly, and turned to the guests. "See there now," he lectured them. "That's what can be done if you but have the will. There is no reason why our young men should not be able to read. Why, even I can read. It only takes deciding to spend a bit of time to learn to do it. This boy has had little opportunity to learn—he lives out on the edge of our realm, up against Saxon lands. He must spend his days attending to our defense needs in that perilous place. And yet he finds time to learn to read! I tell you, we should all be so enterprising. And what a ripping good reading it was, too! Well done, Sebastian. We'll hear more of it later. Keep up the practice, lad." Sebastian bowed his head toward the king and began to breathe again.

Between readings, minstrels sang saucy Frankish ditties and jugglers performed, balancing a chair on their chins or singing a song while keeping several balls in the air at once. Most phenomenal was a diminutive man with a bright red beard and bushy eyebrows, lightheartedly called "Edo the Unwise" by everyone. He was a merry little man, almost a dwarf, with a twinkle in his eye and an impudent demeanor. He delighted in making disrespectful, ribald, or humorous references to every person at the table—with the exception of the king.

On this occasion, Edo drew gales of laughter by describing how each person might be going to bed later that night, mimicking hilariously their imagined likely preparations for sleep or nocturnal liaison. He indicated a pretty young woman sitting near Charlemagne and depicted her as in a state of breathless anticipation, tongue hanging out and hands fluttering to her breasts. She was delighted to have been singled out and winked broadly back at the jester. A burly warrior was deduced as too awash in wine to function and another as too stuffed with supper to do anything but keel over in his bed asleep as soon as his head hit the pillow. The warriors chosen as the jestees were not especially pleased to be singled out, but under the king's eye, they managed to scoff and laugh off the roguish innuendos. No one else seemed to mind Edo's crudeness. Indeed, they encouraged him and laughed the more when he succeeded in getting under anyone's skin with his barbs.

When he came to the end of the table, he raised his eyebrows at Sebastian, threw up his hands and made a pumping motion between his legs. Everyone roared except Sebastian, who turned several colors of red, which was noticeable even in the dim light, endearing him immediately to all the women present.

Chapter 13

Eros

Count Liudegar sat across from Sebastian by the fire. He was an exuberant man by nature, if not a very careful one. It was only midafternoon and he already had a cup of honey beer sloshing in his hand as he waxed lyrical about Sebastian's show of prowess in the practice yard that morning. "Ye did well this mornin', m'boy. By thunder, ye nearly knocked the heads off Grimwold and Beotrand, and they're the best I brought with me! Let me see that arm of yours." He leaned forward and took Sebastian's right arm in his grip.

"By the rood, ye've got an arm like a blacksmith! How'd ye do that? And ye without your full growth yet. It's as big around as my daughter's thigh!" He paused and leaned forward a bit and cleared his throat loudly. "A-humpf! Ah, speaking of my daughter's thighs, have ye thought yet about takin' a wife?"

"No, my lord," Sebastian blurted in surprise. "I am only sixteen, my lord. I scarcely know any women at all."

"Hell, boy, what've ye been doing all this time? By the time I was sixteen I'd bedded every pretty girl in the village and a goodly number of the wives and widows in the county! Ye don't know what ye're missing. Don't ye ever go anywhere? Ye know, ride about the country, visit some other lords?"

"No, my lord. We have little time—the Saxons . . ."

"Blast the Saxons! Scurvy lot of mangy dogs, is all. Let Attalus handle 'em. He can do it in his sleep. Ye come and see me. My daughter'll teach ye a trick or two. And she's beautiful, all men say it, and as fiery as they come. She'll raise yer passions for certain—or if she don't, it'll mean ye're naught but a dead man walking."

"Sir, Lord Attalus is dead," Sebastian said quietly. "He died just before I came."

Sebastian spent his days at the king's court in Worms in the exercise yard engaging in mock combat with the king's retinue of warriors and other young fighting men as they arrived for the council. He spent his nights in the king's library studying and rehearsing the text of *The City of God*. He read at every midday main meal at the king's request and sometimes at the infrequent banquets at night. He consulted with the monk Laidred on pronunciation and meaning and became quite fluent as a reader. Charlemagne was delighted and began to take advantage of Sebastian. The boy's crisp enunciation and sense of timing were already better than most of the clerics who read at meals, and the king was taken with the idea that Sebastian represented a potential new generation of literate laymen.

Adding to that favorable impression, Sebastian was showing up well in the daily combat training exercises. His quickness and the skills Attalus had taught him were soon noted by the younger warriors who practiced each day in the courtyard overlooked by the king's quarters. It was no less a personage than Arno, the palace count, who informed the king that he might enjoy watching the morning workouts as the warriors matched up against each other with wooden practice swords for exercise and fun. Peering out from a crack in the drapes at his window, Charlemagne could see at once that Sebastian was an exceptional fighter—clever, fast, and dogged. He rarely attacked, patiently letting the larger men come at him. Then he would step nimbly aside and use their rush to tag them soundly with a quick riposte to the side of their helmets or the backs of their knees. Furthermore, he seemed inexhaustible as he fought one challenger after another, never asking for quarter or even a rest. Although the youth inquired daily if he might be excused to return to Fernshanz, Charlemagne had no intention of letting Sebastian go home before the campaign and perhaps not even afterward.

Although Sebastian worried constantly about his mother and the community at Fernshanz, the king's court offered plenty of distractions—and compensations. Sebastian had noticed at once how easily the women of the court mixed with the men, and there were many women, several of whom sat nightly at table near the young king. Charlemagne was very comfortable with the ladies of the court, laughing and trading whispered jests with them and encouraging them to sing with him. His vassals, too, seemed to be on as good terms with the women as they were with each other. Sebastian watched this daily undercurrent with considerable confusion. For his own part, he found it difficult to say anything to any of these women. Yet they loved to caress his sword arm and watch the bright red patches rise immediately on the pale skin of his beardless face.

Count Liudegar, true to his word, sent for his daughter Adelaide. She did indeed have the figure he had boasted of, and at only sixteen, she proved to be the boldest woman Sebastian had ever known. On the day she arrived, she sought him out just before the midday meal. "You're the one they call Sebastian, aren't you?" she demanded, as soon as she saw him. "I can tell because you have coal-black hair, and," she added with a mischievous glance up and down his body, "you're pretty." She laughed at his embarrassment and tossed her russet hair. "Where are we sitting?" she exclaimed, taking his arm and looking around at the bustling court gathering to eat.

Adelaide didn't seem to mind what anyone thought about her. She was a confident, single-minded girl, who was used to having her own way. Her stunning good looks and the nonchalant air of privilege she affected allowed her to get away with almost anything she wanted to do. She was much like her father, and unlike most young Frankish women of noble families, she didn't care a whit for social respect or the usual expectations of domestic virtue, and by the time she was sixteen, she was already an enchanting jezebel.

The next few days proved to be a complete bamboozlement for Sebastian. Adelaide came every day to eat with him and hear him read.

The whole court buzzed about the apparent match and watched with keen interest and poorly concealed glee as the daily drama unfolded. Adelaide would smile sweetly at Sebastian and raise her eyebrows coyly as he rose when the king bade him to read. It was already obvious she considered him her property. From that time, the quality of his daily readings began to deteriorate.

Toward the end of the first week, Sebastian rose at the king's request to read the famous last words of King David from Second Samuel. He had begun to color profusely even before he started to read. He stood stiffly, clutching the heavy Bible tightly. Adelaide, hands in her lap, sat directly beneath him, smiling up into his face, creating an engaging domestic tableau.

"*Haec autem sunt verba David novissima,*" Sebastian began resolutely.

Adelaide moved closer to the end of the table, smiling innocently. "*Dixit David filius ISAI . . .*" After a long pause, "*Dixit vir cui constitutum EST!*" Going faster, "*De christo Dei Iacob, egregius psaltes Israel. Dominator hominum iustus, dominator in timore Dei.* UNH!"

As he tried to concentrate, his face became even redder and he began to stumble over words, skipping whole sentences. Most of the dinner guests were unaware of his omissions and mispronunciations, but they caught on right away that something—or somebody—was causing him to shout words, stammer, and otherwise lose his steady cadence and calm voice.

The king was not unaware of Adelaide's covert subversion of the normally solemn readings. If at first he was inclined to disapprove sternly, he soon saw the hilarity of the situation, made more comical by Sebastian's extreme discomfort. He allowed the scenario to play out a bit further to see what Sebastian would do.

Sebastian stopped and started, fidgeting about. Finally he backed up until he had moved himself completely away from his customary place at the end of the table and wound up standing at least several feet out into the open room. All the while Adelaide sat sweetly at the end of the table, as if there were nothing in the world more delightful than listening to Sebastian read from the scriptures. Occasionally, she would inhale deeply and let out a wistful sigh.

The guests held their breath, wondering how long the king would tolerate such an impertinent spectacle. Some of the guests began to snicker openly; some could barely contain their laughter. Finally, an outright guffaw was heard from one of the more audacious younger men on the other side of the table.

Mercifully, halfway into the last words of King David, Charlemagne cleared his throat, which was his usual way of ending the readings. "Thank you, Sebastian. That will be enough for now," the king announced solemnly, and then quickly smothered a chortle into his hands. Thoroughly abashed, the young reader moved reluctantly back to the table and even more reluctantly slid in beside a delighted Adelaide, who grabbed his arm possessively and smiled merrily at everybody.

In subsequent days, Adelaide applied increasing heat to Sebastian's awakening libido. She seemed to be constantly lurking in the halls or near the courtyard watching him practice. Frequently she suggested a walk into the town or beyond, and Sebastian, just as often, firmly declined to oblige her, appalled at the idea of a Frankish warrior walking anywhere in public with a woman.

However, Sebastian was far from immune to Adelaide's persistent attention and titillating suggestions. She never hesitated to whisper some ribald jest in his ear or to touch his body whenever she had the chance. Such intimacy startled him at first, but when she persisted and became more and more familiar with him, he found himself stirred by her brazen behavior and looked forward rather guiltily to her advances. She was, after all, a beauty, fully developed and full of laughter and fun. Furthermore, the scent that radiated from her body was wonderful. Sebastian had never been around a woman who used perfume, and he found it nearly intoxicating.

There was no telling where Adelaide might suddenly appear—pouncing out of a corridor as he walked to practice, lurking outside the door of the king's library, even emerging out of the gloom of the stable as he was returning from a ride. Upon such occasions, Adelaide minced no words nor bothered with preliminaries. She simply backed him into a corner and began kissing his neck or face and running her hands over his body. He began to find her irresistible.

That is, until he saw Adela.

Sebastian first saw Adela during the last days of preparation for the new campaign. She accompanied her father, Count Gonduin, who was

lord of Andernach, a very rich province north of Mayence on the west bank of the Rhine. Charlemagne was very fond of Gonduin, a senior member of the king's own Arnulfing family and thus a partner in the ruling dynasty. Although he went by the title of count, the silver-haired, dignified gentleman had the vast lands and responsibilities of a duke and was one of Charlemagne's most respected generals.

Long before Gonduin arrived, messengers rode in announcing him. Count Arno alerted the king as he was listening to Sebastian read at the midday meal. Charlemagne pulled Sebastian along as he strode toward the main gate to meet the old man. Gonduin rode in with a large retinue of personal vassals, attendants, and family members. Among them was Adela, Gonduin's sixteen-year-old daughter. It was not unusual for the daughters of aristocracy who were of marriageable age to present themselves on the occasion of the assembly. More often than not, such an appearance led to a wedding.

As the party dismounted to pay homage to the king, Sebastian, standing at the king's side, came face to face with Adela. He thought he had never seen such a serenely beautiful face. Because she was wrapped in a bulky, hooded riding cloak, her face was all he could see. Sebastian gazed at it in wonder. *This is how queens must look*, he imagined. She affected a calm poise, but her eyes were alive and animated. They were violet, which was rare among the Franks, and they sparkled with delight as she took in everything. Her lips parted in wonder as she was presented to the high king.

"Welcome, Gonduin, welcome!" the king bellowed warmly as he embraced his old friend. Then his eyes fell on Adela as she was introduced by her father. "My God, Gonduin, what have you been hiding? Do you grow angels there in Andernach? Welcome, Adela! You will have a hard time, young lady, getting out of here without a husband—maybe three or four!" Amid the chorus of cheers and laughter, Adela cast her eyes down and blushed. When she raised them again, they fell on Sebastian, and she smiled engagingly. She seemed amused to catch him staring at her. It was just a brief moment and then the entourage moved on with the king toward the great hall. Sebastian was charmed. Without a word he fell in beside the lovely girl and followed the crowd.

Once inside the great hall, Adela emerged from her cloak, giving it with a smile to a servant. She wore a practical dark blue traveling dress of soft wool, so long that it covered her feet. But her arms protruded from the dress, revealing a bodice of white silk. As they sat, she removed a mantle of the same pure silk, releasing a mass of auburn hair, braided and adorned with bright purple ribbons. She and Sebastian had moved toward the tables together quite naturally, as if they already knew each other, and now the girl turned her full gaze to Sebastian. She looked at him with a slightly elfish smile and leaned toward him a bit.

"And who are you, sir, if I'm going to sit with you?" she said boldly.

With some difficulty, Sebastian found his tongue. "Why, I'm Sebastian. Uh, I'm from Fernshanz," he added hastily, as if that would explain everything about him.

"Well, Master Sebastian from Fernshanz, how is it that you come to be so close to the king?" Adela asked as they accepted cups of wine from a passing servant. "Are you part of his family?"

"Nay, kind miss, I am not," Sebastian replied apologetically. "I am not close to the king at all; I am merely his reader, sometimes, at meals. I was reading to him when you arrived."

"You can read?" Adela exclaimed, seeing the young man with new eyes.

"Yes, I can; not very well, of course," he added hastily. "I often don't understand what I'm reading, but I practice and learn whenever I can. It gets easier the more I do it."

"I'm desperate to read," the girl confided eagerly, as they found a place among the tables and benches. "Could you teach me? I mean, would you think me bold if I asked you just some simple things, such as how to recognize a word? I don't know much Latin, but I would practice. We have books at home, but the priests won't let me use them, and since my mother died, my father won't let me go to a convent to learn. There's one not too far from Fulda, a famous one founded by Boniface himself. But my father says he cannot do without me. I know it's just because he doesn't take my desire to read seriously. I'm sure I could win him over, though, if I could only show him that I really mean to learn and that I have made some progress."

In her excitement Adela leaned closer to Sebastian and grasped his arm. "Please," she entreated, giving him the full force of her striking eyes.

"We may only have a few days before the campaign begins," Sebastian protested, drawing back a bit in surprise. Adela quickly withdrew her hand and looked down in embarrassment. Seeing her disappointment,

Sebastian added apologetically, "But I could teach you the alphabet at least, and how to sound the letters. Then you could start to understand the words."

"When?" she pressed him. "When can we start, and where am I to come?"

Sebastian agreed to meet her an hour after the meal in the king's library, and he explained to her how to get there. "We won't have much time," he continued. "The king comes daily to chapel close by there, and priests will be coming in and out of the library beforehand. I shall have to get permission."

"Permission! Why?" the girl groaned. "If you have to ask a priest, you will never get permission—I have tried it. They don't want a girl to read. They don't want a girl anywhere near their schools or their books. Pah! We might as well forget it," Adela said, sourly.

"It's all right," he hastened to assure the girl. "I will speak to Laidred. He's the priest in charge of the library and he's my friend. He has been helping me learn. I'm sure he will allow you to go in. If necessary, I'll tell him your father is Count Gonduin, a great general and a friend of the king. He will let us study together, I'm sure of it."

Sebastian was sorry he had mentioned the need to get permission, but he felt he could convince Laidred to bend the rules. He was also somewhat shocked to realize how difficult it was for a woman to learn to read, remembering how his mother had always yearned to do so. More than anything, he was acutely aware that he would regret not having the opportunity to spend further time looking into Adela's incredible eyes.

As it turned out, Laidred was not at all sure about having a woman in his library. For one thing, he knew very few women, and the ones he did know made him uncomfortable, especially the pretty ones. He also did not know how the king or the archchaplain—or any of the other clergymen who surrounded the king and his court—would feel about such a pretty young girl handling the books that only they handled. It might even be a temptation for some of them to know she had touched the same pages and covers that they did.

Sebastian had to exert all his powers of persuasion and promise Laidred to copy several pages of a Bible into the new miniscule Latin text before the priest relented. He gave Adela an embarrassingly fleeting tour of the library and shooed them out with a parchment copy of the alphabet and a clay tablet. Laidred did not want to be the first to allow a woman to invade the sacred spaces of ecclesiastical power.

They found a semi-private place inside the chapel on a row of benches reserved for the infirm. The light was bad and the time until Vespers short, but Adela grasped at once how to form the letters and she copied them easily. Still, they managed to practice copying only half of the letters before the chapel began to buzz with priests preparing for the service.

"Hide the tablet and scroll in your cloak," Sebastian whispered. "The priests don't need to know what we're doing. Just kneel and pretend we're waiting for the service to begin. Practice tonight if you can, and I will meet you here in the morning during the breakfast meal. No one will be here then." The girl's radiant smile of gratitude was pay enough for any effort he might have to make on the morrow.

As Adela retreated from the chapel, Sebastian felt a bit like a conspirator, but he found himself in complete sympathy with her desire to succeed. More compellingly, he could still feel the sensation of her fingers under his as he guided her hands to trace the letters, and the brush of her shoulder against his as she leaned forward to see.

On the way back from the chapel to the warriors' barracks where most of the younger men stayed, Sebastian was ambushed by Adelaide.

"Where have you been, you slippery eel?" she exclaimed breathlessly. "I've been searching all over for you—and then I hear you've been sitting with Lord Gonduin's daughter in the king's hall! I won't have it. Doesn't she know—don't they all know—that you belong to me?" She grabbed him by the shoulders and tried to push him back into the lengthening shadows of a gap between two buildings. Sebastian resisted, aghast that she would presume so much and not at all in the mood for this brash, aggressive girl after the subtle, captivating allure of Adela.

"Wait—what are you doing?" he protested, as Adelaide wrapped herself around him and literally pushed him into the narrow alleyway. "We mustn't do this! I can't," Sebastian whispered in confusion, even as Adelaide was overwhelming him with her embrace and the delicious smell of her body. Later he would wonder what might have happened if Varnar, captain of the king's guard, had not been passing by at this crucial moment. Attracted by the scuffling sounds and muffled voices, Varnar turned back and peered into the alleyway. "Here now," he challenged in a commanding tone, "what the devil's going on? Come out of there at once, whoever you are!"

Adelaide swore like a man but broke off promptly and popped out of the alleyway, straightening her skirt and smiling broadly at Varnar. Sebastian reluctantly skulked out behind her, mortified. Varnar eyed them both with surprise but recovered himself quickly.

"Excuse me, young master. I heard noises. And it was my duty to investigate—king's quarters, y'know. Sorry to disturb you." He promptly dipped his head, touched his hand to his forehead, and backed away. Adelaide briefly watched him go and then turned to Sebastian with raised eyebrows.

"No!" Sebastian exclaimed in alarm. "No, no—I have to go," he stammered, backing out of the alleyway. "I'm . . . I am to read again soon. I have to prepare. I have an appointment. I must go. I can't marry you!" he finally blurted out. Adelaide followed him with her hands on her hips.

"Marry me!" she trumpeted, laughing. "Who said anything about marrying? All I want is a bit of fun. After all, I don't get to go to assemblies every day. Besides, I will have to marry whatever man my father chooses for me, and I seriously doubt he would pick you. You must be the poorest warrior in all the realm. You're not a count; you're not even lord of the place you come from. I heard that Fernshanz really belongs to Count Konrad."

Sebastian's ears burned in embarrassment, and he hit back. "Pray tell then, Lady Know-All, why do you have such interest in me if I count for so little?"

"I told you before—you're pretty to look at, silly boy. All the girls say so. I especially like watching you on the training field; it's exciting. The older men say you're the best of all the young fighters this year. Besides that, they say you have the king's ear—and his favor as well. I've heard the story about the Saxon black statue you captured. Oh yes! You're a bit of a prize. That's why I want you." She paused a moment to let her bold words sink in. "So do you want me or not? You're not likely to find anybody else like me—and I guarantee you, you won't forget the experience."

Sebastian's eyes widened. He took a deep breath and fell silent for a moment, mouth open, thinking. Finally, he spoke in a wavering voice, staring at his feet, "Adelaide, it's true; you're the most exciting woman I've ever seen and I am sorely tempted every time I'm with you, but I will soon be going to my first battle. I cannot go with the stain of sin upon me."

"Sin! What sin?" she blurted out. "I'm not married; you're not married. What sin would we be committing? All I want is to find out if you're as good as you look—just a little pleasure between you and me. God knows life will be dull and hard enough for us later. We might as well enjoy our youth and whatever life offers us now."

Sebastian was shocked to realize that he was panting with desire for this luscious young woman who had so blithely forced herself upon him. All he had to do was give in and he could have his first sweet taste of sexual pleasure—apparently completely without consequence. Only the recent memory of Adela—the long looks they had shared, the deep sense of mutual understanding, and the powerful notion he felt that Adela would somehow prove to be his soul mate—stopped him from giving in to his lust. He backed away with a struggle and mumbled stubbornly once again, "I can't go into battle with sin on my soul."

Adelaide erupted in exasperation, "What are you, a priest or a warrior? If you are a Frankish warrior, I've never seen one like you." She paused and took in his downcast face. "Well, priest, I can see I must let you be this time. But I'll tell you this: You will wake up in the morning—and maybe for the next thousand mornings—and wish you'd had the sense to take Adelaide when she came to you, because you will never know a woman like me. I could give you such pleasure you would think you were an angel in heaven." She sighed, shook her head, and caressed his face a last time. "Well, think about it. I may not be done with you. Meanwhile, I don't intend to waste the rest of my time at this assembly. Good-bye, stupid boy. Go back to your snotty little princess. God, what a cold breakfast that one is! What on earth do you see in her? She barely breathes."

"I'm teaching her to read," Sebastian muttered. He was beginning to feel he really might be sorry if he let this vibrant, passionate girl walk away.

"What? So *that* explains it? Why would you want to do that? What good is it if a girl can read? What a bore! Well, go to it, priest. I wish you well, I truly do, but there's precious little joy in it, if you ask me. It sounds about as thrilling as going to Mass every day. Farewell, Father Sebastian. Come and see me if you ever wake up."

Adelaide stormed off, head up, long hair flouncing. Standing stock-still for several minutes after she left, Sebastian could still smell her perfume.

If Sebastian had closed a door on one kind of love, he had opened another. Adela became the focus of his existence for the next two weeks. He saw her every day for several hours as they labored over the Latin phrases in a Bible he had begged use of from Laidred. They started with the Psalms. After they had read a psalm several times over, he had her write it down on her clay tablet. In the beginning it was slow work, but each day Adela proved more and more able to read and then write the psalms they studied.

Sebastian became totally absorbed in the lovely, thoughtful girl who had such a burning desire to read, to talk endlessly about serious and meaningful things, and to enlarge her world. He recognized himself in her drive and inquisitiveness, and he delighted at how fast she learned.

They began each day with a new psalm and worked at it assiduously. "*Dominus pascit me,*" he would say, as with Psalm 23, "*nihil, mihi deerit. In pascuis herbarum adclinavit me . . .*" She would repeat the Latin sentence haltingly. Then he would interpret the psalm for her, and she would read it again. "The Lord is my shepherd. There is nothing I shall want. In green pastures he leads me . . ." Finally, she would write it down, word by word in tiny letters, until she had filled her tablet. Then they would erase it and start again. They spoke in low voices and only now and then looked up at one another. They became lost in their work together, oblivious to all else, although many eyes, as it turned out, were watching them throughout these sessions.

Inevitably, they would digress from the work to discuss what they were reading. The discussion diverged into many subjects.

"Sebastian, teach me everything," she burst out one day. "I want to know everything! And you must know that I am so glad to have found you and so grateful that you are willing to teach me."

"Adela, I don't know everything. I hardly know anything. I can read and write a little in Latin, and Father Louis taught me some stories of the saints. But I know very little about the rest of the world. I've only been to Adalgray and Fernshanz—and here. But I want to know, too" he hastened to add. "I want to know as much as you do. My father told me tales of Spain and Aquitania, and I can't wait to see those places. They are so different. People don't even look the same. Most of them are dark and wear strange clothes.

"And Italy, too!" he continued, warming to the subject of far places. "My mother was there once—with my other father—the one who wasn't really my father. I told you about him before. They went to Pavia with King Pippin. They said it was full of vineyards and fruit everywhere, and the people couldn't even speak the Frankish tongue. They had to talk in Latin to our people."

"I want to go there, Sebastian! I want to see those places. Wouldn't it be wonderful if we could go together?" Realizing she might have gone too far, Adela abruptly changed the subject. "But I want to know more about life—and the afterlife. What is that supposed to be? No one really seems to know. And what about good and evil? What was God thinking when he created such creatures as the Saxons? And what about our own people—why isn't everyone nice? Sometimes I think we act no differently than the Saxons."

"And why is it they tell you that what you think is absolutely wrong when you feel in your heart you are absolutely right?" Sebastian added emphatically. "It's like there are rules that must not be questioned."

"I know," she nodded, "it's far worse for us women; my father thinks I'm incapable of real thought. He only wants me to be concerned with running his household. God forbid that I should want to talk about something that matters to men."

"You have no idea," she continued heatedly, "how dull life can get if all one ever talks about is sewing, food, children, and what men need. I have questions. I have ideas. Why is it so hard for most men to let me share them? They treat me like a child or a stable animal, and they look at me like that, too. You're so different. You actually listen to me!"

Sebastian decided that Adela was indeed no cold fish, as Adelaide had described her. Although she did not put herself on display or reveal her feelings readily, Adela was passionate about many things. Outwardly, she seemed like a very private person who didn't care for most people to know what she was thinking. For the most part, the men she met were indifferent to what she thought anyway, so she rarely looked at anyone until she had been formally introduced. She then knew in an instant whether she would want to share her thoughts with that person. Most of the young men at the assembly did not pass her scrutiny, and she did not favor them with as much as a glance afterward.

Nevertheless, Adela's beauty and poise were such that all men turned their eyes to her when she entered a room. She hardly noticed. With Sebastian, on the other hand, she became completely open and eagerly shared not only her thoughts and questions but who she was. From her frequent laughter and increasingly uninhibited conversation with him, he was pleased to know he had become someone she trusted.

As the time for the general assembly drew near, more and more of Charlemagne's vassals began appearing at the court. Although not all supped with the king or had access to the king's quarters, his table in the evening was filled with newly arrived counts, bishops, and assorted clerical assistants. Many of the counts and highly esteemed vassals brought their wives and grown children, and among them was a good number of fair young women. They all knew that the king had yet to take a woman formally as queen, and they all hoped the king might look their way.

It was rumored that Charlemagne had sired a son with a childhood friend named Himiltrude. But she was not of an important family, and there was some kind of secret having to do with the child not being quite right. Whatever the cause, Himiltrude had not been seen for more than a year, and nobody seemed to have ever seen the child.

The king had come closer to a union with Desiderata, a Lombard princess, whom he married reluctantly at the urgent pleading of his mother Bertrada. She had arranged the match in a complicated political scheme to ward off a war between Charlemagne and his younger brother and co-king, Karloman. The idea was to forge an alliance between

Charlemagne and Desidarius, king of the Lombards in north Italy, as a means of balancing the power of the two sibling kings.

It worked for a while, with an uneasy truce being observed by both sides, and Charlemagne found himself with a Lombard wife for about six months. Many said he never liked her, for she was cold and a bit prickly, and she looked upon the rough nature of his court and a chilly life north of the Alps with disdain. Besides that, many said she was "not pretty enough for the king."

In the previous December, not long after Widukind had taunted Charlemagne about the friction with his brother, Karloman had sickened and died. No one seemed to know why; he was only twenty-one. On hearing the news, Charlemagne had immediately raced to western Francia with some troops and pressured Karloman's erstwhile supporters into swearing allegiance to him. Now sole ruler of the Frankish nation, he no longer needed the uncomfortable alliance with King Desidarius. He therefore lost no time in packing off his homely, unsought, and unwanted Lombard bride back to her father. The rumor mongers insisted that the king, though he dallied with many of the women at court, was truly in love with Hildegard, the sublimely beautiful daughter of the Duke of Alemannia, whom he had met only once. On that occasion, she had appeared well spoken, poised, and completely at her ease with the high king, and the king was smitten. Unfortunately, Hildegard, a blooming, healthy girl who appeared to be exceptionally mature for her years, was only thirteen.

When it became obvious that the king would soon put the army on the march, Adela suggested a ride out into the countryside. She was accustomed to riding daily and was an excellent horsewoman. Once they cleared the town, the two galloped along the river road and then turned off to explore some old Roman ruins at the top of a hill. Adela had brought a light meal of bread and fruit, and they shared a small flask of wine as they sat on a fallen stone and gazed out over the river as it sparkled in the fading sunlight.

"Adela," Sebastian began haltingly, not looking at the girl, "the army will leave soon, and I don't know if I will ever see you again. But I must tell you how . . . how . . ."

"How what, Sebastian? What are you trying to say?"

"How important you've become to me," he concluded lamely.

"Important?" she chided. "Am I merely a connection you've made, some acquaintance who will help you rise later in life?"

Sebastian colored slightly at her teasing and began again. "What I mean to say is I shall be sorry if I do not see you again. Very sorry."

"Why wouldn't you see me again, silly boy? Of course you shall—perhaps as soon as the summer campaign is over. I'll ask my father to invite you to Andernach. We'll resume our lessons," she added playfully.

"But I'm nobody. I have no great property, only Fernshanz, where there's not much land or wealth and constant danger from the Saxons. I cannot simply go away when I like."

"Then you must do a good job fighting them this time so they won't be a threat anymore. Listen," Adela said earnestly, dropping her playful tone, "we'll find a way. I'm sure of it. I haven't met you for nothing. I couldn't feel . . . I wouldn't care . . ." she stumbled and fell silent, suddenly embarrassed by what she almost said.

Emboldened, Sebastian took her hand. "Wait, I feel the same thing. I've thought of little else since I first saw you. I don't sleep well. You fill my head no matter where I go or what I do, and when I think how unimportant I am, how little and narrow my life is, I despair of ever seeing you again. Adela, you are . . . I . . ."

As he stumbled over his words, Adela reached out, took his head between her hands, and kissed him gently on the mouth. "Oh, Sebastian, don't you know I love you? It doesn't matter what you've done or what place you have—I loved you from the beginning. Not only for what you already were but even more for what I knew you could become. You're not like the other men; all the rest of them are so cocky and aggressive. These last few weeks . . . every day I can't wait to see you. I've felt that I might burst unless I knew you felt the same, and now you've told me. It's all I hoped for."

Stunned with surprise and delight, Sebastian sprang up, took her hands in his, and pulled her to him in a long embrace. Then he began to kiss her—her neck, her eyes, the tears on her cheeks, and finally, her soft mouth. It was a gentle, innocent kiss at first, but as both yielded one to the other, it became more passionate and urgent.

Adela pushed away from Sebastian, gasping. "Wait—wait." She leaned back and held his head in her hands. "You know we can't go further with this now, but there will be a time, my heart. For now, it's enough to know what we feel. Is it not so?"

No longer able to contain his emotions, Sebastian stood and gathered her once more into his arms. "It is so, Adela, but I can scarce believe it. I feel that my entire life has changed . . . I feel that I know what it's supposed to be about now—and it's you, Adela. You're what I need. I've been waiting for you."

He felt her mouth against his ear as she whispered again that she loved him. Suddenly, filled with the perfection of the moment, he reached down and swung her up into his arms. Looking out across the river into the spellbinding twilight, he spoke softly, as much to infinity as to Adela, "Thank you. If I never live another day, this will have been enough.

For weeks the king had been chafing to get the campaign underway. Most of the key leaders of the army had arrived, including counts and other mounted warriors from as far away as Aquitaine. Outside the town after dark, the hills were lit up with the campfires of the infantry contingents. Charlemagne waited now for the siege engineers, upon whom the ultimate success of storming the Eresburg depended. Equally important were the commissary officers who were charged with gathering enough food for horses and men in a campaign that might last all summer. It was this latter business that was causing the delay, for warmer weather came slowly this year, and grass and hay were in short supply.

Charlemagne languished impatiently, filling his days with war councils, church affairs, and endless consultations with counts and clerics and even ordinary Frankish soldiers in the outlying camps. He visited them frequently, walking among the cooking fires, inspecting equipment, and talking earnestly to the men in small groups. They knew their king and he knew them.

Charlemagne spent most of his time, however, with the counts and mounted elite who were the heart of his army—the vaunted corps of heavy cavalry. These were the skilled and heavily armored fighters who shattered enemy lines on an open battlefield or went over the walls in a siege. They were his vassals but most of them were also part of the powerful landed provincial aristocracy, who were virtually independent within their own counties. The king spent time with almost every one of them individually, and asked scores of questions about their land, their work, and their problems. Before the campaign ever began, he knew exactly who he could count on and for what tasks.

Konrad of Adalgray was one of the last of the counts to arrive at the palace. He appeared with an entourage of young warriors in the middle of the afternoon, brushing aside the protests of Count Arno and barging unescorted into the great hall of the king's quarters. The room was empty at the time, but Charlemagne soon appeared with several advisors, as it was his custom to greet every count and any important member of the army.

"Well, Konrad," the king began, "I'm happy to see you've come on time for a change."

"Wouldn't miss it, my lord king." Konrad said cheekily. "Not when there's a chance to bash Saxons and collect their treasure. There is treasure this time, is there not, sire? At least that's what my bratty cousin is supposed to have said. Don't know why he thinks that ugly piece of Saxon iron he fished up out of the mud means treasure. He's full of humbug, that boy. The Saxons are just a bunch of poor dumb beasts. But at least they'll have horses and women!"

"I should box your ears, Konrad, you bloody fool. Let me remind you that it was I who made the connection between the black statue and that rumored Irminsul gold. We may find it yet. And then I'll make you eat your words. But go on now, get yourself fed and housed. And stay sober!" In the end, not wanting to waste any more time preaching to a lost cause, he welcomed the young count again, patted him on the back, and passed him off to an agitated Count Arno to be fed and housed.

Chapter 14

Disaster

"Come on, Drogo!" urged Bardulf. "It's just a bit further. Yer such a clubfooted slinker. Wait till ye taste this wine. It's real wine, not the swill made from berries or honey. It come all the way from Andernach across the great river, where they make barrels of it every day."

Bardulf had stolen the wine right from under the nose of Baumgard's vicious guard dog, Hercules, a huge mastiff who guarded the steward's storeroom. It had been easy. All Bardulf had to do was wait until Baumgard left the storeroom and went down into the village on some errand. Bardulf, lounging in the shadow of the nearby pig sty, had sidled up to the storeroom door, cracked it a bit, and threw in a chunk of venison, cut from the leg of a red deer brought in by the hunters just that morning. The dog gobbled it up and sniffed the door for more. Bardulf threw another piece farther back into the storeroom and slipped inside. He kept feeding the dog as he moved toward the three big wine casks in the back of the room, murmuring to the dog all the while in a calming, sing-song voice.

"Oh, 'Ercules," Bardulf crooned soothingly, "ye great pile of *sheise*, only keep eatin' this here deer meat and just let me fill this tiny wineskin with a wee small bit of this wonderful wine that Baumgard won't let nobody drink, not even the lords. I believe he must be savin' it for hisself, don't ye know. So ye won't mind if I just borrow a bit of it to sooth me achin' bones, now would ye?"

Bardulf had managed to turn on the tap and fill a large wineskin almost to the top when the dog, feeling full, emitted a low growl. The bold thief kept crooning as he edged to the door and just managed to slip through it as Hercules decided to object violently to his presence in the storeroom.

Once outside, Bardulf wrapped his cloak around the wineskin and sauntered nonchalantly across the drawbridge down into the village to Drogo's hut. Late in the afternoon, the two youths walked out of the front gate into the forest, as if going to gather wood for the night. They made their way several hundred meters into the darkening woods to a small stream of water running through a deep ravine. There, in a hollow carved into the bank by the stream at flood, they built a tiny fire and proceeded to drink the magic contents of the wine flask.

Drogo had dragged his feet and protested the whole way, sure that Baumgard would somehow know his precious wine casks had been violated and that soon there would be a hue and cry for them and they would be doomed.

"Drogo, ye blasted milksop," Bardulf railed at him, poking him with his walking staff "I'm tellin' ye, nobody saw me. I was so slippery not even 'ercules got a good look. Why, I was in and out of there before he could fart, and I got here the best kind of sweet nectar ye ever tasted in yer life. And once ye've had a bit of it, ye'll feel exac'ly like ye can fly, I'm tellin' ye true."

According to plan, the boys got so drunk they went from ridiculous hilarity to glassy-eyed stares. Giggling conspiratorially, they fantasized about the village girls and traded crude jokes.

"Drogo, me ol' lad, us Franks is the smartest people on earth, don' ye know. An' ol' King Karl, he owns half the worl', by God! But it's peasants like us, hardworkin', long-sufferin' bloody yeomen who are the smartest. Have ye heard the famous tale about Odo, one of our cleverest brothers?"

"I have, Bardulf, but tell it again. I loves to hear it."

"Well, Odo were so smart the king hisself asked him to come to court and give out some of his famous wisdom. They set ol' Odo down at table with the king, and brought such food as you never seen in yer life, one steamin', delicious thing after t'other. But poor Odo didn't know how to eat at table with a king. Ye see, there was this rule that when they sets a dish before ye, ye must eat from the top of the meat and not turn it over or cut from the side or such. So they brought ol' Odo a lovely fish to eat, but he proceeds to turn it over with his knife, seekin' the tenderest part. Well, ye would've thought he murdered somebody. All the lords jumped up and complained to the king that Odo had broke the sacred rule of eatin'. They said, accordin' to the custom, Odo must die. And so the king asked, 'Have ye any last wish, Odo? I swear I'll grant ye anything excep' yer life.'

"Odo thought a minute and says, 'Well, King, I don' mind dyin' for ye, but this is me last wish—that whoever saw me turn the fish over should have his eyes put out.'

"Well, the king swears by God that he never saw Odo do the deed. And then ever' lord and lady at the table swore by Christ an' the holy martyrs that they ain't seen nothin' neither. And so our good ol' Odo winds up eatin' the fish and a dozen other savory meats an' such, and then he walks out the door of the castle whistlin', with the king's blessin' and a big jug of this here lovely wine we're drinkin' right now. An' what do ye think of that, Drogo?"

"I think he were smart indeed, Bardulf, almost as smart as ye!"

"Well, I am smart, Drogo. And yer smart, too, by sweet Jesus. There's no reason why a couple of smart boys like us couldn't have whatever we wants—good food and wine—an' women! By all the saints and martyrs, we should have all the women we wants—like Brigitta in the village there!

"Have ye noticed how her teats get bigger ever' single day? I swear she looks jus' like she might fall over from the weight of 'em. I'd like to put me face right between 'em and go brrrrr!"

"He-he-he," tittered Drogo, unable even in their present uninhibited state to say many words about a woman. But he listened in open-mouthed wonder as Bardulf compared in detail the charms of every maiden in Fernshanz.

At last, wrapped in their cloaks, they fell dead asleep before the moon was up. Mercifully, as it turned out, their little fire went out completely.

Sometime in the pre-dawn darkness, Bardulf awoke feeling cold. He reached for a stick to stir up the fire, but it was dead. He was just about to wrap his cloak tighter about himself and roll his back up against Drogo's broad rear when he heard a low but chilling noise. It was the sound of a Saxon voice.

"I smell smoke, Yura. I'm sure of it," hissed the voice.

"Keep moving, fool. What's out here in the middle of the forest?" said a second voice. "The village is still well ahead of us. We'll lose our place in the line if we don't keep up." The pair moved away from the edge of the ravine toward the fortress.

Bardulf was wide awake by now, in spite of the rush of pain in his head from too much strong wine. He sucked in his breath and listened in terror to the footfalls and muffled voices as line after Saxon line passed above them.

"Drogo," he whispered when the Saxons had passed and the forest was quiet again. He put his hand over his friend's mouth and whispered in his ear. "Don' make a sound! Saxons! Scores of 'em." He had to press hard on Drogo's mouth and cover his body with his own to keep him from lunging up with a shout. "S'all right, Drogo," he whispered, "but we mus' get out of 'ere—now. Jus' grab on to me belt. We got to go deep into the woods and we'll be safe."

They had not gone far when the dawn broke faintly. Then they heard the cries of alarm and the screams of attackers and victims. Drogo began to weep and cry, "We mus' go back, we mus' go back."

"Right, Drogo. Go back and get a Saxon spear up yer arse for the trouble. Just keep movin'," was Bardulf's grim reply.

The wolfmen held back in the forest just long enough to avoid being detected by the sentinel dogs. When they moved forward near dawn with ladders, they broke from the woods and ran the last hundred yards, hitting the walls before the watch on duty had enough time to sound the alarm. They were over the walls just as the townspeople were pouring out of their huts toward the citadel. The first wave of Saxons overcame the sentinels on the walls and opened the gates. Saxon cavalry waiting in the woods then poured through, cutting down the townsfolk as they fled. The drawbridge to the citadel was never pulled up and the Saxon riders reached the citadel keep before most of the villagers. Ermengard and a score or so of Fernshanz sergeants and soldiers made it into the keep and barred the door. Father Louis and his wife and children were already close by and came in just before the door was closed, the Saxons hot behind them.

Those in the keep watched and listened as a massacre occurred in the village and citadel yard. The wolfmen spared no one, cutting down women and children along with the men. They were crazed by blood lust, howling and braying like animals as they slaughtered the inhabitants of the fortress. Some Fernshanz soldiers gave a good accounting of themselves, but in the end it was hopeless. The enemy numbered nearly two hundred men.

As dawn broke, the Saxons set the keep on fire, piling wood from the other buildings of the citadel and from huts in the village around it. Flames licked up over half the height of the building. Finally, when it seemed the keep would collapse entirely, the door opened and Ermengard stepped out. She had one moment of dignity as she moved straight out toward the waiting enemy before a Saxon rushed up and swung his sword with full force against her neck. Two Fernshanz soldiers used the spectacle of her death as cover to race from the keep toward the walls. One was cut down immediately, but the other, Sebastian's young comrade Liudolf, made it to the wall and leaped down from it, disappearing into the thick woods.

Next out of the burning keep came Father Louis and his wife Bertha, followed by the children, crying and clinging to their parents' clothing. Father Louis held up before him a large bronze processional cross; his wife held on to his massive arm and kept her face to the ground. The spectacle of the huge priest holding high the Christian cross and shouting Latin prayers at the top of his voice nonplussed the attacking Saxons for a moment. Some even urged that the priest must be allowed to pass unharmed. Others, however, gorged with excitement and blood lust, simply regarded the priest and his family as new targets. Arrows flew into the bodies of Father Louis and Bertha. She went down at once, but Father Louis continued to stand and shout his prayers into the faces of the Saxons, arrows sticking out of every part of his body as if he were a great tree sprouting branches. Finally, several Saxons ran at him and skewered the priest with spears. He dropped the cross and fell across the body of his wife, as the Saxons hacked the children clinging to his corpse to pieces.

Few survived the carnage. The wolfmen were swept up beyond all reason into the madness of the hour. No slaves were taken, no women were raped, and no one was spared who could be killed. Some Fernshanz soldiers fought their way over the walls and into the forest. Of the villagers who were there at the time of the attack, only Baumgard survived by covering himself with mud and filth in the muck of the pigsty near the keep. Since pigs usually fed themselves by roaming free in the forest, only a farrowing sow was in the pen. Lying flat on his back in the mud and stink, he nevertheless managed to witness through the timbers of the crude structure the death of Ermengard and the murder of the villagers. He lay in the cold muck even as the Saxons let out the sow and sliced her up to be eaten, and he continued to lie there for hours as long as the Saxons rampaged. Only in the middle of the night, after the last Saxon had departed bearing such loot as could be found, did he draw himself slowly from the filth and crawl toward the still burning buildings to warm his shaking limbs.

It was Liudolf who brought the news of the disaster at Fernshanz. He had walked steadily, without sleep, even running much of the way to the Rhine. There he luckily hailed a small troop of the king's messengers traveling from Frisia to the king's court. When he first saw Sebastian, he was unable to meet his eyes. Instead he had knelt before him, head bent, and gave his mournful report in tortured whispers to the floor.

One by one Liudolf recited the names of the casualties he was sure of: Ermengard, his own father—Liudolf the Elder, Olderic, and most of the other sergeants. He did not see what happened to Father Louis and his family when he bolted from the flaming blockhouse, though he feared the worst for them. And he could not account for Heimdal, Baumgard, or any of the household staff.

Stunned, Sebastian collapsed onto a bench in the reception hall of the palace. "It's my fault; I should never have left. This wouldn't have happened," he moaned, head in his hands. Suddenly he leaped up. "I must go back at once," he shouted. "Quickly, Liudolf, find Archambald and Bernard, get the horses. We must go back!"

Grasping Sebastian by the shoulders, Liudolf forced him back down upon the bench. "Listen to me, Sebastian, there may be a few other survivors, but I know your mother is dead and probably most of the villagers. They burned the fortress. I could see it even from the deep woods. There is nothing you could have done if you had been there. And there's nothing you can do about it now."

The word soon spread throughout the palace, and Adela sought Sebastian out at once to console him. She took him to the chapel and held him in her arms while he wept for his mother and his friends. Finally, the king summoned him. Adela kissed him lightly as he prepared to leave.

"Sebastian, it will pass. God will take away this pain. Go now, with all my love. But don't forget a thing. Don't forget what we said to each other by the river. These last few days have been full of wonder—a blessing for us both, I think. Remember them whenever things get bad, and know that I hold you most dear, more than anyone or anything in the world. When this campaign is over, seek me out. No matter what occurs, seek me out."

Chapter 15

What a Warrior Does

The Eresburg Fortress, Saxony, Summer 772

Sebastian sat his horse nervously as the sounds of the battle rose and fell. He was with Count Edelrath's cavalry and it was in reserve. They had not even been allowed to watch the attack. The Saxons could not be permitted to know how many troops stood against them or where any cavalry forces might be located. Only the count and a few companions had gone forward to the edge of the woods to follow the battle and be ready to respond when necessary.

Charlemagne had called Sebastian to him as soon as he had heard the news of the disaster at Fernshanz. He spent only a few moments sympathizing and then wisely commanded the youth to stay constantly with Count Edelrath from that moment on and act as one of his personal aides to prepare for the attack on the Eresburg. Forcing himself to suspend his need to mourn over his loss, Sebastian was grateful for the distraction of being immersed in the details of planning for the march and forthcoming battle.

As one of Count Edelrath's aides, Sebastian was able to be present when Charlemagne announced his battle plans. The high king's preparations had been as demanding as they were simple.

"Comrades," he had begun, addressing his senior captains almost affectionately, "we've campaigned together long enough for you to know my battle strategy; you know I think the best way to win any fight is to have a great advantage in numbers and strike the enemy with overwhelming force. Thanks to you, we have that here and now. It doesn't hurt to achieve a bit of tactical surprise as well. I'll wager old Widukind did not count on us showing up as soon as we did and with so many troops. So far, all he's seen are small groups of scouts and messengers. But he'll know soon enough what's coming." The king walked familiarly among his war chiefs, looking them directly in the eye and talking in a calm, personal tone.

"When the horns blow, comrades, I want the woods on all sides of the fort to explode all at once. I want to see columns of our troops carrying ladders at a dead run while the archers pour a steady rain of arrows onto those walls. I better not see a single Saxon bowman's face pop up over the battlements until we get the ladders in place. At the same time, I want the wheeled battering rams raced up to the gates—quick as you can—at both the front and rear of the fortress at the same time. Protect the driving teams as much as possible with the portable walls, but tell the men I want those gates pounded until they throb. I want to hear it."

"Gonduin," the king had continued, his voice rising with excitement, "make sure another corps of bowmen sends volleys of fire arrows into the buildings inside the walls. I want as much smoke and confusion as we can possibly make. When I give the signal to attack, keep those horns blasting out from all sides. Let's scare the hell out of 'em. Edelrath, you keep the cavalry ready to ride at a moment's notice. I'm sure the Saxons'll try to break out the moment we breach the walls. And you can be sure that bastard Widukind will be with them. All right then, let's do it, let's truly put the fear of our God in 'em."

Up to this point, the Saxons had greeted every sighting of Frankish soldiers and scouts with jeers of derision. But in the face of the tremendous wave of violence that spewed forth the moment the horns sounded, Widukind's troops fell silent and curled up under their shields to avoid a steady shower of arrows. As the Franks quickly threw ladders against the walls on all four sides of the fortress and began to climb, the Saxons seemed almost paralyzed. Only a few pairs of eyes showed over the top of the parapet to note the progress of Charlemagne's men.

By the time they realized the Franks were already climbing up, it was almost too late to rally their mates.

But rally the Saxons did, recklessly demonstrating their vaunted ferocity. They held on tenaciously to their advantage at the top of the parapets, spearing the Franks as they climbed or standing fearlessly atop the battlements to get more force behind the strokes of their broad swords. If they knew fear at the moment the attack unfolded, they quickly mastered it in the heat of the fierce battle for the walls.

The simultaneous attacks severely strained the Saxon replacement plan, and as the defenders fell, one after the other, they could not be replaced as rapidly as necessary. For every Saxon who fell without an instant replacement, a Frank stood on the walls in his place and forced the Saxons to defend themselves in two directions. It took less than an hour of savage combat to capture the walls and force the fight down into the interior buildings below. Knots of Saxons stood together on the walls, fending off the Franks as best they could, while others leaped down and made for whatever buildings offered hope of protection.

No news of the battle came to Sebastian and the cavalry as they waited in a clearing behind a wall of woods. Sebastian kept taking long, deep breaths, fingering his lance and sword and checking every piece of equipment for the hundredth time. He sorely missed Archambald, with whom he had shared so much excitement and change during the past two months. Although the sergeants of the training field liked the carefree lad and laughed at his dizzy, never-ending comments, in the end they declared him not quite ready for "real war," and he had been left behind to help guard the supply base.

Finally, a messenger pounded into view and signaled for the cavalry to prepare to ride. The entire troop was on the road and ready when Count Edelrath himself galloped up and shouted, "The Saxon horses are breaking out. Quickly now—at the gallop!" He wheeled his mount and sped back toward the fortress with the cavalry crashing along behind him.

Early in the battle it had become clear to the Saxons that they could not hold the fort, and Widukind had apparently given orders for every man to fight his own way out. He and a few dozen men had reached the stables, found their mounts, and charged back to the front gate, fighting off Frankish foot soldiers dropping down from the parapets as they raced for the gate. The gate was thrown open, much to the surprise of the Franks on the other side who were still trying to batter it down. They were swept aside as the Saxon cavalry poured through the gate and made for a side trail through the woods away from the main Frankish troop concentration. The last of Widukind's band disappeared down the trail just as Edelrath's cavalry came into view. Immediately they were in pursuit.

Traveling along the narrow forest tracks was slow going at any time, and especially for a large body of horsemen. Although the Saxons knew the way, they often found themselves stymied by unexpected barriers of fallen trees and brush, and it was not long before they could hear the Frankish cavalry closing in. At a small clearing Widukind gave the order to turn and fight. A shower of Saxon arrows met the Franks as they burst into the clearing.

When Sebastian, who was at the end of the column, was finally able to force his horse into the little meadow, a furious melee was already under way. The bodies of horses and men littered the open area and made it impossible to fight on horseback. Sebastian dismounted and rushed into the clearing with his spear held high, just as a slightly built Saxon emerged from a knot of men fighting in the center of the field and made a run for the brush. Sebastian moved at once to cut him off. The man hesitated for a second and then rushed toward the lad. Sebastian launched his spear at the same moment. The Saxon caught the spear easily on his shield and bore down on Sebastian with his sword drawn. Sebastian barely had time to draw his own sword before the man was upon him.

The Saxon tried to bowl Sebastian over with his shield, and when the youth stepped lightly aside, the man whirled around and swung his sword down with all his might. Sebastian smoothly parried the blow, driving his opponent's sword out and away, following with a quick backstroke to the man's head. The Saxon wore an iron helmet but no *brunia*—he wore no chain mail at all. The blow landed on his helmet and stunned him for a second. In that second, he lowered his shield just a bit and Sebastian brought his sword back down from a high guard just above the man's shield. The blow caught the Saxon on his unprotected neck. He staggered backward and collapsed in a heap, his life pouring out of the wound.

Sebastian was astonished at what had happened. It had been so quick—he had not even meant to kill the man. His blows had simply been reflexes from his training, and now the Saxon lay gasping at his feet. Sebastian was aghast and stared hypnotically at the dying man. His dismay almost cost him his own life as a brawny Saxon broke from the fight in the center of the clearing and made straight for Sebastian. The man was fully armored and obviously a veteran fighter. He was also a very large, powerful man who carried his weapons easily. He had apparently seen his friend fall and had come to seek vengeance on his killer.

Although Sebastian had fought many mock battles during his years of relentless training, for the first time he was facing men who were actually trying to kill him. Clearly this big Saxon planned to dispatch his smaller opponent quickly and then break for the protection of the woods. He rushed into the fight confidently and began raining blows on Sebastian's shield as if he would smash it into bits to get to the boy. Sebastian could see clearly what the Saxon would do each time he lifted his sword, but the man was too experienced and careful to be fooled or foiled by any of Sebastian's stock of training-ground maneuvers. He never let down his shield guard, and his blows kept slamming down upon Sebastian's shield, each one a solid shock to the lad's spine. No matter how cleverly he guarded himself and struck back, Sebastian could not get inside the man's shield. He was also increasingly hard-pressed for good footing as the space of the little glade became strewn with more and more bodies and debris. The Saxon pressed him relentlessly, waiting for the moment when Sebastian would make a mistake or lose his balance.

In a flash of desperation, Sebastian took the one course open to him. He waited until the Saxon swung a long downward sweep against his shield and simultaneously swung his own sword wide and had it parried by the Saxon's shield. He stepped quickly inside the shield, as close to the man's body as he could, as if trying to grapple with him by hand. At the same time he dropped both sword and shield, grasped the man at the neck by his chain mail, and slid his dagger into his right hand. The Saxon struggled to shake loose of him. He stepped back and pounded Sebastian on the helmet with the pommel of his sword, but before he realized the trick or the danger it represented, Sebastian had the dagger at his throat. "*In nomine Patris, et Fillii, et Spiritus Sancti*," Sebastian croaked in anguish, as he shoved the dagger home.

For Sebastian, the aftermath of the battle was far worse than the battle itself. He had been raised by Ermengard to believe that life was precious and that killing, although often necessary in the parlous world they lived in, was not the true message of the Christian scriptures. Thus to kill a man was shock enough to feel the weight of God's stern judgment, and Sebastian had killed two before the day was half gone. He could have killed more, for many of the Saxons defeated in the glade by Edelrath's cavalry had been too severely wounded to make an escape. They lay on the ground as they had fallen, shrieking and moaning in pain or waiting in dumb resignation like crippled deer for the violent end they knew must come. At least they were put out of their misery quickly by a simple blow to the head or neck by Frankish soldiers who were combing through the field for useable weapons or any other items of value. A quarter hour after the fight, no Saxon remained alive in the small meadow.

Sebastian watched the slaughter in horror. Then he was suddenly and violently sick, falling to his knees and puking into the grass. He crouched there, shuddering and crying, unable to lift his head from the ground. After a time, he felt a light hand on his shoulder, and a low voice spoke to him calmly, "Right, then, let's get up now. There's still work to be done. There's a good lad."

Count Edelrath helped Sebastian get to his feet and gather his fallen sword and shield. He still held the bloody dagger in his hand. "Wipe that off now, son, and put it away. Clean your face off, and then find your horse. I need you to ride to the Eresburg at once. Find the king and tell him I am coming as soon as I can gather the troop. Can you do that for me?"

"Why . . . uh . . . yes," Sebastian stammered, gradually recovering from the state of shock into which he had fallen. "Yes, I can, my lord—I'll go at once." He turned, disoriented, and stumbled over a body. Count Edelrath helped him to his feet and pointed him toward the edge of the woods where Joyeuse waited, whinnying and pawing the ground.

Edelrath called out behind him, "You've done well today, Sebastian. Steady now. Get yourself past the killing. It's what a warrior does. Hold your head up and finish the day strong. Find the king. Stay with him until I come."

Those last days with Adela in the palace at Worms provided the only clarity for Sebastian in the wake of the battle at the Eresburg. The rest was chaos. Sebastian found the king after the fight in the forest glade, as he had been instructed to do by Count Edelrath. But the fortress was awash with the carnage and confusion of war as Charlemagne dealt with scouting reports, reorganization, and such pressing things as the disposition of prisoners and wounded and the division of spoils.

Sebastian caught the king's eye briefly as Charlemagne conferred with his commanders one by one. "Sebastian!" he called out. "Come here, lad. What's this blood all over you? Are you all right? Tell me quickly. Where's Edelrath?" Sebastian briefly recounted the results of the chase after Widukind and the Saxon cavalry, leaving out his own part in the skirmish but assuring the king that he was unhurt.

"What about Widukind? Did you catch that devil?"

"No, high king," Sebastian reported, standing as straight and still as he could, though he felt his limbs still trembling from the day's combat. "Count Edelrath instructed me to tell you that Widukind escaped. He was not among the dead on the field. The count also said he would come to you as soon as he could regroup the cavalry."

"*Verdammt noch mal!*" the king swore. "More's the pity. We've not seen the last of that arrogant beggar. I wish we'd snared him so I could have hanged him for his impudence. Well, no matter; we'll catch him next time. Meanwhile, I want you to stand by. We have to move quickly and soon to find the Irminsul. There's no Saxon treasure here, nor much of anything else worth having. Get yourself something to eat, and be ready to leave quickly. We'll need you to choose the way, and we'll likely ride as soon as Edelrath comes back. The light won't last much longer today."

Sebastian could not eat. Instead, he collapsed against the wall of a rude building not far from where the king was taking council with his captains. He tried to close his eyes and rest his mind a bit, but thoughts of the battle kept coming back to him. Finally, to cleanse his mind of the bloody images, he thought for the thousandth time of Adela and their last few days at Worms. As he had done then, in the wake of the terrible news from Fernshanz, Sebastian took refuge in Adela's words and in the lovely picture of her that appeared as if by magic whenever he closed his eyes. He fancied he could still feel the pressure of her lips and hear her voice as she had bidden him farewell.

Chapter 16

The Irminsul

Saxony, Summer 772

They found the Irminsul easily enough the next day by following the trail Sebastian had discovered with Anchesigal. Not far from where Sebastian had captured the black statue, they had come upon the sanctuary, surrounded by a circular wooden wall. Swallowed in the gloom of a forest of huge old oaks, it was rather small and inadequate as a fort. They saw signs that Saxon cavalry had been there recently, but not a single guard was visible, and the gates were shut and barred. The place was eerily quiet.

Charlemagne signaled his archers to fire a volley over the walls. There was no response. He then ordered a cautious approach of warriors with ladders, covered by the archers. The men, led by an eager Count Konrad, were up and over the walls quickly, and soon the main gate creaked open. Konrad stepped out and announced loudly, "There's not a damned soul in the place. Looks completely abandoned . . . the bastards!"

Suspecting a trap, Charlemagne sent out security patrols into the forest in all directions, and warriors poured rapidly through the gate with weapons drawn. Moving past several buildings near the gate, they came into the center of the compound. There they beheld a ghastly sight; a massive dead oak, the legendary Irminsul, drooping with gaunt branches. Hanging by the neck from the bare branches was at least a score of bodies, some little more than skeletons, others more recent corpses. It would have been hard to tell who the dead men might have been, Frank or Saxon, except that many of them still had Christian crosses around their necks.

Sebastian was with the king as the troop entered the sanctuary. He was sickened by the sight and dismayed at the sudden thought that one of the grisly skeletons, half-hidden by tattered clothing, might be that of his friend Anchesigal.

The bodies of nine Saxon guardian priests formed a ring on the ground around the tree. Pools of blood connected the bodies, one to the other. It was clear that the bloody ring had been created by the mass suicide of these unlucky wardens, each of whom held a bloodstained dagger of some sort in his dead hands. A fearful stench hung in the air and a sense of horror and profound foreboding pervaded the stillness of the place.

Recovering from his initial shock, the king was outraged by the barbarous scene. "By God, these are a wretched, sinful people! I've never seen such an unholy thing. They must be defeated, these Saxon devils. We must end such profanity forever. It's a horrible offense against God and man." He commanded that the victims be cut down forthwith and their bodies buried. The dead priests were to be dragged away and their bodies burned somewhere in the forest. The king then ordered hasty defenses to be set up lest the Saxons should mount a counterattack.

"And what of the treasure, my lord king?" asked Count Konrad, impatiently. "There's not one bloody trace of it. There's nothing here at all—except dead people and empty buildings. Bah! All of this for nothing."

"Be still, Konrad, damn you," the king said irritably. "If nothing else, we shall cut down this cursed tree and burn it. Then we'll raze these walls and leave this unholy ground a blackened waste. I'll show the Saxons the emptiness of their worship of trees and statues."

"Sire!" Sebastian stepped forward out of the ranks. Surprised, the king turned toward him. "What is it, Sebastian? Do you know something?"

"Sire, when we captured the black statue last year, the cart where I found it was full of digging tools—picks and wooden shovels. There were so many I had to throw them out of the cart to find the statue. Later, when I asked Heimdal about it, he said that the Saxon god Odin was supposed to have sought a fount of wisdom that was under the sacred tree, and he had to leave his eye there as a pledge. Is it possible the treasure is buried?"

The question hung in the air as Charlemagne surveyed the scene again with fresh eyes. The ground inside the circle of blood was strewn with thick straw, yet every few paces, a pointed stone, like a large cutting tooth, protruded from the straw. On the surface of each stone, faint runic letters were visible.

"Bring some tools," the king barked, with growing excitement. "Dig here! Dig inside the circle—under the stones! Beneath the tree!"

They found the treasure in short order. Under each rock, they uncovered a trove of gold and silver that was stored in oaken boxes resting on beds of rock. It was a king's ransom of coins, jewelry, ornaments, and statues. Some gold plates, chalices, and candlesticks were Christian, and some of the treasure, mostly coins with Greek writing, came from Byzantium. It represented the spoils of hundreds of Saxon incursions made either against their Frankish, Frisian, and Slavic neighbors or taken in pirate raids on the ships and towns of the seas to the north.

Incredibly, the Saxons had made no attempt to remove the treasure. Apparently, the defeat of Widukind's cavalry so soon after the precipitous fall of the Eresburg had prevented him from reaching the Irminsul and had forced him to flee for his life. Perhaps the self-murdered priests had been victims of a final sacrifice to the *Yggdrasil*, and their nine bodies, placed so carefully around the ancient tree, were meant as symbols of the nine worlds of Saxon mythos.

Whatever the explanation, the discovery had a sensational effect on Charlemagne's men, each of whom expected to receive a share of the phenomenal treasure. Cart after cart was filled with the gold and silver and parked in a holding area inside the walls. The king placed Varnar and his most trusted personal guards in charge of the laden carts. He then forbade any celebrations until the status of the Saxon forces should become clear. Meanwhile, he ordered the great tree be completely destroyed.

This latter task was far easier said than done. The girth of the tree was broader than a normal man was tall, and the oak wood was still hard. It took an entire day to bring the tree down with axes and another day to chop up the branches so the tree might be burned. On the third day Charlemagne commanded that his principal commanders and any Saxon captives be brought to the site to observe the burning. It took another two days to turn the great tree into ashes.

By the end of that time, a vexing problem had arisen: the army had run out of water.

The king stewed with frustration. "What in blazes is happening? It's always raining in these bloody Saxon woods. And now no rain has fallen for over three weeks! Have you been up to the Lippe, for God's sake? There's got to be some water there."

Count Edelrath kept his distance while the king vented his annoyance and disappointment. "Sire, both rivers in the area, the Lippe as well as the smaller Diemel, are so shallow the current has ceased to flow in them. Pools have become so brackish the water is undrinkable. The stores of water we brought with the troops are almost exhausted. I'm afraid, sire, that thirst has became a central problem."

The king was loath to abandon the campaign at this point; he was determined to take advantage of the overwhelming victory and press the Saxons to sue for peace. The lack of water, however, threatened to force him to move the entire army back to the west, to sources of water near the Rhine. Reluctantly, he prepared to give the order for the army to withdraw.

Then, as if to underscore Charlemagne's victory with an act of divine intervention, it began to rain. For all the men, but especially for the king, it was a good omen.

"Well, Gonduin," demanded the king, "Am I wrong to continue the fight against these Saxons and take their lands? Shall we call this a war and not just another punitive expedition? Edelrath, what do you think? Tell me what to do about the Eresburg. Should we raze it to the ground, or garrison it with Franks and make it as strong as possible? Leudegar, what say you? We have the Saxon gold. 'Tis a tidy fortune, *nicht wahr?* Every one of us can go home now and enjoy being rich for a while. Shall we leave the bloody Saxons in peace for yet another year?"

The council of commanders sat on logs while the king passed around a wineskin filled with strong *schnaps*. They huddled over a small fire in front of one of the barracks buildings inside the Eresburg walls. The rain had lasted two days, and it took another two to move the treasure carts back to the Eresburg. The army was of a mood to leave this gloomy place of dense forests and heavy rains and go home to enjoy the victory and whatever share they might have in the treasure. However, his senior advisors knew that the king had already made up his mind.

Edelrath broke the long silence that followed the king's questions. "Sire, if you decide to stay here, so close to Saxon territory, you will need a much stronger fortress than the one we are in now. The Eresburg must be made into a real castle with higher walls and towers on the corners. We should use stone if we can find it and move it here. You will also need a strong commander, one who isn't intimidated by the isolation or the threat of a new Saxon attack, for I am sure of this, my king: the Saxons will come back. They will not suffer the loss of the Eresburg and the Irminsul lightly or for long."

"Aye, my lord," echoed Leudegar. "They'll come back, as they always do, and we'll have 'em raiding all the way to Fulda again if we don't put a stop to it now. Let us move against them instead. Let us indeed call it a war. Burn every village between here and the River Weser. If they show fight, then we'll beat them again, and this time we'll demand hostages from them."

"One more thing, my lord king," added Gonduin in a somber voice. "We must make them forsake their wretched gods—and take an oath to become Christians."

"And if they won't, Gonduin?" the king asked. "What then?"

"Then, my lord, we must wipe them out. Destroy the whole wretched race, if need be. If they want to serve the devil, then let them go to hell!"

Although Sebastian had recovered somewhat from the shock of his first battle, he remained emotionally troubled by the events of the last few weeks. Killing the two Saxons and the awful news from Fernshanz continued to plague his mind, and he felt none of the exhilaration that coursed through the whole army. He hung back from the strutting and boasting, the raucous celebrations, and the singing and drinking around the nighttime campfires. Instead, he spent much of his time walking or riding the deer paths of the forest. He was surprised to realize that most of these solitary journeys wound up with him drifting in the direction of home, toward Fernshanz.

Eventually the king sent for him. "I've not forgotten you, lad," the king began warmly. "How fares my young warrior now, after he's tasted his first blood?'

"I am well, high king," Sebastian replied, unable to match the king's enthusiasm.

"You're well? Is that all you can say for yourself? The way you say it makes me think that you are sick. What can be wrong? You're one of the conspicuous heroes of this campaign! Edelrath told me how you bested two Saxon warriors in the forest glade; he said one of them was a huge man and a veteran fighter. He feared for your life and tried to get to you but was attacked himself on the way. By the time he was able to free himself, you had already defeated your opponent. Not only that, but without you we might have missed the Saxon treasure altogether. All of us are in your debt for that."

"Thank you, my lord. I . . . it is my duty, I'm honored to serve . . ." was the mumbled reply. Sebastian stared at the floor.

"Whoa, now, something indeed is the matter. Tell me, Sebastian. What in the world can be making you so glum at such a time?"

"I don't know, my lord—I just keep thinking about my family, my people in the village, about Fernshanz. Almost everyone I knew and cared about was there, and now they are gone."

"You can't do anything about that now, Sebastian. It's the way of war; you must go on. At least you can take satisfaction in knowing we have had our vengeance—and we shall have more! I have decided to continue the offensive. We'll drive the Saxons beyond the Weser and bring them to their knees. You want to be part of that, don't you, son? It will be glorious. You will learn so much, and it will help you get over the loss of Fernshanz. When this campaign is over, I'll bring you back to court with me, and you will be one of my personal vassals. I need such young men as you beside me, who are good at many things. What do you say? Is that a contract?"

"My lord king, I am truly grateful for all you have done for me. It would be a great privilege to serve you as a part of your court. Yet, I feel obliged to the people of Fernshanz, and I feel responsible for what happened while I was absent. I've thought of little else over the past several days, and the thing I'd like to do most right now is go back to Fernshanz, gather the people, and rebuild."

"What people, Sebastian?" said the king gently. "I thought they were all wiped out."

"Not all, lord king; my companion Liudolf says that some escaped, and others were not at the village when the wolfmen attacked. There may be many such. It's just that most of what we had—the buildings, the stock, our stores of grain—was destroyed, and I would need to start over. But I have no means."

"I see," mused the king, pulling on his mustache." He paused and thought for a long moment. Then he summoned Count Edelrath and his chief advisor, the newly promoted archchaplain, Bishop Regwald, and bade them be witnesses to what he was about to say.

"Sebastian, you have done me great service over this past year. I have seen that you are both capable and dedicated, not only to me but to your people. That is exactly what I want in the men I choose to help me govern this realm. I am inclined to help you do what you desire. When we return from this campaign, I'll see to it that you receive what you need to rebuild Fernshanz and repopulate it. There are many homeless peasants in the towns along the Rhine who would like a fresh start. We will make an effort to send them to you, along with supplies, animals—cattle, oxen. Seeds, too. It will be your share of the treasure. You have certainly earned it.

"If you are successful," the king continued, "if Fernshanz can once again be my eyes and ears, my bulwark in the north, then I will see that the fort and its lands become yours. But you will be my vassal, not Konrad's. You will answer only to me. One day, when the danger from the Saxons is over, I'll insist that you come to my court. After all, we must get you married. I doubt you know a single woman, *nicht wahr?* Besides that, what shall I do without my reader?"

"My lord king, I am most grateful, truly. But may I set out now, if it please you, with my men?"

"Now, before the campaign is over? I intend to beat these Saxons down once and for all and make them into Christians. They must acknowledge that I am king and that henceforth they owe their allegiance to me. We still have much work to do."

"I know, sire, but I am afraid of what may happen to the peasants who are left at Fernshanz. If we don't begin to plow and prepare the fields, there will be nothing to eat this winter. They will be lost."

"Ah," the king nodded. "Well, go then. Take your friends from Fernshanz, and I will send a troop of soldiers with you."

"It is not necessary, high king. The Saxons will be busy staying alive. They will not likely bother Fernshanz for a long time, I expect."

"Well, you are right," the king said, laughing. "In fact, some of my senior officers are so bloody-minded they want me to exterminate the whole race. What do you think of that?"

"I'm sure they don't mean that, sire. The Saxons are just people, aren't they—like us?"

"Not like us, lad. Not like us. No. They need serious changing, and I intend to do it, by whatever means necessary."

"To be sure, sire."

"Go, lad," the king said, grabbing Sebastian by the shoulders. "Rebuild. Make a place for yourself. You will see that it is a very good thing to have one's own land. Fernshanz will be yours if you can make it thrive. And come to me as soon as you can, at least for a visit. I shall miss you sorely. God go with you."

The Saxons did not show battle again that year. They faded away into their forests instead, leaving their villages unprotected. Charlemagne's troops burned the villages wherever they found them and took captive any Saxons unfortunate enough to stray into their path. If an armed man would not throw down his weapons at once and beg on his knees for his life, he was killed on the spot, and God help any woman or girl who was caught. If she was lucky, she would be fancied by a single Frankish warrior who would keep her for himself and protect her from the other men.

By the time the army reached the Weser, the Saxons sent emissaries. Hostages—the sons and brothers of high-ranking Saxon chieftains—were offered and taken by Charlemagne. He agreed not to cross the Weser and to leave the Saxons in peace. His conditions were few and clear: the Saxons would forsake forever all hostilities against the Franks, and their leaders would stand ready to welcome Frankish missionaries and prepare their people to accept Christianity.

"A good day's work, sire," Gonduin proclaimed heartily, as he rode beside the king on the way back to the Eresburg. "They have accepted all our conditions and we can reasonably assume they will be well on their way to saving their souls by this time next year!"

"We'll see, Gonduin," reflected the king. "I'd feel much better, however, if Widukind had been part of the agreement and had offered hostages of his own. We can't be sure how much those emissaries at the river really represented all the Saxons."

"No matter, sire. They were soundly beaten on all counts, and they lost a prodigious lot of men. They gave their hostages and agreed to accept our priests. We also have the Eresburg, and we shan't give it back. We have them by their testicles."

"Don't be too sure—Widukind wasn't at the river. But it is a good start. I mean to make the Eresburg much stronger. We will send engineers and a large contingent of troops to garrison it. By the way, who would you recommend to command our new fortress?"

"Why, let me see. I would need to think about it awhile."

"How about Count Konrad?"

"What, that arrogant jay? He's a scoundrel through and through."

"Yes," agreed the king in a low voice, "but if anyone can defend this God-forsaken post so near to the Saxon heartland, it's him. He has no fear, and he is ruthless. That's what I want. The Saxons must be shown no lenience. If they step out of line, I must know it at once. If they need disciplining, then he is the one to do it. I don't exactly trust Konrad, but I know he will be tough to defeat and he will enforce my will here."

"But will he take the job, lord king?" exclaimed Gonduin. "It's not likely to be a post he would care for overmuch. Konrad is the kind who likes to drink and carouse. This command may seem too much like work to him."

"Under normal circumstances and given normal incentives, you would be right, Gonduin. But, as a matter of fact, I have already spoken to Konrad."

"And?"

"And he says yes . . . on one condition."

"And what is that, my lord?"
"That he be given the woman he wants in marriage."
"And who, pray, would that be, sire?"
"He wants your daughter, Gonduin. He wants Adela."

Chapter 17

Out of the Ashes

"Oh, most merciful and generous God, who watches over us all, the great and the small alike, bless and keep us forever!"

The voice was unmistakably that of Baumgard, as loud and bombastic as ever, but the fat steward was nowhere to be seen. Near the old keep, Sebastian and his small party sat their horses uneasily and surveyed the ruins of Fernshanz—the burned-out buildings, the wrecked fences, and the residue of the villagers' meager possessions scattered everywhere.

Baumgard's disembodied voice continued eerily. "Welcome, Lord Sebastian! Most Welcome! Welcome, Master Liudolf! Welcome, Master Archambald! Welcome, good soldier Bernard! A thousand times welcome to all! Thank God and all the saints, you have come. We had almost given up hope." With that, a gaunt, disheveled, and incredibly dirty Baumgard emerged from the shadowy interior of the pigsty. Close behind him, smiling broadly, came Lothar.

"We thought it were the Saxons again, m'lord Sebastian," Lothar began, running up to catch the bridle of Sebastian's horse. "We have had no news, m'lord. Nothing. No one from outside the village has come until now."

"Are there no more villagers, Lothar?" Sebastian asked anxiously, dismounting with an effort after a precipitous journey without rest. "When Liudolf escaped, he wasn't sure how many had survived."

"There are, sir," Lothar reported, less cheerfully. "We've a score or so of men but no women at all, except for old Marta. She often goes into the forest alone to look for her special herbs, and that's where she was when the Saxons come. She never even saw 'em. Neither did most of the men who came back. By chance they was away from the village that day on various bits of business—tradin' in other villages, searchin' for bees, or huntin' for cattle or pigs and such. It were very lucky for myself; I had borrowed a cart and a pair of oxen and was in Lippeham by the Rhine, tradin' young pigs for seed. And it's a good thing, too, Lord Sebastian, for we will sorely need the seed if we are to survive."

"Seed? What seed, Lothar?" Sebastian asked absently, trying to shake the discomfiting feeling that he was in the presence of ghosts. He gratefully accepted a ladle of cool water from Baumgard.

"Sir, there is very little left to eat. We mus' plant soon or we will starve."

"I know, Lothar," Sebastian agreed earnestly. "That's why I came as quickly as I could. But we must talk of this later. Right now we are weary and hungry, and I imagine it's been a while since you have tasted bread. There are some loaves in the bags on my saddle—help yourselves. We've also brought four horses with packs full of provisions—gifts from the king himself."

Later that evening, after bread had been made and shared with all the villagers, Sebastian sat around a fire in the area of the old keep with the principal members of his tiny community, his companions and a group of about twenty free farmers and a few serfs. In spite of the welcome food and the initial euphoria at Sebastian's return, the mood of the group was gloomy. Fear and uncertainty could be seen in the eyes of most of the men.

"First of all," Sebastian began reassuringly, "the high king wants us to rebuild Fernshanz so it can become once again his anchor of defense in the north. He promised me personally that he will help us rebuild. He promised provisions, materials for rebuilding, and people. And in place of Attalus, he has made me his personal vassal and lord over Fernshanz."

There was a hopeful stirring among the peasants as they leaned forward eagerly to hear more. Sebastian continued solemnly, "As for the

Saxons, you may be at ease for now. The king has won a great victory over them. The Eresburg fortress has been taken from them, and the army is moving as we speak to drive them beyond the Weser. I took part in the battle, and I tell you truly that the Saxons were badly beaten; they lost many men and will not likely bother Fernshanz for the remainder of this year, at least. For one thing, the king plans to turn the Eresburg into a Frankish fortress."

Sebastian wanted to add that having the Eresburg under Frankish control meant there would be help close by, but he had heard news just before he left that Konrad was to command the new fortress, and he was sure that nothing but grief could come to him now from that quarter. In the meantime, at least, the Saxons would have more serious things to worry about than Fernshanz.

"Let us sleep now and rest ourselves in the knowledge that King Karl himself is our patron. He has sworn not to abandon us, and he will help us build a new Fernshanz. Tomorrow we will talk about how to begin. Be of good heart. We shall endure and survive." As Sebastian rose, the peasants bowed before him as if he had always been lord and disappeared into the darkness to whatever hovels they had managed to erect.

Sebastian awoke the next day, refreshed by a deep sleep and satisfied that at last he was home and could finally begin the work of rebuilding Fernshanz. With Baumgard as guide, Sebastian set out with Liudolf, Archambald, and Bernard to survey the extent of the devastation. Almost as an afterthought, he called for Lothar to accompany them.

They went first to the chapel area, where at least the stones erected over the dead remained. With much waving of hands and stamping of feet, Baumgard began apologetically, "I am sorry to report that much of what we did at first, Master Sebastian, was just bury the dead. It was a great effort, but by the grace of God we persevered, as well we should. It took a very long time. I am ashamed, my lord! I am truly stricken to have to tell you that we were not able to dig a grave for each person. I am mortified to say we had to bury the people quickly because of the truly pestilential smell, and so most of them rest together, sadly, in a common grave." Sebastian shook his head and looked down at the earth as the portly steward paused to wipe his bulbous nose on his sleeve. His out-of-control hair, his outlandish appearance in his dirty rags, and his ever more preposterous statements and dramatic gesticulations made Sebastian almost smile in spite of the somber moment at the graveyard.

"We did bury your mother in her own grave, God rest her soul," Baumgard said solemnly, as he showed Sebastian the site. "There she lies, beside Lord Attalus. We thought it was the proper thing to do, since they were from the same place and knew each other so well. And close by them lies the saintly Father Louis and his family. We knew you were close to them, and so there they also lie."

"And Heimdal, Baumgard? Where have you buried him?"

"We have not, good sir. There has been no trace of the blind man, dead or alive," the steward asserted. "It is possible the Saxons carried him off or found him and killed him at his home in the woods. In any case, we certainly will continue to use every means to find him, dead or alive."

"Naturally, Baumgard," Sebastian replied, his stomach churning. "Very appropriate . . . very thoughtful. Thank you." They stopped for a moment to pray over the plot of Ermengard and Attalus and the graves of Father Louis and his family. Sebastian forced himself not to think of these people whom he had loved so much for fear he would break down in front of his men. Instead, he set his mind on the day ahead and curtly ordered the troop to walk on.

There was not much to see. No building was intact; there were no boats, no carts, and no animals to pull them. The Saxons had not stayed long enough to do damage to either of the walls, but they had taken all the cattle, horses, and sheep. Only some of the chickens had managed to escape and were now pecking around the burned-out huts. Lothar assured them that at least there were plenty of pigs in the forest, which would go a long way toward seeing the village through the winter. And there were two oxen, those Lothar had brought back from Lippeham.

"Where to begin?" Sebastian sighed as they sat down by the river to eat something at midday. As they ate, a small catboat with a single sail appeared, tacking upstream. Two oarsmen provided further power as a third figure sat motionless in the bow, his face covered by the hood of his cloak. The boat grounded beside the group and a familiar voice resounded from under the hood, "It is only when you have lost everything that you are truly free to do that which is new."

"Heimdal!" Sebastian shouted, leaping to his feet and running to the boat. He helped the blind man climb out of the boat and then crushed him in an embrace.

"My good Sebastian, if you please. Be gentle with an old man. You are bruising my delicate ribs."

The group surrounded Heimdal at once, bombarding him with questions, their previously gloomy mood dissolving in his dauntless presence.

"Wait," he implored them, "Sebastian we must pay these good boatmen. Have you any money or something to trade?"

When the boatmen had been rewarded for bringing their dear friend home, Heimdal recounted where he had been. Grieving for his old friend Attalus, he had taken advantage of the improving weather and Sebastian's absence to take to the road again. He simply walked out of the woods one day well before the Saxon attack and set off down the road toward Lippeham. There he had supported himself by begging on the steps of the town church and ensconcing himself at night in a small inn of ill repute near the river. The girls there had found his quick wit and endless stories entertaining and they had adopted him forthwith. In their boisterous company, he was able to assuage his sorrows and live in relative ease until he heard the bad news about Fernshanz and talked some idle boatmen into bringing him home.

Sebastian was profoundly grateful to find Heimdal still alive and to have his counsel as the group settled down once again to chart a new course for the village and its people.

"Where to begin," he said again. "There is so much to be done, and it's almost midsummer." After a long silence, it was Lothar who finally responded. "My Lord Sebastian, I'm sure you will agree, first we needs food. We have neither wheat nor rye; whatever the Saxons did not take was burned. We mus' plant somethin' else to eat for the winter, and we mus' get the seeds in the ground as soon as may be. We mus' plant . . ."

"Lothar, you ignorant bumpkin, what else could we plant that would take the place of wheat and rye?" interrupted Baumgard irritably.

"We could plant barley, Baumgard, if'n you please. And oats. We will need oats for the horses."

"Hmpf," Baumgard snorted. "Have you ever tried to bake bread out of barley or oats? It doesn't rise. It's terrible! No one will eat it. Besides, it is too late to plant."

"It don' have to be made into bread," Lothar continued stubbornly. "Most of our people already use a common cook pot, and they throws whatever they has into it—bits of meat, onions, and mushrooms. The gruel in that pot is what they eats all week, and barley is a big part of it. The pot stays on the hearth, warm and ready all the day."

"That is true," Bernard said in his gravelly voice. "When I was a boy, there was always something to eat in that pot on the hearth. It ain't all that tasty, mind, but one could live on it."

"But, my Lord Sebastian," complained the nettled steward, "there is not enough time now in midsummer to raise even a crop of barley or oats."

"That may be, Baumgard," Lothar conceded. "It is late, but if we starts to plow into the fall, we might get at least a crop of oats for the horses. And . . ." he hesitated, as if about to say something seditious.

"And what, Lothar?" Sebastian prompted, beginning to see some hope in the words of this quiet young farmer.

"There is another crop that don't take as long to grow. We could raise beans. And peas and lentils. Not just in the peasant gardens. We could begin to plant such seeds in the fallow part of our fields that we already cross-plowed last spring."

Like most Frankish manors of the day, Fernshanz used a two-field system: they planted half of the available fields in winter grain in the late fall and harvested it in the late spring or early summer of the next year. The other half of the fields was allowed to lie fallow and was enriched by the manure of grazing or corralled stock. Each peasant's family raised their own vegetables on a private plot around each hut.

"No!" Baumgard almost shouted indignantly. "The fallow land must be allowed to rest. Otherwise we shall wear out the soil. Everyone knows that!"

"Hear him out, Baumgard, please," Heimdal interrupted. "In Lippeham I heard much talk from boatmen and farmers from villages all along the Rhine, even as far as the town of Cologne. Some are using a new system to grow more crops. The land is divided into three parts, not two, with each third being rotated once a year. On one-third of the land, they continue to plant wheat and rye in the fall for harvest in early summer, and they still leave another third to lie fallow. But the final third is planted in the early spring and harvested in the fall."

Lothar jumped in excitedly. "That's it, Heimdal. That last third is planted altogether in summer crops: barley, oats, peas, beans, lentils—all food that can go into the common cook pot and provide food for a whole family all winter long, especially if we can add meat to that pot from the pigs in the forest. There will be more than enough of them now that there is so few of us. We jus' mus' be sure to help the pigs find food this autumn by knockin' acorns out of the trees for 'em and providin' 'em with whatever scraps from the village there may be."

Lothar paused again, embarrassed to have made such a long speech to those he considered his betters. At length he continued, speaking in the same quiet, logical voice but with increasing urgency. "You will worry, good steward Baumgard, that we will wear out the third of the land that we plants in barley and beans. On the river villas they say not so. They say the beans and lentils have somethin' that puts the strength back into the soil instead of takin' it out, as wheat and rye does. They say that even the old Romans knew this and used it to their good. Whatever they knew, it don' matter; we will rotate each field so that it is used different after each plantin'."

At this point, Liudolf spoke for the first time. "Are you sure about this, Lothar? I know little about farming, but I know this: if we wear out the land, we will have to move from here. And even if you are right, how can we plow the land in time to put in such a crop of beans and barley? We have no plows, no animals, and I doubt we can get them in time, even if the king himself has promised them to us.

"It may be," continued Liudolf in a low but determined voice, "that the only course for those of us who are left is to go back to Adalgray or even to the new fortress they are building at the Eresburg and throw ourselves on the mercy of Count Konrad. At least we would eat."

To this dire proposal only Heimdal responded. "Let me sound a note of caution. You all know what kind of man Count Konrad is; his reputation for violence and cruelty to the common folk is widespread. Few Franks can be found now who will willingly work on his lands or fight with him when necessary. Serfs must be conscripted and forced to live and work at Adalgray since Konrad has become its lord."

Sebastian shuddered. He knew there was no way he could go back to Adalgray or to the Eresburg and survive. He turned again to Lothar, who waited patiently, eyes cast down.

"Lothar, even if you are right about the fields and the summer crops, what makes you think we could survive here if we do what you suggest? How can we plow and plant in time? We only have two oxen left and not a single plow."

"Lord Sebastian, I believe we can do it! I can make a scratch plow. We can even make it without a metal blade; all we needs is some good, strong wood. That's how the old people always did it, anyway. We still have two good oxen. We can plow enough land to plant the peas and beans and oats and barley seeds I managed to get from Lippeham afore the Saxon raid. With any luck, we can have a harvest in late October or even November."

"Perhaps," conceded Liudolf, "but what will we eat in the meantime? The food Lord Sebastian has brought will not last until then."

"Ain't there fish in the river, sir?" Lothar ventured anxiously. "The lords and soldiers can hunt and fish. We can gather nuts, mushrooms, and berries growin' in the forest. We can slaughter some pigs."

"And I can go to Lord Gonduin at Andernach!" said Sebastian abruptly, suddenly excited by the idea. "The king has given me leave to do so, and Count Gonduin himself encouraged me to come to him if I had need. He said he would help me until the king could provide for us later."

"In the meantime, sir, if you will, I can begin to rebuild our defenses," said Bernard, adding hastily, "I ain't no good at farmin'."

"Yes," said Sebastian, warming to the plan, "we must organize. I will go for help. You, Bernard, will see to our security and devise a plan to fight if necessary. You, Liudolf, will be our hunter and scout. And Baumgard, you and Lothar must organize the farmers to begin planting. And I want you to consult with Heimdal, do you hear? No arguing. Those who do not plow with the oxen must work with hand tools." Turning to Archambald, he said, "And you, my friend, must once again be my companion. It seems we shall have a new adventure together."

"With all my heart, Sebastian," the lad blurted out enthusiastically. "I believe we shall indeed prevail in spite of everything. And, thank God," he added bluntly, "we shall not have to go back to Count Konrad."

Archambald spoke for them all with these last words. If any had doubt, and not a little fear, about the daunting task before them, at least they realized they had come upon a new idea, one that might work, in spite of its unorthodox provisions. Moreover, his youth notwithstanding, they all had faith in Sebastian, whose leadership had already been tested and whose integrity and determination they respected.

Thus the little Fernshanz community embarked upon a new and groundbreaking era. Heimdal later put their new resolve philosophically to Sebastian. "Be of good cheer, dear boy, and marvel at how fortune sometimes changes dramatically through unlikely agents. Ironically, Fernshanz's fortunes and those of all of us who are part of it rest not on the learning of a scholar or the will of a lord, but on dire necessity and the awareness and inventive ideas of a peasant serf."

"Where are we off to, Bardulf?" Drogo inquired plaintively. "I'm sore afeared of these here dark woods."

"We're off to see the big river, m'boy. I've never seen it," Bardulf replied buoyantly, as they strode along the track. "And after we sees it, we're goin' on to Andernach."

"Andernach! Where's that, Bardulf? Is it far? I'm terrible hungry."

"Well, I don't rightly know where it lays, Drogo, but we're goin' to find it. That's where they makes that lovely wine that used to be in this here skin I got round my neck. You know what they calls it? Baumgard tol' me. They calls it 'Dragon's Blood'! Now, ain't that a ripe name? Well, this here skin'll be full again, if I have my way. I likes feelin' like a dragon. Once we get to the river, we'll jus' ask. I hear there's plenty of people on the river, pilgrims and such. We'll jus' ask 'em."

"Please, let's go back home, Bardulf. Maybe the Saxons have gone." Drogo was becoming more and more unhappy with each step away from Fernshanz.

"Right, Drogo. Let's go back and get skinned by them Saxons. You heard 'em—all that yellin' and screamin'. And later we seen the smoke, din't we? They breached the fort, no doubt about it, and likely ever soul in it's dead. We ain't goin' back, Drogo, and that's final."

"But what are we goin' to eat, Bardulf? I'm so hungry already. It's been almost a whole day since we et last."

"Ye can catch a rabbit, can't ye? I've seen ye do it. Soon as we stops this evenin', we'll build a trap or two. And when we gets to the river, there'll be plenty of people who need help. We'll jus' hire out for our supper. People're always needin' help, ain't they?"

As it turned out, there were no rabbits in the thick woods. And the next day, when they finally struck the river, they found soon enough that travelers on the river road wanted nothing to do with two vagrant youths with their hands out. The common folk they met were as poor as they were and the mounted travelers trotted by rapidly, hands on their weapons, without so much as a look at them.

Toward the end of that day, it was getting harder and harder for Bardulf to keep Drogo moving. The woeful youth kept wanting to sit down, and when they did, he began to weep piteously. Bardulf began to doubt his own resolve, but there was nothing to do but keep moving. Just before dark, their luck changed—for the worse.

Out of the gathering twilight, a company of brigands stepped from the woods in front of the two wayfarers. There were six of them, all rumpled nomads, with wild hair and the odor of animals. Their leader was a hulking hunchback with no front teeth. His long, scraggly hair framed a scarred face, and his bare arms bore the marks of too much time spent in the dangerous life of a freebooter. In his hands was a heavy club.

"What's in that skin, boy?" the robber asked without preliminaries.

"Why, nothin', sir, nothin' at all," Bardulf replied, trying to stifle his terror. "It used to be there was some wine, but there ain't none no more."

"Give it here," the bandit growled and grabbed at the skin. He upended the spigot into his mouth and abruptly threw down the empty flask. "Damn ye, then. What else d'ye 'ave?"

"Nothin', sir. I'm tryin' to tell ye, we come from Fernshanz, up there on the Lippe. The Saxons attacked us. We got away with only our lives, that's all." Bardulf was nervously eyeing the other bandits, who were forming a tight ring around them. Drogo was near to fainting.

"Well, then, I reckon there's nothin' left to do but kill ye," the big man proclaimed, tapping the end of the club in his open palm.

"No, sir, no," exclaimed Bardulf, desperately. "We can work. We works hard. We'll work fer ye. What do ye need us doin'? We can do anythin'."

The leader reflected on the idea a moment. "Well, boys, this might be yer lucky day. I am Teuthardis, and these here is my band of lovely brothers. Do ye know what we does? I'll tell ye, if ye don' know eggsackly. We robs people, and we kills people. What d'ye say to that?" Drogo sank at once to his knees and let out a despairing squeak. Bardulf kept swiveling his head from side to side, searching for an avenue of escape.

"Mebbe we'll give ye a choice," Teuthardis proclaimed. "Ye can join us and be robbers with us, or ye can die. Which'll it be?"

Recognizing his only chance, Bardulf tore off his shirt, proclaiming desperately, "Look at them muscles. I'm strong. I can fight. I fought before on the walls at Adalgray. So did Drogo here. We're good fighters—the best. I expec', sir," said Bardulf, drawing himself up manfully, "I expec' we will become robbers."

"Robbers it is, then," said the bandit with a mirthless laugh. "Remember, I am Teuthardis. Ye answers to me. And ye better hear that good, for I don' stand fer no mischief. Now go with the boys and find yerselves some good clubs. There'll be some business with 'em in the mornin'."

"Sir," Bardulf ventured timidly. "Might there be anythin' to eat?"

"Eat? Eat, he says, boys," he said with a smirk toward his cronies, who howled in derision. "Ye eats after ye works, and ye ain't worked yet. We'll see whether ye eats or not, dependin' on how ye helps us in our business tomorrow. Now let's get us some nods. Tomorrow'll come soon enough, and we'll all have enough work then." He gave a guttural laugh and trudged off into the forest.

The next day, the brigands felled a tree where the river road ran narrowly through a thick wood. Teuthardis and three cohorts hid on either side by the fallen tree. The others, including Bardulf and Diogo, concealed themselves at the rear of the trap, ready to pounce behind any prospective prey. One of the bandits climbed nimbly up a tall elm until he could see the trail behind them. He had not been in the tree five minutes before he hissed to those below. "Riders comin'. Only two! And two pack horses!" And he began to scramble down the tree immediately.

They had not long to wait before the two riders rode into the trap. Teuthardis stepped out, brandishing his huge club. The others broke out of the woods simultaneously, closing the trap around the startled horsemen.

Sebastian did not hesitate. He had been expecting something like this since he and Archambald had left Fernshanz, and they rode with weapons ready. At the moment Teuthardis stepped out of the woods, Sebastian spurred his horse hard directly at the man. Joyeuse leapt ahead snorting, and before the man could swing his club, the big horse had bowled him over. Jerking the horse around, Sebastian hurled his spear into the chest of the bandit leader just as he was picking himself up off the ground. As Tuethardis collapsed, Sebastian yanked his sword out of its scabbard and laid into the others. They tried manfully to get in a blow at Sebastian, but the big horse, its blood up and racing, reared and wheeled and attacked them. Sebastian cut down one man and wounded another before the rest of the band fled into the trees. Only two remained, and they knelt in the road with their hands held high in the air.

"Master Sebastian! Master!" Bardulf screamed. "Don't! It's us. Me and Drogo, from Fernshanz. Don't ye know us? Save us from these crazy men! They're tryin' to make robbers out of us!"

"And we ain't had nothin' to eat in nearly three days!" wailed Drogo, loudly.

Sebastian was hard-pressed to calm Joyeuse, who apparently felt he had just begun to fight. He reared and whinnied, fighting the bit. Eventually, he settled down enough for Sebastian to speak. "Get up here, Bardulf, behind the saddle. Drogo, you get up behind Archambald. Quickly now, there may be more of them. Move!"

While Archambald gathered up the pack horses and Sebastian's spear from the body of Teuthardis, the two youths, thoroughly rattled but enormously relieved, finally managed to climb up on the horses' flanks and hang on as they maneuvered around the log and galloped away down the road.

Chapter 18

Andernach

They crossed the Rhine half a league or so upriver from the town of Andernach to make it easier for the bargemen to maneuver. There was a sharp bend in the river where the town lay, beyond which the river narrowed significantly at a point called the Andernach Gate. It was important for river boats to hit the southern end of the town before being swept into the swifter current where the river turned to the north and narrowed.

None of the Fernshanz men had ever crossed such a formidable body of water in a boat, and all of them, even Sebastian, clung to the sides of the barge as it slid into the current. As Andernach grew larger before their eyes, Sebastian could see that it was not a big town, but more of a boat stop on the way to Cologne, Mayence, and Worms. Still, it had a fine harbor with wharves and a number of barges. Sebastian's heart beat faster because somewhere beyond the considerable activity on the docks was the real reason he had come to Andernach. It required a major effort to control his excitement at the thought of seeing Adela.

Sebastian paid the boatmen at the stock landing with the last of the silver deniers Bernard had received from Ermengard. He had no idea how they would get themselves and the horses back across the river. At least the boatmen assured him he would have no trouble finding the villa of Count Gonduin.

Beyond the harbor area was a small trade center with a tavern, a market, and artisan shops, bounded farther inland by an old Roman wall, no longer in use for defense. On the other side of this wall, directly above the market square, was the sprawling villa. It featured a central stone house, built in the old Roman style with arches for doorways and a red tile roof. Radiating out from the big house were numerous outbuildings and gardens—evidence that a small army of servants and functionaries attended the great estate. Most large Frankish manors were modeled on the old Roman *latifundia*. Surrounded by their extensive fields, they had lain in deep rural isolation. By contrast, Count Gonduin's villa abutted a town directly on the river. Sebastian marveled again at the lack of significant fortifications around the place, although the ruins of an old Roman redoubt, part of the Limes border forts, dominated a rise downriver from the town.

They were met at the villa's entrance by a contingent of armed guards. "What is it ye want?" the surly, uncooperative sergeant of the guard drawled laconically. "The lord is away. Ye can go on down the road to the pilgrims' 'ospice if ye like." He tried to dismiss Sebastian and his little band with a disdainful wave of the hand. When Sebastian showed no sign of moving, the sergeant reported curtly, "I've done tol' ye, Lord Gonduin is on campaign. He won't be back for the rest of the summer. Ye best be movin' on afore I lose me good manners." Sebastian calmly stood his ground and insisted that the sergeant go and tell whoever was in charge that Sebastian of Fernshanz requested an audience.

"Sebastian of what?" said the guard. "Never heard of ye. Besides, ye're too young to be anybody. And I'm tellin' ye, I be in charge, and you can't stay here nor speak to nobody. That's it then, skirr on out of here. There be an inn in the town, if ye've got the means."

Realizing he was in imminent danger of losing his temper and resorting to violence in his impatience to see Adela, Sebastian paused for a moment, took a deep breath, and addressed the man formally. "Sergeant, I am lord of the fortress Fernshanz which lies directly against the Saxon lands to the north. I have just come from the high king's army, where I took part in the defeat of the Saxons at the Eresburg. I have come here with messages from the high king himself. If you make me stand here one moment more, I will charge you with obstructing the king's business and insubordination to an officer of the king's own heavy cavalry. Do you know who I am now, sergeant?"

The sergeant wasted no time in ushering Sebastian and Archambald into the spacious villa, which was almost as luxurious a palace as that of the king in Worms. He led them to the central courtyard and bade them wait while he sent a message. Bardulf and Drogo were bidden to lead the horses to the stables where they might find a bite to eat at the nearby servants' kitchen.

Hardly any time elapsed before Adela came. She burst through a residence door into the courtyard and caught her breath as she saw Sebastian. She would have rushed to him if not for the presence of Archambald. "Lord Sebastian!" she exclaimed. "And Archambald! I'm so glad to see you both. Please come and sit with me. I will send for some refreshments. Excuse me—I'll only be a moment." With that she slipped back behind the door to give instructions.

"Archambald, old comrade," Sebastian said, grasping his friend's arm and looking straight into his eyes. "Will you do me a great favor? When Adela comes back, will you make an excuse and leave us for a little while? Just go down to the stables and see about the horses. Or talk to some of the people around here and gather some news. Find out who's important—you're good at all that. I'll send for you when they bring the refreshments."

Archambald made a face and bent over in mock pain. Sebastian patted his shoulder in feigned sympathy. "I know. You're starving to death again. It won't be long, I promise."

When Adela reappeared, Archambald dutifully mumbled an excuse, bowed awkwardly, and backed away out of the courtyard. Adela rushed to Sebastian and buried her face in the base of his neck. Sebastian almost fell over backward but recovered enough to return her embrace with equal passion.

After a moment, Adela leaned her head back and met Sebastian's eyes. He bent forward and kissed her lips. Though the kiss lasted only a moment, it stirred all the longing he had felt the last time they met. The kiss seemed perfectly natural and the only thing to do at that moment, but Adela pressed her face again into the hollow of his neck, afraid that he would see the confusion in her eyes.

At length, she pulled away and led Sebastian to a bench near a garden of roses in the courtyard. She didn't look at him. Her demeanor changed and she became nervous, distress clouding her face.

Afraid he had made a terrible mistake, Sebastian entreated her, "What is it, Adela? I'm sorry—I didn't mean to offend you."

"Oh, Sebastian, it's not that. That was . . . I wanted you to kiss me. It's something else, something I have to tell you at once. You need to know it now, before anything else happens."

"What is it, then? Tell me. Why are you so upset?"

"I am to marry Konrad," she blurted out the single statement and then buried her face in her hands.

"What?" Sebastian jumped to his feet and instinctively grabbed for his sword handle. His face turned ashen and his eyes darted about the courtyard as if he could find the enemy he sought and kill him. At length, he managed to control himself enough to ask for the details.

"When? And why you? I didn't know you'd even met Konrad."

"We are to be married in the autumn, when the campaign is over. I am to live with him in the new fortress, the one they're building at the Eresburg. And no, I don't know him, really. I've only met him twice. The first time he was a complete animal. He looked me up and down like I was property for sale and said some stupid things, like I was the kind of woman who would need a *real* Frankish warrior. It was disgusting. I wouldn't talk to him again—I wouldn't even look at him. I had no idea at all that he fancied me seriously."

"But why would he pick you, especially if he could see you didn't want him? And why would your father agree?" Sebastian said angrily, his voice rising. "He must know what kind of man Konrad is. Everyone knows."

Adela raised her face, already covered with tears. "My father is one of the high king's generals and his most trusted advisor. They are from the same house, the Arnulfings. The king asked him personally to give me to Konrad because he needs Konrad to command the new fortress being built inside of Saxon territory. It will be a hard, dangerous job, and to reward Konrad, the king agreed to give him what he wants. For some Godforsaken reason, Konrad wants me."

"I still don't see why. You obviously let him know how you feel," Sebastian reasoned, with fading hope.

"Of course I did! Konrad came here briefly with my father after the announcement. I told him to his face that I would make him a very poor wife, that I could never love him or respect him, and that I would certainly come to hate him. He only laughed, as if our conversation were some kind of game. He's perverse. If he thinks someone hates or opposes him, it makes him even more determined to harass and dominate that person. He told my father he wanted a strong woman to bear him children. He said she had to be a 'proper lady,' a virgin, who would bring honor to his house and be a good challenge for him—as if I were some kind of horse to be bred and broken to the saddle," she added bitterly.

"For God's sake, what can we do now?" Sebastian groaned. "I can't bear the thought of you being married to that *schweinhund*. Your life would be hell—worse than hell. I've got to find some way to kill him! I have twice the reason now. I'm sure it was he who poisoned my father."

"Sebastian, sit down. Listen to me. I knew you would react like this." Adela pulled him down beside her on the bench. "A short time after my father and Konrad left, I received another visitor, a messenger from the king himself. It was Bishop Regwald, the king's own archchaplain. He told me in no uncertain terms that I could not refuse Konrad, no matter how I felt. It was the king's wish, he said, and his word must be obeyed. The marriage must take place for reasons of state. And I, like any loyal Frank, must put away my own feelings and embrace what is best for the state and the king. In the end, it is the king who decides, and King Karl does not believe a woman's wishes need be considered in such matters. In fact, he would never even think of it."

"I will challenge Konrad. He won't refuse to fight me; he hates me."

"Wait, stop thinking like that. What if he killed you? Everyone says he's a ferocious fighter. You would be gone and I would still have to marry him. And if you win, you would be in disgrace with my father and the king. Do you think they would let you marry me then?"

"But I can't let you fall into Konrad's hands—he's a brute. He will dishonor you and hurt you. Doesn't your father know that?"

"You know as well as I that every Frankish woman is subject to her husband. It has always been so. But what makes you think that I can't handle him? In case you haven't noticed, I'm a strong woman. I have been managing my father's estate almost since my mother died when I was ten, and I have thought much about this since my father told me.

Konrad only wants me because he knows I care for you. He doesn't need a wife. He is happy with any available wench. I know what to expect from Konrad and I know how to manage him. He will be satisfied if I give him the two things he wants most."

"And what are they, Adela?"

"An heir and the prestige of a virtuous wife who brings honor to his house. I can do that. But he will soon find that he will have no pleasure or love from me whatever, and then he will leave me in peace."

"What if he beats you or rapes you? He is more than apt to do both."

"If he lays a single finger on me in violence," Adela spat out venomously, "I will kill him. And he will know that before we are married. He will fear to go to sleep or drink too much lest he wake up with a dagger in his throat. I do not think God would punish me for defending myself. No, I am no simpering, brainless maiden or servile wench to be treated as any man pleases. From what I know about your mother, Ermengard, neither was she, and you have told me she had no trouble handling that stupid man."

Sebastian leaned closer and covered Adela's hands with his own. "But what about me? I want you, too. Since that time at the king's palace, I've thought of little else than seeking you out, as you told me to do. Whatever troubles I've had since then, whatever losses or trials, have been eased by the vision of you. It creeps into my head at every waking moment. How can I let you go to a man I despise and who is such a monster as Konrad? What about us and what we said to each other in Worms before the campaign?"

"My dearest Sabastian, you will always be my only love. Don't you think I want you just as much? I have thought of nothing else since that time. But listen to reason. If I were to refuse to marry Konrad, my father would disown me and put me in a convent, and Konrad would find a way to kill you, because he would know it was because of you that I refused him. Alas, it was too good. We should have known better than to dream as we did; we should have known we couldn't choose each other, in spite of what your Father Louis told you. We are not peasants in a village, and even in the village marriages are often arranged."

"So what are you saying? Is that all there is? Is that the end of everything?"

"No—a thousand times no!" Adela began to cry and fell into Sebastian's arms as he rose. "I will love you all my life. I will find a way to stay connected to you—somehow. I can read now and write letters. I have a wonderful teacher—Sister Herlindis. You will meet her soon. She can be our go-between. We will find ways to see each other; you will be at the king's court now and then. So will I. Whatever occurs, we will still have each other—at least in our minds and hearts."

"But is that enough for you, Adela?" Sebastian whispered into her ear. "For me, it will almost be as if you died and I will be communing with a memory."

Adela tightened her embrace and murmured finally in a barely audible voice, "No, it will never be enough. But at least we have some time together now. Come to me tonight—in my rooms, after everything is quiet. I won't be asleep."

"Master Archambald," Drogo cried in excitement. "Did ye ever see such a place? It has three barns and an enormous granary full of wheat and rye. And we're to stay indoors tonight in rooms in this here warm stable. And we'll eat in the servants' eatin' hall, right next to where the soldiers eat. There's to be fish tonight, as well as bread and ale!"

Bardulf added suggestively, "If we had some money or somethin' to trade, we could even have a cup of that there Dragon's Blood wine they makes here. There's a whole stone buildin' where they makes it, and it has a cellar full of wine barrels, some bigger'n a cart. And right next door to it is a threshing floor and a brew place where they makes ale. This here is a good place, Master Archambald. I hope we gets to stay awhile."

They were standing in front of a row of several large, clean stables—each one for horses of different usage. Beyond the horse stables were a score or more of other pens and stables, each containing different farm animals. The complex was buzzing with activity as peasants, servants, and soldiers came and went in the course of their duties. Bardulf stared brazenly at the many comely young women hurrying back and forth from the farm area to the manor house.

In the Fernshanz village, most of the stock, except for the horses, had been kept in the peasants' own houses or were allowed to roam in the adjacent woods until winter. At Andernach there were barns, corrals, and fences to pen up the animals for immediate use by the manor house and its large contingent of servants, soldiers, and attendants. The fields, which contained the main wealth of Andernach, spread out from the complex to the west and south as far as the eye could see. Numerous fiefs of land had been granted by Count Gonduin to his personal vassals in return for their service to him, and scores of villages comprised the whole of Andernach manor. It was said that Gonduin himself had no idea how many villages there were.

Archambald found the enthusiasm of Bardulf and Drogo infectious. He began to look about himself at the bustling life of the huge manor farmyard. After the horses had been settled, the three strolled through the muddy streets of the complex, marveling at the wealth that was apparent everywhere. Numerous carts moved continuously between the fields and the farm buildings, several blacksmiths clanged at their trade over an impressive forge, and dozens of hunting dogs in the kennels competed with farm animals to raise a cacophonous clamor.

"We may indeed stay here as long as a week," Archambald replied, watching a handsome young woman crossing from the artisan workshops into the central courtyard behind the manor house. "I reckon we could learn a thing or two from a place as grand as this. And you, Bardulf," he said, turning to the tall, self-assertive youth, "you can do us a service by poking around amongst the servants and farm workers to see if any might fancy new opportunities downriver and a chance to improve their situations. You and Drogo might spread the word that there is plenty of land available at Fernshanz, and a man might be granted as many as two or three manses if he thought he could manage them. You can also say that we have the best of masters in young Lord Sebastian, who is a special favorite of the high king.

"Tell anyone who seems interested," Archambald continued importantly, "that they can come and see me, Master Archambald—Archambald Wolf's Bane, that is." He added hastily, "Of course, we'll have to get some sort of permission to lure them away from Andernach, but I rather think Lord Sebastian has considerable influence in this establishment. Ahem!"

"What sort of folk should we be lookin' for, Master Archambald, ah, Wolf's Bane?" Bardulf added impudently.

"Well, you know—we need every kind of person. You should look for farmers, freemen only; we can't be running off with Count Gonduin's serfs, now, can we? And you should see if there's a blacksmith or two who might be interested. We sorely need a good smithy. Such a man is sure of a high place at Fernshanz. And artisans of every sort—fullers, candle makers, iron mongers, carpenters, weavers, stone workers; why, even a priest," Archambald added, surprising himself with his own insight.

"Well, I reckon we wouldn't be able to hire no priest away from here. He surely wouldn't want to live in no burned-out Fernshanz fort after all this here." Bardulf waved his hand over the busy estate.

"Just do what you can, Bardulf. Spread the word that we're looking for men—and women, too, for that matter. Go down to the marketplace and see what you can stir up there. There may be folk coming off the river, looking for a place to start a new life. Tell 'em to come and find me if they're interested."

At that point, a footman from the manor house caught up with them to request Archambald's presence with Lady Adela in the courtyard.

The afternoon was interminable for Sebastian. Archambald was in high spirits and kept up an endless patter of talk while eating everything that came his way. Sister Herlindis turned out to be as good a teacher as Adela reported. She proved to be a genuine scholar and had read books and treatises that Sebastian had only heard about. She even gave him advice on how to improve his own reading ability and information about where to find the nearest monastery from which he might borrow readings.

Sister Herlindis was herself on loan from a well-regarded convent not too far from Fulda. Count Gonduin had made a generous contribution to the abbess in return for the nun's services as Adela's teacher. Meanwhile, Adela had been an apt and eager pupil. To Sebastian's surprise and chagrin, she could already read better and with more comprehension than he. Of course, she spent much of every day with Sister Herlindis.

At last, the long afternoon came to an end with a twilight supper. The horses were fed and put up, and Bardulf and Drogo had been taken to their little room in the stable. Sebastian and Archambald were given rooms in the guest residence across the courtyard from the main manor house. Adela herself showed them to their quarters, making sure to casually point out to Sebastian her own rooms as they passed by.

Arrangements were made to meet with Andernach's steward the next morning to confer about provisioning Fernshanz. Adela's forthright and confident manner concerning the management of Andernach made both young men feel their mission would bear fruit beyond their expectations.

The Andernach manor house sat on a rise facing the river just beyond the old Roman wall. Between the wall and the house were an orchard of various fruit trees and a large garden of vegetables and flowers next to the house. It was a stone building, with three large sets of rooms on the ground floor and ten smaller rooms for attendants and family guests on the floor above. Across from the spacious central courtyard behind the manor house was a complex of wooden buildings used primarily for important guests. The largest of the buildings was reserved exclusively for the king. Count Gonduin was a close friend and family member as well as a trusted advisor, and Charlemagne often traveled down river by barge to visit the lovely estate. He particularly liked to come for a few days during autumn to sample the new wine.

Because the king was in the habit of traveling with a large entourage of family members, clerical administrators, and friends, playing host to him was no light matter. The row of "king's quarter" houses on the courtyard included a separate kitchen house, a bakery, a storehouse and wine cellar, a public house where guests could meet in common, and a second large visitors' lodge almost matching the king's suite on the other side of the courtyard. Sebastian and Archambald were quartered in this second lodge, directly across the courtyard from Adela's rooms in the manor house.

Since Count Gonduin was away on campaign, the only guests at the manor were Sebastian, Archambald, and Sister Herlindis, whose quarters were on the second floor of the manor above those of Adela. The entire manor, including the animals, seemed to shut down as soon as darkness fell. Accustomed to taking the opportunity to sleep whenever it presented itself, Archambald was soon snoring.

Sebastian stationed himself at a window overlooking the courtyard. There were small guardhouses at both the eastern and western ends of the manor house, with two guards each during the night hours. While one guard stayed in each of the two guardhouses, a third patrolled the farm and artisan buildings and the fourth spent most of his time in the central courtyard. Even in the dark, Sebastian could make him out as he strolled slowly along the covered ambulatory framing the courtyard. As he waited for the guard in the courtyard to go to relieve himself or trade places at the guardhouse, Sebastian kept imagining and reimagining his impending tryst with Adela. There was no doubt she expected him to come, and once they were together it seemed clear what would happen. The prospect made his head pound and his blood run so hot he felt he must surely have a fever. Alternately, he contemplated the cold consequences of taking advantage of these tantalizing circumstances.

At last, the guard made his way out of the courtyard in the direction of the guardhouse. As quietly as possible, Sebastian slipped through the main door of the guesthouse and crossed the courtyard at a run. The stone manor house had three entrances, one for each set of rooms. Count Gonduin, when he was home, occupied the eastern wing and Adela the western one; the middle rooms had been for Count Gonduin's wife but had rarely been occupied since her death. Sebastian tried the latch of the door to Adela's rooms. It opened at once, and he was inside the small anteroom in an instant. A single candle was burning to give him light. Down a corridor between two sets of rooms, he could see another light coming through a partially opened door. Barely daring to breathe, he made his way to it.

Two candles gave light on either side of a low bed in the middle of the room. Adela sat in the bed against a bank of pillows, her arms hugging her knees against her body, her eyes wide as Sebastian slowly pushed open the door and slipped inside. Her thick hair was undone and fell loosely over her bare shoulders. She wore only a loose linen shift that hardly concealed her budding figure. Even in the low light, Sebastian could see the flush in her face and her wide eyes glistening with excitement.

"Come," Adela whispered, holding out her arms.

Sebastian stopped, his hand still on the door latch, holding his breath, mouth open, too paralyzed by the beguiling scene to move or even speak. Finally, his voice husky with pain, he muttered, "I cannot."

"Why? What's the matter?" Adela rose to her knees in the bed, still holding out her arms to him. "It's all right, Sebastian. It may be the only time we'll ever have together. It's all right—I love you. Come, sit here beside me and let me hold you."

Sebastian said raggedly, "No, I can't! I cannot hold you or even touch you. I should not even look at you like this, though I will never forget it. If I sat on the bed with you, I could not control myself, and I must!"

"For God's sake, why? Tell me. I must have at least something of you before my fortunes change forever. I don't understand. Don't you love me? I was sure you must . . ."

"I've never felt closer to anyone or wanted to be with anyone in my life so much as you."

"Then what is wrong? There is no one to disturb us. No one will ever need to know."

"But that's exactly the point, don't you see? You will know."

Sebastian knelt on the floor beside the bed, finally grasping her outstretched hands. "Listen. Since this morning I've had time to think, and I know now what we must do. You are my beloved. You are part of me. I know you well enough to realize what will happen if I make love to you now. For one thing, I know how close you are to your faith. I saw it every day at Worms. It was no false piety, like so many of the nobles in the high king's court. It was real. You are no ordinary woman, no middling soul. I saw how that soul soared during those long conversations we had at Worms. You told me that you even struggle with God—remember? You recounted the story of how Jacob wrestled with God and how much you felt akin to him. Isn't that so?"

Adela nodded, tears welling up in her eyes. Sebastian continued, "If I took you now, which I want to do with all my being, I would rob you of that relationship and of the peace it gives you. God knows you will need all the divine support you can get for the next part of your life."

"But I'm willing to forego even that peace—for you."

"I believe you. I can see you would give up everything, and that is a gift I will treasure all my life—however sweet and never given."

He reached out to her, and for a brief moment she fell into his arms. With a great effort, he let her go and fell back upon the floor. "No! I won't jeopardize you. It's not only your peace of mind, it's Konrad. He will also know."

"I don't care," said Adela balefully. "I hate him already. For him to know he is not the first is at least one blow I can strike against him."

"You must not!" Sebastian said in alarm. "You don't know Konrad. He is capable of anything—he might kill you. That you are 'a proper wife' who brings honor to his house is the one thing you have in your favor. It gives you a place above him. He will respect that. But if you betray him, you will lose that advantage, and you may even lose your life. He would at least be certain to hurt you greatly. I will not be the one who puts you in that peril."

"God help us," Adela moaned. "How can this happen? I know you are right. But, still, I long for you. I want you even more. I can't bear the thought of never being with you!"

"We cannot, Adela. I will not see you harmed even more. I have to go now while I still have the will. If I stay a moment longer . . . We will speak tomorrow. Pray for me now. And try to think how we might always be together somehow, even if not as we would wish. Remember, I will love you always." With that Sebastian slipped out of the door into the dark hallway, leaving Adela still kneeling on the bed, weeping and holding her arms out toward the door.

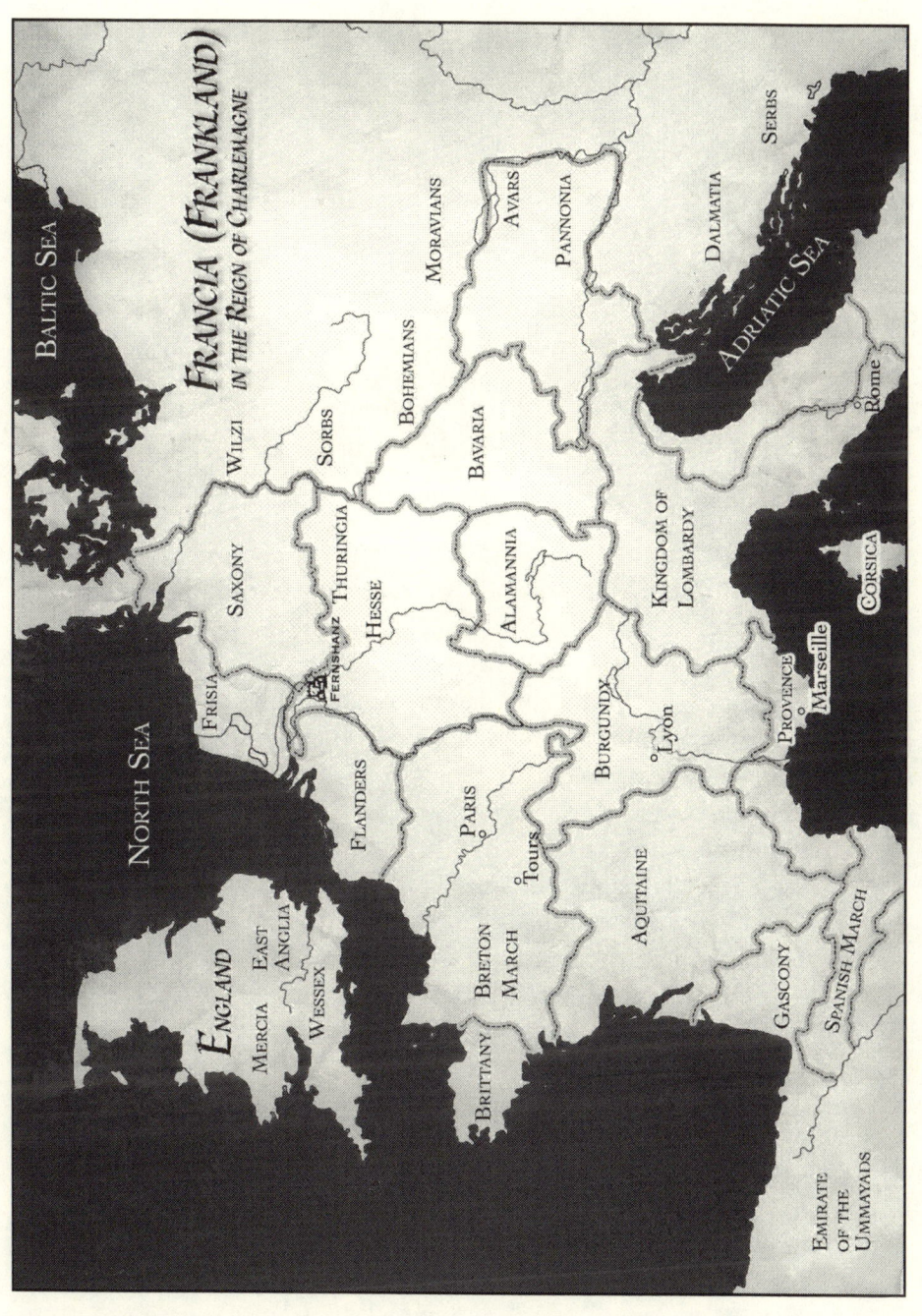

Chapter 19

The Pilgrimage

The Road to Tours, Late Autumn 772

As they set off on a fine day in late September after the small harvest was in, Heimdal took up his habit of reciting in Latin as he walked.

"*Messis quidem multa; operari autem pauci,*" he chanted as Fernshanz fell away in the background.

"Yes," Sebastian sighed in relief, "indeed the laborers were few, but the harvest was sufficient, thank God. At least there will be barley and oats to last through the winter, and the harvest of beans and peas in the new field was more than we could have hoped for. We'll see what happens next year when we try to plant wheat on it."

"*Ite; ecce ego mitto vos sicut agnos inter lupos,*" went on the blind man, with wry intent.

"Yes, indeed, you and I will certainly be sheep among wolves. Well, you were the one who said not to take any weapons," Sebastian observed ruefully, "so if we meet any wolves, animal or human, it'll be your fault, not mine."

"*Nolite portare sacculum, neque peran, neque calciamenta . . .*"

"Right," Sebastian groaned uneasily. "Take no money bag, no sack, no sandals. At least you agreed to wearing boots—it'll be winter before we know it—though I don't understand at all why they had to be such old boots and already so worn."

Unperturbed, the blind man retorted, "Sebastian, this journey will not be about safety—or comfort. You are the one who needed to be purged. You are the one who says he is sick with love, loss, and hate. You are the one who lamented to me that life no longer held any meaning for you. By the end of this trip, my lad—if there ever is any end and we do return to this place—you will find that this journey will have been about far more than any girl."

He blithely resumed chanting the verses from Matthew's Gospel, smiling broadly at how appropriate they seemed for the present moment.

Now that they were on the road and were so completely vulnerable, Sebastian trudged along in silence, glumly thinking how ridiculous it was to have undertaken such a foolishly impractical adventure. All he really wanted to do was go wherever the army was and find some way to kill Konrad. For weeks after the visit to Andernach, he had been sick with regret and longing for Adela. His moods alternated between fits of towering anger and disgusted lethargy. Even his body ached. He spent hours every day running the memories of her over and over in his head, desperately seeking a way to change their destiny. Finally, after a week of frustration, he had emerged from his room at the urging of Archambald and Liudolf and thrown himself into the task of preparing the small Fernshanz community for the winter. Still, he slept little and spoke only when necessary, numbing himself with hard work alongside the peasants from dawn to nightfall.

Their last few days at Andernach had truly been a kind of hell for him. He had seen Adela every day, almost all day, as she went about fulfilling every need Fernshanz might have. He couldn't sleep at night, knowing that Adela was in her bed only a few seconds away from him. He resorted to running furiously, pell-mell down the river road in the dark until he was exhausted and then plunging into the cold waters of the river, repeating this ritual over and over until it was almost dawn. More than once he was nearly carried away by the river's strong current.

He gave the Andernach night guards stern orders that they were to perform the changing of the guard in the courtyard and not at the guardhouse so that at no time would the courtyard be without eyes. If it were not so, he was sure he would succumb to the gnawing temptation to race across the few yards to Adela's bedroom.

Adela proved generous to a fault in providing for Fernshanz. Sebastian worried that her father would disown her once he returned and realized how much wealth she had heaped upon Sebastian and his people. A flotilla of boats had been filled with animals, grain, wool, and wine. She provided iron strips for plows and oxen for three teams, and she gave Sebastian two of her own mares for breeding, one of which was her personal mount. Sebastian had been embarrassed by her largesse. However, she refused to listen to him and continued to cram the boats with everything she could think of that he might possibly need, saying that the king had required it and that Sebastian must have his full share of the Irminsul treasure.

Adela had even provided the Fernshanz community with a blacksmith, a carpenter, a cooper, a potter, a brewer, and a priest. All of them were also farmers and all save the priest came with their families. There were nearly two score, all of whom were freemen. Sebastian took pains to explain to them the precarious situation at Fernshanz, but those who came were swayed by the promise of good land and a fresh start.

The priest, Father Pippin, had not been long at Andernach and had only been a priest for three years. Most of that time he had spent as a wandering mendicant. He had washed up on the prosperous shores of Andernach only when his health had failed and he had been weakened almost to the point of death from dysentery and starvation. Adela had heard about him and rescued him from the servants' quarters. She took a personal interest in the quiet, humble cleric and gradually came to enjoy long conversations with him as he recovered.

Father Pippin was a slight mouse of a man, emaciated and a bit hunched over, with limp strands of thinning hair hanging down over his ears and forehead. He never raised his eyes while walking from place to place and seemed almost invisible when entering a room, so unassuming and unattractive was his physical appearance. Most of the people he met during the course of a day paid him no notice.

Adela, however, discovered that Father Pippin was not only an intelligent, learned man but was almost mystically devout. After a time she began to think of him as the most Christ-like person she had ever met. For one thing, he refused to subscribe to the common notion of hell that plagued the peasant mind so doggedly, labeling it to intelligent intimates like Adela as merely a state of mind. On the other hand, he was recklessly unselfish. He cared nothing at all for himself, bending his efforts to the needs of whomever he met, whether man or woman, peasant or lord. He was not physically able to help many, being small and weak in stature. He tried anyway, lending a hand without comment to help with the harvest or to load a cart, just as if he were a peasant himself, until he was exhausted. Then he would collapse and need others to come and care for him.

Adela found that he was best at helping people think through their problems. He was good at listening, and he lent an ear as long as anyone wished to pour out their troubles to him. He then went away and prayed, returning the next day to provide a precise diagnosis of the distressed person's situation and suggest a way out of the difficulty. Adela found his intuition almost magical.

It was thus a painful sacrifice for Adela to suggest that he relocate to Fernshanz. It wasn't that Andernach had any scarcity of priests or that Father Pippin had a high place among the several clergymen there. He did not. But Adela had come to regard him as her personal chaplain. She was very sad to see him go, but the possibility that he would become for Sebastian the close friend and confidant that he had been for her was consoling. And so he had proved to be, in a number of momentous ways.

Leaving Adela to her fate with Konrad had been excruciating for Sebastian, and he might have gone mad thinking about it if not for Father Pippin. The little priest had known Adela so well by the time he left with Sebastian that he could speak as though he knew her thoughts.

One night on the trip home to Fernshanz, Sebastian fell into despair. He raged and shouted furiously at Archambald and the others as they tried to set up a camp for the night. In a fever, he was on the point of saddling Joyeuse and racing back to Adela's side, whatever the consequences. Calmly and without looking at Sebastian or saying a word, Father Pippin came and laid his hand on Sebastian's as the lad fumbled with the saddle straps. He then gently took the horse's bridle and gave it over to Archambald, who was waiting timidly in the shadows. Then he led Sebastian to a place by the fire and sat down quietly.

At last, haltingly and wretchedly, Sebastian unburdened himself to the priest, including all the details of what had happened at Andernach. Father Pippin merely listened, nodding his head and encouraging the tortured youth to talk himself out. At length, when Sebastian had run out of words and sat holding his head in his hands, the priest began to clarify to Sebastian exactly what both he and Adela had accomplished by their self-denial.

"It is true, Sebastian," he explained, "that I do not personally know about love between a man and a woman. But I know this about love: it cannot be separated from sacrifice. There is a cost to love of any sort, if it is truly love and not self-gratification. For love, if it is true, is concentrated on the beloved. If it were not so, our good Lord would not have offered his son to us."

Uncharacteristically, he looked directly into Sebastian's eyes and continued in a low voice, "The same is true, I think, of the love between a man and a woman. Think about it; you refused to succumb to your desire for Adela to save her from dishonor, and she did the same to save you from danger. There was no other way. Be happy that she loves you to that extent. You could find no relationship between a man and a woman nobler than that.

"Be at peace, then," he went on. "And if you cannot be at peace, then go on a pilgrimage. Go all the way to Tours in western Francia, to the shrine of Saint Martin. After all, he is the patron saint of the Franks. All of us should go there at least once in our lives. Let the hunger and hardship of a long and arduous journey teach you. Go on foot and without much means. Pray. Ask God to give you peace. By the end of such a journey, it will become clear to you exactly what you and Adela have done for each other, and you will purge yourself of your sins."

"But, Father," Sebastian protested, sweating with emotion and struggling to control his restless body. "I have committed no sin with Adela, and now we can never be together. I cannot bear it. The loss of her has made me empty like a tomb inside, except for one thing: this awful hate—this crazed anger—I feel toward Konrad. It's become my only reason to live. I dream of killing him with my bare hands; I want to rip his evil heart out. I owe him already for my father's death, and now he is robbing me of one who is even dearer."

"And that is precisely why it is imperative that you go, Sebastian," the priest exclaimed, grasping the tormented youth by the shoulders. "Not because of what you have done, but because of what you want to do and may eventually do if you don't change what you feel so strongly—if you don't find a way to give up this murderous rage in your heart. You will suffer on this journey—I already foresee that. But I see, too, that you *must* suffer if you are finally to rid yourself of this poison living inside of you."

That is how Sebastian happened to be on the road with Heimdal at the end of the summer. He would have preferred to have Father Pippin as his pilgrimage partner because it was the diminutive priest who had convinced him that on this pilgrimage God would intervene, and he would find a way to cleanse his soul of its bitterness and discontent.

Unfortunately, Pippin was frail and almost always in ill health. Heimdal, on the other hand, was spoiling to go. As soon as the blind man had exhausted the possibilities of a place, he was ready to move on, and in spite of his handicap, he loved nothing more than the thrill of setting out on an adventure and living entirely by his wits. Sebastian's pilgrimage was no more formidable than many he had already undertaken, under the same dangerous circumstances and with similar poor resources.

"Go in peace—no, go and *find* peace," Pippin had said as Sebastian and Heimdal set out on the road. Following tradition, he blessed them as pilgrims and said, "Have faith and God will provide for you and protect you."

After a month or so on the road, plagued by blisters and aching legs, Sebastian could not help feeling it was reason more than faith that had sustained them thus far. Heimdal was far more about logic than he was about morality or religion. Unlike everyone else around him in this age of brooding fatalism and superstition, he believed in cause and effect. That was the gospel he preached to Sebastian constantly as they walked the seemingly endless road together.

"Think, Sebastian," Heimdal would say, "does the cow sicken and die because God is punishing its peasant owner for a dalliance in the bushes with one of the village girls? Or does the cow suffer from having eaten poisonous weeds? Does the horse go lame because God is punishing the horse for some reason? Is the horse guilty of sin? Or is he lame because he has been ridden too long over a rocky road?"

Heimdal went on, "Men and women are simply animals, like the cow and the horse. Bad things happen to them because of what *they* do, not because of what God does. If a young lad seduces his master's wife and the master discovers it and kills both the wife and the lad, it's not so much God's vengeance as the master's, *nicht wahr?*"

"But don't you believe in the holy commandments given to us through Moses, Heimdal? Why else would God give them to us and tell us to live by them?"

"Perhaps, my good young man, God wanted to warn us of the consequences of selfish acts and give us the chance to think over some sensible rules before acting," was Heimdal's casual answer. "It may be no more complicated than that, Sebastian. God knows we are animals but he has given us the power to choose. That makes us much higher than the animals and even a bit like God himself."

"Heimdal!" Sebastian exclaimed in shock. "Don't blaspheme."

"Well, you can think what you like, but ask yourself why God gave you the power to think, which the animals do not have, and why the power to choose is at once the most interesting thing about us and yet the most vexing. Thinking and choosing is what makes us only a little less than the gods. It's a great pity and such a waste that we do so little thinking and let others do our choosing for us."

Caked with dust and his throat swelling for want of water, Sebastian mechanically moved down the rutted track toward the next village. He and Heimdal had been on the road already many weeks, and they were now in strange territory. Sebastian could not even understand the language being spoken in the villages through which he passed. This was the land of the West Franks, who had been so long in the old Roman part of Frankland that they had adopted many of the customs and much of the Gallo-Roman way of speaking. They dressed differently from the East Franks and lived a life that seemed to Sebastian easier and less intense.

"Take no money or other valuables," Father Pippin had said in that fateful conversation on the way home to Andernach. "Above all, take no weapons." At the outset Sebastian had been beset by his vulnerability, but Heimdal merely said, "Relax. Imagine yourself to be a brainless peasant. Beg, as I do. Do not speak if we are confronted. You don't sound like a peasant. Act the simpleton. I will find a way to get us out of trouble."

Heimdal was as good as his word. Sebastian became the mute, simple-minded companion to Heimdal, the blind beggar. They survived by begging and occasionally working for anyone along the road who seemed to need assistance or a little muscle power. Sebastian squelched his impulse to take charge of any situation, realizing that he had little advantage in such circumstances and was better off pretending to be a harmless idiot.

Crossing the Rhine at Cologne, they planned to walk west to Aachen and south to Rheims and Paris. They identified themselves as pilgrims on the road by wearing long, coarse tunics and monkish cloaks. They carried no extra clothing or tools, not even a bread knife. Heimdal explained that the brigands they were bound to meet would relieve them of anything besides the wooden staves they used to pick their way over the rough terrain.

They often traveled in groups. When possible, they stayed at hospices specifically established for pilgrims at monasteries, convents, and rich villas. However, these hospices were few and far apart, so they passed most of their nights in the open fields and forests. As colder weather loomed, they threw themselves on the mercy of farmers in villages along the route, mostly poor people who took them in despite their own poverty. Whenever they came to a town, Heimdal took time to beg at the gates or at churches built on the sites of sacred graves. When no town could be reached, Heimdal begged at the crossroads of a village while Sebastian foraged.

Sebastian found he had little talent as a beggar; he had no knack for chanting or for engaging passersby with friendly banter, as Heimdal did. He could only try to stare vacantly and hold out his palms, but he looked too fit and healthy to be a beggar in spite of poor rations and continuous walking. He contented himself with gathering wood, looking for fallen grain in the fields, and seeking a shelter where the two of them might sleep. Eager for anything at all to do, he worked with a will whenever Heimdal could find someone who was willing to pay for labor with food or lodging. It took awhile, but he finally became used to not saying a word from one end of the long day to the other.

The exception to the ban on speech for Sebastian was the occasional day when the two traveled alone. On such days, Heimdal took advantage of Sebastian's eagerness to talk to impart his unorthodox ideas and unconventional wisdom.

"Take, for example, your obsession with training and fighting," Heimdal began without preamble during one morning's hike. "You've told me you drive yourself unmercifully because you hate to lose in the silly mock combats you engage in with the other young men. You never wish to lose a bout, and that, presumably, will help you in a real fight. But did you ever consider that somewhere out there lurks a man who is your better and that if you meet him, he may kill you if he can?"

"I cannot help that, Heimdal," Sebastian replied. "You are right, of course; there may always be someone better. But I must believe that I will never meet him and that I am the best in any contest, no matter what. And I must train to make it so. That way I will improve my chances of survival."

"Amen, amen, I say to you again, my boy, if you fight, there is always a chance you will lose, but if you don't fight, there is no chance you will lose, is there?"

"Now what in blazes does that mean, Heimdal?" Sebastian asked irritably. "I must fight if I am called to do so. It is what a warrior does. I cannot simply choose to tell the king or my sword brothers that today is just not a good day for a fight."

"I only mean to say, Sebastian, that perhaps you should seek ways to avoid fighting unless you must. That also increases your chances of survival, does it not? Find other ways to get what you want without fighting. Don't you think that's a much more Christian approach?" he added teasingly.

Sebastian trudged along in silence for a while, thinking about what Heimdal had said. Eventually he returned to the argument. "Give me an example of what you are talking about, Heimdal."

"Well, what about the siege at Adalgray?" Heimdal suggested.

"What? We had to fight at Adalgray. There was no choice," Sebastian exclaimed heatedly. "They attacked us."

"Only after Attalus refused to parley."

"But he had to say what he did. We couldn't just give in to them!"

"Perhaps, but there might have been a third way. Listen, Sebastian, it might be best to parley as long as possible, especially if you are the underdog. Possibly, something will turn up. If you had delayed long enough, Athaulf might have come back, or you might have thought of something else if you had time."

"In this case, my cousin Konrad never would have stood for it."

"True enough. But at least you can remember the lesson, which is never fight unless you must, and fight only as long as you must. If you can remember that, you may indeed live a long time and help your people avoid disaster."

After awhile Heimdal began again, "Sebastian, you may not wish to consider it, but you also should learn how to deal with defeat. When you've been beaten or you are sure that you will be because of numbers or circumstances, you must learn to negotiate with honor. It is foolish to throw your life away out of pride."

"How could I do that, Heimdal? It would be dishonorable and cowardly."

"Not necessarily, Sebastian—not if your enemy is reasonable and is willing to give you terms. He may wish to avoid the cost of defeating you completely, and you can get away with your skin while keeping your honor.

"But I must say," Heimdal continued on a different track, "though I may seem to contradict myself, some things are worth fighting for even if there is a good chance you will lose."

"What things, Heimdal" Sebastian asked.

"Well, what do you value? What would you fight for if it were only up to you? What do you think is worth dying for?"

Sebastian replied without hesitation, "Home, family, those I love, the king's decree."

"Good, Sebastian. Perhaps later you will think of other things. But let's consider what you said. I agree with you about home and family, those you love, and your friends. Strangely enough, you may find that you would die most willingly for those who fight beside you. But what about the king's decree?"

"What of it?"

"Do you believe the king is always right? What if the king is wrong? Would you still fight?"

"I must."

"Even if what the king wants is not what you believe God wants?"

"Doesn't the king always know what God wants?"

"Does he?"

"You're talking treason, Heimdal."

"Sebastian, there is a very fine line between right and wrong. The angel of darkness often appears disguised as the angel of light.

Discerning what is right and what is wrong is probably the most difficult thing you will ever have to do in this life. People like Konrad have no problem with that. He gives it no thought at all. He does whatever he wants or whatever the king says he must do. He loses no sleep choosing between right and wrong."

The blind man stopped and tugged at Sebastian's cloak. "But you, my friend, you will be a man of true integrity. Your choices will be hard. All I can tell you is that in the end, you must do what you believe is right. The trouble is that sometimes what you believe is right may turn out to be utterly wrong. Still, you must live with yourself, even though the price you pay for being wrong is high. You will find that our failures have much to teach us if we are willing to acknowledge them and not blame others for them."

After that, Heimdal said not a word for the rest of the day, leaving Sebastian to plod on in the face of an increasingly cold wind from the north, his mind churning with Heimdal's uncomfortable assertions.

Chapter 20

Wayfarers

Their route took them across the Rhine at Cologne and then to the king's villa at Aachen, where they stayed in a pilgrim's hostel. The days were golden and mild, the best weather of the year but the last of the good days. After the harvest there was a spirit of goodwill and generosity in the villages through which they passed. Heimdal begged and Sebastian fetched and carried. They found it easy to support themselves, and they often enjoyed pleasant circumstances. Sebastian began to learn about the peasants among whom they lived and traveled. Most of them took Sebastian for what he seemed to be, an unfortunate simpleton who had never learned to speak. For the most part, they treated him indifferently but not unkindly.

Their fellow travelers were mostly peasants. A few were making a real pilgrimage, but most had been uprooted by some kind of misfortune. They traveled in groups for safety and assumed the identity of pilgrims. Some who had been freemen had lost their crops or had not been able to pay their rents, and rather than become serfs, they had taken to the road. Some men hated their lords or had left their land rather than go into the army. These men had to travel far to find anonymity. Others were serfs or slaves who were escaping their bondage. They fled into the forest at the sound of horses' hooves. Some traveled with small families—never more than one or two children who could walk on their own. The road took its toll on infants.

They met one such family while negotiating the crossing of the Rhine. Sebastian had worked all day at Lippeham, loading a boat with harvest goods for the right to sit on it as it traveled upriver to Cologne. A family of four had arrived late on the second day and was refused passage. The father was desperate to cross the river, and he approached Heimdal to persuade him to intercede with the boat captain for their passage.

"Good and generous blind man," the peasant began earnestly, "I see that ye are on good terms with the boat captain and crew. They love yer singin' and yer stories. Who would not? Ye are most wondrous cheery to listen to. Will ye not help a poor family get a crossin'?"

"Why would I want to, my good man?" Heimdal countered casually. "What might be in it for me?"

"We mus' get t'other side before another day. If ye'll only help us do that, me family and me'll be beholden to ye. We'll cast our lot with ye. I see that ye're alone except for that young idiot. We'll help and guide ye."

"Ahem," Heimdal sputtered. "My man Sebastian may be cleverer than you think. At least he is strong and does what I ask of him."

"Can he cook, then? Is he good at gatherin' grain and cabbages at night from the fields and kitchen gardens we pass? My son can do that. And my wife and daughter'll cook for ye when there's food. We can help ye in hard times if it should come to that."

Heimdal considered the proposal and decided with Sebastian that it was worth giving the man a chance. He had only to promise the boat captain to sing and tell stories all the way to Cologne, which he would have done anyway for free.

Their new traveling companions were a simple lot but had an air of mystery about them. The man had the strange name of "Ubrigens," and he would not say exactly from whence he had come. "Somewhere in Frisia," he had muttered. Sebastian immediately suspected he must be a runaway serf. He seemed honest enough, but somewhat secretive and anxious. His wife, Bova, was a sturdy peasant with bright blond hair and a florid face, who displayed a sharp disposition and intimidating muscles. She obviously knew how to manipulate her husband, though she kept quiet around others because of her accent, which was strange among the Franks.

The son, Lutz, was a quiet, skinny lad of thirteen or so who did his parents' bidding cheerfully enough but was far happier rummaging about in the nearby woods. He seemed to scour the forest floor and had an uncanny knack for finding herbs for making tea along with various roots and nuts. He also could slip into a peasant's vegetable garden at night without so much as raising a hair on the back of the family dog.

Gersvind, the daughter, was little more than twelve but already a striking beauty, with the thick golden blond hair of her mother and the slender, willowy body of her father and brother. She minded her father carefully and did not seem to let her mother's bullying spoil her serene and sunny disposition. She worshipped her brother and was always tousling his towhead or challenging him to wrestle. She was as playful as he was somber.

The road west from the Rhine led through Aachen, or Aix, as some of the western Franks called it. It was a rather unremarkable town of only a few hundred souls, but it included a royal estate. It was said that the king was partial to it because of the sulphur springs found there. Sebastian took advantage of their brief stay in the small pilgrims' hospice to have a swim in the warm pools, which were outside and unguarded when the king was not in residence. In the cold morning air, steam rose from the springs as Sebastian stripped off his monk's garments and dove in head first.

He found that the springs were not really hot, as some people claimed, but if one splashed about vigorously it was exhilarating. Attalus had taught Sebastian to swim almost before he could ride, and Sebastian found the occasion bracing and refreshing in spite of the cold.

As he climbed out of the pool, he began to dress quickly in the brisk air and tangled his wet body in his rough linen shirt. A burst of giggling sounded from the bushes surrounding the pool. Sebastian continued to dress calmly, as if he had not heard the outburst, but as soon as he had himself covered, he raced for the bushes and caught Lutz and Gersvind trying frantically to make an escape. He cut them off and turned them back toward the pool. He caught up with one after the other, picked them up, and made as if to toss them spinning into the water but relented at the last second, sending them shrieking and laughing round and round the pool. At last, exhausted, they sat on the edge of the water and dabbled their hands and feet in it but cringed at the thought of having a bathe in the tepid water when Sebastian playfully mimed the suggestion.

The road west from Aachen led to the old Roman town of Lidge and then southwest through the thick forests of the Ardennes region. Heimdal had not wanted to take this route, but their departure from Fernshanz had been so late that now the winds of November were threatening snow and they needed to get down to such larger towns in the southwest as Rheims and Paris, where they would have a better chance of finding food and protection.

By this time, their little band had swelled to almost twenty souls who were all anxious to get through the brooding forest as quickly as possible. A few men knew the way and the route was not particularly difficult, only depressing in the gloom and gathering cold. Sebastian, however, was impressed and excited by the signs of animals he saw everywhere along the road. He envied the lord who had the hunting rights to this vast larder. Wild boar and red deer tracks abounded, as well as those of bear and wolf.

After several days on the road through the forest, the pilgrims suddenly encountered a barrier across the road and a sullen band of men with cudgels, staffs, and a few bows standing athwart the path. Remembering his first encounter with outlaws, Sebastian shifted the long staff in his own hands and prepared to fight. Heimdal soon discerned the crisis and held on to Sebastian's arms.

"Do not, Sebastian," he hissed, feeling the tension in the young man's arms. "Let us see what this is. We may be able to disarm the situation. Remember, there might be a third way."

Holding on to Sebastian's arm, Heimdal made his way to the front of the pilgrim group and listened as the situation unfolded.

The outlaw leader, a short, stout man with a grim visage and more bluster than menace, began to speak hesitantly to the group in an incongruously high voice.

"I'm Boldering, leader of these men here. This here is our road. Ye has to pay ter use it, that's all. It'll cost ye—money or food, one."

Although they bristled and brandished their crude weapons, it was clear that Boldering and most of the men with him were not real brigands, only poor farmers on the move and down on their luck, like so many in Sebastian's own group.

"By whose authority do you claim these woods, fellow?" Heimdal asserted, taking the lead. "I imagine the lord of this forest might object to having his road blocked by the likes of you."

Boldering stepped forward, flaunting his staff before him. "As far as I knows, there ain't no lord in this place, on'y us. We be the lords of this here forest. And our 'awthawruty' is these here clubs." He grinned back at his men, who agreed with rough laughter.

"Well, as you can see, we are pilgrims, my good man," said Heimdal. "And if you know anything of your Church and the faith that stands behind her, you will know that those who molest pilgrims are doomed from the moment they raise their hands against them to the everlasting fires of hell and the tormenting damnation of the devil himself!"

Boldering fell back a few paces, looking aghast. Some of his men muttered nervously. Gathering his courage, he stepped forward again. "Well, we mean ye no harm, ye pilgrims. But this here woods is where we lives, and we must earn our livin' somehow so's we can eat. So we have set a tax upon the road, just as the lords themselves do. So it follows that you must pay somethin' in order to pass," he finished in a righteous tone.

It was clear that the small group of aspiring brigand-landlords would stand by their new tax law and continue to obstruct the road. Heimdal held up his hand. "We must deliberate," he announced in a dignified voice. "We shall fall back a bit and decide whether your terms must be honored or not. In the meantime, do not forget my warning, Boldering. If you cause us harm without justification, you will burn for it." With that, he led the small group back a hundred paces or so and settled them on the side of the road. He called Sebastian a short way into the woods beyond the group's hearing.

As soon as they were alone, Sebastian whispered, "I can take them, Heimdal. They're only a bunch of farmers. They'll run as soon as I give them a few bumps on their noggins."

"Shh, Sebastian, have you learned nothing? There may be no need to fight. We may be able to use these would-be brigands to our advantage. We desperately need a break from these endless woods, and it would be a blessing if we could find a comforting fire and a safe place to sleep for a day or two.

"Listen," he continued, "I have a plan. You've been telling me for the last several days that the forest is full of big game, isn't that so?"

"Most assuredly, Heimdal; there are tracks everywhere. We crossed red deer spoor only a league or so back. What of it?"

"Did you see a bow among those men there that might be serviceable?"

"Well, now that you mention it, Heimdal, I did look carefully at their weapons. Their staffs are little more than hacked down branches, and the bows they have are clumsy and poorly made, better for shooting hares than men."

"What about a red deer? Could you shoot one, if they lent you a bow?"

Sebastian took a deep breath. "Now I see what you're up to, old fox. Yes, perhaps, if I could get close enough. But how will you get that Boldering fellow to let us have a bow?"

"Leave it to me. Risk is a compelling consequence of hunger. We will see when last they ate."

As it turned out, the pathetic band had experienced few paying customers on their road of late, the year was far along toward winter, and the weather was threatening. Heimdal was at pains to convince them that the pilgrims had no money at all and very little else to offer, barely enough food for a few more days.

"But," Heimdal hastened to assuage their grumbling disinclination to believe him, "there is one great asset among this group of simple wayfarers, a great hunter, who from a babe was deprived by God of his wits but gifted in exchange with supernatural knowledge of the forest and its denizens and a superb ability to shoot a bow—any bow. He can bring down the charging boar or fell the hind in full gallop at two hundred paces," he hastened to add, clearing his throat at the end.

Sebastian shifted uneasily on his feet as everyone's eyes fell upon him. He knew full well that no bow among the farmers was likely to be capable of accuracy beyond a few meters. He'd be lucky to find one with enough power to penetrate the thick hide of a red deer at any distance. But the die was cast. The peasants deliberated and finally brought forth a bow, without arrows. As Sebastian tested its pull and examined the wood for cracks and the bow sinews for weakness, every pair of eyes in both groups was upon him. Finally, he held up the bow and gestured for an arrow. The bandit leader was reluctant.

"How do we know he won't turn the bow ag'in us?" he demanded snappishly.

Heimdal reassured him. "Have two of your men stand behind him as he shoots. If he turns a hair in either direction, your men can knock him senseless. All right?"

Boldering agreed. Sebastian walked a pace or two away from the group, with the two guards behind him, and pointed toward a tree a few strides off the track. He fitted the arrow, raised the bow, and shot quickly. They gaped in surprise as the arrow quivered in the middle of the tree. Sebastian retrieved it and shot again several times, each time from a longer distance. Finally, he nodded to Boldering and handed the bow back to its owner.

There was humming in both groups as everyone began to grasp what might be possible. Finally, Boldering emerged from his band and approached Heimdal.

"Well, blind man, if he shoots a deer like he shoots a tree, we could all be eatin' tonight. I'll tell ye what, if he will go huntin' with my two stout men and their staves, we'll lend him our bow. And if he brings back some meat, we'll all have sommit', share and share alike. Agreed? But if he but try anythin' at all of a crooked nature, my men'll brain him good."

"My good man Boldering, our Sebastian is completely incapable of dishonesty—you will see. Let them go at once, and the sooner we will all eat. Meanwhile, you and your men might best be building a great fire to accommodate the carcass."

It was a bold venture on Heimdal's part, but he had known Sebastian from his birth and knew him to be a clever, instinctive hunter and a dead shot with any decent bow. It was just a matter of whether the bow was heavy enough and whether Sebastian could hunt with two clubfooted peasants trailing behind him.

As it happened, they quickly came upon the tracks of the herd of red deer Sebastian had noted an hour before. They led along a trail parallel to a creek, with heavy timber on one side and a meadow on a gentle hill on the other. Sebastian could see that the light brush on the edges of the meadow would provide perfect bedding grounds for the big deer once they emerged from the timber at twilight. He bent down, plucked a handful of dry grass, and threw it up high into the air. The wind blew the grass back into his face, an essential factor if he were to have a chance of getting a shot.

The problem was that the meadow was on a hill. When the deer emerged from the woods to eat, they could just as easily emerge onto the far side of the hill or so far away from him that no shot with this bow would be possible. He could stalk them but not with his two clumsy guards. He had to find a way to move the animals to him.

The day was getting away from them and Sebastian had to make a decision. He decided under the circumstances that it was better to drop his mute idiot guise and trust that he and Heimdal could move away from this group later when they emerged from the wilderness.

He turned from the meadow and put a hand on the shoulder of both of them. "My good men, listen to me now."

They jumped back as if they had been struck a blow. "No, no," Sebastian said soothingly. "It's all right. I'm not a mute nor have I ever been. It's just a way of becoming an ordinary pilgrim on the road. In truth, I am a lord and have my own land beyond the Rhine. But I'm making a pilgrimage for my sins and I want to remain unknown. Can you understand this?"

They nodded dumbly but still held back in amazement at this unsettling turn of events. "Listen to me, friends. We can have meat tonight, for sure. There are signs of *rotwild* everywhere. But you must help me. This bow will not shoot far, and the deer will not come to us unless we drive them. Here is my plan. We must cut evergreen boughs and build a blind here. The wind is blowing toward us. When it's twilight we'll wait to see on which side of the meadow the deer emerge. They're certain to do so for there's good grass here. Then one of you—you, Bertram, must go around the hill through the wood and come out on the far side of the hill behind the animals. Then you must walk slowly over the hill and down toward the deer, being careful not to alarm them. It's possible you won't even see them, but they will certainly smell you and if we're lucky they'll move straight down this path toward us, because they use it often. You, Fredigis, will stay with me to perform your duty. I promise you, on my honor as a king's warrior, I won't betray you. Are you agreed?"

After shuffling their feet and looking furtively at each other, Bertram finally spoke. "Do ye swear on yer mother's life ye won't betray us?"

"I cannot, Bertram, for that blessed lady is dead. But I'll swear on the life of my beloved, whom I care for more than anyone else in the world."

"What be her name, then?"

"It is Adela, and she is a great lady. I swear on her life that I won't betray you."

With that they agreed and immediately began to help Sebastian cut boughs and form a rough blind. Sebastian found three trees close together in a triangle on the edge of the meadow, near at hand to the deer trail. He cut long saplings and braced them parallel to the ground between the branches. He then cut evergreen boughs and draped them over the crossed saplings, contriving in a short time a crude but effective blind. Finally, Sebastian cut small holes through the branches to see through and a slightly larger, square hole through which to shoot.

When it was twilight, the big red deer appeared almost magically on the edge of the forest, a herd of fifteen cows with one old bull. They were just suddenly there, as if they had not even moved. Sebastian quickly signaled Bertram to slip out of the blind and crawl quietly on his belly until he was out of sight and sound. He then would make his way in a circuitous route through the woods and come out on the far side of the hill. There he would wait a few moments until there was no sound and then walk slowly over the hill to the meadow where the herd grazed.

Meanwhile Fredigis, who was a man of little nerve, was so excited by the spectacle of a large deer herd that he could scarcely sit still in the little blind. Sebastian heard him shuffling his feet and snuffing through his nose. He turned to him, gripping both his shoulders.

"Fredigis, you mustn't move about or make a sound. Not at all! You must imagine yourself to be a stone. You're a stone, do you hear? Close your eyes and think of yourself as a big grey stone that never moves. That's your job, not to move at all. Do you understand?" Sebastian tightened his grip on the man's shoulders until he winced.

"I will not move," was the meek reply. "I am a stone."

The herd gradually moved onto the hill and began to graze. Suddenly, the head of the bull went up and he gave a loud snort. Led by a large cow, the herd began moving downhill toward the end of the meadow where Sebastian waited. At first, they moved slowly as they began to get a faint whiff of the human approaching on the other side of the hill. As his scent grew stronger, the herd began to move more purposefully toward the path, the big bull on the far side snorting and urging them along.

At last the herd reached the creek trail and began to trot toward Sebastian. He waited, remembering the first lessons Attalus had ever taught him about shooting.

"Take a deep breath before the shot, let out half of it, and hold. Release the bowstring as imperceptibly as possible," Attalus had cautioned over and over. "Try not to know when your fingers will let go. When the arrow is released, follow through with your bow hand forward and your drawing hand rearward. Follow the shot with your eyes. Lean into it. Practice this over and over, until following through becomes instinctive."

As it turned out, the shot was easy; the herd moved steadily toward the blind and never suspected a predator until the lead cow crumpled in the middle of the path, the arrow through her heart.

There was a wonderful feast that night in the camp of the erstwhile brigands, but Sebastian was uncloaked in his simpleton's disguise. Ironically, instead of resenting the deception, the other travelers began to regard him almost as a mystical hero who was to be much admired in the moment but quite distinctly from a distance. Lutz and Gersvind crept up behind him to hear him talk, now that he had broken his silence, and every now and then Gersvind reached out a small hand to touch his arm.

Chapter 21

The Plague

Paris and Tours, Winter 772-773

Sebastian managed to provide the little band of pilgrims with one more feast of red deer meat before they left the forest. Borrowing the same bow from Fredigis and Bertram, who, along with their leader, Boldering, had decided to throw in their lot with the pilgrims, Sebastian stalked a herd that crossed their path purely by accident as they set out early in the morning. This time he went alone, keeping carefully at a distance from the herd until it began to graze by the side of a stream. Hidden in a stand of low brush close to the stream, he waited an hour while the herd grazed peacefully. At last, a young cow wandered back toward his hiding place. Rising slowly while her head was down, he made the shot when she looked up toward him. According to Frankish custom, he knelt by the side of the fallen animal and said a prayer of thanksgiving. He then dipped a sprig of evergreen in her blood and stuck it through a small hole in his hat. He would wear it until every part of the big deer had been completely consumed.

The road from the Ardennes led to Rheims, where Frankish kings had been anointed since the days of Clovis. Heimdal was pleased with the trip thus far.

"This has been too easy," he crowed, when they struck the road to Rheims. "We've had reasonable weather and plenty to eat thanks to you, O Great Huntsman, though I shudder to think what the lord who owns that part of the Ardennes woods would say if he discovered you poaching his game."

"It is not wrong to take food if one is starving, Heimdal. You said so yourself," Sebastian countered sanctimoniously.

"Yes," Heimdal agreed with a grin, "but were we starving or just being expedient, my good young apologist?"

He continued jauntily, "And now it appears we have almost a whole village to walk along with us. Ubrigens and his family have turned out to be a treasure. It's almost like having your personal serfs back in Fernshanz. If I'm hungry, I send off Lutz to steal a cabbage for me from a kitchen garden. If I want my tunic washed, Bova will do it, with only a little complaining. And Ubrigens himself is a jack of all trades; he can build anything, even a cart from the wood of a dead tree. And he's a fair hand at cooking, I'll attest. He makes everything taste better with just forest herbs and roots. It's odd that he's the one who usually cooks and not Bova. By the way, my boy, I think that woman's a Saxon."

"What?" Sebastian exclaimed. "What makes you say so?"

"Well, listen to her. Does any Frank you know talk like she does, with all that spitting and snarling? She doesn't talk much, but whenever she does, she can't say a single word correctly. And didn't you tell me she has a mass of yellow hair? I believe, my lad, Ubrigens is hiding a refugee of some sort."

There was no particular reason the score and more of pilgrims clung to Heimdal and Sebastian; they simply felt more secure with them, and they had confidence in Heimdal's resourcefulness and glib tongue. They also admired Sebastian's healthy good looks and his quiet, serious demeanor.

For his part, Sebastian became more and more comfortable with the peasants and even came to trust them a bit, although not unconditionally. Most of them were innately self-oriented, having been at the brink of starvation or some other disaster too many times. Although they seemed loyal and honest, many of them were actually quite devious and clever. When they camped each evening, everyone pitched in to make rude shelters and prepare the fire pit, but they would fight in a heartbeat for a scrap of food or a sleeping place by the fire at night. They were loath to share their meager resources, even when they saw that Sebastian did so regularly. They laughed and joked together and ate and drank like boon companions whenever there was plenty, but they always held something back and truly trusted only their immediate family. Only Ubrigens's family was completely open with Sebastian. They had come to regard him as their patron and champion.

When the group finally arrived in Rheims, everyone wanted to visit the cathedral to see the Holy Ampulla, the "oil of the sacred phial," which was said to have been brought to the city by the Holy Spirit in the form of a white dove. In the turbulent days of King Clovis, it had been used to crown the king and give him legitimacy, and since then many future Frankish kings were anointed with the sacred chrism. Heimdal immediately set himself up to beg at the church where Clovis had been crowned while Sebastian took the rest of the faux pilgrims, including Ubrigens's family, to find a shelter somewhere nearby. He eventually settled the entourage in a common house where the poor and sick came, hoping for a miracle or at least a handout from wealthier pilgrims.

Almost immediately an altercation broke out when Bova began to prepare a meal for her family. On the road, some of their fellow travelers had begun to realize that Bova was a Saxon woman. Many of them had suffered at the hands of Saxons, some in disastrous ways, and resentment began to build against Bova and her family. For her part, Bova did not help the situation; her response was combative. She became furious when they derided her and fought back when they baited her. The angrier she became, the more her speech betrayed her—the Saxon curse words came out, along with the strange dialect. The more they taunted her, the more aggressive she became. She began to throw things at the others and produced a short, heavy cudgel with which to defend herself.

Sebastian left the common house soon after arriving to escape the smell and close quarters. He returned just in time to see Bova backed into a corner with the cudgel in one hand and a long knife in the other. Standing before her, also armed with knives, were Boldering, Bertram, and Fredigis. Other Franks from the band prevented Ubrigens from going to his wife. The children cowered on the floor at his feet.

Just as Sebastian came in, Boldering lunged at Bova. She easily dodged his wild thrust and swung her knife full at his face, ripping his cheek from eye to chin. Boldering leaped back, bellowing in pain and rage.

"Stop this at once," Sebastian commanded, stepping quickly in front of Bova, holding his heavy walking staff with both hands across his body. "You men step back. Bova, leave this room at once and wait for me in the street outside. Ubrigens, take your children and go. Go!" he shouted. Bova immediately slipped out from behind him and made for the door. Surprised and somewhat intimidated by Sebastian's commanding presence and voice, the peasants allowed Ubrigens and his family to escape.

"Get her!" Boldering howled, holding his hand to his bloody face. As Bertram and Fredigis reluctantly tried to edge around Sebastian, he warned them, "Don't do it, friends, or you'll regret it." The two hesitated as Sebastian backed away to the door. He warned them once more, "Don't follow us. If you do, I shall thrash you both until you can't walk. Do you understand?" They nodded sullenly, and Sebastian quickly slammed the door shut behind him.

They left the town at once, stopping only to pluck Heimdal off the steps of the cathedral. He came unwillingly. "This was an excellent place to beg. I could have made enough to see us all the way to Tours, and now this," he complained irritably. "From now on, have the woman cover that damned yellow hair, and tell her to keep her mouth shut. After this, we'll have every Frank on the road on the lookout for her." They hurried from the town and made a forced march for Paris.

Sebastian had never seen so many people in such crowded conditions. Although the old walled city branched out somewhat, mostly on the left bank of the Seine, Paris consisted mainly of the *Ile de la Cité*, and the majority of the people lived behind the walls on the wedge-shaped island in the middle of the river. Even Sebastian could tell as soon as they crossed over the bridge that the place had been a town for a very long time. But the ancient Roman grid pattern had long gone by, and the streets struggled to provide a straight passageway because of the shoddy dwellings built directly on the street frontage. Once a stranger left the main road, he quickly lost his sense of direction because of the sameness of the close-packed, jumbled houses.

Every street was incredibly dirty, as night soil and garbage were pitched into the winding passages every day before dawn. It took Sebastian a whole morning to get used to the foul smells of the streets and marketplaces, which seemed to be everywhere, even in the innermost parts of the city. He marveled that there was a public tavern on almost every street corner and a large number of churches, more than he had ever seen in one place. For the first time, Sebastian became aware of prostitutes, for many plied their trade openly on the streets, calling out suggestively to passing men and even grabbing their arms as they walked by to pull them into a squalid street-side shanty. Heimdal seemed most intrigued by them, stopping frequently to banter and enjoy their spicy repartee.

They found lodging in a common house close to the famous cathedral. People said it had been built on the very site of the Roman Temple of Jupiter. The lodging house was only a large, bare room where pilgrims and the poor could come in out of the weather in exchange for a coin of any kind or a morsel of food. The dour, toothless landlord's wife kept a sharp eye on the comings and goings to be sure no one slipped by without paying. When it fell dark, they moved into the cathedral itself for security and the warmth provided by scores of other paupers and pilgrims. They slept on the floor against a wall if they had come early enough to find a place by it. Surly guards with cudgels and an occasional dark-robed priest kept the people back from the altar area.

Sebastian was anxious to get out on the streets at the first hint of daylight. He spent his time wandering the narrow passageways until he came upon an open square where there was a marketplace and a few dingy shops. He could generally find his way back by looking for the tall, massive walls of the cathedral or asking for directions. He struggled to understand the language of the majority of the people he met in the inner city because the local dialect contained few truly Frankish words. However, he never went far without finding a tall, red-bearded Frank from the eastern part of the realm who could point him the way.

They had been in Paris only a week, and Sebastian had found work as a laborer building a new church. Heimdal was happy begging and singing in Latin on the steps of the cathedral, and Ubrigens and his family kept busy helping a carpenter build crude tables and chairs. As the weather had become much colder, they agreed tentatively to remain in Paris until the early spring before going on to Tours. Once Sebastian had been to the shrine of the great Saint Martin, he felt he could go home and take up his life again. As Father Pippin had suggested, amid all the clamorous activity and danger of surviving on the journey, the bitterness and ache in his stomach every time he thought of Adela had begun to subside.

Late one afternoon, Lutz found Sebastian at the building site. He ran up out of breath, crying, *"Mutti, meine Mutti! Bitte hilfe!"*

"What? Calm down, Lutz. Take a deep breath. Now look at me." Sebastian put an arm around the boy and steadied him. "What about your mother? Tell me slowly. What has happened?"

"They came . . . the men from the forest. They hit her and hit her, and she fell down. They dragged her away."

"Where, Lutz?"

"I tried to follow but they shook their clubs at me and said they'd dash my brains out if I followed. I ran to find you."

"Tell me which way they went, Lutz. Did they say anything?"

"River. I heard them say river," the boy murmured and began to cry again.

"Lutz, look at me now. Listen—you must be a man now. Find your father and sister and go at once to the cathedral. Tell Heimdal that we're in danger and that he must come with you as quickly as possible to the bridge that leads to the road to Tours—the other bridge, not the one we crossed when we first came into the city, do you understand? You must wait there until I come—do you understand? Can you do that, Lutz?"

The boy stifled his sobbing and nodded silently. "Go, then, as fast as you can. Bring the others and meet me at the bridge. Go!"

As the boy fled down the street, Sebastian headed toward the river, dreading what he might find there. It was only a few hundred yards, but the winding streets halted his progress time and again. Finally, he reached the thick walls overlooking the river. Luckily, he came out at one of the several sally ports in the walls, which were open now during the daylight hours. Guessing, he ran in the direction of the bridge. He had not gone far when he saw what he had been seeking. A crowd had gathered by the riverbank, and there in the shallow water of an eddy he saw Bova, face down in the water, her bright yellow hair streaming out into the current.

Sebastian burst through the crowd and waded out into the water, scooping up Bova's lifeless body. The crowd gasped when he rolled her onto the grass. Deep bruises showed on her face and arms and her throat had been cut from ear to ear.

Sebastian covered the body with his own cloak and swung it up into his arms. He marched away toward the bridge as quickly as possible. Luckily, Lutz had found Ubrigens and Gersvind and they had no trouble picking up Heimdal along the way. The group crossed the bridge at once and made off down the road toward Tours. At the first copse of woods along the road, they stopped to bury Bova's body. Gersvind wept piteously over the shallow grave, which Sebastian laboriously dug out with a flat rock and a stout stick. Strangely, Lutz shed no further tears and instead stood stoically against a tree staring at the scene, saying nothing. Ubrigens fell into shock and could only sit rocking and weeping quietly by the side of his wife as Sebastian worked. They buried her body in Sebastian's cloak and piled whatever stones they could find over the raw earth.

Not wanting any trouble over Bova's death and fearing an attack by Boldering's gang, the group set off at dark and walked down the road through most of the night.

After a few days on the road, Sebastian fell ill. His head began to ache, he developed a fever, and he descended into a spiraling malaise. He could hardly keep up even with the children, and when they stopped to rest, he collapsed and was hard to rouse. The last thing he wanted to do after every break was get up and get back on the road, but he forced himself, groaning and holding his head in his hands.

"What is it, Sebastian? Tell me what's wrong," Heimdal urged, alarmed at Sebastian's sudden breakdown.

"I'm sick, Heimdal. I can hardly stand. My body feels like it's on fire, and my skin tingles and burns terribly. It's all over my head and neck. All I want to do is tear at it and make it stop."

"Do not touch it, Sebastian. Do anything you can to keep your hands off your skin, especially your head. Above all, do not stick your fingers in your eyes. Do you understand?"

Sebastian grunted. "But what is it, Heimdal? Why am I hurting like this? Is anyone else sick?

"No one. I don't know what it is, but I'm not surprised. Paris was a pesthole; you could have picked up anything. Can you go on, or must we stop?"

"I'm desperate to stop. I just want to lie down. My head hurts and my skin burns!"

Heimdal felt Sebastian's forehead and could tell he had a high fever. "We'll stop at once in the very next village. Chin up now—only a little farther and you can rest, I promise. We'll find something to help you."

The last few leagues were torturous for Sebastian. Without a cloak, he was chilled to the bone, but his head and neck burned and he could hardly see. He put one foot in front of the other by sheer willpower, praying to God at every step that the pain might stop. Finally, they arrived at the outskirts of a small town. Luckily, Heimdal was able to persuade a farmer to allow them to stay the night in his small barn. For a few precious coins, the farmer went into the town and came back with a warm cloak for Sebastian, who lay in the straw of the barn shivering and burning at the same time until, mercifully, he fell asleep.

The next morning, as light slowly crept into the barn, Gersvind lingered over Sebastian, her eyes full of tears. "Papa," she called in a wavering voice, "he is turning all red and puffy."

Ubrigens crept to her side, fearing what he might see. There, in the dawning light, he could make out long bands of red dots breaking out all over one side of Sebastian's face, from his forehead to his neck. The youth continued to sleep restlessly, thrashing every now and then, his breath coming fitfully and his brow contorted with pain. Ubrigens recoiled in fear and pulled his daughter away and out of the barn.

"He's got summit', Heimdal, summit' terrible!" Ubrigens muttered almost incoherently. "We mus' get away, we mus' leave 'im and go on at once, else we'll all be sick with it."

"Calm yourself, Ubrigens, you lout. Don't frighten the children. We don't even know what it is yet. It might be nothing. Tell me what you saw." Ubrigens described what he had seen in the half light, highly exaggerating Sebastian's appearance.

"Go into the town at once, and see if you can find a healer. Ask for a woman who knows herbs, understand? And pull yourself together, man. We mustn't let Sebastian down, now that he has saved us all thus far. Go on then, and take Lutz with you. See if he can find us something to eat."

Heimdal spent a nervous hour afterward manufacturing conversation with their host, the farmer, who came into the barn several minutes after Ubrigens left. Heimdal covered Sebastian's face with his own cloak and convinced the farmer that the youth was simply exhausted after many weeks on the road and needed to rest. The blind man regaled the farmer with a highly embellished tale of their journey thus far, exaggerating Sebastian's role as if he were a great warrior instead of a wandering pilgrim. Heimdal's talent for spinning a tale charmed the simple farmer, who had never been more than a few leagues from the village where he had been born. At last Ubrigens showed up, bringing with him not one but several peasant women and two of their husbands. They immediately crowded around the sleeping youth. One woman, the eldest and presumably the village healer, lifted the cloak from Sebastian's face and recoiled. The peasants fell away at the sight of Sebastian's inflamed face, across which small blisters had now begun to appear.

"Buboes!" someone gasped. A woman screamed, and all of the peasants rushed out of the barn shouting. Their host turned at once on Heimdal. "Get him out of here at once, d'ye hear? That man has the plague!"

At the outset of the disease, Sebastian spent most of his time in a semi-conscious state, slipping in and out of dreams full of struggle and frustration. He discovered later that Heimdal had intentionally drugged him so he would rest and stay immobile. The situation was grim everywhere they went. If a passing pilgrim or villager on the road saw Sebastian's face, there was immediate alarm as frightened villagers armed themselves to ward off the small band of erstwhile pilgrims.

To his credit, Ubrigens had overcome his own fear that Sebastian might have the dreaded disease and had fashioned a crude travois—two long poles held together with strips of a blanket, upon which they dragged Sebastian out of the village and down the road. At the first convenient forest they stopped to spend a night, and Ubrigens used the time to carve an ingenious pair of wooden wheels by cutting rounds from a thick branch and whittling holes through them. A makeshift axle was secured on both ends by leather strips cut from Sebastian's boots. Although the device had to be repaired frequently, it became far easier to move Sebastian down the road, his face concealed by his cloak at all times.

Sebastian slipped in and out of consciousness as the rickety conveyance was towed slowly down the old Roman road toward Tours. He endured so many repetitions of nausea and vomiting that he became too weak even to lean his head to the side when the bile rose up in his throat. Heimdal insisted on making him drink, though he struggled to deny the water. He simply wanted to die and end his misery.

Most of his fitful dreams were of Adela—reaching out to her in desperation only to experience the pain of watching her fade away in a fog. Sometimes she would appear smiling calmly, as if it were the most natural thing in the world for them to be together. That dream never lasted, however, ending always in her tearstained face fading away from him. Oddly, he also had dreams of Adelaide, haughty and laughing or smothering him with her kisses. He struggled to escape at first and then went limp in her arms, unable to will himself to move—no strength, no willpower.

Other dreams were even more compelling and unsettling. He saw Konrad's sweaty face and a bloodstained sword. He saw Attalus in full armor, sword and shield in hand, standing firmly with his legs apart at the open gates of Fernshanz and then again in the same posture but looking inward toward the barred gates of Adalgray. He saw Father Louis, his body shot through with arrows, speaking incongruously to him as the blood spilled from his mouth: "Don't be discouraged, lad, life is good, life is holy, protect it. Do not become a brute. Be optimistic and trust in your God. Be joyous!"

He saw Heimdal, too, speaking in his best Socratic manner, "If the king gives an immoral command to his warriors, does the king still rule by God's will?"

His mother came to him as well with tears in her eyes "Don't be like them, my sweet boy. Pray always. Read! Learn!"

Finally, Father Pippin was there, adding his humble voice to the restless dreams. "Seek the truth, Sebastian. Don't claim to be more or less than you are. Renounce your pride. It is not you who conquers, it is God. You are merely his agent."

After nearly two grueling weeks, they arrived in Tours and went immediately to the famous basilica built over the bones of Saint Martin. Sebastian was better. His fever was gone, but he was so weak he could barely walk, and he stumbled as they led him up the steps and into the church. He crawled the last few yards to the altar and sank down before the crypt holding the saintly relics. Other pilgrims fell away as they saw the gaunt youth crawling determinedly toward the altar. Some whispered, "Plague!" as they saw his swollen face. Others made the sign of the cross and shrank back from the sight.

When Sebastian awoke the next morning, he was in a pilgrims' hostel near the basilica. The blisters on his face had burst during the night and scabs were already beginning to form over them. His head was clear, but his body was so weak he felt he couldn't move. Heimdal and Gersvind hovered over him, periodically ladling sips of water or broth into his mouth. Gradually, he began to recover.

"It wasn't the plague, damn you, Ubrigens!" Heimdal exclaimed for the fortieth time. "If he had the plague, he'd have far bigger buboes and they would be on his neck and under his armpits, not just across his forehead and one side of his face. It's just that everybody who sees it thinks it's the plague, and that's what put us in danger."

"But what was it then, Master 'Eimdal?" Ubrigens whimpered, reverting to his usual timorous state.

"It was something else. I don't know what, damn it all! But I know this—if it had been the plague, he would have been stone-cold dead a long time ago. So stop telling everyone the saint cured him of the plague."

"But he were cured, were he not, 'Eimdal? And weren't he cured after he crawled up on the altar? And if it weren't the saint who cured 'im, who, then, might it be?" Ubrigens insisted.

As soon as Sebastian was strong enough, they started for home.

Chapter 22

Lothar the Magician and Simon the Radhanite

Spring and Summer 773

"Welcome home, Master Sebastian! A thousand times welcome!" By chance, Baumgard had been near the front gate at dusk when Sebastian returned with Heimdal, Ubrigens and his family, and a scraggly band of nearly forty peasants, all free farmers with their families, whom Sebastian had convinced to leave their temporary and precarious lodgings in various towns along the way.

After the newcomers had been settled for the night and Sebastian sat down to eat, Baumgard pontificated: "We have been so long without a lord, Master Sebastian, 'tis a shame! It's a wonder anything at all has gotten done since you've been gone and that we have not starved to death. I'm afraid you will find things much worse than when you left, and, sir, I must tell you it is not my fault. I am steward here, 'tis true, but since you've been away, we have all been taking orders from a peasant! And he's worse than a lord!"

"And what peasant might that be, Baumgard? I seem to recall leaving a number of people in charge of various tasks."

"Why, Lothar, who else? You told him he was to help me with the farming and the organization of the peasants. But he has taken over and convinced the others that he is right."

"And what has Lothar done that is so outrageous?"

"What has he not done? He has created chaos in this village and thrown the peasants into utter confusion. He has a new idea every day, and uses what little labor we have to scratch away at these outlandish ideas. Why, for one thing, he used all the metal you brought back from Andernach to make a newfangled plow. He says it must be bigger and stronger because our soil is too thick!"

"Well, he's right about that, Baumgard, our soil is too thick except on the higher ground. It is impossible to turn the soil down by the river with a scratch plow. Tell me, does the new plow work?"

"Well, it certainly does not work with just one team of oxen. Therefore he has pulled right out of the air the preposterous notion that since we have only four teams of oxen and so few peasants, we must cultivate the earth in a different way. To do this he has commandeered all the oxen teams and yoked them together. I don't know how he does it, but now they follow along, one team behind the other, and all pull only the one plow."

By this time Baumgard had worked himself into a sweat and was rolling his eyes toward heaven and gesticulating wildly. However, the more agitated Baumgard became, the more elated Sebastian began to feel. Hiding a smile, he got up and began looking out over the dark fields expectantly as Baumgard ranted on.

"You should see this plow! Not only does it have a coulter to dig the soil, but it also has a kind of large knife to cut into the soil from the side and a curved board to push the earth to one side. And now Lothar is saying that what he needs to make the work go much faster is wheels. Wheels for a plow! Who has heard of that? Such a lot of nonsense!"

"I certainly must see this plow," Sebastian mused, staring out over the fields.

"But that is not the worst, my lord. You will be astonished at where he has been plowing."

"And where is that, Baumgard?

"Why, in the good grassland directly down by the river! I am ashamed to tell you, Lord Sebastian, that he has ruined the wonderful grasslands where you and the good Attalus were pleased to raise your splendid horses. He says the earth is much richer there where it gets plenty of water and that if we plow it, it will yield ten times the grain we get on the high fields away from the river.

"But that's still not the worst, my lord, he has upset the whole way the peasants tend the land and distribute its produce. That's what is going to cause the real trouble. Sir, I humbly beg your pardon. I did everything in my power to stop this madness before it erupts into disaster, but Masters Archambald and Liudolf supported Lothar."

"Calm yourself, Baumgard—nothing is your fault. I myself instructed Archambald and Liudolf to allow Lothar to implement his ideas if he believed strongly they would truly benefit Fernshanz and its people. Tell me why you think what he has done is so dangerous."

"Sir, instead of the square fields we have always assigned to each peasant, Lothar says that for the time being we have to pool our resources and plow the land together, in common! Imagine that! Everyone is to use the plow and the oxen by turns and even the produce of the fields must be shared in common. The peasants are to plow as far as the oxen can pull before they have to blow, then they are to turn around and plow back again. Now we have long fields instead of many square ones, and I have absolutely no idea how to divide up the harvest—if there is any at all."

"Strips."

"Sir?"

"We will divide the long fields into strips. Each peasant will have so many strips, and some will be mine, which the peasants will work for me in exchange for their strips. I have seen this done in a few fields along the Rhine and some in western Francia. I wondered at the time how they managed it. We will assign separate strips to each peasant in different fields, according to how good the land is and to make it fair for all. Then we'll mark the strips with stones and perhaps a wedge of unplowed earth between each strip. Each man will plow his own strips and harvest them, too. We will simply have to use the oxen we have in common—at least until we can afford to buy more of them. And you, my good steward, will have to see to it that we all plant, weed, and harvest at the same times."

Sebastian clasped the dumbfounded steward by the shoulders, smiling. "Baumgard, I have not been so pleased in a very long time. You have done exceedingly well in my absence, my good man. I can well imagine how hard it must have been for you to allow this tremendous change. Only a rare steward would have been so farsighted as to see what had to be done for Fernshanz to survive. I believe that only you, good and faithful Baumgard, would have had the wisdom to seize opportunity when it appeared, and in spite of all your reservations, allow good ideas to emerge from unlikely sources. I congratulate you, and I thank you."

Sebastian's praise took Baumgard completely by surprise and he stepped back, mouth agog and hand over his heart. He sputtered for a moment, coughed, and recovered adroitly. "Well, my lord, I must admit I did have reservations, very grave reservations, and at first I slept little at night when contemplating such extraordinary changes. But I said to myself, we have to step out into the unknown if we are to survive, we must be bold enough to go where no one else . . ."

"Yes, yes, Baumgard, you're quite right. Well done! We'll talk more of it tomorrow. And now, I really must get some sleep."

"Lookee there, Drogo. Don' ye see it? It's a boat, by God."

"I don' see no boat, Bardulf—I jus' see a big, fat log lyin' low in the water."

"That's the boat, ye idjit! It's just turned over. Somebody's wrecked it and turned it over. Let's get it out."

They worked for an hour, pulling and straining until the old boat was safely up out of the river. Turning it over, they discovered they had found a primitive cargo boat, which was made from overlapping slabs of rough boards held together by iron rivets and waterproofed with tarred moss. A large oak block secured between the ribs in the middle of the boat contained a broken-off mast for a single sail. A round hole through the strakes on both sides of the boat showed that the boat could be rowed, and protruding on the right side at the back of the boat was a wooden slot and hook, but the large steering board it was meant for was missing. At the front of the boat, a gaping hole told the story of its misfortune.

Bardulf was fascinated with the boat despite its condition. Finding it seemed providential, a sign that the time had finally come to change his fate. Since Sebastian had left in the fall the year before, Bardulf and

Drogo had been conscripted like everyone else who remained in the village to bend their backs for the survival of the Fernshanz community. Every day held a myriad of work details and chores, and Baumgard was a fierce taskmaster. If they were not winnowing from the fields, they were cutting wood and thatch to make sheltering huts. If they were not scouring the woods for edible roots and nuts, they were fishing in the river or snaring rabbits for the cook pots. From dawn to dusk Baumgard and Lothar occupied them with an endless list of urgent work to be done.

As spring arrived, the winter wheat crop looked luxurious and bountiful. Soon they would harvest it. Everyone breathed a sigh of relief. Now the most urgent business was plowing for planting the summer crops of oats, barley, and lentils. They had so few workers that every man of the village had to take his turn at the plow. Only the old soldier Bernard, who was exclusively assigned to rebuilding the fort's defenses, was excused from the plowing.

When they only had the old scratch plow, cross plowing had to be done, sometimes two or three times across the same section of field, even in the uplands. Because of the heaviness and thickness of the soil, the earth required so much effort that the men were completely exhausted by the end of each day. Things were better now that they had the new plow, but Bardulf was desperate to escape the drudgery. He recognized the potential of the little cog boat immediately and pounded Drogo on the back enthusiastically until the poor lad shouted in protest.

"We're goin' to be boatsmen, Drogo!" Bardulf declared triumphantly. "We're goin' to become very important people here at ol' Fernshanz. We'll be the ones who carries the pigs and nuts and honey to the towns along the big river and brings down goods from there to Fernshanz—seeds, and salt, and the like, and . . . and wine, Drogo! We're goin' to become wine merchants! 'urrah! We'll be tastin' some of that Dragon's Blood again before the leaves fall this year, ye mark my words."

Calming himself, Bardulf stared at the boat and pronounced pensively, "All we has to do is figure out how to make us a mast and a sail. We can get down the river fine, but comin' back'll be the tricky part. I don' even know what kind of cloth they use to make a sail. We mus' find out, Drogo. It'll be the difference between a life of back-breakin' scratchin' in the dirt or rollickin' on the river, doin' ac'zactly as we please and gettin' thanked fer it by ever'body!"

"And he has created a thing he calls a 'wheelbarrow'— a kind of a box on a wheel so one can push things instead of carrying them."

"Sounds eminently useful, don't you think, Baumgard? One can probably move twice the amount of things with it, *nicht wahr?*" Sebastian said, tongue in cheek.

"Yes, I suppose so," Baumgard said peevishly, "but it will make the peasants devilishly lazy and weak," he concluded.

Baumgard continued, "And he has harnessed the river and makes it flow through a small house where there is a large wheel. And the wheel turns a lever and the lever moves a grinder, and the thing actually grinds up grain. He says that it is a present for you, and that you will control the milling from now on."

"No, *you* will control the milling for me, Baumgard. We shall grind grain much faster now and every peasant will have more time to do his or her other chores and raise more grain and other food. By thunder, we shall be able to store up plenty for the winter. If we do this right, no one will ever starve in Fernshanz again!" And Sebastian leaped on his horse and went off toward the new mill with a wide grin on his face.

"He's also built an oven house for the whole village in your name," Baumgard shouted after him, "so all the peasants can bake their bread there if they pay you for the privilege."

"Wonderful, Baumgard," Sebastian shouted back. "Well done, again! But don't charge the peasants too much!"

The trader came up the Lippe just before sunset in a shallow-draft, single-mast longboat rowed swiftly upriver by a dozen Danish sailors. The boat was packed with trade goods inside small wooden chests upon which the oarsmen sat as they skillfully drove the boat up onto the sandy bank beside the small wharf.

Several peasants still in the fields noticed the craft and ran at once to announce its arrival. Boats on the Lippe were rare except when they arrived on the king's business, and they had never seen a foreign trade vessel. By the time the boat pulled up to the wharf, a crowd of villagers had assembled and the news had been brought swiftly to Sebastian, who was in one of the barns where Lothar was helping a cow deliver her calf.

Sebastian rode to the wharf just in time to meet the master of the boat and the owner of its contents. He was a tall, olive-skinned man of slender but muscular build. With his remarkably white teeth, framed by a thin black mustache and goatee, he would have been called handsome in any country. He wore high boots and flowing trousers, a tunic of bright green silk and a fur-trimmed cloak. His shiny black hair was mostly concealed beneath a round cap of eastern design. Leaping nimbly from the boat onto the wharf, the man bowed extravagantly to Sebastian in a sweeping gesture.

"Good day, sir," the merchant ventured, speaking fluently in the Frankish tongue. "I am called Simon, and I come in peace to trade with you, if you are willing. What a beautiful horse! Would you be interested in trading for him, perchance?"

Sebastian dismounted slowly, trying to assess whether the man and his Danish crew signified a threat or an opportunity. He wore no armor, nor did the Danish oarsmen, though all had weapons near to hand. Sebastian was glad to see a number of his own warriors arriving with weapons and shields.

The merchant continued, smiling, "I hope, good sir, you will believe me when I say we come in peace and only to trade. We are on the way to Mayence to offer our wares, but we heard of this place from the merchants in Frisia and thought to try our luck with you. May we come ashore?"

Sebastian hesitated. Meanwhile, Liudolf came up quickly with some soldiers and whispered in his ear. "We don't know them, Sebastian. Those are Danes. They're on good terms with the Saxons, and they're known for thieving and piracy."

"A moment, sir, if you please," Sebastian said courteously to the waiting merchant. Turning to Luidolf, he said calmly in a low voice, "There are only a dozen, Liudolf. What's the harm in allowing them to show us what they have? I have never seen such a man as this Simon."

"Sebastian, he is no Frank, nor even a Christian. Look at his dark face and what he's wearing. I believe he is a Jew—or a Syrian, one of those traders who go from place to place selling anything they have and spying on everybody. Send them away at once, or we will find a raiding party in their wake."

Sebastian turned back to Simon, who stood smiling sardonically, one hand on the hilt of a long curved sword and the other on the side of the boat.

"Your king has given me permission to trade in this land," said the merchant. He reached inside his belt and drew forth a parchment. "See, here is the king's writ; look at the seal." He held up the parchment for all to see.

Sebastian stepped forward quickly and took the parchment out of the trader's hand. Simon frowned and stiffened, grasping his sword hilt more firmly. Sebastian held up a hand, palm outward, and then turned his attention to the document. He could not read all of the words, but he could make out clearly the Latin letters for "Simon" and for the word "MARCHANT" written large in the middle of the page. At the bottom was, undeniably, the king's seal embedded in red wax.

Sebastian slowly handed the scroll back to the merchant, who grasped it tightly and returned it to his belt. "Well, then, Sir *Marchant*," he said looking Simon in the eye, "We will parley with you—but only with you. Your men must stay on the boat. Is that satisfactory?"

"This is dangerous, Sebastian," Luidolf whispered again. "He only wants to see our defenses and how many men we have." Sebastian shrugged him off and spoke courteously to the trader. "Come, sir, but I can offer you little hospitality, I'm afraid. We live in danger of attack here, and my people are wary of strangers. We cannot be too careful when the Saxons still raid in these parts."

"I understand, sir . . . ah . . . sir . . ."

"I am Sebastian, master of this fortress. It is called Fernshanz. You are welcome to sit with me awhile and we will talk. But I cannot take you inside the walls."

"No matter, Lord Sebastian, no matter at all. Have your servants bring us two benches and perhaps a small table. We can sit here within sight of the boat and in the shade of your walls while I tell you what I can do for you—and perhaps what you might do for me."

Soon they sat together as Simon had suggested, just the two of them. Simon kept within sight of his boat and Sebastian kept his men at a distance. Baumgard brought bread, cheese, and some newly brewed beer to the table.

"You would, of course, not sell me your horse, I'm thinking," Simon began, smiling once more. "He is a beauty indeed. Reminds me of Spanish horses I have seen."

"Joyeuse is a Spanish horse, or at least he comes from that stock. My father brought his forbearer back from beyond the Spanish mountains. And, yes, you are right, he is not for trading."

They ate and drank in silence for a minute, and then both began to speak at once. Simon deferred to Sebastian. "I want to know where you are from and why you happen to be here, of all places. There are far richer towns along the Rhine. I doubt we could afford to trade for anything you might have."

"Don't be confused by the way I dress, Lord Sebastian; my clothes come from the far places to which I have traveled. But I was born in the same land you were—in Metz, on the River Moselle, to be exact. Your king is mine as well. It just happens that my people are different. They call us Radhanites, which is just a name having something to do with the Far East, our frequent trading destination. I have relatives—business partners, really—in Egypt, Baghdad, and Byzantium, as well as in Metz and along the Rhine in Worms and Mayence. My people came into these lands with the Romans and have lived in various parts of Francia far longer than you Franks. We trade for a living. We own no land, so I travel a great deal."

"I presume all of this means you are a Jew," Sebastian ventured. Simon nodded and smiled. Sebastian continued, "I know of your people, but I have never met a single Jew. I hear you are not Christians, but you believe in the same God."

"That is correct, sir. We have believed in that same God for thousands of years. In fact, we were the first people to believe in the one God, the Invisible One, the Maker of heaven and earth. We have much in common, Lord Sebastian. The main difference, you see, is that you have found your messiah, while we still wait for ours."

With that the Jew, smiling broadly, leaned across the table and touched his cup of beer to Sebastian's before quaffing it down.

As they talked, Sebastian found himself intrigued by the man and enormously curious about the places he had been and the people he had seen. Simon had in fact dealt with high officials in the lands of the two greatest kingdoms on earth, the fabled Byzantium and the vast desert empire of the Arab and Persian peoples. Even Sebastian knew of these two great empires. Simon had walked the streets of Constantinople with its impregnable walls and incomparable wealth. It was the elegant and powerful capital of the Greeks, who called themselves the New Rome. He had been to the old Rome as well and knew the confusion of politics in that struggling center of western Christianity, but he disdained it in comparison with the might and prosperity of Byzantium. Nevertheless, he reserved his greatest praise for the Baghdad Caliphate, the so-called Arab Empire, saying it had an energy and inventiveness like nothing he had seen elsewhere. So much was being discovered in its cities—medicine, astronomy, geography, and even a new way of counting with numbers, including a number called "zero," which made every business transaction incredibly easy. In every Arab land, learning was prized more than gold.

As Simon talked, Sebastian was awed by his stories and profoundly attracted by the opportunity to learn something more of the fascinating world in which Simon traveled. Against his better judgment, he invited Simon to have supper with him inside the fortress and to pass the night as his guest. He ordered that food and drink be brought to the Danes but would not allow them to debark from the boat. Simon merely smiled and posed no objections.

The two spoke together by firelight well into the night. By morning they had become friends.

"I haven't found many Franks like you, young Sebastian. Even the king doesn't think as liberally as you do; it's almost as if you had studied in a monastery. You would love to meet some of the people of the great empires to the east—the Greeks at Constantinople and the learned men of the great Mussulman Empire beyond the Middle Sea. Those people are not like us here, where everything is tied to the land and a few poor cities. Their world is knit together by ties of trade, with scholars following the trading vessels and sharing their knowledge with men like themselves in other cultures."

"How do they treat you, Simon? You are neither one nor the other."

"Ah, they see us Jews as a very necessary link between their worlds and others. That's our great advantage. They use me and others like me to learn about those other worlds, to carry state messages to them, and to invite them to discourse. If there were not already so much suspicion and bad blood because of religion, they would welcome the emissaries of every land—Christian, Mussulman, or pagan—to meet with them in Damacus, Alexandria, or Baghdad every year. They would exult in it, and everyone who came would travel there in complete safety and leave with lavish gifts and the thanks of the caliph."

"Well, if you're so important to the great leaders of the Mussulmen, why are you here? Surely we are at the end of the world for you. There is very little for you to gain here among our cold forests, *nicht wahr*?"

"Sebastian, I will tell you something that I hope will not make you dislike or fear me: I make my way in this world by knowing. The more I know, the more I prosper. I can use what I know to turn a profit through trade; I can make myself welcome in many places by sharing what I know; and I become a much enlarged man because of what I know. It makes me happy to know. It gives me power. It's a fine and satisfying way to live."

"Besides," he added with a grin, "I turn a handsome profit by trading Frankish swords in Al Andalus. They're the best in the world. And there is even more to be gained by buying the pagan Saxons and Slavs you capture and selling them on the slave markets in Baghdad or Constantinople."

"Ah. Hmm. That's why so many look askance at what you do. I'm not sure the king would approve of you selling Frankish swords to a potential enemy, nor would the Church look so kindly on the sale of slaves to the Mussulmen."

"Nonsense, Sebastian, the Church is only concerned about slaves who are Christian—it doesn't care a fig if the slave is a tree-worshipping Saxon or a Wilzi Slav or ignorant Sorb. By the way, it's comical how many pagan slaves are suddenly converted to Christianity just when they are about to be sold."

"But such work must be dangerous, isn't it? In addition to all that, my men think you are a spy for the Saxons or the Danish pirates. They would kill you, or try to, if I let them."

"Ah, that is the price I must pay for my exotic life. Danger is the sauce upon my plate of knowing. I live largely by my wits and by a very valuable talent for sizing up the people I meet. I have met many people over the years of all types, and I must be able to know what kind of men they are. Are they dangerous to me? Must I beware of this one or that one? How can I appeal to one or another? I must judge a man quickly and find out what he most wants. Everyone wants something. I am willing to trade anything—goods, people, information . . . whatever works, whatever gives me an advantage."

"That's a very frank confession, Simon. I wonder that you would confide in me. How do I know now that you won't sell information about me and Fernshanz? How do I know you won't sell out my king?"

"Good questions, Sebastian. And I would not have been so frank with most other men, but you are obviously able to think and reason. Surely, you must see that to live like I do I must be careful about whom I take into my confidence—but you will also be able to see that I reason well, too. Information about Fernshanz does not represent much value to me, but a man like you is rare. I am exceedingly glad to know you."

"Why, pray tell? I have no power or influence."

"Not now, perhaps, but you will—you'll have both power and influence one day. The king is no fool. From what you tell me, he already sees in you a commodity of value. So do I. You can read; you have good ideas. From what you have told me this night, you have already proven your value to the king several times over. Most importantly, you cannot be bought, nor can you be swayed from your innermost values. Yes, I'm glad to know such a man. You would be a good and loyal friend to have. If I do good things for you and your people, you might return that favor to me. Who knows when I might need such a friend?"

"What good things could you do for me, Simon? We are too poor to trade with you for even the cheapest goods."

"Yes, but it will not always be so, Sebastian. You've told me tonight of your hopes to rebuild your town and increase the prosperity of your people. You've spoken with such enthusiasm and conviction about the new things you're doing here, the new ideas, the different methods you're trying. That is how I know that one day you will achieve what you want for your people and become an important man among the Franks. I can help you—and I want to."

"How?"

Simon pulled a small leather bag from his belt, pouring out a pile of silver coins. "I can lend you a little money, and you can buy some of the things you need. You've said you need iron for the spokes and axles of your new plow, *nicht wahr*? And you want to buy more oxen for the plowing? I'd wager you also want to find more weapons for your soldiers and horses for them to ride. Isn't that what's constantly in your head?" He pushed the pile gently toward Sebastian.

Sebastian took a deep breath. "I've never seen so much money, Simon. We never have any but the smallest coins." He hesitated and then deliberately pushed the coins back toward the smiling merchant. "But if you truly know me, as you say you do, you must know that I can't accept such a gift. I could never repay you. Even if Fernshanz prospers beyond my dreams, we would still have very little you would want."

"It's not all about things, Sebastian. Someday I may simply need a friend. I am happy to help such a man as you, and one day it may be that such a small investment will pay great dividends one way or another. At the very least, when I'm in this rough edge of the Frankish realm, it would be good to have a warm place to sleep and a friend to talk with well into the night over a cup or two of ale."

"And you want nothing more from me? No information in return? No guarantee that I will stand with you against my people or against my king, if it would ever come to that?"

"Sebastian, Sebastian, you do me an injustice. There's nothing here in Fernshanz I want except perhaps a good friend. God knows, I have too few I can trust. But after talking to you tonight, I'm sure that I could trust you and come to you if I were in trouble. Such a man as me, who lives on the edge of fortune, good and bad, must find his refuge and make his friends wherever he may be. Trust me; I know a good investment when I see one."

At that, Simon got up, stretched, and strolled out of the room into the yard to relieve himself, leaving the pile of silver coins on the table.

Chapter 23

Of Silks and Success

The pair of riders declined to dismount as Sebastian rode up to meet them at the fortress gate. They seemed nervous and unsure of themselves. Sebastian saw immediately that they were soldiers from the Eresburg. He had seen them before in the halls of Adalgray, a pair of Konrad's personal entourage, who were always around when there was drinking and carousing to be had.

Sebastian made them wait a bit and then slowly rode up. "If you will not get down and take some refreshment, gentlemen, then I must ask you forthwith what business you have with me." He eyed them steadily as they looked nervously around themselves and made a show of steadying their horses. "We may not linger, Master Sebastian." He noticed they declined to call him Lord Sebastian. "We are only here to find out . . . ah . . . to ascertain . . . to inquire if you are well and back from . . . your pilgrimage." This last was said almost with a snicker.

"I am, as you see," Sebastian said calmly. "What else?"

"Ah, we . . . we are to inquire if you are well enough and ready to fight should Lord Konrad need you against the Saxons."

"Why, did the Saxons rise up? Is the Eresburg in danger?" Sebastian's voice rose slightly in alarm as he suddenly realized that Adela might be at risk.

"No, no—it's just that several weeks ago we thought they might and we rode out against them, burned some villages, that sort of thing. Seems we stirred 'em up and there might be movement among them soon."

"If Lord Konrad has gone against them without provocation, they are sure to retaliate. You may tell Lord Konrad that I am fit to fight but that I have only a few warriors to bring with me, since we are still recovering from the Saxons' attack last year. I am training new men, but none are ready to fight except in defense of Fernshanz, which we are still in the process of rebuilding. I will come if he insists, but unless it's a full Saxon uprising and the Eresburg is in danger, I can better serve our cause by remaining here to rebuild the fortress and train my men."

Sebastian watched the pair ride off with a growing sense of unease. One would return to Konrad with his answer and the other would ride to the king at his winter headquarters in Thionville on the River Moselle. It was doubtful that he and the Fernshanz community would appear in good light in either report. With that thought in mind, Sebastian summoned Archambald.

"Listen, my friend, you must go to the king for me and tell him how we're faring here at Fernshanz. Tell him that our population is growing, not only with new farmers and craftsmen but with soldiers as well, whom we are training. He needs to know the rebuilding is proceeding well, and we'll soon have a strong fortress again. You should also tell him that I am building a moat."

"A moat? What moat?" Archambald asked blankly, suddenly dumbfounded at the prospect of going by himself on a mission to see the king.

"I hadn't told you yet, but it's been going around in my head. It's something Simon said we should do. We can divert the river around the citadel so an attacking enemy would have to cross over the water to get to us." As Archambald labored to understand the idea, Sebastian pressed on, "Never mind, just tell him that I intend to build a moat—he will understand. Tell him as well that the planting has been successful and we look forward to a bountiful harvest this year. Thank him for all the goods and animals we were able to bring back here from Andernach—it has made all the difference."

"But, Sebastian," Archambald protested, feeling more and more apprehensive, "I don't even know where the king is, and if I did, I doubt I could find him."

"Don't worry, Archambald, I'll send Bernard with you. He can find anything. Besides, it's not hard—it's right on the River Moselle. You just follow the river upstream from where it meets the Rhine. Bernard will know. You just need to go along and make sure you paint a rosy picture for the king. Say we're well on our way to full recovery and that I will be stronger and better off than before, as long as I can stay here awhile and get it done. You'll do fine, and I daresay, you'll even enjoy it. Can't you see yourself at the king's court, giving a report in front of all those important people? What an audience—what an opportunity! It will bring out the very best in you."

At that, Archambald suddenly grabbed his stomach and turned away, making a noise as if to vomit. Observing from under his arm Sebastian's look of concern, Archambald suddenly spun around, laughing. "Of course I'll go. Who wouldn't? What a journey! What an embassy! I shall regale the king with such stories of our hardship and heroism and of the miraculous recovery we have made that he will be astounded and will wish to travel here at once and see for himself!"

"You will do no such thing, you deceitful lout," Sebastian said, giving Archambald a good-natured thumping on the chest. "Just tell him we're doing well and have hopes of a full recovery. Do not lie to the king, do you understand? Above all, don't entice him to come here or send anyone. He comes with hundreds of people. We can't afford it. We just need to reassure him and then hope to be left alone. Don't brag or be downcast—just show confidence, and don't be a clown."

At the end of the summer, Simon the Radhanite paid another surprise visit to Fernshanz. This time he stayed three days and was welcomed into the citadel by Sebastian. In spite of the grumbling of some of the villagers and soldiers, his Danish boatmen were allowed to pitch a camp on the riverbank near the wharf. Bardulf and Drogo befriended them instantly.

"Bardulf, we mustn't do this. Fridl's father wouldn't like it, and I don' think it's very nice."

"Shut yer mouth, Drogo. Don' ye understand? We mus' find a way to fix the boat. Not a soul here knows how to do it, but the Danes know. Look at their boat. They built it, and it's a thousand times better'n ours. We jus' mus' get 'em to tell us how to fix our boat. Fridl is what they wants. They'll do anything for her. We jus' mus' get her to go to 'em, and I think some of that there silk they got on board will do the trick. I'll just promise her a kerchief of fine silk. And damn her father, he don' care nothin' for her anyway, and he'll be mighty pleased when she brings him back some wine and a haunch of that sow we slaughtered in the woods last week."

"But where are we goin' to get any wine? Baumgard don' have none no more. We can't steal it like before."

"The Danes have it, ye stupid. Don' ye see 'em drinkin' it ever' night? We'll just tell 'em that in exchange for the woman, they mus' give us some wine and the silk. Then we'll tell 'em if they want to see her again, they mus' help us to fix the boat. It's awright, Drogo. Fridl don't mind. She's been with ever' boy in the village anyway. She likes it. Makes a change from her old dad workin' her to death, like he does."

"I don' know, Bardulf. Seems wrong to me."

"Do ye want to be a boatman or not?"

"I do, Bardulf, I do! I want to go to Lippeham and have adventures and such, jus' like ye said."

"Well then, keep yer mouth shut about this. Our Fridl with her fine big tits is the answer. We'll be fixin' that boat afore summer."

This time Sebastian was delighted to be able to present Simon with a three-month-old colt sired by Joyeuse with one of Adela's gift mares. The young stallion showed every bit of the spirit of his sire, and Sebastian was pleased to think Simon would find him a worthy return for the silver coins he had so generously given.

He was not disappointed. Simon was delighted with the gift and immediately began to coax the colt into trusting him with treats and a calm, soothing voice. He showed Sebastian a special delicacy that he called *sucher*, a ball of a brownish-white substance that proved incredibly sweet to the taste, sweeter by far than even the purest honey. Simon said it was made from a plant that grew by the great river in the land called Egypt. The colt was mad for the treat and came prancing to meet Simon as soon as he appeared.

If their first meeting had charmed Sebastian, he was enthralled by the fantastic tales Simon told during the three nights of this visit. Many of the stories were of a fabulous city in the east called Madinat al-Salam, the City of Peace, known more simply as Baghdad, where Simon had obtained his strange curved sword.

"It is truly a rich, magnificent place, Sebastian. You have never seen a place like it. Do you remember how impressed you were when you first saw the city of Worms? Well, Baghdad is one hundred times more beautiful and more impressive. One of the four gates into the city is made of gold.

"And there are all kinds of people, Sebastian, from every part of the world, who have so many different colors of skin and ways of dress. They come with thousands of items to trade: leather, silk, brocade, and precious gems such as rubies, pearls, and amber. You can buy anything in the bazaars of Baghdad: iron, glass, perfume, spices, slaves of any type and from any land, and every kind of food, delicious in every way."

"What kind of king governs such a place? He must be a giant among all men. How has he managed to build it?" Sebastian asked, incredulously.

"He is called Al-Mansur and he is Caliph of the Empire of the Arabs. He is like our king, and his realm is at least as big as the one the Franks rule and many times richer. But, strangely enough, no one ever sees him. He resides behind the walls of a great palace and only his most trusted advisors may approach him. His city—and indeed his empire—is ruled by a 'vizier,' a kind of wise man with special powers. I met this man, and he is as clever and learned a one as I ever expect to meet. He is of the family they call the *Barmakids*, and he goes by the rather comical name of Yahya. They say it is his family that has built the great empire of the Abbasid caliphs and that he is the most powerful of them all.

"I had come to sell fine Spanish leather to the court. I was made to wait while Yahya sat on a pillow on the floor of his assembly room listening to a storyteller while a musician played beautiful music on a stringed instrument called a lute. I got on well with this Yahya. He likes the people of my race, their practicality and daring, and he liked me. In appreciation for the trade goods I had brought, he gave me a gift before my departure. Let me show it to you."

They strolled out to Simon's boat and he went on board to draw a rough woolen blanket from one of the chests upon which the oarsmen sat. He opened the blanket to reveal a bolt of the purest raw silk of a blood-red color. "This, my friend, is one of the most sought-after trade items in all of your Christendom. And do you know why? Because your ladies like it. They want to have fine dresses and cloaks made from it. I daresay you could woo almost any young Frankish maiden successfully with enough of this fine stuff. It's my most successful trade item, and I'm almost out of it. Your king bought a great deal of what I had. I'm afraid I must soon make the arduous journey back to Baghdad if I wish to make myself truly rich with silk.

"In the hopes that you will one day have a fine Frankish lady, I wish to gift you with a few lengths of this precious material. If you ever fall in love, you may thank me profusely for it one day. In the meanwhile, let me give you something else you will like—a toy." At this, Simon pulled from underneath the bolt a rectangular piece of the same material, in the same deep red color. In the middle of one end it had a long tassel made of cords of silk woven together. Simon then produced a few sticks of wood he called bamboo and a long rope of interwoven silk thread wrapped around a stick.

"My good Sebastian, this is what they call a *gabelweih* or 'kite.' The idea for it comes from the same place this fine silk does—from a place so far away to the east, they say it is where the sun rests each night and rises each morning. The land is called Kitai. Let me put it together, and then I will show you a thing which will delight you."

Simon began to attach the bamboo strips through loops on the edges of the fabric until the kite stood stiffly straight within its wooden frame. He then attached the end of the light silken rope to the upper middle of the kite, released a few lengths of the rope, and began to lope away into the wind blowing from the river. The kite at once began to dart up deftly into the sky as the silken rope played out. Finally, Simon stood still, with the kite soaring high in the sky above the meadow, jerking back and forth as he moved the cord.

By this time, the eyes of every villager were on the kite, all mouths open in wonder as the dainty piece of silk danced and weaved against the brisk breeze.

"It's yours, my friend," Simon said, once the kite had been brought gently back to earth. It's only a play toy, but one day you may find a good use for it. They say such a device was used by a famous general in Kitai to win a battle. He painted magical signs on the kite and flew it in front of his enemy, who became so frightened by the flying images that they ran in terror before him. If nothing else, you can use it to amuse your children, if you ever have any."

The next morning, the trader was gone, having carefully led his blindfolded new colt into the middle of the boat, where he had constructed a small corral behind the main mast.

"I may not be able to keep the colt, Sebastian," he said, as the boatmen prepared to pull away from the bank, "though I'd dearly love to have him for my own. But I travel mainly by boat, and I couldn't take him as far as I would wish to go. Nevertheless, I will trade him most carefully and only for the most important reason and the best return, you may be assured. You have done me a very great favor, and you have once again offered me your hospitality and friendship. I won't forget it. May the God who watches over both of us keep you safe until we meet again. *Auf dem Wiedersehen.*"

The king did not fight in Saxony the year Sebastian returned from the pilgrimage or the following year, nor did he send for Sebastian. Instead, he sent word by Archambald that he was pleased with the progress at Fernshanz and that it should be continued at all costs. However, he charged Sebastian with the obligation to support Konrad at the Eresburg with as many men as he could muster if the situation there should become critical.

Sebastian was greatly relieved and poured himself into the restoration work and helping Lothar and Baumgard coax ever more production from the land. He found he could once again concentrate on the land and work before him. He had managed to store away his thoughts of Adela in a sacred place in his mind where their love would endure forever. They had paid the price for this pure and timeless love, and it would always be there, no matter what happened, even though he felt it was likely he would never see her again.

To rebuild Fernshanz and make it prosper, they had to reconstruct the entire farming system based on the use of the new plow and the reconfiguration of the cultivated land. New peasants arrived almost weekly, having heard of the opportunities and innovations at Fernshanz. The money Sebastian had "borrowed" from Simon was used to buy more oxen and as much iron for tools and weapons as they could afford. On a rare trip to Frisia in the north, Lothar and Sebastian spent a good portion of the precious silver to acquire a small herd of excellent horses, which they would pass on to the new warriors at a greatly reduced cost. It turned out to be a very good summer.

The king had moved against the Lombards in Italy at the urging of the new Bishop of Rome, Hadrian. The Lombard king, Desidarius, had usurped papal land and had become a threat to the pope himself. The king tried to negotiate, but Desidarius dissembled and delayed answering Charlemagne's demands. In exasperation, the king gathered a large army, and in a bold winter crossing over the Alps, came into Italy and laid siege to the Lombards at Pavia.

Sebastian expected to be called, but for two summers, as it turned out, none of the Frankish chieftains on the Saxon March were summoned. Sebastian gained yet another blessed summer to build and grow. By the end of the second summer, nearly five hundred souls worked the soil of Fernschanz, and Sebastian could count a cohort of over a hundred warriors. He began to feel that he was firmly and rightfully lord of his land.

Chapter 24

Gersvind

Summer 774

Sebastian woke late on the Monday following a church high holy day, at which there had been feasting and more than a little drinking of honeyed beer and the sweet wine the peasants made from berries. At first curious and then delighted with the way the wine made him lighthearted, Sebastian had drained too many cups before he realized how unsteady it made him.

As the peasants danced and sang around the bonfires on the green in front of the village church, he had gradually eased himself back into the shadows and stumbled up to the manor house. He had fallen into bed and slept like a stone until midnight, at which time he awakened with a headache and a terrible thirst. Sleep came again only as the stars faded and the eastern sky began slowly to push back the dark.

It was past midmorning when Sebastian stirred. He was shocked to see how much of the day he had already wasted and he hurriedly arose. He was halfway dressed when the door to his room opened and the peasant girl who helped old Marta, Sebastian's housekeeper, slipped into the room.

"Forgive me, my lord, Marta told me I was to clean your room today," she said shyly, with her head down and only the barest glance at the disheveled state Sebastian was in.

"Where is Marta, anyway?" Sebastian growled, not at all comfortable with this young woman in his room.

"She has gone to the village, sir. I didn't know you were still here," replied the girl, still looking at the floor but making no move to leave the room.

Sebastian stared at her, not knowing exactly what he should do in this situation. On the one hand, he thought he should dismiss her summarily with a curt warning never to come into his room again while he was there. On the other hand, he was having a hard time pulling his eyes away from her. She was remarkably attractive for a serf's daughter, not at all dirty or foul smelling. In fact, he fancied that she smelled of flowers. Her hair was long and full and as yellow as the wheat in early summer. Her sky-blue eyes occasionally glanced up brightly, and the red patches on her cheeks and the golden skin of her face and neck spoke of her radiant health and vigor. Sebastian stood transfixed, mouth agape and dumbstruck.

At last the girl broke the silence. She said, almost under her breath, "Does my lord wish me to continue?"

Sebastian, coming to himself with a start, muttered, "What? Oh! Why, I suppose . . . Yes, do go ahead. I shall be out of here in a moment." But he did not move from the corner of the room by the rough, low bed where he had been dressing. The girl began to move around the crude, straw-filled mattress, straightening the skins Sebastian used for covers and plumping the eiderdown pillows. She kept her back to him as she edged around the bed, sensing his presence rather than seeing him. She bent over the low bed straightening and smoothing until she stood directly in front of him. Still he did not move, unable to take his eyes off the girl's hair and her bending figure.

She could hear his shallow breathing behind her. Finally she stood straight up with a pillow in her hands and stepped back as if to shake it out, her shoulders barely brushing his chest. She froze. By this time, the blood was pounding in Sebastian's head, his mouth was dry, and his fingers were tingling. He scarcely breathed. Later he could not remember making any conscious decision, but his hands rose to grasp her shoulders and pull her gently back against him. His face bent into her hair and his lips found her neck. He inhaled her scent, striving almost to breathe her into his body.

For a long time afterward, he stayed immobile with his head buried in her hair, breathing in her scent and trying to clear his mind. Gradually, she rolled him away from her and began to tenderly stroke his face and chest. For the first time, she looked directly into his eyes and kissed him lightly over and over. Into his ear she blew her name, "I am called Gersvind, my lord." After awhile, she gently disentangled herself from him, arose, and slipped away quietly through the door.

Of course, Sebastian remembered the girl, the same shy, skinny girl he had teased and played with on the road to Tours four years before, a modest wildflower, now become a luminous rose. But the realization came upon him slowly. He had lost track of her after the trip in the press of work, training, and planning. His contact with the villagers was almost wholly limited to the key men—Lothar, Baumgard, and the soldiers, primarily. At the weekly Mass and at holiday celebrations, he generally kept his distance and retired early, aware that the lord's continued presence might spoil the festivities.

Sleeping badly and assaulted by erotic visions, Sebastian held out valiantly for the next several nights until he could no longer stand to be without her. On the fourth day after she had come to him, he made an excuse to go up to the manor in the middle of the day, a thing he almost never did, being in the habit of coming to the manor house only to eat and sleep at the end of the day. He busied himself with pretending to look for an item of his battle gear until he found a moment to take Gersvind aside. He grasped her hand and entreated her to come to him that night as soon as the house was quiet. She said nothing but raised her eyes briefly to his own and pressed his hands.

Thereafter, Gersvind came to Sebastian as often as she could find a way to slip out of her father's hut, and Sebastian knew a pleasure he had never dreamed of. But his passion and increasing affection for the girl were spoiled by the voices that intruded increasingly upon his brain in the bright light of day. They told him frankly that she was a peasant girl, the daughter of a serf. Though they were tender with one another and lay in each other's arms as naturally as the sun rose, they had very little to say to one another. Sebastian felt ridiculous when he tried to explain his work and the decisions he had to make about his duties and the manor. Gersvind was sweet and loving but so limited by her menial background that she could think of nothing to say outside of the routine of her own daily existence.

Added to that dearth of common experience and the obvious differences between them were the voices in his head that mocked him. Most Frankish warriors would not think twice about deflowering a village girl. For them, a woman was merely the reward of power and victory. Other voices, however—those of Ermengard and Father Louis—accused him of his sin. Then there was the voice of Heimdal, laughing wryly at his hypocrisy.

He knew he could never marry Gersvind, and he realized that his liaison with her deprived her of finding an appropriate mate among her own class. Whenever Sebastian mentioned something like that, she shook her head and began kissing him all over, eventually thrusting her body against his until he could think of nothing else.

Their liaisons went on for many weeks, all through the summer months and into the harvest time. Then, one early morning when the light had just begun to creep into his room where Gersvind lay naked and spent on his bed, Sebastian discovered the unmistakable swell of her belly and knew she was with child.

When he could decently leave her, he made his way to the chapel, filled with remorse and anguish. What could he do? What was to be done? Although she was precious to him, he could not make Gersvind his wife; it simply wasn't an option. The peasants would disapprove of it as much as his peers. But neither could he cast her away as if she didn't matter to him. As he knelt in the dark chapel, Father Pippin came in and began to prepare for a feast day Mass. He came at once to Sebastian and inquired if he had any need.

"Father, I have sinned," Sebastian blurted out. Slowly, he told the priest what he had done and how miserable he now felt because of it, imploring the priest to tell him what he must do.

"For one thing, my son," the priest said, immediately taking on his customary role of confessor, "you are only a man, and you are alone. You are no worse than any other man. Men lust. Even I, a priest, and a poor specimen of a man, find it hard to be without a woman. One must pray constantly and mortify one's flesh. It is a battle that lasts a lifetime, I assure you."

The priest laid a hand on Sebastian's shoulder and whispered gently, "I must prepare for Mass now. But you have made a good confession. Are you truly sorry for your sins?"

"Oh yes, Father, but what can I do? I have ruined her life," Sebastian groaned.

"No, my son, you have not. You assuredly have not. You do not know these peasant women. Much can be done. But I must prepare for Mass now. Let me give you absolution and your penance. Then, later, come back to me here and we will plot to bring you right again. It will not be easy and it may cost you more than you realize, but all is not lost. We shall find a way."

Sebastian had never had as difficult or painful a decision to make as in those next days after his confession. Being without Gersvind was excruciating. Talking dispassionately with Father Pippin about what must be done filled him with self-loathing. The solution they eventually arrived upon indeed included a price he was almost unable to pay. Not only did he lose his lovely girl, the first experience of uninhibited passion in his life, but the solution included giving her to another man, a man he loved almost as much as Gersvind—Lothar.

During the time he had been at Fernshanz, no man had helped more than Lothar to solve the myriad problems of being the lord and adjusting to a life full of loneliness and doubt. Lothar had been an inexhaustible source of ideas and optimism. Not only had they turned Fernshanz from a struggling to a thriving manor, they had created the beginnings of a modest prosperity. Fernshanz was an example for the people of other manors and farms around them, and it was Lothar who had been the engineer of all of it.

Father Pippin revealed to Sebastian that Lothar had long had his eye on Gersvind. After all, she was the most beautiful maiden in the village. He had longed for her from the first moment she emerged from her girlhood, lovely and vivacious, standing out amongst the rude girls of the village as a pheasant among magpies.

Sebastian was shocked and mortified to learn that the entire village knew of his liaison with Gersvind. Lothar was so despondent he had become sick and stayed away from his work for a week. Sebastian had remarked how sad and distant he had seemed at that time. However, Lothar never wavered from his wholehearted loyalty and support of Sebastian. He labored even harder to find ways to make the manor work better and achieve even more. He approached his lord with a rueful smile and a residual sadness that Sebastian could only puzzle at.

Now the priest's revelation made all things clear, and Sebastian grieved to know how badly he had hurt this good man who had already given him so much. But Father Pippin was quick to connect Lothar's sadness to his eventual joy. He proposed that Gersvind be given as a bride to Lothar and that they both embark on another life in a different place, perhaps one where Lothar could attain a position in which he could excel and grow into his potential.

Sebastian listened with hope and growing determination to create a fortunate ending to the baleful situation. As soon as the priest's suggestions had sunk in, Sebastian realized that this was the solution he sought, and he made plans at once to travel to Andernach, where Lord Gonduin's vast lands might offer a favorable situation for a talented man. There, he intended to extol Lothar's virtues until Lord Gonduin could do nothing else but establish him as a steward on one of his many estates. Sebastian was as sure of the outcome as he was of the sun rising the next morning. As luck would have it, Lord Gonduin needed little convincing, for he had recently lost a good steward and was already seeking another. The arrangements were made; it only remained to convince Lothar that he should marry Gersvind and take her into a new and more promising life.

Upon his return, Sebastian wanted to go to Lothar himself and confess frankly his sorrow and remorse at what he had done. Father Pippin refused to allow him, saying that at all times he must act as the lord of the manor. He could not be seen to have the weaknesses of common men. He could, however, be generous and show his pleasure at the happiness of his people. Thus a celebration was organized in the village for the wedding of Lothar and Gersvind, which was almost as lavish as a wedding celebration for a prosperous lord. Sebastian spared no expense, and the couple's vows were celebrated for three whole days, after which they immediately departed with an escort for the estate of Lord Gonduin.

Father Pippin had proved his value as an advisor and friend to Sebastian in the skillful way he had convinced first Lothar and then Gersvind that their marriage was the only good solution to the present situation. He persuaded Lothar of Sebastian's complete unawareness of his love for Gersvind and of his abiding affection for both her and

Lothar. What he said to Gersvind, Sebastian never learned. Whatever it was, Gersvind never again looked directly at Sebastian. Nor did he ever manage to touch her again, not even to hold her hand, or speak to her directly to say good-bye or wish her well. It was as if she had died and was now only a memory. After they left for Andernach, Sebastian could not believe how much he missed her. He grieved for weeks. Only the hard work and activity of harvest and a return to the brutal regimen of the practice yard gradually relieved his mind and allowed him, at last, to sleep through the night.

Chapter 25

Old Wounds

The Eresburg Fortress, Spring 775

"Well, I'm off. Scouts are saying there's much movement starting up among the Saxons. We'll just ride out and ring their bells a little—give 'em a warning to keep away from Frankish territory."

"Wonderful, Konrad," Adela said caustically. "What will you do, burn another village and rape some more Saxon women? I've noticed you've brought several of the prettiest ones back to live with us—thankfully, in your part of our quarters."

"Bitch! You'd better be glad I keep the Saxons away from this place, otherwise they'd be here to rape you."

"Hmm, perhaps I might enjoy that a great deal more than your occasional drunken pawings."

"You insufferable slut! As if I want you anymore! I don't know what I ever saw in you in the first place. Just look at you—you're as pale as a ghost and skinny to boot. Where have your damned tits gone? Your clothes look like they've come off a peasant woman's back, and your hair's a bird's nest—not a ribbon in it. Doesn't even smell good anymore. Pah! Who would want to lie with you now? Besides, I've already gotten all I want from you."

"I'm so glad that we've come to this amicable understanding. Now you have plenty of time to play with your whores and I can concentrate on raising little Hugo."

"His name is Hugobert, damn you, after my grandfather. I want him called that, do you hear? And listen to me, woman, if you turn that boy against me, I'll kill you—slowly—which I am inclined to do more and more these days anyway."

"Go ahead, Konrad—I'm sure you're capable of it. Just be sure to make it look like suicide, or at least an accident. Otherwise my father and perhaps the king might be a bit upset about it."

"Just keep on, you worthless slag, and you'll see how much I care what they think. I am lord of the Saxon March now. They need me; I can do anything I want. I can rip off your clothes right now and have you on the floor in front of the servants if I care to. How would you like that?"

"Oh, perhaps you'd like our sweet Hugo*bert* to watch that. It might give him a good start at becoming just like you—an ignorant, vicious lout. Let me tell you something, Konrad," Adela said, her voice becoming husky and menacing, "if you ever do such a thing, you must finish the job and kill me—or you will never have another peaceful night within these walls. And don't think I care much about living anymore. I'd rather risk my life to see you dead."

"Oh, I know what you live for . . . you're still hoping that bastard Sebastian will come riding to your rescue, isn't that so? I saw how you looked at him that time in Worms before the Saxon campaign. And your own father told me how badly that bitch's whelp wanted you and was willing to give up anything and everything for you."

Adela feigned indifference to conceal the emotion she felt anytime she thought of Sebastian. "He was just a boy; there was never anything between us except a mutual desire to learn how to read—which is more than I can say for you, O Great Warrior."

"Bah—reading indeed. The guards at Andernach told me how he came to you that time after the battle of the Eresburg. He wheedled the king into letting him leave before the campaign was over so he could "take care of his people." Instead he went straight to you. The guards said he acted funny the whole time he was there and you escorted him everywhere and treated him like a prince. And then you gave away half of Andernach's possessions to that miserable beggar. My God, was your father hot over that one!"

"I did nothing more than reward Sebastian for his part at the battle for the Eresburg and for finding the Saxon treasure. My father later told me I had done as I should have, and even the king thanked me."

"Well, what were they going to do? The deed was already done. Besides, the idiot would have done better to keep his part of the treasure and buy what he needed. No matter. I suppose you heard what your little turd of a lover did next?" Konrad paused to sneer, "he marched off to western Francia on a pilgrimage, just like a beggar! They say he dressed up in monk's clothes. Took nothing with him—no weapons, no money, no baggage. He just up and disappeared down the road, walking away from Fernshanz one day with that old blind beggar. They say he caught the plague. Didn't kill him, more's the pity, but you can't kill a rat, even with the plague. I should have petitioned the king right then to let me name a new lord for what was left of Fernshanz. Now he's home again and it's too late. But I'll catch him out sooner or later, and I'll find a reason to kill him."

"By God, Edelrath, we've got to teach these bloody Saxons a harder lesson, damn them. They've broken the treaty again. I had to send four detachments to Konrad when we got back from Italy, and he barely beat them at that."

"With all due respect, sire," Count Edelrath began cautiously, "they say it was Konrad who stirred them up this year. Saxony was quiet enough when we left for Italy."

"What? He's only doing what I told him to do—keep the bastards off balance and make them know who will punish them if they break the treaty."

"Aye, lord, that he did. Konrad loves to punish."

"Well, Edelrath, it's what the devil is needed. They only understand force, and you know it. How many times have we gone against them already? They hate Christianity, they don't respect any treaty, and they don't care a fig for the notion of peace."

"That may be, my lord king," joined in Gonduin, who recently had been recognized by the king as duke of the northern region of the kingdom. "But we can ill afford this new distraction with the tremendous effort and cost of Italy so fresh behind us. They say Konrad unnecessarily stirred up the Saxons. They say he ordered ruthless, unprovoked attacks, and all of his columns came back with rich treasure chests of Saxon plunder."

"Bollocks, Gonduin! It was Widukind who raised the Saxons. It's always him, the devil. One day I will stretch his hide between two of their bloody sacred trees, if it's the last thing I do. And I don't care what Konrad plunders from those heathens. He and his men deserve every bit of it."

The two captains fell silent, recognizing that the king could not be reasoned with when he was angry. If his mind could be changed, they knew it would have to be when the storm in him had subsided.

"By thunder, I cannot endure this," Charlemagne burst out, smacking his fist into his palm. We shall go against the Saxons. Don't preach to me about Italy—I know what it cost. And the Lombards shall pay for it, too, not us. By the saints, why do you think we conquer if it doesn't pay? Aren't we putting Frankish counts into the Lombard duchies? And the bloody Saxons will pay, too!"

The king got up and paced around the room, his mind already racing ahead into the Saxon campaign. Suddenly, he stopped, straightened himself, and became calm, almost solemn. "I have a responsibility, gentlemen, to protect this realm against its enemies, and I have a greater responsibility to defend the Holy Church—indeed all of Christendom—against the devil and his agents. I take those responsibilities most seriously, gentlemen."

"We will start planning at once to go against the Saxons. Assemble the eastern army. We'll have the *Maifeld* at . . . at Dueren this year—there's a good place. It's near the Rhine, near Aix; it can be reached easily by troops from the west. And I want a lot of troops this time, do you hear? Send a general muster to every count in our ancestral lands west of the Ardennes and north to the Frisien border. And I want 'em all there in the first days of May. This time we'll take the war into the heart of Saxony. If they think Konrad is bad, wait till they see what a scourge the king can be."

The messenger arrived from Quierzy in the early days of March, just as the snows were beginning to melt off the land. Sebastian was already hard at work, preparing for the spring plowing. Incredibly, he had enjoyed two full summers of concentrating on the rebuilding of Fernshanz and he was looking forward to a third. The king, however, could not be denied. A general assembly of the army was to be held at Dueren the first week of May, and Sebastian was instructed to arrive early.

The messenger reported that the king had called for Sebastian by name and wished him to read at table. The news threw Sebastian into a panic. After the Saxon raid, he had absolutely no books or parchments. Rarely had Sebastian been able to read anything since the fires. He sought out Heimdal to help him think and Father Pippin, who had collected a few readings he used at the Mass.

"Well, Sebastian, this will teach you to do something too well," Heimdal began wryly. In deference to Sebastian's distress, he added, "It's nothing, dear boy. We simply have to think of what the king likes and then plot how to get it. So what is it, Pippin, that the king likes? You were at his court."

"He likes David," the priest said without hesitation. "He fancies that God has put him in the same circumstances as King David and has given him the same challenge. He is king over God's people, and his sacred charge is to make war on God's enemies and defeat them." After some deliberation they determined that the Eighty-Ninth Psalm and some passages from Samuel might be most well received, along with a reading or two from *The City of God*.

"But where can we get a copy of these readings?" Sebastian groaned. "It's too far to go to Paris and ask Fulrad again, and if I go to Fulda or some other monastery, there's no guarantee they would let me borrow anything.

"The Eresburg," Heimdal said calmly.

"What?"

"You must go to the Eresburg. Isn't Adela there? Isn't she the only person you know who is likely to have a Bible on hand and who is also likely to lend it to you?"

Sebastian was taken aback by Heimdal's suggestion. Every day he thought of trying to see Adela again somehow, but he despaired of it because of Konrad's hatred and jealousy. Now, however, he had an excuse to go—the call-up for the campaign. After all, even if he was the king's vassal now, the agreement was that in an emergency, he would strengthen Konrad's forces with whatever soldiers he could muster from Fernshanz.

"You're right, Heimdal," Sebastian exclaimed, "I have a reason to go there now. In fact, I must go. I need to confer with Konrad about bringing my men to fight with his cohort if need be. I'll go at once!" Sebastian jumped up and began pacing around the room, talking excitedly about the details of the trip—what he would say and who would go with him.

"A moment, Sebastian," Heimdal warned. "You cannot simply barge into the Eresburg and expect to see Adela; you mustn't even ask. Konrad is not likely to let you see her even if you do ask; it will give him pleasure to prevent it. You must go there strictly to discuss military affairs, and you mustn't stay more than a day or two. Every hour you are there with that maniac, you put yourself at greater risk."

"Then, how am I to see her—to get the books, that is?"

"Pippin must go with you. He is her old confessor and counselor, and it would not be counted amiss if, while you confer with Konrad on army affairs, Pippin requests an audience with Adela. She will be sure to lend him the books and, if it's at all possible, she will know how a meeting with you might be arranged. I'm sure she won't attempt it if the risk is too great. And you must abide by her decision, do you understand, Sebastian? You will be risking your life and perhaps hers as well, if you aren't very careful."

"I understand, Heimdal. I will be content to wait and see. At least Father Pippin can convey my words to her, and," he mumbled almost as an aside, "perhaps it will be enough just to breathe the same air as she."

The approaching visit to the Eresburg stirred up all the emotions Sebastian had tried to control since returning from the pilgrimage. He had come to regard the long journey to Tours and his subsequent sickness as a sign from God himself. He bore no outward marks of the plague or whatever illness it had been, but inside he felt he had a wound that had been inflicted by his near-death experience. He called it his "sacred wound," for it had changed what he thought and what he intended to do with the rest of his life.

He had become reconciled to the loss of Adela, knowing that she, too, had accepted her fate and regarded it as her own sacred wound. She would grow stronger from it and make her life count in other ways. Somehow the wound he bore trumped his former lust for Konrad's blood. He even felt sorry for Konrad, knowing that he would eventually descend into a hell he would no doubt create for himself. Sebastian's ambition now was just to live and work for his people and be at peace.

"Well, will you bring any soldiers, or is it just you and a handful of your old playmates?" Preparing for a hunt the next day, Konrad was in a surly mood, not having anticipated the arrival of Sebastian.

"I can bring a small detachment of perhaps twenty men. We are still replacing our losses," Sebastian replied.

"The devil! Is that all you can bring? And I'll wager they can't fight either. Bloody farmers is all you've got. The next thing you'll be telling me is you want to bring your serfs to fight for you. Bah!"

"Count Konrad," Sebastian began quietly, "we do not have enough freemen at Fernshanz to defend the fortress and at the same time send a large detachment to the field. I must leave some behind, but I assure you the men I do bring to the campaign will be warriors. All will be mounted, all will have weapons and some armor, and all will be well trained. I've worked with most of them for over a year, and I assure you they can fight."

"Oh, of course they can," Konrad said sarcastically, "though they've never fought before, and most likely they've never even seen a Saxon. No matter—I don't need 'em to fight. I'll use 'em for my transport and as camp soldiers. They can take care of my horses and cook me something to eat. But you, dear cousin," he added, "will stay with me, though you haven't seen a real fight as yet."

"I was at the Eresburg when we took it. I fought in the cavalry battle when the Saxons broke out."

"Oh, that. You think that was a battle? That was a skirmish, and from what I heard you were lucky you weren't killed. No matter—I'll protect you. We'll give you a good look at how the Franks of the Saxon

March can fight and see if you can learn. It won't be like reading a book, I can assure you."

Sebastian rose. "I'll send you the twenty men a few days before you set out for the assembly," he said, ignoring Konrad's deliberate insults and hoping to end the consultation as soon as possible.

"What? You'll be with 'em, won't you?"

"No, the king has called me to Dueren early. I must be there before the assembly begins."

"Why?" Konrad burst out loudly, obviously angry at this new manifestation of Sebastian's favor with the king.

"The king wants a report about Fernshanz—and he wishes me to read to him again."

Konrad burst out laughing. "Is that it? Well, of course you must go and 'read' to the king. That's what a good warrior does, ain't it? I'm sore ashamed I cannot do the same. I would dearly love to stand up and read some lovely psalms to the king. Well, run right along then and impress the king with your Latin phrases. Perhaps he'll make a monk out of you after all." Konrad laughed again and then clapped his hands for a servant.

"Go along now; I don't have time for any more of this. There's a big hunt tomorrow, and I need to prepare for it. I'll give you further instructions when we're at the assembly." Looking away, he waved his hand as if dismissing a servant. Sebastian only too willingly nodded his head and made a quick exit from the room.

Meanwhile, Father Pippin had sent word to Adela that he and Sebastian had come. Her reply came swiftly. Pippin was to meet her immediately in the chapel, the one place she was fairly certain Konrad would not be likely to enter.

"Father Pippin!" she exclaimed on seeing the little priest. She took his hands at once. "I am so happy to see you. Sit down here, beside me. I cannot believe you came—it has been so long. And Sebastian, how is he? I didn't send for him; Konrad would . . . well, never mind. Tell me about him and about yourself and Fernshanz. How is life for you there?"

Her questions burst from her unabated as she squeezed Pippin's hands in excitement. Finally, she allowed him to speak. "Sebastian is well," he began in a matter-of-fact tone. "He wants to see you, but he knows it would not be wise. He sends his warmest regards to you and begs you to lend him your Bible. He must read before the king soon, and the Saxons burned all the books and parchments at Fernshanz."

"Of course I will," she exclaimed passionately, "and he can have some other readings as well, with my blessing. I have quite a library now, thanks to my good father, who looks after me by sending me books. But tell me of Sebastian? Does he fare well? Is he married yet? I get so little news here in this Godforsaken place, and Konrad tells me nothing. I rarely even see him." She looked away. "As long as I'm his caged bird, he pays me little attention—he only comes in once in awhile to make sure I'm still here. It's just as well," she sighed. "I'm afraid, Father, ours is not a happy marriage, but at least I have my son."

"And how is he, madame; how fares young Hugo?"

"Oh, well enough, I suppose. He has no playmates here, and his world is a very small one. It's just me and Sister Herlindis and a few servants . . . except when Konrad bursts in on him. He comes so seldom, though. It's almost as if he forgets to visit the boy. And then when he does come, he thinks that Hugobert should love him and be happy to see him. He picks him up and whirls him about and talks to him so loudly it frightens him. He brings him inappropriate gifts, like knives or other weapons he couldn't possibly handle. It invariably results in the boy crying and holding out his arms for me. Usually, it ends with Konrad becoming enraged and storming out of the room. The boy already dreads seeing him."

"I am sorry indeed to hear that, lady. You and the boy are in my prayers every day, I assure you. I'll continue to offer my Masses for you. I wish I could do more."

"It's all right father, truly. I have my books and Sister Herlindis. She has been so good to me, a treasure, so kind and understanding. And she's so wise—she has helped me understand what I must do and even how I can be happy in this life. You will be glad to know that I have come much closer to God here in this prison than I ever could have done at Andernach or elsewhere. It's almost as if I was brought here by the finger of God to learn what is important. I've learned to praise him every day and be glad I am alive so that I can serve him and teach my son to serve him. I understand how small and insignificant this life is, and I am preparing myself joyfully for the next."

"I am truly glad and grateful, my lady Adela. I will pass this on to Sebastian. He worries about you and would like nothing more than to see you, but of course, he does not wish to compromise you in any way. We will return to Fernshanz tomorrow."

She paused and took a deep breath. "Tell Sebastian it may be possible. Konrad has a hunt tomorrow, and he will be leaving early. There's a chance I could see Sebastian here in the chapel, if you will say Mass for us tomorrow before you leave."

The day proceeded as planned. Konrad left on the hunt with many of his companions before daybreak, and Father Pippin began to say the Mass at first light, with Sebastian, Adela, and Sister Herlindis as the only participants. Archambald readied the horses and waited outside with them. Herlindis had the grace to sit on a bench near the altar, where Father Pippin slowly said the Mass, his back to the small congregation. Sebastian and Adela sat like plotting confederates in whispered dialogue near the back of the chapel.

"I would become a nun," she whispered as the Mass began. "It's the only life I want now. But I cannot escape from this place with Hugo, and I can't leave him to Konrad's gentle ministerings."

Sebastian tried to take her hand to comfort her. She resisted, saying, "Don't, my dear. You must not even touch me. He has spies everywhere; they watch everything I do. They could easily be watching through some chink in the walls—who knows? And he would use any excuse to kill you. You've taken a terrible risk just to come here. You must leave as soon as the Mass is over."

"We shall, but I had to see you, my sweet lady. It's been so long. I cannot forget you, no matter what I do or who I am with. I've tried, believe me. Nothing works. I feel we were meant to be together, and I would risk anything for that to be true."

"Oh, my friend, my only love, I've not changed either. You'll always remain at the center of my heart. But I would rather love you from afar than see you dead by the hand of that devil. I couldn't bear it if you were killed. At least I know that you're alive somewhere and that there is someone in this world who returns my love and makes me complete, even if I never get to see you or hold you. I'd rather have that distance than the emptiness that would come with your death. Promise me, Sebastian, that you will not die, not by Konrad's hand or anyone else's. At least if you say it, there's still a chance that someday we might be together. It's worth hoping for and dreaming of. Promise me!" She almost reached over to touch his face but pulled her hand away at the last moment.

"I promise, Adela. I must do what is required of me as a soldier, but I will take no unnecessary risks. God knows, I don't deserve it, but I will hold on to that hope, and if God lets me live, perhaps the dream will live as well."

Toward the end of the Mass they shared communion together and remained standing before the altar. Father Pippin gave them a special blessing, almost as if they had taken vows and were now embarked on a perilous journey. They paused a brief moment at the end to look one more time into each other's eyes and then followed Father Pippin to the door.

The light blinded them for a moment as they emerged from the dimly lit chapel, but when their eyes adjusted to the bright sunlight outside, the first thing they saw was Konrad. He was there with his entourage, directly in front of the chapel, still mounted, glowering down at the small party as if he had just caught them all in bed together.

"So this is what it is, then, an assignation as soon as my back is turned! I knew you would try something, you bitch's whelp. What did you think—that I wouldn't suspect something? And you, deceitful priest and hollow nun, did you turn your heads away and busy yourselves with false piety as they made love to each other in the shadows of the chapel? Did you really think I wouldn't know?

"Well, it's time to put an end to all this—no more lying. You're a bitch and a whore, Adela, and your lover is a piece of putrid dogshit. He deserves to die, and now is as good a time as any. You can watch while I kill him. We have good cause. Arm yourself, whore's bastard! Let it not be said that I did not give you at least the chance of a cornered rat." Konrad dismounted in a murderous rage and drew his long sword, waiting for Sebastian to respond.

Father Pippin rushed forward to stand in front of Sebastian, and Archambald seized Sebastian's arm to keep him from drawing his own sword. Sister Herlindis clutched Adela to her breast in fear.

Before Konrad could take a step, Father Pippin held up his pectoral cross before him and moved forward, surprisingly calm and fearless. "If you do this thing, Count Konrad, you must kill us all. You are greatly mistaken. We attended Mass together, nothing more, and we shared the Lord's Supper. Had you been there, you would have felt God's presence, and you would have also been welcome.

"Do not persist with this absurd threat," the priest continued, moving steadily toward Konrad with the cross held high in his hands. "Sebastian has done no wrong. If you kill him, you will kill an innocent man, and you must kill me, too, or the king will know everything. Think what you are doing, Count. The king has summoned Sebastian for a special purpose. He holds Sebastian in some esteem. If you kill the king's friend, you will find it hard to avoid his wrath. Leave off now, sir, before you make a grave mistake."

"Konrad," Adela wailed from behind the group, "for God's sake, nothing happened. He never even touched me. There is nothing between us—we only attended Mass together. What could be more innocent?"

"Hah!" blurted Konrad. "Innocence is something you've never known anything about. I know you want him. You would lie with him in that chapel if you thought you could get away with it. But I know you didn't—at least not this time. So I will let the pig go, but there will come a day . . ." Konrad glared once more at Sebastian, turned on his heel, and vaulted into the saddle. Shouting to his comrades, he clattered away in fury, leaving Sebastian, sword half-drawn, shaking in frustration.

Sebastian was grateful for the long ride home. It gave him time to control his rage and listen to the counsel of Father Pippin. After all, for the moment there was nothing to be done either about Konrad or Adela. It was best to set his mind to preparing the men for the coming campaign and himself for the journey to the king's court. Konrad's time would come.

Standing once again in a familiar place by the corner of the table nearest the king's dining platform, Sebastian began the ritual reading.

As soon as he began, the king raised his head with a start, listened a moment, and then joined Sebastian in a lusty recitation of the psalm.

"I have set a leader over the warriors;
I have raised up a hero from the army.
I have chosen David, my servant;
with my holy oil I have anointed him.
My hand will be with him;
my arm will make him strong.
No enemy shall outwit him,
nor shall the wicked defeat him.
I will crush his foes before him,
strike down those who hate him.
My loyalty and love will be with him;
through my name his horn will be exalted.
I will set his hand upon the sea,
his right hand upon the rivers.
He shall cry to me, 'You are my father,
My God, the Rock that brings me victory!'"

"Splendid choice, Sebastian!" cried the king, obviously delighted by this first choice of readings. "How did you know I like this one so much? You must be a seer. It's quite my favorite, and it's just what we need right now. Perhaps it should be the message, the fundamental essay of this campaign 'the king will crush his foes before him . . . God will make his arm strong, no enemy shall outwit him!' And now let's say the psalm in the Frankish tongue. Do you know it?"

Chapter 26

Changing the Way

Saxony, Summer 775

The thin, blond girl of thirteen or fourteen years cowered by the stump she was bound to, a short, thick rope noosed around her neck and the end tied in multiple knots to the stump. She had been trying frantically to pick the knots apart, but her small fingers could not budge even the first knot. She was weeping in desperation, her pale face contorted with effort.

Sebastian had left the village as soon as the raping started. He had already seen too much of it and it sickened him. It was as if the warriors did not see the enemy's women as people but only as prizes to be plucked and used as quickly as possible before someone else did. A few—the prettiest ones—like this girl, were swung up on the riders' horses and spirited away to the forest, to be enjoyed later at leisure and then sold as slaves.

The girl jerked her hands away from the knots as soon as she became aware of Sebastian. Her mouth gaped open and she cringed low to the ground, gasping in fear. Sebastian felt great pity for her and wished to sweep her up into his arms and comfort her like a child. In a burst of rage and compassion, he leapt from his horse and slashed at the rope with his short sword until it came free of the stump. Then he gently removed the noose from the girl's neck and carefully pulled her to her feet, guiding her slowly to his horse, all the while speaking softly to her as to a child. He mounted and swept her up quickly behind him. Turning the horse, he galloped down the forest path toward Saxon territory.

They rode for a league or so until Sebastian began to notice signs of another village, a widening of the path, wood stacked beside the road, fresh horse manure, and a hastily abandoned cart barely concealed in the trees. It was clear that some of the defeated Saxons had retreated this way. Sebastian halted and swung the girl down. He pointed down the road toward the village.

"Go, you will find your people there. Tell them Sebastian, the Frank, has set you free. Go!" With that he wheeled the charger and cantered back into the forest.

Fernshanz was awash with celebration. Warriors swaggered everywhere, shouting with exhilaration, made completely prodigal by their great victory. As the wine flowed, war songs filled the great room, and tables and benches stood in immediate danger of being wrecked.

With staggering force, the Franks had charged into Saxon territory. At Syburg, they smashed the one fortress the Saxons had been trying to establish on the Frankish border and captured the entire garrison. They paused briefly at the Eresburg, where Charlemagne vowed once more to Konrad to strengthen that outpost so that it could never again be taken, and then they drove deeply into Saxon territory all the way to the Weser River in the middle of Saxony.

On the Weser, Sebastian decisively became a true veteran of the grim business of war. The Saxons made a stand behind hasty earthworks, their backs to the river. They attempted a cavalry charge as the Franks approached but ran up against a wall of large horses and iron. Their cavalry was cut to pieces, and the remnant retreated ignominiously back behind the earthworks. The Saxons lacked the armor, the horses, and the leadership to put up a good fight. At the end of the day, when the earthworks had been overrun, they gave up in droves. Many were roped together in long lines of captives, bound eventually for the slave markets. Others were corralled behind makeshift fences to await parley stipulations and a hostage exchange. Any who resisted or tried to escape were summarily executed.

Sebastian was with the king's cavalry, again commanded by Edelrath. He had been afraid at first, but in the heat and clamor of the first clash, he lost himself in the fight, unconsciously reacting almost automatically to the threat in front of him, as he had been trained to do. Visions of the infamous "rope" of his training days flashed coincidentally into his mind as he fought. He was surprised at how easy it turned out to be. There was the initial jarring crash and boom as the two sides met with a flurry of blows, and then each new opponent somehow incredibly fell away as he slashed and jabbed with whatever weapon he chose to use. He found he knew exactly what to do, and he did it with increasing skill and confidence. At the end of the day, even after they forced their way over the earthworks amidst deafening cheers and screams, he found himself acting instinctually, in a state of complete concentration, blocking out all else but the man in front of him. When it was over and they told him he had killed at least eleven men, he thought he had killed only one, and in the night that followed, he mourned that single man, whose face he could not remember.

At Fernshanz, the king again called Sebastian to his side. "Well, the fight at the river was spectacular, Sebastian. Edelrath says you fought like a lion to overcome the barricade. And then, as if that were not enough, he says you distinguished yourself again during that midnight scrape at Lubbecke."

The Saxons had sought revenge through a surprise night attack against Edelrath's troops as they recovered from the grueling battle on the Weser. They had waited until Edelrath sent out foragers to bring in needed water and supplies, and then they slipped into the sleeping camp along with the returning foragers.

"It could have been much worse for us," the king continued warmly, "if you hadn't roused the camp and fought back. As it was, we lost a lot of men unnecessarily. By God, it took a Saxon with a large pair of bollocks to come into our camp like that."

"It was Widukind, my lord," Sebastian replied quietly.

"What? Widukind! How do you know that?"

"I saw him, my lord. I spoke to him."

"By God, Sebastian, what are you saying? The Westphalians weren't even supposed to be there. You spoke to him? Absurd! He could have killed you."

"No, my lord. As it was, I almost killed him."

The king was flabbergasted. "You almost . . . what? What are you saying, Sebastian? Are you drunk? Explain at once."

"My lord king, I woke up when I heard a man cry out in pain. I saw the Saxons striding among our sleeping men, hacking at them to the right and left as they went. I shouted the alarm at once and rushed to the fight. Thank God there were not many of them and we soon turned the tide, but as they were running, one stood his ground to cover the retreat. It was Widukind. I saw him clearly in the moonlight, the same big, blond man who met with you that time in front of the Eresburg. I engaged him with a will, and as he backed away to follow his men, he stumbled over a body and fell. I had my sword at his throat."

"Well, what happened? Why didn't you kill him?"

"I don't know, my lord—I couldn't. I said to him, 'Are you Prince Widukind?' He answered, 'I am. And if you are going to kill me, you had better do it quickly before someone else does. You will be famous.' And he laughed."

"Then what?" said the king, mouth agog.

"I stepped back and let him get up. He asked me who I was and when I told him, he tapped his breast once with his fist and said 'There lies my sword. Take it. Consider it a hostage for my life.' Then he turned and disappeared into the forest. This is the sword."

The king took the sword gingerly and examined the runic marks upon the haft. Later, he would ascertain that they were indeed the marks of a Saxon prince.

"Why did you let him go?" the king said in disbelief. "We've been after that devil for years. Why didn't you finish him?"

"My lord, he was a prince. If it had been you and I was a Saxon, I could not have killed you either."

Later, in another part of the villa, Sebastian huddled alone in a tiny room. He could no longer stand to be a part of the reveling or to listen, as the wine removed all reserve, to the raucous boasting and minute recounting of the details of every battle or skirmish.

As far as his "sword brothers" were concerned, the camaraderie of campaign and the crucible of battle had indeed bonded him to some of them, but he was repelled by their cruelty in war, their avarice and unbridled excesses after a battle. For them, strength, courage, honor, and loyalty were the major virtues of a man. There was not much room in their minds for mercy or compassion. With few exceptions, they were proud, sanguinary, and ruthless, delighting in warfare. The great majority were illiterate semi-pagans, Christian more in name than in reality. Although his mind was more open, even the king was much like them.

To add to Sebastian's dismay at the outcome of the battle, he narrowly avoided a fight with Turpin of Mayence, a mercurial young warrior from a county on the upper Rhine. Turpin flew into a rage when Sebastian admitted freeing the young girl after the fight on the Weser.

Irked by Turpin's belligerent arrogance and galled by his loud threats about what he would do if he discovered who had taken the girl, Sebastian had stood up and without bothering to offer a reason calmly announced, "I did it. I let her go."

Turpin's mouth fell open, his face contorting with indignation and rising anger. Sebastian met his furious gaze with an expression of contempt.

"You what? How could you let her go? She was not your captive," Turpin shouted, going red in the face. "That was Widukind's bastard daughter, you damfool! One of his chiefs told me where she was hiding in exchange for sparing his life. She might have been worth a fortune in ransom. You had no right!

"What's the matter with you?" Turpin shouted. "Don't you know the rules? I think you must be crackbrained!"

"I don't give a damn what you think," Sebastian replied offhandedly. "I would do it again."

Only the intervention of Count Edelrath, who happened to be in the great hall at the time, prevented a brawl, as both men's hands moved to their swords. Holding both hands high in the air as a gesture of restraint, the count moved quickly between them, turning first to one and then to the other with a look of warning in his eyes.

"Stop this at once," he commanded. "Take your hands off your swords or I will have you seized. You, Turpin, leave this room immediately and return to your cantonment area. I will join you there presently. You, Sebastian, come with me."

The count made it clear in the uncompromising conversation that followed that Sebastian was in the wrong. It was strictly against the established practices of Frankish warfare to steal or otherwise tamper with another man's war spoils. If left unreconciled, such a breach of the custom could lead to feuding and bloodshed.

"You must make amends. Do you understand?" the count admonished sternly. "What have you got to give him in exchange for the loss of his prisoner? Any gold? Any prisoners he can use as hostages?"

"No, my lord. I instructed my men to take only weapons, iron objects, and horses. No people."

"Then you must give him horses. How many did you take?"

"I think my men rounded up about thirty after the battle."

"That's good," the count grunted in satisfaction. "Give him half."

"Half, my lord? These are good horses—warhorses. They would go a long way toward helping me equip all of my soldiers with mounts."

"Sebastian," the count said gruffly, "you must play by the rules unless you want to make enemies of your own comrades. Like everything else in life, if you want to be different, you must pay the price. Now give Turpin half of what you've got. You are lucky that girl was only Widukind's bastard daughter; if it had been his son or one of his legitimate daughters, it might have taken you years to pay Turpin back. As it is, that girl was worth the price you're going to pay."

In the end, Sebastian sent Archambald to Turpin with the horses and instructions to let him choose the ones he wanted. He would not go himself, and he would not apologize to Turpin.

Chapter 27

God's Punishment

Syburg, Summer 776

Autumn and winter passed without further fighting. Fernshanz prospered, Lothar's innovations took hold, and peasants of all sorts began showing up to enlist in Sebastian's growing community. The majority were men who could prove they were free. They brought their families and their weapons, for they knew they would have to defend any land they might be given to farm. They came for a chance for more strips of land than they had worked previously and because they heard the master was fair to his people. All serfs and runaway slaves were turned away.

Sebastian had hopes of passing another summer without a call-up. The moat in front of the citadel at Fernshanz was almost finished, and they would soon be able to fill it with water. The winter wheat crop on the new fields of the bottomlands near the river looked marvelous, thanks to the work of the deep plow. The three-field system had worked, and there would be enough to eat for everyone. His profound pleasure and pride in the achievements of his thriving community were soon dashed by frantic messengers riding furiously from Count Konrad.

That year the king was forced to campaign in Italy to put down a Lombard rebellion against Frankish rule. To spite Sebastian's hopes, there was to be no peace on the eastern frontier either. Widukind had raised the Saxons again. They broke their oaths, abandoned their hostages, and brought a host of the various tribes together. Through an incredibly bold ruse, Widukind actually succeeded in winning back the Eresburg fortress without losing a man.

The Saxon prince waited until his spies informed him that Count Konrad had left the fortress to look after his interests at Adalgray, taking a sizeable portion of the garrison's soldiers with him. Widukind then appeared without warning before the fortress gates with a swarm of screaming Saxon soldiers and an impressive array of siege machines, including catapults. With his usual daring and bravado, Widukind rode up to the gates alone and called for a parley.

When a trio of Konrad's lieutenants naively honored the request and emerged on foot through the main gate, Widukind parleyed with them for less than a minute and then rode them all down and cut them to pieces in a ferocious attack that took full advantage of their astonishment. Only one of them even managed to draw his sword before he died. The gates slammed shut just before Widukind managed to jam his spear into the closing gap. He galloped back to his lines whooping, a sword in one hand and his spear held high in the other. Everything happened with such jaw dropping speed that not a single Frankish arrow followed Widukind's exultant retreat.

That night, as the Saxons drunkenly celebrated their leader's daredevil courage and skill in anticipation of the next day's conquest, the entire Frankish garrison, every man, woman, and child, including Adela and little Hugobert, slipped out of the rear gate and escaped through the woods to the fortress at Syburg in the west. Riders intercepted Konrad's returning column and diverted it to Syburg only a day later.

Sebastian and the men of Fernshanz arrived at Syburg the next morning after riding all day and a night.

"Well, it took you long enough, damn you; we could have been overrun while you dillydallied. How many troops have you brought me?" demanded Konrad, as Sebastian led the Fernshanz men through the gates.

"I came as soon as I could get the men together, Lord Konrad. We brought more than half the garrison, nearly a hundred men," Sebastian replied calmly, long used to Konrad's churlish manner.

"By God, why didn't you bring the whole garrison, you idiot? Don't you realize that if we lose here, your precious Fernshanz will be next?"

"There are women and children at Fernshanz, Lord Konrad."

"Damn them to hell. All the more for the Saxons to rape if the Syburg is taken. You're a fool. Get your men in place, damn your eyes, and quickly! You're responsible for the western and rear walls, and you better not neglect them or I'll cut you down myself, you stupid pup. Widukind will be here before we can take a morning shit tomorrow, or I don't know him."

Made overconfident by the easy conquest of the Eresburg and reveling in their victory, the Saxons missed a golden opportunity to take the Syburg fortress as well. The refugees managed to slip into safety behind the walls at Syburg just ahead of both Konrad and Sebastian, who rushed their troops by forced march into the fortress in plenty of time to prepare for the Saxon attack. When the Saxons finally showed up, they paraded arrogantly and loudly before the walls in a brazen attempt to intimidate the defenders into giving up as at the Eresburg. When they finally mounted an attack, it was haphazard and poorly organized. As a result they were soundly thumped and thrown back in disarray.

"Are you mad?" shrieked Adela. "You can't take Hugo up to the battlements—he's three years old! Have you completely lost your mind? Give him to me at once!"

Konrad shoved her roughly, causing her to trip over a bench and fall to the floor. "I will take my son where I will, you slut. He needs to experience a bit of the warrior life and see his father in command. He will be a great Frankish warrior, and it is not too soon to show him what his life will be like. Besides, the Saxons are already beaten. All their assaults have failed, and they don't even know how to use their own damned siege machines. Most of them didn't work at all, and with the one they did get to work, they flung a huge rock right on top of their own front ranks. My troops nearly fell off the walls laughing.

"No one's seen hide or hair of Widukind, either. I don't think he's even with 'em. This fight is already finished." Konrad moved confidently toward the door, singing as he bounced the boy up and down in his arms. "*Huppa, huppa, der Reiter . . .*"

"Please, Konrad, don't take him," Adela pleaded. "He's just a baby. It's too soon for him to see all that fighting—he'll be frightened to death."

"All the more reason for him to see it now. He must get over his fears and learn to be a Frankish warrior—fearless and eager for battle. Right, boy? Besides, there's no danger now. I'll bring him back directly. Meanwhile, you will stay here. I won't have you opposing me in front of my men."

Hoisting the boy onto his shoulders, Konrad slammed the door in Adela's face as she desperately tried to stop him. As she heard the key turn in the lock, she collapsed, sobbing against the door.

Up on the walls, Konrad was in for a surprise. There were suddenly many more Saxons in the field before the fortress, twice as many as before. The catapults had indeed been abandoned, but Konrad could see that a heavy battering ram was being rushed forward toward the main gate, accompanied by makeshift walls of wood being carried along the sides and held above the soldiers to ward off arrows as they advanced. A courier from Sebastian had warned that there might be a simultaneous attack from the rear. Many Saxons were seen gathering at the edge of the woods, and Sebastian himself had caught a brief glimpse of a white horse.

The attack began with fire arrows. Then horns sounded. Scores of screaming Saxons raced toward the fortress, each man seeking to be the first over the walls. Konrad was so taken aback he seemed frozen with the boy in his arms. Hugo was now thoroughly alarmed and began wailing for his mother. Konrad came to his senses with a start, grimaced fiercely at the screaming child, and roughly handed him off to one of his personal bodyguards. "Take him for Christ's sake. How can I run a battle with a baby in my arms? Take him back to his mother, damn her, and damn him, too, for a squalling brat." In a heartbeat, he had forgotten the boy and become totally absorbed in the unfolding battle.

Meanwhile, Sebastian had all he could do to hold off Widukind's attack on the rear wall. The prince was indeed there, mounted on his white horse just beyond the front wave of attackers, his banner-bedecked spear raised high in the air for all to see. The men of Fernshanz found themselves in a desperate fight to fend off the rampaging Saxons. Sebastian was obliged almost at once to take every second man from the western wall to reinforce the rear wall. For almost an hour a furious battle raged. A few Saxons succeeded in climbing over the walls but were met immediately by Sebastian with a small reserve. Finally, the horns sounded again, and the Saxons withdrew into the woods. There was no doubt in Sebastian's mind that they would be back.

Calling Archambald and Liudolf to him, he announced, "Well, my friends, it's time to play the game."

"What game, lord?' Archambald wheezed, still breathing heavily from the excitement of the fighting. "You can't be joking at a time like this?"

"You know, the game with the kites, the one we practiced so many times—about confusing the enemy."

"Oh," Archambald mouthed absently, the light dawning in his head. "Aye, Sebastian," he said, suddenly enthused with the idea, "I know it well. I ought to; I had to run enough to learn how to keep the bloody thing up in the wind. What about it?"

"Well, go and fetch the kites, you dunce, and hurry! And send me that little troop of boys I spoke to before the attack began. They should be waiting right by the little chapel. *Um Gottes willen. Mach' schnell!*"

The boys arrived before Archambald, and Sebastian set them to work at once building piles for bonfires on either side of the chapel. Under Sebastian's eye they had worked all through the previous night gathering the wood and branches.

Now, as the bonfires began to catch hold well, the boys threw evergreen boughs on top of the piles so that the smoke billowed up copiously, dark grey in color. Archambald trotted in, puffing. "Here they be, Sebastian, cords and tails and all."

"Finally! Good. Quickly now, put them together and take this pitch and paint a big black cross on each kite, so big that everyone will be able to see it, especially the Saxons. And then raise them up— as quick as you can now. There's no time to lose. Liudolf, when you're finished, take one of the kites and fly it on the far side of the chapel. Hurry now, both of you!"

As fate would have it, a breeze helped them raise the scarlet kites quickly. The long black crosses were clearly visible as the kites danced in and out of the billowing smoke just as the Saxons launched their next attack, once more against both the front and rear walls. Liudolf and Archambald moved the kites skillfully back and forth around the fires so that they seemed to be both a part and a consequence of the smoke.

The effect on the Saxons was immediate. They stopped in midstride, awed by the apparition. Some began to falter, not daring to go a step further toward the eerie sight. At that point, Sebastian ordered horns to be blown continuously and as loudly as possible as the kites swooped through the smoke.

"They're running, by God," Konrad shouted exultantly, his sword still dripping with the blood of the first wave of attackers. Those Saxons who had managed to reach the front wall leaped down from their scaling ladders and crashed into the backs of the retreating ranks of their fellows. Some were in such haste they almost ran upon the spears of the ranks that were still advancing. In minutes, there was unmitigated confusion.

Konrad saw the opportunity at once and wasted no time. "Order the reserve to hie to their horses," he barked to a young courier, "and tell 'em to be ready to ride straightaway. Run like the devil, boy!" Unable to wait, he, too, leaped down from the parapet and made for the stable as fast as his bulky body and short legs would allow him.

As soon as he was sure the Saxons had indeed retreated, Sebastian hastened to the women's quarters to make sure Adela was safe. She began screaming as soon as she heard him knock on the door. He had to break it down to let her out. She grabbed him and cried. "We've got to find him, Sebastian! We've got to bring him back, get him away from here! Please, oh God, help me!"

"Who, Adela? Who is it you're talking about?"

"It's Hugo!" she wailed. "He's taken my baby up to the walls. We've got to find him, Sebastian—we've got to save him! Help me!" She already had Sebastian by the arm and was dragging him with her through the door and toward the front wall.

"Who has taken Hugo, Adela? Tell me! What has happened?"

At that moment the cavalry swept past toward the main gate with Konrad in the lead, entirely swept up in the moment, his mind and body focused on the counterattack. The gates swung open and the force threw themselves after the retreating Saxons.

"Oh God," Adela groaned, "where is my poor child?

They found the boy eventually, his small body crushed beneath the parapet by the main gate, his neck broken by the fall. Later Sebastian pieced together what had happened. According to the accounts of two surviving soldiers on that part of the wall, the praetorian into whose arms Konrad had thrust the boy had paused a fateful moment to look over the wall at the rapidly advancing Saxons. In that one second an arrow struck him in the eye before he could even start toward the ladder. He had staggered backward and fallen into the courtyard below, bringing Hugo down with him to his death.

Konrad returned in the middle of the night, exhilarated by the successful counterattack. He immediately began preparations to continue the pursuit of the Saxons as soon as he could reequip and reinforce the cavalry and see to the reorganization of the fortress defenses. He sent couriers to the king and Duke Gonduin, bragging of a huge victory over Widukind, and then he was gone again at first light, apparently not having given a single thought to the fate of his son.

Adela would not bury the child. She kept his body wrapped in blankets on her own bed and stayed there with him, rocking back and forth on the edge of a bench by the bed. Sebastian was so concerned he called on one of the medicine women of the village to give her a potion in a hot herb drink to make her sleep. In the middle of the night, Adela finally fainted into the bed beside her son's small body and slept until noon the next day. Sebastian stayed by her side, only stepping outside the door occasionally to get a report from Liudolf or Archambald.

"I've got to get away from here, Sebastian," Adela said when she regained consciousness. "I must go before I kill him or die trying. He has murdered my son, and he isn't even aware of it. I want to scream my cries for justice to all the saints and angels, and beseech God to condemn Konrad to burn in hell. I cannot bear it that he still draws breath."

"We will go, Adela," Sebastian said, holding a wet rag on her forehead as she lay in the bed. "Calm yourself now—it will serve no purpose if you become ill. Rest now. Sleep some more if you can. Tomorrow, we'll talk of going."

He left her in the care of Sister Herlindis and made his way around the defenses. In spite of the odds and the initial ferocity of the Saxon attack, the garrison had not fared too badly. The Fernshanz troop had lost twelve men, with two more too severely wounded to be moved. All the walls continued to be manned at nearly full strength.

At last, Konrad returned on the morning of the second day since his departure. His cavalry force had enjoyed initial success, but halfway to the Eresburg, his troop was ambushed and very nearly surrounded. In the end they wound up ingloriously, showing their horses' rumps to Widukind as they scurried back to the fort.

When Konrad strode into Adela's bedroom, visibly shaken and alarmed at the news he had only just received, Adela attacked him at once and without warning. She grabbed the first thing at hand, a bronze candleholder, and rushed upon him with a fury. Her first blow broke a finger in his left hand, and he narrowly avoided having his head bashed in with the second. He finally managed to wrench the candleholder away from her and threw her back onto the bed with an oath and a roar. Only the intervention of Sister Herlindis stopped him from dashing her brains out with her own weapon. Instead, he flung it into a corner and fled from the room, holding his wounded hand with the other. Adela's curses followed him down the hall.

"You must take her," Konrad later insisted to Sebastian. "She's gone completely insane. I can't reason with her; God, I can't even talk to her, and I can't stand her anymore. She screams at me and calls me a murderer—I, who saved this fortress and all in it from a Saxon ravaging! I am innocent. As soon as I saw the danger, I gave the child to my most trusted guard. How could I know that he'd be killed? I didn't even see it; the Saxons were upon us."

"I can take her home, Lord Konrad. I can take her to Andernach. She has told me she wants to become a nun."

"Good! And good riddance! Let God have her, and see how he does with her. Finally, finally I'll have some peace. Take her. Take her at once. I don't care what happens to her. You can ravage her yourself if you want to—it matters not a whit to me now. I can't wait to see the back of her and all her bitterness and accusations. I'm not a murderer. I couldn't prevent what happened to Hugobert. If anything, she should have come up to the battlements with me—then I could have just given him back to her straightaway once I saw the danger. Besides," he added petulantly, "it's just one child. We could have made others if she had just been a true wife to me, the witch. I haven't slept with her in a year."

"We will leave in the morning, Konrad. If you don't object, I will bury the boy's body at Fernshanz."

"I don't give a damn where you bury him. Just get him—and her—out of here as soon as possible. I want to be quit of the whole business, and the sooner the better."

"We're goin' back to Andernach, Drogo! And we're takin' the daughter of the Duke of Andernach in our boat! Do ye know what a honor that is? They say she can't ride no more, bein' sick and all, because of her on'y child gettin' killed like that durin' the fight at Syburg. I saw 'em plantin' the little lad there in the church graveyard. The young master says we're to get the boat ready double quick and be waitin' to go at any time."

"Aw, Bardulf, I don' want to go back to Andernach. I'm afeared of that big river. We ain't never crossed over it before in our own boat, and it's big—bigger'n anythin'."

"Don' you worry, Drogo. It'll be easy. When we gets to the Rhine, the master'll hire horses to pull us upriver in the shallows, and then it's a quick crossover to Andernach. Why, we might even sail across on the ferry barge and leave our boat on this side since they knows how to do it better. And then, when we're done there, we'll just drift on back with the current and use our sail to get us home on the Lippe. It's goin' to be easy—ye'll see."

"Ye go, Bardulf. I'd just as soon stay home this time. I'm afeared even when we sail up to Lippeham. Ye know I can't swim."

"Listen, you lump, I'm goin' to need ye, so yer goin' and that's a end of it. And besides, Drogo, don' ye remember them pretty girls down there at Andernach? I'm thinking of bringin' one back with me this time, as well as some of that lovely Dragon's Blood wine. Why, we might even find a roly-poly little splitter for ye. Wouldn't ye like that now? Come on, Drogo. This can be the kind of trip we've been dreamin' of ever since we got the boat."

They buried Hugo's little body beside Ermengard and Attalus. Adela was content with that, knowing that the place would at least be near Sebastian. She stayed in bed three full days before she was ready to travel again.

Meanwhile, Sebastian saw to the fortress and the fields, mindful that this might be the last chance he would have this summer to see personally to the affairs of Fernshanz. He visited the families of the men he had lost and conferred with the village council about their welfare. He inspected the barns and building projects and rode over every foot of the Fernshanz lands. He commanded Bruno to double the training for the Fernshanz detachment until such time as the king brought the army, and to ready the horses and supplies. Then, reluctantly, he settled Adela into Bardulf's boat and headed down river toward the Rhine.

Adela was strangely distant with him on the trip. She stayed mostly in the makeshift bed he made for her in the boat and waved him away whenever he tried to touch her or comfort her. "No, Sebastian," she said, "we mustn't start something we can't finish. I'm married still—it will not do. What has happened is already God's punishment because of our desire for each other. Besides, I cannot think of your love now. I lost my little boy, whom I loved so much. My soul is in shreds and my body is sick."

"You'll heal, Adela," he whispered to her, holding her hands. "I'll bring you back; one day you will be happy again. You'll see. This will pass away, as all bad things do. And I will always be there for you. I don't care if you are married. It means nothing, certainly not in God's eyes; it has never been a marriage."

"That is not what the Church or the king would say, or even my father, though he hates that bastard who was my husband and knows him now for what he is. It is the way things are," she sighed, and let go of his hands. "I'll go to the convent with Herlindis. Perhaps that is what God has wanted for me all along."

"No, Adela—God does not wish to punish you, and that's what the convent would do if it prevented you from loving me as I love you."

"I can't love you like that again, Sebastian—not now. That's why we have suffered. We sinned, don't you see? Even if only in our hearts. We longed for each other and sinned each time we imagined ourselves in each other's arms. And now I must pay for never trying to be a wife to Konrad, for hating him as I do. I was never a good wife; I never even tried. God knows."

"That is not your fault—Konrad was a beast! No woman could have made him a good wife. You were forced to marry him and he treated you like a slave. Besides, we loved each other first and promised ourselves to each other—before Konrad and the king intervened. God knows that, too."

"True enough—Konrad is the devil himself, and being with him was the worst trial I could have had. But I think now that I had to endure Konrad to know what God wants; He wants me for Himself. I'm not sure, but I think I lost Hugo because of my sins. That is why I must go to the convent now and try to understand. I must discover what it is that God wants of me."

Sebastian left Adela at Andernach in the care of Sister Herlindis. Duke Gonduin was already with the king, who, having returned victorious from Italy, had immediately called a new assembly at the town of Worms. King Karl was infuriated that the Saxons had revolted again and that they had even managed to take the Eresburg and burn it down. He was determined to bring down his thunder upon them.

Sebastian joined the king at Worms with a contingent of Fernshanz men just before the army set out for the Saxon frontier. Word had spread about the ingenious part Sebastian had played in the route of the Saxons at Syburg, and the king was eagerly awaiting the full account.

"My boy, you are full of surprises! Sometimes I think you dabble in magic. Where'd you ever get an idea like those . . . what do you call 'em? Kites?"

"Yes, my lord king," Sebastian said. "Kites. And I got them from your *marchant*, Simon the Rhadanite."

"Oh, him, is it? Right. Clever fellow. Bold for a Jew. Sold me some beautiful silk. But he didn't give me any of those kites, by God. How dare he keep such a secret! How'd you worm 'em out of him?"

"He just came to see me one day in his boat. We stayed up all night talking. He's a well-traveled man and knows much that I wanted to learn. By the end of it, he called me his friend and gave me the kites, along with the story of how they had been used in a place called Kitai."

"Yes, I've heard of that place. It's even much farther to the East than that Baghdad everyone says is such a rich and powerful city. I should like to know more about all that—and you shall tell me all you know.

"By the way, I saw you putting your cavalry through its paces yesterday. Regwald told me I ought to see what you're up to. Quite a show, from the little I saw of it. But what was all that business about the charge—shields high, spears low, front line riding cheek by jowl? Hardly any room between 'em."

"Sire, I have trained the Fernshanz men you saw for more than a year. They're well disciplined and devoted to the unit and to myself, if I may say so. We use a tight formation with all horsemen using stirrups and charge in a very straight line, with all spears couched until impact. We use heavier spears, more like lances. Then we wheel and charge again, in line, and as many times as it can be effective.

"It's the stirrups that make it work so well, my lord king," Sebastian continued fervently. "Attalus brought them back from Spain years ago."

"I know, it's those silly ropes you put your feet in," the king said dismissively. "I've seen 'em. Wouldn't use 'em, myself. I tell you what, boy, if you get your feet tangled in those ropes and fall off your horse, he'll drag you to death."

"But sire, that's just the point. The stirrups keep a warrior from being knocked off his horse. They give him a solid seat. He can lean into the charge, with his feet anchored in the saddle, and put his whole weight and the weight of the horse behind his spear. I believe, sire, that no cavalry in the world could stand against us if we could learn to fight like that."

"That's a bold boast! Can you prove it? Have you tried it?"

"No, my lord king, I have not. We haven't had an opportunity as yet."

"Well, you shall have one, Sebastian. Bring what cavalry you have, and you'll fight with me this time. We shall have many nights together on this campaign. I plan to run the Saxons into the ground and not stop until they are prostrate before me. By God, I'll have their heads this time."

As it turned out, the king had to do little fighting on this campaign. The Saxons faded before him like snow in the spring sun. It was said that Widukind got wind of the king's approach and immediately took his entourage back into the forest sanctuary of the Danes.

Charlemagne got as far as the source of the River Lippe and was met there by a large delegation of Saxon leaders pleading for mercy and offering hostages and allegiance to the king. The Saxon capitulation was so great that Charlemagne felt emboldened to build a new fortification at a place called Paderborn. It was the first outpost so deep inside Saxon lands, and the king felt he could at last see the end of the Saxon wars and the incorporation of his ancient pagan enemies into Christendom.

Chapter 28

Alas, Adelaide

Summer 777

"M'lord Sebastian!" Bardulf shouted in alarm. "Look downriver. A boat's comin'. See it? There, by the bend?" Sebastian rose up from inspecting the rotten seed Bardulf had just brought back from the port at Lippeham. He was angry at the merchants for having traded the mess to him and angry at Bardulf for not making sure of what he had in his bundles. He had just finished blistering the lanky youth with acid comment on his abilities, first as a trader and secondly as a boatman—one, he opined, being as disastrous as the other. Bardulf was only too happy to spy a distraction, even one which might mean danger.

Sebastian immediately blew a signal horn to warn the fort and waited. It soon became clear that only one boat, a low-lying Frankish cargo vessel, was approaching. As it drew closer, Sebastian began to make out the banner flying from the mast. It was the badger crest of Count Luedegar, and standing foremost in the bow was his daughter, Adelaide.

She swept off the boat as if she owned the land she trod upon and approached Sebastian laughing, as if she had only seen him yesterday, though in truth it had been almost five years. She ran up to meet him and threw her arms around his neck, much to his embarrassment, as his men were looking on. "My dear old Sebastian, how pretty you still are! In fact, you've become even more handsome—filled out now, big muscles, ummh!" And she raised a shapely arm and, scowling, clapped her bicep as if to show her own fierceness.

"My God, Sebastian, but you live in the wilderness!" she exclaimed, waving an arm at the forest around them. "Not one settlement did we see or even a house between here and the Rhine. I began to fear we would run right into the bloody Saxons before we found you. Well, are you going to stand there? Aren't you going to invite me into your . . . uh, castle?"

Five years had made little difference for Sebastian as he found himself tongue-tied again in the presence of this bold, vibrant woman. She had grown into her full beauty; even though she wore a traveling cloak, the buxom, captivating curves of her body were still stirringly evident. As before, he could also detect the siren smell of her before she got down from the boat.

Somehow, Heimdal heard of Adelaide's presence and hurried out of his lair in the woods to be present at supper in the manor. Sebastian was quick to welcome him as a buffer between himself and Adelaide, who had already assumed an uncomfortable familiarity with his body, patting his face whenever he came near her, squeezing his arms, and even occasionally, while standing or walking beside him, letting her hand run down lightly over his buttocks. "My dear young woman, how generous of you to grace us barbarians with your presence," Heimdal began as the wine was being passed around. "You have no idea how boring this place can be. There are absolutely no women here, none at all, unless you count the peasant wenches— which . . . ahem, I'm ashamed to say, I must do upon occasion. But you, my dear, appear to be a gift from Olympus, and may I be so bold to say you have the voice and scent of an angel."

Adelaide rewarded the blind man with a melody of delighted laughter. "Sebastian, where did you find this lovely fellow? And why aren't you more like him? I mean, you could at least greet me with a lustful look or two. Heimdal can't even see me and he 'looks' at me that way. If he weren't such an elderly gentleman, I should be tempted to encourage his flirtations."

Heimdal stayed long after supper, regaling Adelaide with tales of his youth and the adventures he had with Attalus, as well as those of his more recent pilgrimage with Sebastian. Adelaide had heard of the trip, of course. It was common knowledge among the Franks after Sebastian had stopped at Andernach on his return. Most were of the opinion that the young man was crazed by the devastation of the Saxon attack on Fernshanz or by the fierce fighting at the Eresburg. Since then he had endured worse. Adelaide had come to see for herself.

What she saw reassured her that Sebastian was thoroughly himself, serious, steadfast, and fully in charge of everything around him, except herself, of course. She spent a good deal of the evening bantering with Heimdal and listening to his stories, but her eye kept wandering back to Sebastian, as if she were measuring him, applying his plusses and minuses against a hidden scale in her brain.

Finally, Heimdal begged to be excused and retired to the pantry storeroom, where he slept when he was at the manor. Although Sebastian immediately offered to settle Adelaide in for the night, she was not ready to sleep but began at once to put herself as close to him as possible. She urged him to sit down beside her on the bench before the fireplace and plied him with yet another beaker of wine, saying she had so much to tell him and to find out about him. Feeling like a rabbit in a snare, Sebastian could offer only weak protest.

"Sebastian," Adelaide whispered, after laying her head on his shoulder and caressing his face and neck, "do you know why I'm here?"

"I do not, Adelaide. But it doesn't matter. I'm glad to see you under any circumstances, and you are welcome. We get very few guests here at Fernschanz."

"Sebastian, what if I said I'm here not as a guest but as your . . . potential wife?"

"What?" Sebastian said, as if she had struck him, and he slid out from under her arms. "What are you talking about? What are you thinking?" He tried to stand, but she pulled him back down beside her.

"I must marry," she said forthrightly, becoming suddenly earnest. Her voice took on a new tone, one of dread and supplication. "Please hear me out. My father threatens to send me to the convent if I do not marry as soon as may be. He's serious. He says I'm an embarrassment to him and he can no longer bear to have me in his house. Sebastian, the convent would kill me. I couldn't bear such a life—I'd rather die."

Realizing fully now where the conversation was leading, Sebastian said with foreboding, "And that . . . has to do with me, then, Adelaide?"

"It does. You see, I know you came to love Adela in those days at the high king's court in Worms. I can tell by the way you shrink from me that you still love her. That whole silly pilgrimage was about her, wasn't it? Well, you can't have her. She's in the nunnery, and she's still Konrad's wife. In spite of what he says, he's not going to let her go, even though he hates her now, I'm told. Oh yes, I know the rumors. It's common knowledge what happened after they lost the little boy at Syburg. But Konrad would die before he'd let such a valuable possession as her get away from him—this upstanding, noble daughter of one of the great houses of Francia. He would kill her before he would let anyone else have her. You know that, don't you?'

"Yes," Sebastian groaned and stood up by the fire. "Yes, I do know it, the bloody devil. He changed his mind about letting her go after we left, but at least I got her safely to Andernach. I would kill him if I could."

"But you can't, love, even if you could beat him in a fight, which is doubtful. He's an important commander in the high king's army and he's Count of the Saxon March. The king doesn't care what he does with his women, but he would care if you killed him."

"I know. Resignation is one thing I got out of my pilgrimage, Adelaide. At least I can stand it now."

She rose and came over to him, pressing her body against his. "Well, what about me? I'd make you a good wife. You would want for nothing, and you would be the most fortunate man in all of Francia. I've always liked you. You're honest and kind, and you're the most desirable unmarried man in all the king's land. I might even be happy with you," she teased, "that is, if you'd let me travel around a bit from time to time. After all, you can't expect me to stay out here in this wilderness indefinitely, with only you and old Heimdal for entertainment."

He backed away, protesting, "This is ridiculous. I hardly know you, and you don't know me. Besides, you've already had half the men at the king's court, *nicht wahr*? Why don't you ask one of them?"

She took a deep breath, raised her hands to her face as if he had slapped her, and sank to the floor. Sebastian was taken aback when she began weeping; he had assumed she was incapable of it. He bent over her and caressed her hair awkwardly. "It's all right, Adelaide. I didn't mean to hurt you. I just thought . . . well, I'm not the type of man you usually like."

"How do you know what I like, you bastard?" she said angrily, raising tearstained eyes to his. "I tried to get close to you at Worms, but you wouldn't have me. I might have had a chance for a different fate if you had. It's true, I've been with a lot of men—that's why my father wants to put me away. And none of those whoresons want anything to do with me now. I thought, at least, you were decent and might see that I could be something more than a courtesan—that I'm intelligent, interesting, and alive, that I'm capable of great love. What else does a man want?"

"Adelaide, I could never make you happy. This is all I have and all I know. I'm not one of those pretend warriors you see at the king's court, one of those 'dancers,' full of tall tales and witty stories. I have serious work to do here, and if I marry, I'll want sons to help me and daughters to bring me joy. I can't marry you just because you need someone to do so."

She moved away from him and stamped her foot in frustration, "Well, who then would you marry, Master Sobersides? Your precious Adela will never be yours, and I'll wager you don't even know any eligible maidens—isn't that true?"

"Yes," he said mournfully, "I don't know anyone. I don't travel much."

She rose and came over to him and began her conciliatory tone again, caressing his chest and running her fingers through his hair. "Well then, am I not pretty?" she whispered. "Don't you like to feel my arms around you, my bosom against your chest? Marry me, and let me make you happy. I am so good at giving pleasure.

"And I could adjust to this place," she went on as she began to fumble with the cloth belt around his waist, "if you allowed me just a few trips now and then to see friends and family, you know? I might even give you a son or two if it would make you happy. What do you say, my love? You have no one. Am I not worth your consideration?" She wrapped herself around him and began to kiss him on the neck.

Late that night, or perhaps in the early morning, Sebastian whispered in her ear as she lay sprawled upon his chest, "All right,

Adelaide. I'll . . . I will marry you." She moaned and smacked her lips softly. "Mmm, that's nice. I knew you would." she murmured drowsily and fell asleep again.

Simon's boat pulled up to the wharf the very next morning after Adelaide had arrived. Sebastian welcomed him at once into the fortress and allowed his sailors to bivouac on the small beach by the wharf.

From the moment she first saw him, Adelaide was utterly captivated by Simon, indeed stunned by him. She loved his flamboyant, adventurous manner, his exotic clothes, his confidence, his vast collection of stories, with which he entertained her and Sebastian at every opportunity, and of course his dashing good looks. Sebastian could not help but notice the startling change in her manner and attentions, and though she continued to sleep in his room, her previously careful solicitation of him and adoring behavior cooled rapidly. He began to feel like a spectator in a drama in which Simon and Adelaide were the only actors. Ironically, although his pride was injured and he felt some jealousy at first, Sebastian was amused more than anything else and curious to see how the drama would play out.

Simon did not seem to notice how outrageously Adelaide was vamping him, cooing at his stories, flattering him on his every remark, and touching him to emphasize her admiration. Sebastian was at first indignant but then gradually relieved. He now saw Adelaide clearly, with some chagrin that he had been so taken in by her charms, but more and more with a sense of escape. Oddly, he still liked her and could not simply ignore her great beauty or disregard the power of her charms when she chose to bring them fully to bear on him. But he felt enormously grateful to Simon for opening his eyes to a potentially disastrous alliance.

On the evening of the third day, Simon announced his intention to leave before dawn the next morning. Sebastian expressed his regret, said a hearty farewell to his friend, and begged Adelaide to excuse him for the rest of the night, as he needed to ride out and attend to business in an outlying village. She was more than gracious and embraced him heartily and with genuine warmth as he made ready to depart.

In the predawn half light, Sebastian walked Joyeuse quietly up to the Danish longboat just as the sailors began to shove off into the current. Simon already stood in the prow—and in the middle of the boat, perched on a pile of rugs, was Adelaide.

"Good morning, friends," he hailed softly. "I see you have decided to travel on together."

Simon immediately signaled the oarsmen to hold up, leaped out of the boat, and grasped the bridle of Sebastian's horse. "Sebastian, I swear I did not intend for this to happen. The last thing I would want is to hurt or offend you. I just could not persuade her to stay, and I felt if she wanted to go so badly, she might not turn out to be such a good thing for you after all, my friend."

Sebastian let out a merry laugh. "You have not offended me, Simon. In fact, you've done me a great favor, I think. But I worry that you will find in her the same problems you saw that I might have. Adelaide is not easily satisfied."

"Oh, have no fear, Sebastian; she will soon see that I'm no fonder of monogamy than she. The life I lead would not support it, even if I preferred it. I have no doubt that somewhere along the road we take together she will find a good reason to get off my boat."

"Sebastian!" Adelaide was standing, unable to abide any longer a conversation between the two men that she could not hear. "I really do love you," she called out earnestly. "I admire you tremendously. You're such a good man. But you were right—you're not the type of man I'm used to. You're really too good for me. And, as God is my witness, I could not live here. It would be almost as bad as the convent. And I'm frightened to death of having children. I would be so bad for you, Sebastian. Forgive me, my dear. Forgive me and let me go with your blessing."

Sebastian called back with a laugh, "You have it, Adelaide, and most gladly. I wish you nothing but good, a rich life and the fulfillment of your dreams. Go indeed with my blessing, and may God watch over you."

Simon grasped Sebastian's forearm and gave it a firm shake, and with a parting grin, waded back to the boat and vaulted in. Sebastian watched as the slim craft swiftly caught the current and disappeared into the early morning fog on the river. He felt some regret at the loss of such beauty and excitement and a little emptiness, as at the end of things, but he turned his thoughts immediately and resolutely to the day before him.

Chapter 29

The Suntel Mountains

Saxony, Spring 782

"Why have you not married yet, my boy?" the king demanded one morning after Mass, as the army gathered at the new fortress in Paderborn for the year's campaign. "How old are you?"

"I believe I'm twenty-six, my lord king," Sebastian replied with downcast eyes, knowing what was coming.

"By God, that's old for a man to be still unwed. What's wrong with you? By now, you should have a pretty wife and a shedload of babies. You could have any maiden in the land if you wanted—they all know about you and want you. Why, you're almost as famous as me! People still talk about the Irminsul treasure and your trick with the kites at Syborg, and you have half a dozen campaigns in Saxony under your belt now. You distinguished yourself in every one, and you've come to be one of my best fighters. Now you need to reap some rewards from it all, by thunder. You're not a eunuch, are you, lad?"

"No, my lord."

"All right then, I've said enough. Start looking or I shall look for you."

"Yes, my lord."

As they strolled together on the wall walk, Sebastian remained quiet, pretending to be absorbed in the features of the new fortress. The king continued, "I wish you'd gone to Spain with me, Sebastian; you would have loved it. It's a land like no other—warm, beautiful mountains, lovely rivers, interesting people. Vineyards everywhere. And olive trees—I love olives. Can't get 'em up here. Different from us, though, those people. Not much discipline. They like to play a bit too much, and they never go to sleep at night. Damnedest thing I ever saw. What kind of man sleeps past daybreak? If we lived there, though, we'd be the same, I suppose. The land's as seductive as a beautiful woman."

"I wish I had gone, sire," Sebastian mused. "I'd like to see such a different land. Attalus told me many stories about it."

"I still dream about it," the king sighed, "though I hate the way it ended—losing Roland and all that. Bad luck all around! Spoiled my victory. At least we laid the groundwork for a bulwark against a dangerous potential enemy. My grandfather, Karl the Hammer, thought the Saracens would be our worst nightmare, but he drove 'em back across the mountains, and now, God willing, I've plugged the hole they came through.

"It's been four years since then—hard to believe. And the Saxons have been almost quiet during that whole time. Every time we go against them, they give up without much of a fight. And we haven't seen that rascal Widukind in all that time. I hope he's dead."

"I doubt it, my lord. He's like a ghost—you never know when he's going to turn up. They say his Westphalians and some other Saxon tribes have made league with the so-called Vikings in Nordmannia, and they've been plundering with them on the isle of Britain."

"Well, better them than us. He can stay there for all I care," the king said scornfully. "If he stays gone, we have a real chance to bring all the Saxons around finally. Did you know we already have several units of Saxon cavalry who have agreed to fight with us?"

"I did not, sire. Do you think they'll be any good?"

"Hell, I don't care, as long as they're not fighting against us. Meanwhile, I'm pleased to see such progress here at Paderborn. I was right to choose Count Leudegar to build it and command it, instead of Konrad. Konrad wanted it badly. But I've been put off by that scoundrel lately. For one thing, he drinks too much wine, just like his father, only he's at it a lot earlier. I'm afraid it's affecting his judgment. Ah, well, he's still a good fighter, and I don't give a fart if it does make him mad that I gave Paderborn to Leudegar. Maybe it'll teach him a lesson."

The king put an arm around Sebastian's shoulder as they walked along. "You know, I might have given this fortress to you if you'd only acted a bit more interested in it, but I can't pry you away from Fernshanz. Why is that, lad?"

"I don't know, my lord—I just like what I'm doing. We're prospering, and I love my people. We grow in numbers every year. There are now as many people in Fernshanz as at Adalgray and almost as many soldiers. The people keep coming. It's hard to say why or from where they come. We've had some success with the crops. I guess that's what brings them. Nobody goes hungry. Most of them are freemen, though I did accept some serfs from other lords in return for help or goods."

"Ah, it's true you've done well, Sebastian. All men say it. I don't blame you for wanting to see it all through. Your place is a model I wish others would follow. I've come to see clearly now that the better off the peasants are, the stronger the kingdom will be. I used to think the peasants would survive no matter what we did. But I see now the Franks are stronger if their base is stronger, and that base is the peasant farmer. You've helped me see that Sebastian—you and some of the others. I've been scouring the country for wise men—learned men, with different ideas—and I'm bringing 'em up to be at my court. By thunder, if it hasn't made my court a great deal more lively and interesting. You should come and stay awhile with me, Sebastian. You'd be stunned by what some of 'em say—and the ideas they have!"

"I would like to, my lord, very much. Maybe this winter, after the harvest."

"All right, then, it's a promise. I'll expect you. Perhaps we will find a bride for you at long last."

"Oh, my lord, I wish you wouldn't—I mean, I wish you wouldn't bother yourself. I, uh, I'm just not . . ." Sebastian's voice trailed off.

"I know what's wrong with you, young man. You needn't try and hide it. You're still pining for Gonduin's daughter, aren't you?"

"I'm sorry, sire. I just . . . she's just all I ever wanted."

"I'm sorry, too, my son. But look here now, you're a warrior, and already a famous one. You can have any number of beautiful maidens, and from good houses, too. I love my Hildegard—that's a fact, and I'm glad I married her, even as young as she was then. But the world is full of beautiful women, and it's a man's world. So pull yourself together and start thinking about taking a mate, you hear?"

"Yes, sire."

"There they are, Adalgis. Don't you see 'em? They're right there at the base of the mountain, already drawn up for battle between those two copses of trees. And out in the open, by God. They've only got crude breastworks to fight behind. We can probably jump the horses over the thing. Can you believe it?"

Konrad could scarcely control his excitement. He had urged his contingent of East Franks to separate from the larger army, commanded by Count Theodoric, a close kinsman of the king and a pretentious aristocrat, whom most of the leaders of the East Franks despised. Konrad burned to find the Saxons and defeat them before Theodoric's army of West Franks could deploy.

Charlemagne had brought Theodoric and many other distinguished West Franks to Paderborn to get them involved in the expansion of the realm to the east. The West Franks hated to fight in the gloomy forests of Saxony, and whenever they could, they claimed the necessity to defend their own piece of the realm as an excuse to stay out of the grueling Saxon wars.

This year's campaign provided the king with an opportunity to impress the West Franks, not only with the ongoing successful pacification of Saxony, but also with the flourishing reputation of the empire. At the assembly in the new and imposing fortress at Paderborn, they had already been treated to the spectacle of emissaries from the King of Denmark and from the Avar Khagan bowing before the high king and presenting gifts. Delegations of headmen from every Saxon tribe had also been present to pay tribute. Among the leaders of the Saxons, only Widukind did not appear. The West Franks were duly impressed and expressed their eagerness to contribute to the further aggrandizement of the realm.

The Rhineland Franks, however, distrusted those from western Francia. They hated their bastardized speech that was hardly German anymore and their fancy ways gleaned from Aquitaine and the southern climes of Spain and Italy. For the East Franks, Theodoric was just the type of affluent, effete, and courtly nobleman they abhorred, an artificial warrior looking to enhance his status with the king with an easy victory against an inferior enemy. The opportunity was provided at the moment by a tribe of wild Slavonic Sorbs who had been pillaging and burning with impunity in eastern Saxony and along the border of Thuringia in the northern part of Frankish territory.

The king had sent a large combined army of West and East Franks, including some Saxon cavalry units, against the Sorbs. Along the way, however, the news came that Widukind had suddenly returned and once again raised the Westphalians and several of the other Saxon tribes. As soon as the king had left Saxony for the upper Rhine, Widukind took the opportunity to assemble the Saxon leaders before they scattered. He took advantage of their disgruntlement at being given a subordinate place at the Paderborn meeting, and he whipped them up with promises of unity and a return to their beloved pagan religion. He boasted of his ties with the Northmen and hinted at the possibility of an alliance between Saxons and Danes against Charlemagne.

The news was electrifying. Led by Konrad, the East Franks immediately lobbied to abandon the punitive mission against the Sorbs and attack Widukind before he could raise a larger army. Theodoric reluctantly had to admit that Widukind constituted the greater threat.

Nevertheless, Theodoric was no fool. He had never fought against Widukind, but he knew of the man's dangerous reputation. As scouts reported the Saxons assembling north of the Suntel Mountains, Theodoric elected to pitch camp on the western side of the deep and swift-flowing Weser River and probe the Saxon defenses before attacking. Konrad persuaded the East Franks to push on across the river and reconnoiter in force. They had come upon the Saxons just north of the mountain complex.

"Let's do it," Konrad shouted. "It's not even a large force. We can ride right over them, and that bastard Theodoric can suck eggs. We'll have all the glory and the satisfaction of showing him up."

Konrad was not the only Frank whose head was turned by the lure of an easy victory and a chance to steal a march on the despised West Franks and their imperious leader. No fewer than three of Charlemagne's personal military staff, Counts Adalgis, Worad, and Gailo, along with four other regional counts, were among those who were convinced by

Konrad to strike at once against a Saxon force that appeared to be caught dismounted and in the open.

And so they had done it—they rode full gallop across open ground against Saxons entrenched behind concealed pointed stakes. What Konrad and the others had not seen were shallow, carefully hidden pits that had been dug in just before the lines. Later they would surmise that Widukind himself had commanded the Saxons, so cleverly was the trap set and so steady were the Saxon lines in the face of the charge.

A firestorm of arrows greeted the Franks at close range, and the front rank of horses went down at once in the pits. Saxon cavalry waited in the woods until the Franks collided at the pits, and in the chaos, as wave after wave of the Frankish warriors crashed into each other, horses spinning and rearing in confusion, Widukind struck out of the woods on both sides, his cavalry plowing into the churning mass, while a third force circled around behind to close the trap completely. Saxon infantrymen leaped screaming over their own breastworks, spearing riders and horses indiscriminately.

Charlemagne's emissaries, Counts Adalgis, Worad, and Gailo, were killed outright by Saxon spearmen as soon as their horses stumbled and went down in the pits. Konrad's horse, too, was killed as it tried to leap across an open pit and was impaled on a stake. Konrad slid off at the last moment and found himself in the middle of hellish mayhem. He struck out wildly in sweeping sword strokes against anything that moved around him, narrowly managing to avoid the hooves of maddened warhorses and the spears of berserk Saxon soldiers. He was cut through his chain mail in a dozen places in the first minutes of the battle. Choking with panic, he desperately caught the mane and bridle of a rearing horse and dealt its wounded Frankish rider a resounding blow to the helmet. The man fell off with a grunt, and Konrad vaulted into the empty saddle.

"Franks—to me!" he bellowed, and began to cut his way out through the path of least resistance. Other riders joined him until there was a wedge of Franks cutting and slashing in desperation toward the rim of the conflict. Finally, Konrad and a few others emerged and raced away toward the river, praying that their exhausted horses could stand the pace of the wild gallop. A few more men and horses were lost in the crossing, but a dozen or so managed to limp into Theodoric's encampment just before dark.

The next day, Widukind was gone. He declined to give battle against Theodoric's larger force, content just to savor the massacre.

At Paderborn, the king received the news in disbelief at first, and then as the news sank in, he began to boil into a state of fury. He could not sit still. Every word he spoke was shouted. He wanted to know everything, every detail—how many men had been lost, why they hadn't reconnoitered first, and who had ordered such a reckless charge. When he was told he had lost seven counts, including three of his most trusted advisors, he was almost beside himself with rage and on the verge of ordering a general call-up of forces, no matter the cost or level of preparation. Count Edelrath and Bishop Regwald, among others, prevailed upon him to wait at least until further reports were in. The king remained adamant about one thing—he wanted Konrad in front of him as soon as humanly possible. When he was told that Konrad had not returned to the army but had gone home to Adalgray, he summoned Sebastian forthwith.

"I want you to go to Adalgray and bring that stupid animal back here to me, do you hear? What does he mean by going back to Adalgray? He owes me an explanation, and by God, he'd better have a good one. By the Cross, I'll have his head if he doesn't come immediately! Go down there and tell him at once, Sebastian. Take two hundred good men and my personal banner. If he resists, bring him any way you can—I don't care if you have to truss him up like a pig for market. Hell, I don't even care if you have to kill him! Just bring him back here. He has to answer for this disaster."

As they rode toward Adalgray, Sebastian felt a rush of excitement and apprehension. The king had just given him leave to do the thing he had been burning to do for the last seven years—kill Konrad. If Konrad resisted, Sebastian was empowered to take him, alive or dead, and if Konrad's character ran true to form, it might very well have to be the latter.

"The sand in the ointment, Archambald, is that we only have two hundred men—good men, to be sure, some of King Karl's own personal entourage of warriors and the bulk of our own best trained warriors. Still, if we can't get in through the gate, we will have no hope of taking the fortress by storm. Konrad is an experienced and formidable fortress commander. Adalgray is as good a stronghold as any, and we have no siege equipment whatever."

"You have a plan, don't you, Sebastian?" said Archambald, with a note of alarm. "I can see it in your eyes. You're going to challenge him, aren't you?"

"Well, what else will work, Archambald? Confound it. I can't go back without having tried."

"Yes, you can," Archambald exclaimed emphatically. "You know what kind of a killer Konrad is, and he'd certainly relish killing you. The king knows you don't have siege machinery. I don't know what he was thinking when he sent you."

"The king was distraught and angry. All he could think of was punishing those responsible for the Suntel massacre. Good God, we lost Adalgis and Gailo! Both of them were the king's friends and close advisors, and five other counts died as well. When was the last time a disaster like that occurred? No wonder he's angry. It won't do at all if I go back empty-handed and the king has to come here and deal with Konrad himself. I don't want to fail him. Besides, it's high time Konrad was brought down."

"Aye, Sebastian—but not by you, and not by any two hundred men without siege equipment. It's insane. Just ride up to the gate and tell him what the king wants. Offer to escort him. Don't make it sound too bad, and for God's sake, don't make him mad. You won't get anywhere, except maybe dead, if you do that."

"What do you think, Liudolf? What should I do?"

As usual, Liudolf's answer was short, to the point, and decisive. "You must do what you have to do, Sebastian. The king sent you to bring Konrad back." It was clear to the single-minded, practical Liudolf that if Konrad would not open the gates, Sebastian's only recourse would be to challenge him to single combat.

Chapter 30

Day of Reckoning

Summer 782

It was a long ride to Adalgray from Paderborn, made longer by Sebastian's growing conviction that death awaited him at the end of the road. No matter how he tried to distract his thoughts from that awareness, his mind kept returning to the finality that this journey represented. Hour after hour, with nothing to do except think of the coming confrontation, Sebastian's initial excitement turned to foreboding and then to fear.

The final day of the trip was warm, his armor uncomfortable. He began to sweat, not only from the heat of the day and the weight of the chain mail but from thoughts of the coming confrontation. He felt sick to his stomach.

Konrad was formidable—more than formidable. He had never been beaten in a fight, and he delighted in killing. Sebastian saw himself going down before Konrad's blows, heard his curses, and felt his hatred as he was being hammered into the ground. Uncharacteristically, the dread in his bowels filled him with self-doubt and depression, and sweat dripped into his eyes as the horses cantered along. In midafternoon, the troop dismounted and walked to give the horses a rest. Eventually, the heat, the sameness of the road, and the rhythm of trudging along in the relative stillness of the surrounding forest lulled Sebastian into a strange waking dream—a vision, actually. He never lost consciousness or felt that he was viewing himself from outside his body, but it was as if everything else faded away as he plodded along, putting one foot in front of the other. He was not even sure how long it lasted, but the vision was uncannily real. It became for him one of the most profound spiritual experiences of his life.

As on the pilgrimage when he had became so ill, the important characters in his life appeared in his vision, one by one.

Heimdal was the first. "The fault of violence," the blind man expounded, "is that it only begets more violence. Where does it end?"

The king then appeared, sitting on his throne. Sebastian spoke to him passionately, "Sire, I'm tormented about continuing to fight for you against the Saxons. To what purpose? Just so you can crush yet another tribe of people and force them on pain of death to bow in deceit before the cross? What would be the price of that in terms of blood and death for so many?" The king continued to look beyond him and sit silently with no expression.

Father Louis appeared. "Your sin, my son, is that you are trying to run away from your disappointment. Your life has not worked out the way you wanted, so you presume to blame God for that, assuming that you know better than God. That is a sin of pride. There is no joy in you in spite of all that God has given you. That is a sin against God's goodness."

"What joy can there be for me, Father? I have lost Adela and all my family. All I do is work and fight. I have nothing to look forward to."

The priest faded away and Ermengard took his place. "Sebastian, my beloved son, don't be afraid, don't grieve. Look at all the good you have already done with your life. Look at Fernshanz. You care about your people, and they are no longer starving. In fact, they even prosper now. You have so much promise; even the king listens to you. You are a window to those around you, and your vision changes the way others look at things. It can change the way things are."

"What if Konrad kills me, mother?" Sebastian asked. "All that is lost, isn't it?"

The face of his mother changed smoothly into that of Adela. "My precious friend, my other self, I will be with you, no matter what you do. It doesn't matter to me whether you win or lose. If you love me, you will do what is right. That is enough. I will always love you."

The image of Adela was replaced by the slight figure of Father Pippin. "Most of us, Sebastian, are simply echoes of those who went before us. We repeat their sins, we mimic their mistakes, and we embrace their flawed way of life. The hardest thing in the world is to be different from those around us. But nothing changes unless one chooses a different path. You know that because you are different. Do you suppose God put you here for nothing? Have faith that you have a purpose, and God will not let you fail. Have faith!"

Upon coming to his senses, Sebastian was astonished at how real the dream had seemed and how clearly he could still recall it. He began to feel better. The fear he had felt before fell away from him, and he found that he could submerge his foreboding into thanksgiving and the routine of the march. His usual confidence began to return and he became almost lighthearted. At the end of the road, he would simply do his duty, whatever it turned out to be, and that would be enough, whatever the outcome.

The sergeant on duty challenged Sebastian's forces at the gate, even though the king's banner flew alongside Sebastian's in the front ranks. "Who goes there?" he called. "Hold and identify yerself."

"I am Sebastian of Fernshanz, here on the king's business. Open the gates."

"Beggin' your pardon, m'lord," came the reply, "but I cannot, unless my lord Konrad gives me leave to open. He give me strict orders to open to nobody without his approval."

"Are you a fool, Sergeant, or just stupid? Don't you see the king's flag? Open the gates at once."

"Sir, beggin' your pardon, sir, again. I would truly love to open these here gates fer ye, but I do so at the risk of me life. The count said he'd have me head."

Resigning himself that he wasn't going to gain access to the fortress easily, Sebastian called up to the guard, "Then go and get your master and be damned to you for ignoring the king's standard. You'd best not be seen again, Sergeant, once this business is done."

"Aye, m'lord, beggin' your pardon once again, sir, but I hope ye will see it's die now or die later, one way or t'other."

"Get on with it, Sergeant—you've made your choice."

"Aye, m'lord."

After a restless wait of nearly an hour, Sebastian pulled his troops back to the edge of the woods. Finally, Konrad appeared on the ramparts above the gates. "Who wants Konrad, Count of Adalgray?" he bellowed. "Show yourself and speak up. I've not got all day." From his slurred speech, Sebastian could tell that Konrad had already been long into his cups.

Sebastian rode forth immediately, alone. In answer to the question, he called out loudly while still cantering toward the gates. "Open the gates, in the name of the king! I am Sebastian of Fernshanz, come to bring King Karl's summons to you, Konrad."

When Sebastian brought his horse up a few meters from the gate, Konrad leaned over the parapet, and with a violent motion, made a lewd gesture down at his old nemesis. "That's for you, Sebastian, you stinking bastard. And it's *Count* Konrad, boy! I can't believe the king sent *you*, of all people! It's an insult—even the king should understand that. So go back and tell him to send someone of equal rank and status as me, not some drizzly little shit who shouldn't even be allowed to sit a warhorse, let along bring me a message from the king."

"Open the gates, Count. It doesn't matter who brings you the message—I come in the name of the king. That's enough. He demands that you come with me at once to Paderborn. Do you dare to defy him? You know that if you do not open these gates you stand to lose all you own and perhaps forfeit your life."

Konrad paused a moment as if weighing the consequences. Finally, it was the wine that answered. He pulled out his sword and shook it erratically at Sebastian, shouting, "I think I will not, bastard! I'm a count—a great warrior. Tell him . . . tell him . . . I can't come. I'm wounded—wounded at Suntel. 'Twas a great battle. Have to recover."

"I will tell him, Count Konrad, that you did not seem wounded to me—only drunk." After a pause, Sebastian added, "As usual."

"You cheeky bastard!" Konrad erupted. "I'll have your blood for that! And this time there'll be no woman to hide behind!"

"Humbug, Konrad," Sebastian scoffed calmly. "I could have beaten you then and I can beat you now. Your day is over, Count Bacchus.

Do you know what the king will do to you now, you drunken sot? I expect I can take this fort, and fairly easily, given the sorry state of its commander. But if I cannot, the king will bring his whole army against you. He will drag you out in front of all your soldiers and cut your limbs off one by one, and then he will post your head above these gates. Those are the consequences of refusing the king's orders."

"Bah, yourself, you stinking donkey pizzle. The king can't do without me—everybody knows that. I am Count of the Saxon March, by God."

"You *were* Count of the Saxon March. When I ride back and tell the king that you defied him, you will be count of nothing and your head will be on a post. Think it over, Konrad. You are playing with your doom."

Konrad blinked and seemed to consider again the consequences of his defiance. Sebastian took advantage of the moment. "As for me, Count, I don't care what you do. One way or the other, I stand to profit. You made a terrible mistake at Suntel by leading that foolhardy charge. Those who survived all say it was you who urged them to do it. Because of you, seven counts are dead, along with scores of other good warriors. I'll tell you now, whatever you decide, the king intends to take Adalgray away from you, along with all your other lands and properties, and give them to me."

Konrad's face turned purple. He clutched his sword with both hands and held it high over his head as if he would jump from the parapets right onto the warhorse and rider circling below. "YOU BASTARD!" he raged. "You, sneaky, filthy bastard. You drip of cum from a stinking lowborn stable groom. Yes, that's right, I know all about you and your whore of a mother. I should have killed you long ago."

"Come and fight me now, Konrad. We'll settle this in single combat. You always said you could kill me—now's your chance. If you succeed, perhaps the king will acknowledge that you are still a great warrior, one who can't be vanquished by anyone. Perhaps he will realize once more that he cannot do without *his best warrior*." He paused, letting the words sink in. Then he said, "But perhaps you really aren't his best warrior anymore. Perhaps I am."

"You! You couldn't beat the flies off a cow's arse. I could kill you one-handed and blindfolded."

"Come down, then, and let's see. Single combat. Only you and me, here before the gates for all to see. If you win, my troops will return to Paderborn—I promise it."

Again, there was a long pause as Konrad struggled with his decision. Once more Sebastian spoke up, "If you don't come down, I shall be forced to pronounce to all my troops and to yours as well that you are a coward. Frankly, I've always thought so myself. And I have never thought much of your so-called battle prowess. You're clumsy and reckless. You think you can win just by charging and screaming at the top of your voice. Your techniques are old-fashioned, your movements are transparent. You're a stupid fighter, Konrad—that's all there is to it."

Sebastian's remarks had an immediate impact. Konrad's limit of tolerance had been reached and exceeded. The slur on his reputation as a fighter was the last straw. No matter what the consequences, he could not let the challenge pass.

"You!" he shouted. "You stay right there. I'll give you what you want, and more—much more! Say your prayers, bastard. You have less than a quarter hour to live." With that, he disappeared from the parapet.

Konrad burst out of the gates mounted on a great black charger, with his spear and shield set for battle. He charged in the old manner of the Franks, with his spear held high above his head and his shield centered before his body. As he came on, he let out a continuous loud and guttural bellow. Sebastian had been signaling to Liudolf to hold the troops in place and barely had time to turn and face Konrad's attack. Joyeuse screamed as the black horse emerged and rose up on his hind legs, but Konrad was upon them before the stallion could gain any speed. Sebastian had no time even to couch his lance.

The charge of the heavy black drove Joyeuse back on his haunches, and Sebastian nearly lost his seat. At the point of collision, Konrad drove his spear with all his might into Sebastian's shield. The head of the spear went completely through the wood and leather, and as Konrad spurred his horse past Sebastian, he turned with the spear still in his hand and jerked violently. As he guessed, Sebastian's shield was attached by a cord to his wrist. The momentum and Konrad's great strength was enough to drag Sebastian perforce out of the saddle and into the dirt below. Luckily, the cord to the shield broke free as he crashed to the ground.

Tossing his entangled spear away, Konrad wheeled instantly to trample and finish his fallen foe, but Sebastian rolled to his right just as the black was on him, giving Konrad no opening to swing his sword. In an instant Sebastian was up. He recovered his spear as Konrad turned for a new charge. Just as the great horse closed the distance to a single spear length, Sebastian reared back and flung the spear with all his might at the charging horse. It struck the stallion just above the saddle's neck strap and went in up to the lateral wings of the spear blade. The great horse stumbled, his knees gave way, and he crashed headfirst into the dust, spilling Konrad precipitously over his head.

Konrad smashed into the ground on his right shoulder but rolled immediately upright and raised his sword. He was just in time to parry a blow from Sebastian's own sword that would have taken off his head. He struggled to his feet, wielding the long sword with both hands, as did Sebastian. They circled and feinted at each other, looking for a weakness. Konrad was hurt; it soon became apparent that he was able to raise his sword into the high guard only with difficulty, and he limped slightly as he sought an opening in Sebastian's defenses. Still, he chose an aggressive tactic, roaring like a bull and rushing at Sebastian in an attempt to overwhelm him. Each time Sebastian ducked, parried, or stepped lightly aside and cut at Konrad as he passed. Soon bloody wounds were oozing in half a dozen places on Konrad's back and legs.

After several ferocious charges, Konrad slowed and finally settled into a cautious defense, waiting for Sebastian to initiate contact. He blinked as sweat rolled down into his eyes, and his counterstrokes became slow and uncertain. Sebastian stepped up his attack, raining short blows from every direction and avoiding a heavy blow that would require him to drop his guard. Konrad was breathing heavily and hiccupping. At one point, he attempted a powerful side slash, causing Sebastian to leap back to find room to parry with a downward blow. The effort caused Konrad to vomit a foul mess of wine and meat all over his chain mail. He wiped at it briefly with his left hand, realizing by the expression on Sebastian's face how badly he was looking in the fight. His shame propelled him to renew his wild slashing attacks as if to prove he was still unimpaired.

Konrad's blows, however, were becoming more feeble. Sebastian bided his time, concentrating on counterstrokes, keeping himself well away from Konrad's headlong bullrushes. Before long, Konrad needed to pause to take a deep breath after every rush. As he did so, he lowered his sword slightly, sometimes letting the point touch the ground. Sebastian began to exploit those moments. When Konrad rushed, Sebastian stepped aside, and as Konrad paused to breathe, he moved in quickly to strike above Konrad's lowered guard. The tactic worked. It gave no time for Konrad to recover, and Sebastian began to score more frequent hits against Konrad's helmet and exposed left shoulder. Soon Konrad was bleeding from multiple wounds, and his steps become more and more plodding.

The end came unexpectedly, almost comically. Konrad raised his sword as high as he could and rushed forward, trying desperately to catch Sebastian off guard. He slashed sideways with all his might and the sword simply flew out of his hands. He staggered, refusing to believe what had just happened. Finally, he made an attempt to rush after the sword. As he did so Sebastian thrust his own sword between Konrad's legs and spilled him into the dirt. As Konrad turned and tried to raise himself, jerking at the same time for his only remaining weapon, the small sword on his right hip, Sebastian hit him squarely in the face with the pommel of his own weapon. The blow sent Konrad's helmet spinning off his head, and Sebastian hit him another blow against his exposed temple. It was enough. Konrad collapsed, stunned, onto his back.

"Kill me. You've always wanted to. Finish it, bastard." Konrad coughed and spat a tooth from his mouth. Suddenly Sebastian was seized with the desire to cut the throat of this man who had been his enemy for so long. For a tantalizing moment, he weighed the thought.

"Why not?" he reasoned. "The king gave me leave to do it. This rotten beast certainly deserves death. He's an evil man who does nobody any good, and no one would miss him. I owe him a death—three deaths, one for each of the people I loved who were taken from me by him one way or another." His hands tightened on the sword.

In the end, Sebastian could not do it. For one thing, it was too easy and too cold-blooded—something Konrad himself would do. For another, mercy seemed a better revenge—a way of rising above Konrad's own sordid level.

He stood up and signaled to Liudolf, who was waiting a bowshot away. At once, the whole contingent of Sebastian's men came cantering forward. On the ramparts of the fortress, no attempt was made to come to Konrad's aid. In fact, no one moved as the king's men surrounded their leader, mute testimony to how little Konrad was loved at Adalgray.

Sebastian had the worst of Konrad's wounds quickly bound up and then trussed him like a pig, as Charlemagne had suggested, and slung him over a saddle. No attempt was made to enter the fortress; Sebastian hardly glanced at it. Instead, he turned and gave orders to return at once to Paderborn. Happily, as he rode, his mind began to clear itself of chronic concerns. Old burdens began to lift like clouds after a storm. Somehow he felt, as never before, completely free.

Charlemagne refused to see Konrad upon his arrival at Paderborn. Instead, he put off a decision about Konrad's fate and ordered the erstwhile count to be confined until his wounds had healed. Meanwhile, the king plunged into plans for the new campaign. He was determined to drive deeper into Saxony than ever before to find Widukind at long last and exact his revenge for the Suntel massacre.

A single day after Charlemagne led his huge army toward the Suntel region, Konrad escaped with a small retinue of disgruntled warriors. He rode posthaste north toward Denmark, brazening his way through hostile Saxons and Danes alike with the enormous lie that Widukind himself had called him to an alliance against the High King of the Franks. When he at last blundered onto Widukind's camp, the prince wasted little time listening to Konrad's whining account of the king's injustice toward him and dismissed with a wave his preposterous proposals for an alliance of Saxons and dissident Franks. Widukind was in a hurry to continue his journey northward for an important meeting with the Danish Vikings. He paused briefly before mounting his horse, and with eyes ice blue in their resolve, pronounced his judgment on Konrad.

"I know you, Count Konrad, you scum-sucking swine. You have plagued and oppressed my people for years. No Frank is more hated than you. Whatever made you think that I, a prince of Saxony, would have anything to do with you?"

Turning to a lieutenant, he gave a simple order: "Take this wicked fool to the nearest grove of sacred trees and hang him as a sacrifice to our gods. Hang him slowly and burn him while he hangs, but make sure you don't burn his head. When he's dead, cut his head off and send it to King Karl with my compliments. Leave his body hanging for the crows." Widukind didn't even bother to look at the horror-stricken Konrad before he rode off.

Chapter 31

The Third Way

Late Summer 782

"My lord king," Sebastian began as he entered the king's tent, more nervous on this occasion than he had ever been, even after many years in the king's service.

They were in the Bueckegau, deep in Saxon territory, near where the Aller flows into the Weser. Charlemagne had moved inexorably toward the Weser River, hunting Saxons and burning their camps and settlements. The Saxons had put up no resistance in the face of the overwhelming force the king had brought with him. Instead, astonishingly, Saxon warriors with white flags, braving death, had burst out of the woods near the Weser in front of the vanguard of the marauding Franks, begging for a truce. They were taken to the king. Their message was that the Saxons would fight no more. All the tribes had agreed to stand down, proclaiming they were ready to submit once again, not only to the king but to the king's religion. Charlemagne accepted their surrender with the caveat that the rebels of Suntel must be handed over.

Thousands of Saxons had come forth to surrender and submit to the king's justice. Little did they realize at the time how harsh that justice would be. Charlemagne had all the Saxons disarmed and their leaders interrogated. Widukind, however, was not handed over, and no one would say where he had gone. They acted as if the elusive prince had vanished from the earth. Their reluctance to cooperate would cost them dearly.

Among the Franks, however, the Saxon capitulation was cause for great celebration. Given the number of Saxon chieftains present, including representatives from all five of the major Saxon tribes, it appeared that these ancient enemies had finally been reconciled to their fate and were now ready to be absorbed into the Frankish realm.

Sebastian chose this moment of triumph to ask the king for an important favor.

"I humbly beg your pardon for seeking an audience at such a time. I know it is a great occasion and you have heavy decisions to make now that the Saxons have ended the war."

The king, who sat at ease in a large tent, was genuinely pleased to see his young protégé. "Nonsense, lad. Of all my officers, I owe you more than most in terms of the Saxons. The least I can do is find out why you look so serious when you should be celebrating like the rest of us. Much of what we have accomplished we couldn't have done without you."

"I am proud, sire," Sebastian continued, rather formally, "to have played a part in these grand happenings. It has always been my supreme wish to serve my king. Nevertheless, though I wish not to spoil your joy at such a moment, I make bold to beg a small boon from you."

"What is it, Sebastian? Out with it, man! Don't be so stodgy. You know there's little I could refuse you now. If it were not for you, we'd still be in those bloody Saxon woods picking fleas off our backs. Name it, son—it's yours."

"Sire, it is as you have often said to me. I am alone. I need a wife. Now there is a woman I would have if you would but allow it."

The king roared with laughter. "Is that all? Well, finally! I had wondered if perhaps you were indeed a eunuch. I've not heard of you having a single dalliance. Well, that's wonderful. And it's high time. Name her, Sebastian, and you shall have her so far as it's in my power to give her to you—that is," the king added teasingly, "if she's unmarried. I cannot let you have someone else's wife, now can I?"

"My lord king, she is unmarried for a certainty."

"Well, who is it then?"

"My lord, does it really matter whom I marry, as long as the lady is free? May I simply choose for myself, no matter what her station in life?"

The king hesitated, narrowing his eyes at Sebastian. "You may, my boy, but I cannot see why you're being so secretive." Finally, in measured tones he announced, "Sebastian, you may have whomever you want. I don't care if it's a peasant's daughter or a count's. Whoever it is, I shall be overjoyed for you."

"Thank you, my lord king—many thanks. I am greatly in your debt," Sebastian stammered and backed away quickly toward the door. "If you don't mind, sire, for personal reasons I should like to withhold her name for a while, just until I can make arrangements with her. Please understand, sire, the lady must also be consulted."

"Well, then, go and do it, Sebastian. It's high time you learned something about women. I daresay you've spent too long not knowing, and let me tell you," the king said with a grin, "it might greatly enhance your life. Yes, I think it would, although I almost fear to let the fairer sex loose upon you. I don't want to lose my best fighter."

"Oh no, sire, of course not. It's just that I must . . . this woman is . . . I need this woman . . . she is . . . excuse me, sire."

"Sebastian, do you really think I don't know who it is? Go on—she's free now, thanks to our old friend Widukind and the charred head I received from him. You can finally have her, with my blessings."

"Thank you, sire, thank you!" Sebastian bowed and moved quickly through the door with the king's delighted laughter ringing in his ears.

The convent at Bischofsheim on the River Tauber boasted high masonry walls and a thick gate. Although no sentries were posted above the walls, the place looked particularly unwelcoming in spite of its reputation as a refuge for some of the most important women in the Frankish kingdom. The highborn daughters and widows of famous men gravitated toward this place, where they knew it was possible for a woman to study and think more independently than almost anywhere else in the realm.

Even so, it was not a place that welcomed travelers or entertained many men of any sort. The place was cloistered night and day, and only the briefest of communications could be had at the gate.

After a week of hard riding, Sebastian rode up to the gate with Liudolf and Archambald and a handful of other soldiers, including Bernard. He pounded on the gate several times and waited patiently. After a time, in frustration, he had the men dismount and begin pounding on the gate with the hilts of their swords. At last, a window behind an iron grate in the gate opened part way.

"This is a convent," a strong male voice announced. "We do not accept visitors, except on special occasions. You must send a letter, be invited, and recognized. We never admit men without special dispensation from the Church or the king." With that, the small door in the gate slammed shut.

Sebastian motioned for the pounding to commence again. After a moment, the small window opened. "What is it you want? And beware—you will be cursed into hell if you have come to do harm to this holy place," said the hooded guardian.

Sebastian dismounted and strode to the gate. "I seek the Lady Adela. I have permission from the high king himself to speak to her. Do not stand in my way if you value your life."

"I do not value this life," said the hollow voice behind the gate, "it is the life beyond that I value. And that is true for all who reside within these walls. Go away. Send a letter from the king, and then we may believe you. The Lady Adela has taken preliminary vows and soon will be a bride of Christ. You dare not intrude upon her solemnity." The man closed the window again. More beating ensued on the gate.

"Open up at once, you whoreson," Sebastian shouted, "in the name of the high king. If you do not, you will be liable for the consequences."

No response.

In frustration, Sebastian mounted and gathered his men in the nearby woods. "I will not wait. I will not suffer any more delay. Are you willing, my friends, to storm this place with me?"

"It will be a pleasure, Sebastian, to capture a convent," Archambald remarked merrily. "I can't say any of us have ever done it. Should be a good deal easier than storming the Eresburg!"

"How should we do it, Bernard?" Sebastian asked. "Shall we break down the gate?"

"No, sir," the old soldier rasped. "Too strong. Take too long. You must go over the top."

"With what, Bernard? We have no ladders."

"Trees. Cut a tree and use the branches to clamber up. Be over in a trice."

And so they slashed a small tree down with their swords, lopped each branch to within a foot of the trunk, and clambered up while Archambald stood below bracing the tree. Because it was a simple wall, with no parapet or wall walk, they simply dropped down the other side into the garden. Waiting there for them was the gate guardian. Despite his deep, gravelly voice, he was a miniature man, a dwarf actually, bearded and short-limbed. He held a heavy staff in his hands and began to use it on Sebastian and his friends, surprising them all with the alacrity with which he bounced between one and the other, belaboring their backs with the stock, all the while chanting in a strange language.

Sebastian found himself in an embarrassing dilemma, not wanting to hurt the little man but frustrated at the delay. He was on the verge of ordering his men to rush the fellow all at once and pinion his arms and feet when a voice at the door to the garden stopped them.

"Lorenzo, stop this at once!" A stately nun in full habit stood at the door, her hands tightly gripped together in front of her. "Pray, what is the meaning of this, gentlemen?" she asked, her voice only a trifle shrill. "This is a convent, as you well know. It is sanctioned by both Church and king, and you will do well to have another thought before continuing."

Sebastian stepped forward immediately, brushing aside the dwarf's cudgel. "Madame, I beg a thousand pardons, but I have . . ." Then he stopped, suddenly recognizing the woman. "Sister Herlindis? Is it you?"

The nun started at Sebastian's voice and then took a step toward him, one hand reaching out. "Lord Sebastian?"

As it turned out, the "siege" of the Bischofsheim convent was not such a frightful event after all; no blood was spilled and no damage was done to the premises. Lorenzo, the gate guard, remained hostile for the duration but was persuaded to return to his post. As for Sister Herlindis, she had recently become mother superior of the convent. She quickly and quietly led the chastened marauders to her chambers where she sat them down, served them some wine, and began a gentle interrogation.

"Lord Sebastian, why did you not simply announce yourself?" she began.

"Sister . . . ah . . . Madame Mother Superior, I tried to do just that. I said my name several times, but your little man . . . ah . . . your faithful gatekeeper would not listen. He kept slamming the window in our faces. I had to do something."

In spite of herself, Herlindis smiled and looked down at her hands. When she looked up again, however, there was sober resolution as well as pain in her eyes. "Well, I suppose you are here for the Lady Adela. You know, Sebastian, she has already taken preliminary vows. I know her husband is dead, God rest his tortured soul; they say you killed him. For that reason alone, among others, I cannot simply release her to you, even if the king has given you permission. God stands higher even than the king."

Sebastian took a deep breath and waited a long moment before speaking. "Madame Mother Superior," he said in a calm, low voice. "I did not kill Konrad. In fact, I spared him, and on the king's orders I took him to Paderborn. He escaped from there and was killed by the Saxons. I did not plan to kill Konrad in order to have his wife. In fact, I gave him a chance to live. There are many who will confirm what I have said. Before I came here, I saw the king at Paderborn, where he is on campaign against his greatest adversary, the Saxon Prince Widukind. In recognition of my services to him, King Karl gave me permission to take in marriage any woman of the realm, provided she is unmarried. I have come here for Adela."

"But I must have proof, Sebastian—I must have something in writing from the king. This is highly irregular; the Church will not sanction it. I must have an irreproachable reason to give Adela permission to forsake her vows and leave this convent," Herlindis said with mounting concern.

At that moment, the chamber door opened and Adela herself stepped in.

"Sebastian!" she gasped as she saw him, and then collapsed against the wall and slid to the floor in a heap.

Sebastian rushed to her side, knelt, and supported her with an arm around her shoulders. Archambald brought water and a cup of wine. When Adela opened her eyes, she said, "I'm all right, Sebastian, really—I'm just weak and shocked. Here, let me stand."

Suddenly, Sebastian made up his mind. He gathered Adela into his arms and marched through the door to the gate. The dwarf made as if to oppose him again. "Get out of my way, little man. I won't be so kind to you this time." Liudolf ran ahead and opened the gate, while the rest of the men hurried to gather the horses. Mother Herlindis swept along behind Sebastian, begging him to stop and consider the consequences of what he was doing. She implored Adela to make him release her.

When they reached the horses, Sebastian put Adela in Liudolf's arms, mounted, and reached down to draw her up beside him. He turned to the nun and said in parting, "Mother Herlindis, you may tell your superiors that the Lady Adela fell ill—as you saw yourself, she fainted. I have merely removed her from the convent to restore her to health. You may also say that I have the sanction of the high king to marry her. I'm sure the Church will agree that for the good of the kingdom the king's wishes in this matter will take precedence over whatever preliminary vows this lady has spoken —especially if the lady herself sincerely wishes it." He turned to Adela. "Do you wish it, my love?"

Adela looked up at him and then at the mother superior. "I do. I wish it with all my heart. I came here only because I believed that it was God's will that I should do penance for my sins. Then Konrad died. And now, just before I am to take my perpetual vows, Sebastian appears. I think it must be a sign that God considers I have suffered enough and that he now wills me to be free, finally, to follow my heart."

The troop rode off at once. As they disappeared into the trees, Mother Herlindis lifted her head and haltingly raised a hand in farewell.

Father Pippin married Sebastian and Adela as soon as they returned to Fernshanz. Their union was not immediately complete, however. Adela still bore scars from her life with Konrad and the loss of her beloved Hugo. She admitted to Sebastian that, though she loved him dearly, she abandoned her promise to the convent partly because she was afraid her grief and terrible memories would drive her further down the dark path of depression she had already begun to walk.

Sebastian was well aware of how fragile Adela was, both physically and mentally, and he treated her with great caution. He insisted on nothing, letting every overture toward intimacy come from Adela. He responded to her need to be held gently and carefully but he only lay down beside her at night when she had fallen asleep.

She began to recover fully on the Feast Day of Saints Peter and Paul. Honoring these leading pillars of the Church was a high holy day and a cause for joyous celebration, with the festivities lasting all day and late into the night. As Lord of Fernshanz, Sebastian was expected to be in attendance at everything, beginning with the early morning celebration of the Mass and ending late in the night when the dancing began around the bonfire. Adela remained at his side throughout the long day, partaking in the promenade through the town to show off the young lord's bride and greet the villagers and their children. She sat with Sebastian on primitive benches in the village green when the feasting began and enjoyed the songs and antics of the self-appointed village jesters, who occasionally moved her to laugh out loud. She even took a cup or two of Andernach wine during the evening.

They stayed only long enough at the bonfire to watch the dancing begin. From the outset it exuded an air of sensual expectation. Adela was fascinated when the young girls of the village began with modest, almost dainty steps to circle around the bonfire in time to the flutes and makeshift drums. They moved tentatively at first, only occasionally and shyly raising their glances toward the watching young men. After a time the men began to clap their hands and utter a guttural rythmic sound in their throats, such as they might do when pulling a heavy load. When the pace of the dancing increased and the women began to move more boldly, spinning and turning, their hands fluttering invitingly toward the men, Sebastian took Adela by the arm, raised a hand in farewell, and passed gently out of the circle of firelight.

"But why did we have to leave, my love?" Adela complained as they returned to the manor house. "Things were just beginning to get exciting."

"My dear girl," Sebastian replied with a grin, "as interesting as it appeared to be, you don't really want to see what might happen next. It might truly be a shock for a lady like yourself. Besides, it isn't fair to the villagers. They would feel constrained to have their lord and lady watching this part of their revelry. You see, on nights like this, good marriages often begin."

Whatever Adela saw that day and evening was enough. She came at Sebastian as soon as they entered the great room of the manor, where a cheerful fire had been built up by Marta before she left for the evening. Flickering shadows on the walls mimicked the motions of the dancers. "Oh, Sebastian," she exclaimed, hugging him tightly, "I have not had such a good time since I was a girl at Andernach. Come and dance with me," she called as she twirled away on her toes around the fire, mimicking the young girls.

Sebastian clapped his hands and tried to imitate the sounds of the village men. Adela laughed in appreciation and reached out to touch him each time she spun by. Dancing faster and faster at each rounding of the fireplace, she collapsed finally into his arms, and then led him eagerly toward their bed. Bounding into the middle of the nest of covers, she looked boldly into his eyes and held out her arms to him, laughing impishly as he stumbled into them. She pulled him down beside her and began at last an awakening that neither of them had ever known or imagined.

They had little more than a week together, hardly believing that they could finally love each other openly and that life could be so perfect. And then the calamitous news came from Saxony—the king had ordered the execution of the rebels responsible for the massacre at the battle of the Suntel Mountains—four thousand five hundred of them.

At first, Sebastian refused to believe what he had heard from a wounded soldier who had returned home from Paderborn. But the soldier was from Fernshanz and had no reason to lie or even exaggerate the news. Later, his report was confirmed by other returning wounded men. They all said that Paderborn had been buzzing with the word from the army even before the king returned. After that, the execution of the Saxons, which some of the men had seen, was all anyone talked about. Most were astonished at the king's draconian response to this latest Saxon rebellion, but those who had fought for many years against the Saxons or had lost friends at Suntel felt the Saxons had finally gotten what they had long deserved and applauded the king's grim judgment.

Sebastian, however, did not. The reports snatched him roughly out of the euphoria of his idyll with Adela.

"I can't stop thinking about it, Adela," Sebastian said passionately, pacing back and forth in the small garden behind the manor house. He smashed a fist into the palm of the other hand. "I can't believe the king would command such a thing to happen. They were unarmed, defenseless men. They had stopped fighting. They came in and surrendered by the thousands. He disarmed them and then . . . and then he just killed them. I'm told that many of the men he killed weren't even at the Suntel battle. He has ruined everything. Does he really think this will deter them now?"

"My love, please calm yourself. It does no good to rage and shout at me—I have done nothing."

"Ah, my sweet girl, I'm so sorry," Sebastian said, dismayed that he was taking his frustration out on Adela. He came and sat down beside her, stroking her long hair absently.

"I just thought he would listen to me, Adela. And I'm not the only one—Edelrath and Bishop Regwald also counseled him to go slowly and think it through. Before I left, I talked with many of the Saxon chieftains who gave themselves up as the army moved toward the Weser. Almost all of them said they were tired of fighting and that they had been divided about continuing the war. They said that four of the five major tribes had already decided not to fight this year, and then Widukind came back from Nordmannia. They said it was only Widukind and the Westphalians who laid the trap at Suntel. Of course, the king doesn't believe them. But I do; it's Widukind we must attend to, not the others."

During the next several days, as much as Adela tried to persuade him that what had happened was beyond his control, Sebastian grew more and more restless. Finally, he left Adela's side, where he been constantly since they had ridden off from Bischofsheim, and sought out Father Pippin. Conscripting a startled Bardulf, they bade him sail them downriver toward the Rhine while they talked.

"You have to go, Sebastian," the priest reasoned calmly. "You must tell the king how you feel. If you do not, you will be no different from the rest of his warriors, and nothing will change. If you want to stand by the virtues you have lived by thus far, if you want to continue to live a righteous life, and if you want that life to please God and count for something in the end, then you must go and speak your mind to the king, no matter what the cost."

Sebastian went next to Heimdal, seeking him out in his forest retreat. The old man listened without saying much as they sat by an open fire. Sebastian talked into the night about everything— the campaign, his strong convictions regarding the course to take with the Saxons, how his high opinion of the king had suffered perhaps a terminal blow, and how he felt about Adela. He was tortured by the thought of having to leave her to go and face the king's wrath, now that they were finally united after so many years.

At length, the old blind man cleared his throat, poked with a stick at the fire, and pronounced his judgment. "You must go, of course, my son. You will not be happy if you do not, you will not be able to resume the joy you have known in having your Adela at long last. It's simple—you must do what needs doing, according to your conscience. It will surely be a perilous undertaking. The king may condemn you; you must be prepared for that. But remember this, just because the thing seems difficult to you, do not think it is impossible to achieve."

Sebastian left at dawn the next day. When he told her what he planned to do, Adela announced firmly that her place was beside him when he faced the king and that she would go with him. It was all he could do to convince her that her presence would only make his task more difficult, that the king and his comrades would think he was hiding behind his wife's noble birth and her position as daughter of Charlemagne's chief advisor. At first she argued violently, and then she tried to reason with him sweetly. Finally, she broke down and cried with abandon. In the end, late into the night, he swung her up in his arms and carried her to their bed. At dawn, she clung to him briefly as he went out, tears welling again in her eyes, but at the door, she managed a smile and raised her hand in farewell as he and Archambald rode away.

Sebastian was gone a month. The king had left Paderborn and gone back across the Rhine to Thionville on the Moselle, where he intended to stay through the winter. Sebastian wound up making a long detour to Paderborn and arrived too late to catch the king. While there, however, he learned the particulars of the massacre of the Saxons. Charlemagne himself had cut the heads off several of their leading men. Sebastian was filled with disgust and was more determined than ever to voice his objections to such savagery, even though the subsequent confrontation with the king at Thionville almost cost him his own head.

Chapter 32

Idyll's End

Fernshanz, Spring 785

"Will ye get that worthless loafer out of me house?" Gradually, Bardulf heard the shrill voice of his wife through the fog of his slumber on a Sunday morning following a night of drinking with his friends. It was a rare occasion when wine and beer flowed freely at hardworking, no-nonsense Fernshanz, but it had been a grand celebration, the birth of the Lord Sebastian's first son with his Lady Adela.

"Wha . . . what's wrong, Liesel, m'love? Can't ye let a man sleep on a Sunday?"

"Sleep, nothin', ye lazy fool. It's no time before the bells will ring for Mass, and ye mus' go. They'll be baptizin' the babe. But right now, there's yer no-account Drogo hangin' around me front door again, lookin' for a handout. I swear I won't feed 'im no more. Let 'im get his own wife and leave yers alone."

"Aw, *mein schatz*, Drogo don' eat much," Bardulf groaned as he gingerly raised himself out of the nest of blankets on the floor in the corner of the room. "And him and me're partners on the boat."

"Partners! What kind of partners is that? Ye do all the work," she screeched. "He don' even know what to do. You just carry 'im along on your trips so ye'll have sommon' ter yammer at. I never saw such a worthless, stupid man."

At that Bardulf bristled and roused himself. Drogo might be all she said he was, but he was Bardulf's best and almost only friend, and he would not have him vilified in this way. He stumbled across the floor in his semi-nakedness and confronted his buxom wife through bloodshot eyes. "Now ye *halt's maul*, ye fishwife! Ye hear me?" Bardulf threatened, breathing his fetid breath directly into her face. "I've enough of yer sharp tongue, especially now, this early in the mornin'. I won' have ye runnin' down poor Drogo. He never done nothin' to ye, and he's a good friend to me." In a lower voice he added, turning away, "Why, O God, did ye ever let me marry?"

Liesel knew when it was prudent to leave off badgering her testy and mercurial husband. He was lazy, untrustworthy, and innately dishonest, but she had been charmed by him the first time she saw him at Andernach. He had swaggered around the place buying food and goods for Fernshanz as if he were the master and not Lord Sebastian. Every time he passed a maiden, he stood by grinning and staring boldly. When he got to her, he had taken her breath away by sweeping her up in a bear hug and whispering in her ear that she was the prettiest maiden in all of Andernach and her body drove him mad.

Bardulf had brought Liesel home with him on that very trip, although her departure had been more like a kidnapping than a betrothal. Liesel's father had refused to allow the marriage and had forbidden Liesel to see the brash boatman again until a bride price might be arranged. Bardulf waited until her father was in the fields and simply sailed off with her. He had not been able to return to Andernach since then.

As for Drogo, Bardulf had pleaded with him to look over the bumper crop of unmarried girls at Andernach and choose one. But Drogo was far too shy and could not even raise his eyes when one of the maidens walked by. Bardulf even picked out one of the girls, homely and a bit cross-eyed, to be sure, but willing. Drogo took one look, turned, and ran back to the boat.

Meanwhile, Liesel had become the steadying influence Bardulf needed in his life. He loved her, though he could never bring himself to change his ways for her. He ate better and was proud of Liesel's energy and industriousness. When he was at home, he lacked for very little. Liesel tolerated him because he was, after all, a big, handsome man and a good provider. She was much better off than she had been at Andernach, and because of the boat trade, she found herself to be one of the most prosperous of the village wives. Poor Drogo, who hung around Bardulf as much as before, was her only complaint, and he was not really much of a problem after all, only irksome and always underfoot.

Almost three years had passed since Sebastian's fiery meeting with the king after the Suntel incident. True to his word, Charlemagne had left Sebastian alone, and he had received no word from any of his old comrades. Even Adela's father had not contacted them. It was as if they had all dropped off the edge of the earth and now lived in a completely different world.

It was a time like no other in Sebastian's life. With no interference from the king and no campaigns to go on, Sebastian could concentrate on the land, and they made great progress at Fernshanz. Many of the innovations Lothar had suggested but never had a chance to implement were put into operation. The moat was finished and the river was diverted into it. The dirt walls of the citadel were replaced by stone, and towers were built on all sides, including two overlooking the river. A much more convenient port was created along the riverbank so that at least seven large boats or barges could put in at the same time. Bernard, the old veteran of many a siege, even contrived to build several catapults inside the walls, so that baskets of stones could be flung at attackers. Pits for heating oil were dug at intervals along the walls.

As for food, the supply gradually grew out of all expectation. In the autumn, they planted cereal grains, much as before, but the spring planting was the surprise. Sebastian took a chance the first year of his exile, divided up the land, and had the peasants plant a second field full of legumes—peas, broad beans, and lentils, in addition to oats. Rotating the crops through three fields, planting one in the fall, another in the spring, and leaving the third field fallow became the annual routine of Fernshanz.

In their private plots, the peasants included more of these legumes among their vegetables than ever before. The result was healthier, more productive gardens and fields wherever the legumes had been planted and healthier peasants. The death rate among children of peasant families became lower than in anyone's memory.

In addition to filling the moat, the river also was harnessed to drive the wheels of a second mill and to provide the power to pound wool with wooden fuller's hammers to make cloth. The river was even diverted into a third building where it filled a primitive boiler for the making of beer. The reputation of Fernshanz grew along with its crops, and by the second year, no more land was available; Sebastian increasingly had to turn away peasants seeking to become a part of the community. With the addition of so many new people, Fernshanz had become more of a town than a village, and Sebastian found himself so busy with his duties as lord that he was obliged to designate Liudolf and Archambald as his deputies in organizing the community and arbitrating its disputes.

Conspicuous and joyous change occurred in Sebastian's private life as well. Adela slowly recovered the healthy good looks she had possessed so strikingly when Sebastian first saw her at the king's court in Worms, and she soon proved to be a fertile field herself, presenting Sebastian with two healthy sons in quick succession. They named their first son Attalus, after Sebastian's real father, and the second Karl, in deference to the king.

Gradually, Adela had emerged from her spells of despair and abandoned her long-held conviction that she was a lost soul whose only chance at redemption was to pay a heavy price for her sins. After the ordeal of her life with Konrad, Sebastian and the boys made her happy. And in her happiness she reached out to all. She flung her net far and wide and launched herself into a life of service at Fernshanz. She became greatly loved and that made her even more content.

Sebastian loved her to distraction. She looked hardly older than when he had first met her, and a wonderful change took place in her outlook on life. When he found himself watching her during an ordinary day, he could see clearly how poised, effective, smart, and at the center of everything she was becoming at Fernshanz, so well loved by everyone. He still could not believe his good fortune, that every night, this lovely, passionate creature would slip into their sleeping place to warm his body and wash his soul with her love.

Their joy seemed complete when, to their great surprise and initial consternation, they became parents of yet a third son, already ten years old, who showed up literally on their doorstep.

One early morning as Sebastian prepared to go out on his daily rounds, Baumgard came to see him and said in his usual obsequious manner, "My esteemed lord and noble protector, Bardulf is on the doorstep without. He has a boy with him. He says he must see you at once."

"What? What are you talking about, Baumgard? I haven't got time this morning for riddles."

"No, sir—no, my lord. It is no riddle. There truly is a boy on the doorstep. He has just arrived on Bardulf's boat, all the way from Andernach. I think you certainly may wish to see him."

News from anywhere was a rare but welcome commodity at Fernshanz, but news from Andernach was always of particular interest. Sebastian hurried to the door. There on the stoop was a slight, comely lad with bright blond hair holding a bulky leather bag in his hands. The boy was striking in appearance and demeanor. In contrast to his fair hair, he had dark brown eyes and his gaze was solemn. He seemed completely unafraid and offered the bag confidently and without a word to Sebastian.

Bardulf hastened to explain. "If you please, m'lord. We just come from Andernach. I been up there to make amends to me father-in-law and sell some of our grain. And, lo and behold, they gives me this boy and says take 'im to you. This here is Milo, m'lord. He come with us all the way from Andernach. And he is a good sailor, I might add. Never give us a bit of trouble. That there is a bag of seeds he wants to give ye as a gift."

"Bardulf," Sebastian said in exasperation, while hesitatingly accepting the bag from the boy, "will you please explain why we are being honored with the presence of this fine young man bearing gifts?"

"Well, m'lord, this here is Milo, like I said. I wouldn't have took him, excep' he was given to me by a woman who said she was his mother, and she swore to me that this here Milo's father was none other than our old friend Lothar. She said ye would want to know this boy."

Sebastian knew at once that the boy was Gersvind's child—and his own. Still, he played out the initial subterfuge. "But, Bardulf, why is he here? Why did she send him?"

"Well, sir, it seems like our good old friend Lothar caught some kind of ague and went and died of it. The woman, that is, the boy's mother, said ye would know what to do with the boy better than she would, that he were a smart boy and ye would want 'im to have a chance to grow up good. I weren't goin' to take the boy, even then, but she kissed 'im real quick and run right off the boat, just leavin' 'im there. I couldn't just leave 'im on the dock; we was all ready to go on and go. He never made a peep when we pushed off, and he din't shed no tears neither. He jus' din't say much at all on the trip up here. But here he is, sir, and I hope I ain't made no mistake bringin' 'im."

"You have not, Bardulf. It was the right thing to do. This boy is special, and I will take care of him. Go on back to your duties now. I mean to reward you later for bringing Milo to me."

"Sir, ye ain't got to do that. He weren't no trouble. I liked 'im, and he's a brave little man."

"I imagine he is indeed, Bardulf. You have my gratitude."

Adela liked the little boy immediately and took him straight to her bosom. After Sebastian painfully explained who he actually was, she never breathed another word about Milo's origin but treated him as if he were her own. Eventually, Milo began to feel at home. He would not talk about his mother and father except to say that they had to go and be with God and that he was to remember them "by being a good servant to Lord Sebastian."

"Well, you are not a servant, Milo," Adela told him. "Your mother and father loved you very much, and they sent you to us so that you would be safe and have a good life. That makes you a gift to us, and you must think of little Attalus and Karl as your brothers, do you understand? You're part of this family now."

Gradually, Milo came to be accepted by everyone at Fernshanz. No one named him openly as Sebastian's son, but it was understood that the boy was special and must be treated as such. It soon became clear that Milo was as good looking as his beautiful mother and as smart and talented as the well-remembered man who raised him. Sebastian wasted no time in teaching him to read, and the boy took to all learning naturally and with ease. He spoke little, but when he did, it was clear to all that he was exceptionally bright. Sebastian's only concern was that he had no liking or aptitude at all for the warrior's life. He could not bring himself to kill anything, even a rat, and he simply hung his head in silence whenever Sebastian suggested that they go to the training field or hunt in the forest. He did not even like to ride, though

Sebastian presented him with a beautiful sorrel gelding that was gentle and already well trained.

Raising Milo was a challenge for both Adela and Sebastian because he was so different from the other boys. However, as long as they allowed him to follow his curiosity and pursue his own interests, he flourished. Sebastian marveled at the intellectual understanding he developed at so young an age, and Adela loved him dearly for his gentleness and increasingly spiritual nature.

Meanwhile, the king was preoccupied with events in his own family. Hildegard, his beloved and beautiful young wife and mother of eight of his children, had died. In the same year he lost his own mother, Queen Bertrada, his staunchest ally. For the next two years, the king, restless and grieving, threw himself into a relentless war in Saxony, almost desperately trying to end the chronic revolts that occurred every year no matter how many victories Charlemagne's troops won. Finally, during the third year of these frustrating campaigns, the king sent for Sebastian.

"Sebastian, my boy!" the king called out joyfully at the sight of Sebastian striding into the great room at the king's fortress at Paderborn. Charlemagne acted as if the three years of Sebastian's exile had never occurred and as if there had never been a lethal reason for that exile. "I can't believe you could pull yourself away from your marriage bed," the king continued in a jovial tone. "They say nine months don't go by without your having another babe. I don't blame you, my boy—that girl is a stunner. I wouldn't leave her bed either!"

Sebastian knelt briefly before the king and stood up, worried and unsmiling, before him. Charlemagne saw at once that Sebastian had not changed his mind. "Ah, blast, I've seen that look on your face before. I was hoping things had changed after so long a time and that you had finally come to your senses."

"My lord king," Sebastian began, reciting the speech he had pondered and practiced over and over throughout the long journey, "You are a great ruler, one without parallel in the world. All men say so. I have always been grateful to be counted as one of your warriors, and my most cherished wish has always been to serve you all the days of my life."

"All right, all right, get on with it," the king said, dreading what he knew would come next.

Sebastian paused, took a deep breath, and cleared his throat. "That is why, my king . . . that is why it's so hard for me to tell you what still lies so heavily in my heart. You know, sire, that it concerns what happened on the banks of the Aller at Verden after the Saxons surrendered three years ago. I . . . I believe, sire, that what we did there was wrong, terribly wrong, and that is why the Saxons are still fighting."

The king's mouth dropped open. Sebastian continued, speaking more rapidly, "Sire, if we are ever to have peace with the Saxons and convince them to give up their pagan gods, we must reflect the values of the Christ we profess, not those of some Old Testament king, who wiped out whole peoples in order to appease a vengeful god. Sire . . ."

"Stop!" the king shouted.

Sebastian continued, imploringly. "Otherwise, sire, we are no better than they are. We must, great king, show them a better way. We must . . ."

"Sebastian! Stop at once or I'll have you bound and gagged!" The king was furious. He regained control of himself with difficulty and said in a voice of deadly calm, "Do you even realize what you have presumed to do? You have just committed high treason again, you sanctimonious, presumptuous, disrespectful whelp. How dare you speak to me in such terms?"

Sebastian went to his knees. "I am truly sorry, my liege. You asked me for a reason. Once, years ago, when I was little more than a boy, when Attalus and I helped you overcome the Saxons at the Eresburg and find their treasure, you told me that I was always to speak my mind and tell you the truth as I see it, no matter what. I do that now, sire, though my life may be forfeit for it."

The king paused and swept his hands through his hair in a distracted gesture. He took a deep breath, and the redness gradually receded from his face. "Get up, Sebastian. I don't know why I let you stir me up like this. You're like a bad conscience. No one can make me feel guilty like you do. No one even tries, not even my sons."

"Actually," the king continued in a milder tone, "if you had just waited for me to tell you . . . I've decided to try it your way. The moment may have come; we have them on the run again. Perhaps they'll listen to you, especially if you know Widukind as well as you say you do. But I've not decided this lightly. I know, and so do you, that your chances are small. It's very likely I will sadly regret this decision." The king hesitated, then reached behind him for an object wrapped in a blanket. Drawing it out, the king cleared his throat and handed it to Sebastian. "Here is your sword back. I pray you won't have to use it, and I also pray that I will not have to take it from you—ever again."

It was Sebastian's turn to be speechless. It was everything he had hoped for. "My lord king," he finally managed to say, "I am most grateful. I believe . . . you will never have need to take the sword back. I have faith that the plan will work. I'm not afraid. With God's help, Widukind will come to you."

Chapter 33

Widukind

Summer 785

From Paderborn, they rode directly north toward the Danish border. At first, they were accompanied by Saxon guides who swore to lead them safely through Saxon territory to a point in the Danish lands where Widukind had last been reported to be. The guides, however, became more and more nervous as they approached the Danish border area, and one morning Sebastian awoke to find them gone.

It was already a considerable risk for three Franks to be so far into strange and hostile territory. Now, without guides or firm knowledge of the way ahead, Sebastian's heart sank at the prospect of continuing the journey.

Heimdal spoke up in the early morning fog as the three pieced together what had happened and tried to collect themselves for the next step. "Well, Sebastian, it isn't as if we're any worse off than yesterday. The Saxons didn't really provide us with any better security. If Widukind wants to kill us, they couldn't have stopped him."

"Yes, but at least they could have pointed the way for us before they ran," Sebastian remarked in disgust.

The blind man yawned. "What difference would it have made? If we keep going north we are sure to find some Danes—more likely they will find us—and if they decide to let us live, they will know where to find Widukind."

"I shouldn't have let you come along, either of you. It should be my risk alone."

In his terse manner, Liudolf now put a precise cap on the conversation. "We've been all over this already. From the moment you decided to go ask the king if you could do this, we have been with you. In fact, we were the ones who convinced you that you had to go, and from the moment we set out, we all understood there would be no going back. There's no sense talking about it again."

Three days later, simply by riding north along whatever trails led in the right direction, they ran into Widukind's band—or, rather, Widukind got word of them and sought them out. Liudolf, who was in the lead, immediately showed fight, but they were quickly surrounded and Sebastian cried out for him to stop.

Widukind was a spectacle to behold. He was bare to the waist, and his thick mane of blond hair was unbound and trailing halfway down his back. His piercing blue eyes were still his most dominant feature, and muscles still bulged in his arms and shoulders despite his years. He was decorated like a Viking with heavy silver armbands and bracelets and a leather coronet studded with jewels around his temples. The Saxon sat his small horse almost casually in spite of the stallion's high spirits, calming it with his legs and low, guttural assurances. When his horse stopped prancing and rearing, Widukind moved closer, with a sardonic, sideways grin on his face, creating the weird impression that only half of his face was smiling. Nevertheless, there was a light of pure enjoyment in his eyes. Sebastian could see why Widukind was respected. He looked and acted in a completely free and unorthodox way, and he took delight in surprising or shocking anyone he engaged. He also had the imperturbable manner of one easily in command. He was both engaging and clever, brimming with energy and cunning. At this point, he was like a big tomcat having surprised a mouse out in the open.

By contrast, Sebastian sat Joyeuse bolt upright and absolutely motionless, making a supreme effort to control the animal lest he mimic the wildness of Widukind's mount. His plan was to give the impression of deliberate grace in adversity, conceding to Widukind no obvious advantage. Out of habit, Sebastian studied the warrior on the dancing horse before him as a potential adversary. He concluded that Widukind might be a handful in a fight and that he would need to be lucky or very tricky to win.

Nevertheless, though Widukind was still powerful, Sebastian discerned that the wily prince seemed to have lost a bit of quickness and might no longer have the stamina for sustained personal combat. His neck and the inside bends of his elbows had tell-tale wrinkles. Great veins stuck out on the sides of his forehead. His naked belly protruded grossly from his body like a melon beneath his powerful chest and shoulders. His temples and cheeks showed the brown spots of a man far past his prime. Sebastian concluded that the legendary prince had long since seen his best days.

"Well, unfortunate Frank," the Saxon began with a laugh, "what have you got to say before we kill you? Oh, but first, perhaps I should give myself the pleasure of seeing you watch your friend, who was so ready to fight just now, and this strange old blind man you have brought with you die before your eyes." With that, he jerked his head toward several warriors, who began to circle around Liudolf and Heimdal.

"Do not!" commanded Sebastian. He spoke quietly, looking directly into Widukind's eyes. "If you kill my friend and servant, you had better be sure and kill me as well, for I will become your worst enemy from that moment."

"Ah, what have we here, a Frank with some spirit? I certainly did intend to kill you as well. Have you any reason why I should not?"

"Yes, a grave one. You will be throwing away a great opportunity—to become the friend of Charlemagne."

"Ha! And why would I want to? That great tyrant has killed half my warriors and chased me out of Saxony a dozen times. Such a friend he would be!"

"Hear me out, Prince. I may have an offer you will find hard to refuse."

The effort Widukind had taken to find them said much more than his elaborate threats to kill them. The Saxon prince was a curious man in more ways than one. He couldn't bear not knowing why the King of the Franks would go to such trouble to seek him out with a message. He had to know what the message was. At the bottom of his curiosity was the inkling that there might be a new smell in the wind.

"Well, it's been a slow morning. I suppose I have two minutes to listen to a fairy tale. Make it good, though, young Frank. If you bore me, these may be your last words."

"Prince Widukind, what if I could guarantee that you could live out the rest of your days in peace, on good land, where you and your people could prosper and no longer be under threat of extermination? What if I could promise you that the king would treat you with utmost respect, as if you were a brother, and give you high honor among all the Franks?"

"You could do this? And who are you, Sir Herald, that you stand so high among the Franks and can speak with the mouth of the king? Are you his son, perhaps?"

"I am not, Prince. My name is Sebastian of Fernshanz, son of Attalus, the Horse Master. I am only the king's messenger, but he cares for me, I think, like a son. I have defied him in earnest because of what I believe, and he has let me live."

Sebastian paused a moment and surveyed the menacing ring of Saxon warriors, suddenly frozen in anticipation of what would come next. His heart rushed out to Liudolf, who sat his horse so calmly by his side, pale as death but ready in an instant for a last desperate fight.

Sebastian continued quietly, "You and I have met before, Prince Widukind, but it was dark, and you might not recognize me. You lent me your sword that dark night. I have it here—in this bag across my saddle. I've come to return it. Wouldn't you like it back?"

He pulled out the long sword and handed it over. Widukind squinted in surprise, admiring the poise of this bold young messenger, but suspecting, nonetheless, some kind of trick.

Sebastian went on in the same calm voice. "And I believe, Prince, that I have met your daughter—one of them, at least. She was a captive and I set her free."

At that Widukind grunted and looked hard at Sebastian, turning the sword over and over in his hands. "I do know you. You are *that* Sebastian—'Sebastian, the Frank,' she called you. Your reputation precedes you. Is it possible you are different from the rest of your cursed race?" He paused to consider this unexpected turn of events. "Tell me,

Sebastian the Frank, you said you believed something so strongly that you defied your own king. What was it that made you do such a foolish thing?"

"I believe, Prince Widukind, that there can be peace between our two peoples."

"Hah! Well, you are the only one, Frank or Saxon, who believes it. We've been killing each other for a long time. What makes you think we could stop now?"

"You are in a losing game, Prince. Karl is king over lands from here to the great sea in the west, and he has ten or even twenty warriors for every one of yours. Your losses have been severe in the past few years, *nicht wahr*? And King Karl's strong fortresses keep marching deeper and deeper into Saxon territory. When was the last time you won a battle against the Franks? Suntel, right? And that victory cost your people forty-five hundred warriors."

"So what would you have me do, brave bringer of old news? Should I tell all the Saxon tribes to lay down their weapons and submit to slavery under the hated Franks? Should I myself crawl on my knees to Karl and lick his feet, begging for pardon? He would cut off my head, as he did to our brothers after Suntel."

"I think not, Prince, not this time. King Karl is also tired of the fighting. He does not wish to lose another man in these endless wars with your people, and I believe he is genuinely sorry for what he did after Suntel. At least he realizes now it was a mistake and solved nothing." After a pause, Sebastian went on, "I think King Karl has been convinced to try a different way."

"And what way might that be, my young Frankish friend?" Widukind said, laughing harshly. "Does he wish to share his kingdom with me, perhaps? Or maybe he's willing to pay us a yearly tribute to stop attacking him. Now, that's an idea I would favor."

"He is willing to give you land—good farmland inside of Francia, on the other side of the Rhine—and honorable places in his army. You know some Saxon units already serve alongside King Karl's soldiers."

"Bah," Widukind spat vehemently. "Traitors, all! Lickspittles and old, frightened women—they're not worthy to be called Saxons."

"They have prospered, Prince. And they do not go hungry."

"That may be, but now they bow and kneel to that weak man who let himself be tortured and nailed to a tree. What kind of pitiful god is that? Why would we want him?"

"You might feel differently, Prince, if you knew even the least thing about him. He is a prince, too, the Prince of Peace. What you see on that cross of wood is his sacrifice so that we might all hope to live in peace."

"So that's your message, is it? You want us to give up our free way of life, our noble warrior's way, all our own ancient gods, and submit to your spineless god and your grasping priests. I do not understand at all why Karl fights so hard for a god that he claims wants only peace."

"Prince, I came here willingly to bring you the king's message and to offer you a chance to end this long war with honor. In our camp, there are some who say the only way to stop the fighting is to wipe the Saxons off the face of the earth—men, women, and children. The future of the Saxon race may depend on your answer."

"Well, Abbi, shall we continue the fight?" Widukind grunted the question into the campfire as he sat drinking a rough brand of *schnaps* into the night with his old friend and longtime companion. "How many years have we fought now? Twenty, is it? I can't remember."

"Too many, Widu. I am tired. And not so good at killing Franks anymore."

"Ah, you're as good as you ever were, you old bear. So am I, by Thor. They can't kill us. They're too stupid."

"That may be, but there are too many of them. They keep coming every year, as many as the stars, and they keep building forts in our land. I'm feeling too old for all this now. I just want to sit in the sun somewhere."

"All right, then, Sebastian the Frank. Your boldness has convinced me. We will parley with your king."

"You must go there, Prince. He will not come to you—not this time."

"I'll go, I'll go," Widukind conceded grudgingly, "though he will probably waste no time cutting off my stupid head. But if he does, it will be the end of you as well. You realize you are my security, don't you? You will have to stay with my men, wherever they may be. We will see how much your king loves you, won't we?"

"I understand, Prince. But I ask one favor of you—let my friends go back with you."

"We will take the young warrior, for we need a guide. But the blind man stays. He would just slow us down. Besides, you will need somebody to talk to, and from what I've heard already, you won't need anyone else. Ye gods, the man never shuts up."

Sebastian smiled. "He's a good friend and counselor, nevertheless, and he doesn't expect to survive this in any case. I will be glad of him."

"Do you expect to survive, Sebastian?"

"I do indeed, Prince. I think you will find that King Karl has had a kind of . . . epiphany. Since the Suntel episode, he has regretted his past harsh methods. I think he understands now what he must do to bring peace."

"Well, he had better, for both our sakes. I don't know about these so-called epiphanies. I suspect he's too old a skunk to change his stink, but I'm betting he loves you enough to try and save your worthless arse. If not, then we will see each other in whatever hell awaits us."

"Are they gone?" Heimdal asked as he and Sebastian sat by the fire waiting for the next move. "Yes, God help us," Sebastian grunted. Now that Widukind and Abbi had decided to take the big gamble and let Liudolf lead them to the king, Sebastian and Heimdal had to reconcile themselves to the status of hostages, a role they knew might last an interminable time. Their Saxon jailers were just beginning to show signs of moving the camp, and the word was that they would go deeper into Nordmannia to join with their Viking allies, since every village in Saxony was still being threatened by the presence of Charlemagne's army. The band consisted of Westphalian Saxons, the hard core of resistance to Frankish rule. They were dedicated to guarding Sebastian until word came from or about Widukind, one way or another.

"How do you feel, Sebastian? Now that the die is cast, are you prepared for the consequences?"

"I am, Heimdal. I've never felt surer that what we're doing is right. It's exhilarating to think that we actually stand a good chance of ending the Saxon wars."

"But are you that sure of your king? He's very proud. He won't tolerate any license of behavior on the part of our friend Widukind. The first time Widukind makes a jibe at the Christian religion or pokes fun at Charlemagne's ample girth, it's probably off with his head. Or don't you think so?"

"That may very well be, Heimdal. I suppose we are in God's hands from now on."

"And what about your family? Until now I reckoned they were the most important thing in your life."

"They are. I love them with my whole heart and my entire being. They are in my thoughts at every waking moment. All I want now is to return to them and stay with them for the rest of my days. If I could do that, I would ask for nothing else in this life."

"And yet you do this! Why did you make this sacrifice? We talked about it over and over, but you have never said why you would choose to stay here when clearly your family is what is most dear to you, not the king."

"It's not just for the king that I do this. It's for my family—my sons, and all the sons of other Franks and Saxons. If I can play a part in stopping the war, then this endless cycle of violence, this bloodbath that occurs every year, may finally stop. Then perhaps my sons will have a chance to do something else with their lives besides going to the *Maifeld* every spring to spend their whole lives killing others."

"But that is what Franks do, is it not? That's been the pattern ever since Karl took the crown, and it was the pattern before him of Pippin, of Karl the Hammer, and of all the Frankish kings, all the way back to old Clovis the Butcher."

"You're playing with me, Heimdal. Wasn't it you who taught me to think like this? You're the one who always told me to question the way things are—that there's no rule that says everything must stay the same." Sebastian stirred the campfire and looked off into the forest and continued, "I believe the king has truly changed. He's not a bloodthirsty man at heart—he'd rather laugh and tell tales and swim with his friends.

He'd rather hear a ballad sung well or a poem prettily written. He loves life and his friends."

"And his women," added Heimdal wryly.

"Aye. But he also loves his people. Look at what he's trying to do. I've heard he wants schools in all the cathedrals, as well as in the monasteries, and not just for those who want to be in the Church—for the sons of warriors as well. You know how he loves reading and wants everybody to learn. He is different. If we can just stop fighting all the time, I believe he will make an enormous change in the way Franks live their lives. Remember the things you taught me about the old Roman era? It may be that he will truly lead us back to those times, when men thought of many things, not just killing and conquering."

"Humpf! I'm afraid you still have much to learn about history, my young scholar. The Romans did their share of killing and conquering, and they were better at it and for a much longer time than Karl. But they did leave a legacy of learning and law and a sense that a man has a mind and must use it to the best of his ability. They also suggested that there is another level of law, beyond war and conquest, to which we might one day aspire."

"Well, that's what I want—I want us to rise to that other level. And I think the king does, too."

"What if he does not? Do you know him that well? What if all he really cares about is his own power? Don't you think it might be wise for you to try and escape from here, just in case?"

Sebastian hesitated, but only for a moment. He poked the dying fire and said confidently, "The king will keep his word."

Epilogue

The Torchbearer

The King's Court at Attigny
on the River Aisne, Western Francia, 785

The celebration at the king's court at Attigny was like nothing Sebastian had ever seen. The king had brought half his army to the small village on the verge of the great Ardennes forest. It was a beautiful place, though it was soon crowded beyond recognition. The camp followers and entourage of singers, musicians, jesters, and jugglers quickly transformed the quiet village into a festival. Widukind's fame drew Saxon and Frank alike to witness the historic event.

Every doubt Sebastian might have had about the king's intentions toward Widukind had been dispelled by the magnanimous way in which the king treated the Saxon chieftain and the many elders he brought with him to share the occasion. For more than a month, the leading men of the Westphalians and several other Saxon tribes had been gathering at Attigny as the word got out that Widukind had made peace with the king. Every arrival had been greeted by the king himself, and every Saxon was treated with deference and dignity. Hunting parties went forth daily to bring in enough game from the dense forest, and the king hosted two or three banquets every week in the Saxons' honor. It was as if they had never been such sworn enemies.

Sebastian and Heimdal had bolted from Saxony as soon as Liudolf and one of Widukind's most trusted lieutenants arrived at the Danish border to report they were no longer hostages. They stopped at Fernshanz only long enough for Sebastian to present himself safe and sound to Adela and bring her the dramatic news that Widukind had been pardoned by the king and would be baptized within the month. The king ordered Sebastian to make haste to Attigny to witness the great event, and Adela was to prepare herself and the family to join them as soon as possible at the king's court.

Sebastian arrived at the end of the third week of the celebration and was astounded by the king's benevolent attitude and largesse. His first meeting with the king left him nearly speechless.

"Well, lad, you have done it! You have brought the old wolf to bay. And he's brought with him almost all the headmen of those blasted Westphalians. They keep pouring in every day. There are so many already it almost makes me nervous, and it's costing me a fortune to feed them all.

"You're just in time," the king continued effusively. "The baptism is day after tomorrow. And I swear it looks like he really means to do it! Along with every man who came to join him. You know what he said to me after I showed him the lands I intend to give to him? He said 'Well, king, I'm not sure yet I believe in all this conjuring and Christian wizardry you've got planned for me, but in the end I reckon all that land you said you'd give me is worth a Mass or two.'" The king guffawed lustily as he remembered the moment.

"And it's you who did it, my good young hero! You took a terrible chance, and I let you, God forgive me. But it paid off, by all the saints! I wish I'd believed in you three years ago. It might have saved me a huge fortune and hundreds of Frankish lives. Sebastian's Way, indeed! I should have trusted you. I'm truly sorry now that I didn't. It's just that we never tried buying them off before."

"Sire, begging your pardon, but that's not exactly the right term. It's not really 'buying' them. What you're doing is investing in their future—and ours, too. You are spending in order to build. The Saxons will become part of us. They will be counted among our troops. They will help us fight our future battles. We shall marry among them and become one people!"

"Hmm, quite a speech," the king mused. "I hope you're right, Sebastian. I trust you now. But it's them I don't trust; I've fought them for so many years it's hard to believe I won't have to do it again. They're like skunks; you can still smell their stink long after they've gone. But at least old Widukind is not likely to see those Saxon woods again. He'll be a long way from them, and he'll never go back now. I think he really likes this new land I've promised him, and he's tired of fighting."

The king paused to consider the young man before him. "Sit down a minute, lad, and tell me something. Did you ever doubt that I would redeem you in the end? Did you think I'd let you rot up there in the Saxon wilderness?"

"Never, my lord king," was Sebastian's immediate reply.

"Well, I thought about it, I'm ashamed to say. Many's the time I have sworn to God that I would tack Widukind's cursed hide up on the gates of the nearest Frankish fortress after we'd killed him. But, no, I couldn't do it. I love you too much, Sebastian, lad. There's no one like you. From the beginning, when you decided to be a warrior in my cavalry, you've been a part of almost all of my triumphs. Truth is, you're invaluable to me. So listen to me, I want you at my side from now on. Do you understand? I want you as a personal aide, starting right after this little party is over. Will you come? You can bring your family. By all means! Move Adela and the boys down here to my court. Travel with me, advise me. You've certainly proved wise enough, young as you are. By the Holy Cross, I'll even make you one of the *missi dominici,* if you like."

"I'd like that very much, sire. Adela is already on the way here. And she's bringing the children. I can't wait to present them to you. Two of them are born warriors, I'd swear it. They are bound to be in your heavy cavalry one day, and I daresay they will grow to be among your greatest warriors. And the other one is already an astonishing scholar, and he's only ten years old. This one will never make a warrior, I fear. He's just not the kind, but he's very bright."

"Ten years old? That can't be right. You only married Adela two or three years ago. What have you been up to, you rascal?"

Sebastian cleared his throat and looked away. "Milo is adopted, my lord king."

"Oh. Well, that's fine then. And don't worry about him not becoming a warrior. We've come to a time now when we finally can think of other things besides war and conquest. Why, we can learn something about the world and about what makes a good kingdom. We might even prove to be better at it than the Romans. We could do more, build more, learn more, make good laws that last. I have already started to create a school in every town where there is a bishop. We will call them 'cathedral schools.' And one won't have to be a clergyman to learn something in them. I want all of us to learn to read. Well, maybe not the peasants. But as many as can. I'll bring in scholars from all over the world. You have never seen such a collection of wise men than what I intend to gather around me. They will truly be a fountain of ideas, so many we won't have time to consider them all. And books everywhere! And trade! We need to revive it. We need to be able to use money again instead of barter. And we need to be able to buy the things we don't make. Why, it takes your man Simon years to bring me more of that silk he peddles so dearly."

"And you will be at the heart of it all, lad. By the saints, you will be at my right hand when I build this new kingdom! An empire, like the Romans, only better—a 'Holy' Roman Empire, if God wills it. For we will make the Church a part of it. And where the Romans went wrong, we will have the Church to help make a kingdom that God will bless and allow to prosper."

"That will be wonderful, my lord king. I hope with all my heart to be a part of it."

"You will be, son, I promise you," the king said affectionately, and then he frowned as if an unpleasant warning had intruded in his thoughts.

He went on in a serious tone, "There's another reason I want you with me. I am going to need your sword again when we begin to do something about those Vikings."

"Vikings, my lord?"

"Yes, the bloody Danes and their allies to the north, the so-called Norsemen. They are coming out of those cold, wild forests around the northern sea like a plague of rats, like there are too many of them for their own lands to contain. They know how to build incredible ships that apparently don't ever sink, and they've learned to navigate those ships for days out of sight of any land."

"I know them, my lord. Or at least, I've seen some of them. The merchant Simon first came to me in such a ship. It was so well contructed it could come all the way up my shallow river without a problem. And Simon said it could go around the whole of Francia down to the Roman Sea without ever having to come ashore."

"Well, I don't know about that. But this I do know. They are using such boats to raid into the British islands. They rape and steal and murder wherever they go. And those are Christian kingdoms now. They are going to have to be stopped eventually. It is only a matter of time before they turn on our own ports and those of western Francia."

"I agree, my lord. But I know very little about them at this point. I think we must begin by gathering all the information we can on them. And, sire, if you'll pardon my presumption, I think you will need to start building such ships yourself if we hope to stop them."

"Right on both counts, Sebastian. And I have already begun the process. I have spies in all the ports of Denmark already. They report to me regularly. In fact," the king paused and continued in a lower voice, "they recently sent me a very disturbing piece of news. They say they saw your old friend Konrad in one of the ports the Danes use to raid into Britain—or somebody very like him: a burly, wicked fighter who killed three men in a tavern brawl before escaping to one of the Danish ships."

"What!" Sebastian sprang up, clutching at his sword, a cold trickle of dread spreading through him. "I thought he was dead."

"Calm down, son. It's very unlikely that the man they saw was Konrad. After all, I saw the man's severed head." He frowned. "True, it was so charred it was hard to tell, but the Saxons who brought it to me also gave me his sword and that amulet he always wore around his neck. I admit, I didn't think much about it at the time except to be glad that the beast was finally dead."

"But, sire, that's terrible news. What if he's not dead? If it was Konrad your spies saw, then Adela is still his wife. At least that's what the Church will say."

"Oh, now, wait a minute, Sebastian. I'm sure it wasn't Konrad. Why would the Vikings have anything to do with him anyway? The Saxons hated him."

"Precisely because they are not Saxons, sire. The Danes don't care what Konrad did to the Saxons. What they would see in him is a great fighter, a formidable ally to have on their raids. They could use him. And he would have no allegiances whatever now—except to anyone who can help him murder and plunder.

"Easy, lad. No need to get so worked up. It was only one report. Never rely on a single report. As I said, it is very unlikely. And even if it was Konrad, he'd never come back here. I'd hang him myself if he did."

Adela arrived too late for the festivities, but she did get to meet Widukind before he disappeared to take possession of his new lands. The Saxon prince was so charmed by her that he swore if he ever had another girl child—and he was "still quite capable of it, mind you"—he would be most pleased to name her Adela. In return, Adela thanked him sweetly for not killing her husband and for having the "wisdom of a great leader" in trusting Sebastian with his own life.

The king, too, was smitten by Adela's magical charisma. Once he had seen her, he drew Sebastian aside and declared to him, "My boy, God must really love you; he not only spares your life in every dangerous circumstance, he gives you a woman who is half Aphrodite and half Virgin Mary. She is clearly as good as she is beautiful."

It was true that, more than her face and figure, Adela's happiness and goodness made her beautiful. Not wanting to change that in the slightest, Sebastian could not tell Adela the unsettling news about Konrad, and he implored the king to say nothing as well. Gradually, in the days that followed the joyous celebration of the apparent end of the long Saxon wars, Sebastian was able to put Konrad out of his mind and enjoy the prospect of becoming a royal vassal and living at the king's court. The king put it all into perspective.

"I want you to forget about Konrad now, Sebastian. It's probably just a rumor anyway. Think of all the good that has befallen you instead. You have a beautiful wife, lovely in every way. You have strong, smart sons, and a distinguished reputation in my army. You can look forward to devoting the rest of your life to making our mutual dream come true—a peaceful realm full of learning and prosperity. You are to be at my side from now on. You will help me preserve the good things we have worked so hard to achieve and we will build far more. And you, Sebastian, will be my torchbearer. You will help me see the way."

ACKNOWLEDGMENTS

Writing this book was a long journey, and I was very glad to have friends who, in one way or another, provided indispensable inspiration along the way: Wayne Gray Alfred, Frances Porteous Macdonnell, Jo Ann and Don Stovall, Brigadier Winter Anstey, O.B.E., Father Edward Hays, Sisters Mary Lenore Martin and Marie Brinkman, SCLs, Teresa Williams and her boys, Karen Fernengel, and, of course, the transcendant Mary Jo.

I am also grateful for the skilled hands of those who helped me craft the novel: Jen Halling for getting me out of the morass of the first draft, Gayla Williams and the literary gang at the Zona Rosa B&N, Karoline Banasik for the cool maps, and Jennifer Quinlan, my matchless final copy editor, whose consummate professionalism and splendid advice kept me on track and pulled the whole story together.

Finally, thanks to those faceless monks or priests who laboriously scratched out the limited accounts, year by year, of the *Carolingian Chronicles*, woefully poor in detail but vital for providing most of what we know about the extraordinary and fascinating era of Charlemagne.

Edwards Brothers Malloy
Oxnard, CA USA
November 20, 2013